THE
SPELLSHOP

THE SPELLSHOP

SARAH BETH DURST

BRAMBLE

TOR PUBLISHING GROUP
NEW YORK

THE SPELLSHOP

Copyright © 2024 by Sarah Beth Durst

A Bramble Book
Published by Tom Doherty Associates / Tor Publishing Group
120 Broadway
New York, NY 10271

www.torpublishinggroup.com

Bramble™ is a trademark of Macmillan Publishing Group, LLC.

The Library of Congress Cataloging-in-Publication Data is available upon request.

ISBN 978-1-250-33397-1 (hardcover)
ISBN 978-1-250-32461-0 (ebook)

Our books may be purchased in bulk for promotional, educational, or business use. Please contact your local bookseller or the Macmillan Corporate and Premium Sales Department at 1-800-221-7945, extension 5442, or by email at MacmillanSpecialMarkets@macmillan.com.

First Edition: 2024

Printed in the United States of America

0 9 8 7 6 5 4 3 2 1

For Adam,

with love and raspberry jam

CHAPTER ONE

Kiela never thought the flames would reach the library. She was dimly aware that most of the other librarians had fled weeks ago, when the revolutionaries took the palace and defenestrated the emperor in a rather dramatic display. But surely they wouldn't touch the library. After all, there were *books* here. Highly flammable, irreplaceable books.

The Great Library of Alyssium, with its soaring spires, stained-glass windows, and labyrinthine bookshelves, was the jewel of the Crescent Islands Empire. Its hallowed stacks were filled with centuries-old treatises, histories, studies, and (most importantly, in Kiela's opinion) spellbooks. Only the elite, the crème de la crème of the scholars, were allowed to even view the spellbooks, as only the rarefied few were permitted, by imperial law, to use magic.

She was responsible for the spellbooks on the third floor, east wing. For the past eleven years, she'd worked, slept, ate, and lived between the shelves, which perhaps explained why, when she first smelled smoke, she thought she'd simply left toast on the cookplate.

Just to be on the safe side, earlier in the week, Kiela and her assistant Caz had begun securing some of her favorite tomes in crates and stowing them on one of the library boats, though she'd never truly believed evacuation would be necessary. Cocooned within the stacks, far away from any whiff of politics or violence, it was a pleasant game: if she were stranded on a deserted island, which books would she most want to have with her? Certainly *The Grimoire on Plant-work*, compiled in the year 357 by scholars Messembe and Cannin, as well as *The Manipulation of Weather Patterns, a Study of the Effects of Spellwork on the Breeding Habits of Eastern Puffins*, which was a fascinating and groundbreaking work that—

Caz swung by his leaves into the aisle where she sat, cross-legged, in front of a pile of books. A spider plant, he was roughly the size of a farm dog but comprised entirely of greenery, with a knot of roots holding soil at his core. He was the smartest assistant she'd ever had, though also, perhaps not coincidentally, the most anxiety-prone. "We're going to die," he informed her, his leaves rustling so badly that it was challenging to pluck out the words.

"The fighting won't come here," Kiela said in the soothing voice she'd perfected after years of working in such a sacred space. She added another book to the pack-in-the-fifth-crate pile, then reconsidered and shifted it to the pack-only-if-it-fits pile.

He shook his leaves at her. "The fighting is *already* here. They've battered down the front door and are ransacking Kinney Hall."

"Goodness!"

The door to Kinney Hall was a monstrosity built of brass and secured with bolts made of the sturdy lumber used for the ribs of ship hulls. She tried to calculate the amount of force required to batter down a thirty-foot door, then blinked. "Ransacking, did you say?"

She'd expected the rebels to secure the library and its treasures—that was only sensible—but *ransacking*? These were freedom fighters, not feral animals. She wasn't even opposed to their goals. On Caz's recommendation, she'd read a few of their pamphlets in the early days of the revolution, and the call for elections and the sharing of knowledge seemed quite appealing . . .

"The North Reading Room is on fire," Caz said. "They lit the tapestries first, and it spread to the scrolls."

She felt sick. All those old manuscripts!

He tugged on her sleeve with a leaf. "Come on, Kiela, we have to leave."

Leave? Now? But she hadn't finished—

"If you make a leave-leaf joke," Caz warned, "I'm going without you."

She got to her feet. The fifth crate was only half-filled. Kiela dumped an armload of books into it without even checking what the titles were—*"Enough, Kiela!"* Caz said as she went for a second armload—and then maneuvered it toward the lift. On wheels, it scooted between the shelves, and she felt a lurch in her stomach as they passed all the full shelves of beautiful, wonderful books. She snagged a few more favorites as they hurried past.

Reaching the lift, she shoved the wheeled crate inside and yanked down the gate. Caz pushed the button with a leaf and turned the crank. The lift lurched and then descended.

As they traveled between the floors, Kiela heard the sound of metal clashing on metal, and her stomach flopped. She didn't know firsthand what a battle sounded like, but she *did* know what a library was supposed to sound like, and all of this was terribly, horribly wrong. Caz crept closer to her, and she wished the lift would go faster.

What if it stopped on one of the floors with fighting?

What if it stopped altogether?

She pushed the sublevel button again and again, as if that would encourage it. The lift continued to inch downward with clanks and squeaks and whirrs. The stench of smoke grew stronger. Looking out through the grated gate, she saw haze shrouding the stacks.

"We should have taken the stairs," Caz said.

"We'd have never been able to carry the books," Kiela said.

"We won't save any books if we're dead." He shook so hard that several of his leaves detached and floated to the floor. "Gah, I'm shedding!"

"You need to think about something else," she said. "Oak trees are struck by lightning more often than any other tree. Apples can float because they are twenty-five percent air. You can count the number of cricket chirps per second to calculate the outside temperature."

"Unless the outside is on fire," Caz said. "How fast do they chirp if it's all on fire?"

The lift lurched as it reached the lowest level. Kiela yanked the gate open while Caz maneuvered the crate with his tendrils. Shoving the crate outside, they exited the elevator.

This far down, water-level, she couldn't hear the clang of metal or smell the stench of smoke. It was overwhelmed by the ripe fish odor of the canal that flowed beneath the library. All of the city of Alyssium was riddled with canals. It was part of what made it one of the world's most beautiful cities, the jewel of the empire. Kiela remembered when she'd first arrived, very young, before her parents died, and how impressed she'd been by the sparkling canals, the lacelike white bridges, the spires, and the flowers that blossomed on every balcony, draped from every window, and framed every door. She wondered how much of the city she remembered was left.

Hurrying through the narrow stone passageway with the wheeled crate, she listened for any other movement. But all she heard was the slosh of water against stone and the drip-drip-drip of a leak somewhere nearby. Ahead were the boats.

Anchored in slips beneath the library, the boats were used to transport books to and from select patrons on nearby islands. Each had silver sails, tied tight around its boom, and a black-cherry hull wide enough to transport multiple crates of books but sleek enough to be sailed by a single librarian. She herself had used one just last winter to deliver a full set of scholar Cypavia's *Examinations of the Function of Forest Spirits in Fact and Fiction* to a bedridden emeritus sorcerer. He'd had his housekeeper offer her a cup of tea as thanks, but she'd declined, wanting to hurry back to the comfort of her stacks. *At least those books are safe.* That was only a slight consolation, though, compared to the wealth of knowledge in peril above her.

She'd already filled her boat with the first four crates of books, secured beneath a tarp. Maneuvering the half-filled fifth crate onto the boat, she strapped it in. There was room for at least three more crates, but there wasn't time to fetch them. She wished she'd sorted books faster. Or been less picky. She wished she'd packed more provisions. She'd stowed a few jugs of water, as well as jars of preserved peaches, a bag of dried beans, and a sack of pecans. For Caz, she had a tub of fresh soil that he could replenish himself in, and she'd also hidden a couple changes of clothes for herself, as well as a few blank notebooks just in case. But she hadn't emptied her cubicle in the library of her personal items. She thought wistfully of all she'd left—her old journals, her best quill set, a wooden carving in the shape of a mermaid that her parents had given her when she was a child. But Caz was right: better to save themselves. And the books.

We'll come back when it's safe, she thought. *This is just temporary.*

Climbing into the boat, Kiela untied the line and pushed off. She pulled out the pole for navigating the watery tunnels. The sails were wrapped up around the boom. They'd stay down until they reached the open water.

She wasn't technically supposed to take the boat. Or the books. Or Caz. But there had been no one left to ask, and she reassured herself that they'd thank her later, when she returned. It wasn't theft. It was her job: taking care of the collection. *I'm just . . . broadening the definition.*

She poled through the tunnels until they flowed out into the open canals of the city.

"Well, this is absolutely horrible," Caz said.

Kiela had to agree.

The stars were blotted out by the smoke that rose from the bridges and spires. The flames cast everything in a ghoulish light, and the sour taste of the smoke coated the back of her throat. She felt it invading her lungs with each breath. Her sky-blue skin looked sickly in the unnatural light, and her dark blue hair soaked up the scent of smoke. Down on the canals, Kiela and Caz were free from the worst of it, but they weren't free from the sights and sounds of death.

Later, she'd block out most of that horrible night: the screams, the corpses in the canals, the fear that choked her worse than the smoke. The trip through the canals felt endless, and the sounds traveled across the water even as they broke into the open sea.

With Caz's help, Kiela raised the silver sails once the water was too deep for the pole. She'd learned how to sail as a small child and had delivered enough books scattered over the years to stay in practice, so she thankfully didn't have to think to perform the tasks. Her hands remembered what to do, how to catch the wind in the canvas, how to speed away, away, away.

Behind them, the great city burned, with its people (both good and bad) and its history (both good and bad) and its books and its flowers. And she knew she wasn't coming back.

As the sun rose over the sea, all pink and yellow and hopeful, Kiela resolved to look forward, not backward. There was no one in Alyssium who'd miss her—which was a depressing thought in and of itself. Really, no one?

Absorbed in her work, she hadn't left the library for anything but the occasional book delivery in . . . Had it been years? Yes, years. After she'd finished school, she'd simply moved directly into a cubicle sandwiched between the stacks. It had been simpler that way. She hadn't had to waste any time traveling to and from her work.

She had no family in the city, and she'd lost track of her classmates—they'd drifted off into their lives, and she'd fallen into the routine of hers. All her meals were delivered, prepared fresh at any hour. Scholars often kept odd hours, and therefore so did librarians. She merely had to send a request down the chute, and everything would arrive via lift in a timely manner. No interaction with anyone required. She'd considered it the perfect system.

The other librarians ... They had their own work on other floors and in other wings. Kiela never liked to disturb anyone, and she had gently—so gently that she hadn't even realized she was doing it—discouraged others from disturbing hers. As the sailboat bounced over the waves, she realized she hadn't even spoken to another soul besides Caz in three weeks. The last person she'd talked to was a janitor whom she'd shooed away for stirring up dust near some particularly fragile manuscripts.

It wasn't that she didn't like people. It was only that she liked books more. They didn't fuss or judge or mock or reject. They invited you in, fluffed up the pillows on the couch, offered you tea and toast, and shared their hearts with no expectation that you'd do anything more than absorb what they had to give.

All of which was very lovely, but it left her in a bit of a quandary: where to go, now that her old life had quite literally burned down. "Caz . . ." she began.

"Mmm," he said, muffled.

She glanced across the boat to see he'd wedged himself between two of the crates and had wound his leaves tight around his root ball. "Caz, what are you doing?"

"Fish eat plants," he said.

"Some fish, yes." She wasn't overly familiar with the dietary preferences of fish. She knew there were fish who liked kelp. She supposed they ate plankton too. Also, insects? "Some fish eat other fish."

"Who eat plants."

"I suppose so."

"Everything eats plants," Caz said. "But barely anything eats books. That's why I'm positioning myself between the crates. No one will think of looking for a fresh, tasty morsel of green next to so many dead trees. So I am just going to stay here, with the books, until we get to wherever we're going, which I hope won't have fish, sheep, cows, or goats." He shuddered at the word "goats," and Kiela wondered if he'd had a bad experience with a goat or had just read about them. *Most likely the latter.* Livestock wasn't permitted in the Great Library, for obvious reasons.

"That is what I wanted to talk to you about," Kiela said. "We need a destination."

"You . . . didn't plan that out?"

"I didn't think we'd really have to leave," she admitted. "Or I thought, if we did, it would be just for a few hours or days. A week at most." She'd thought they could rent a slip in a harbor at one of the nearby islands, perhaps Varsun or Iva, and stay for a couple days at one of the charming inns where the lesser nobles liked to vacation.

Caz sagged, his leaves drooping as if they'd never tasted water. "So did I."

They sailed silently. It was a gloriously beautiful day for a sail. Light breeze. Cheerful lemon light flashing on the water. Seagulls flew overhead, cawing to one another. The many islands of the Crescent Islands Empire—if it was an empire anymore, thanks to the revolutionaries—looked peaceful from the distance, if you didn't look back to where smoke still stained the sky over the capital city. The islands' gray, white, and black cliffs were majestic, and the sweet little fishing villages looked quaint, with their brightly painted houses, cheerful gardens, and cobblestone streets. She and Caz could sail into one of their harbors and then—do what? She couldn't afford an inn for more than a couple days. The coins that Kiela had brought with her wouldn't go far. Even if she could pay the harbor fees, she didn't relish living on the boat, day in and day out.

She resolved not to panic. She'd think as she sailed. And an answer would come to her.

Across the water, she saw a herd of merhorses rise and fall with the waves. Her breath caught in her throat. Half horse and half fish, they were a magnificent sight. She watched, mesmerized, as they cantered through the water. Their hooves crashed through the waves as their powerful fish tails propelled them forward. Covered in jewellike scales and made of solid muscle, they were the living embodiment of both beauty and strength. *Like the sea itself,* Kiela thought. One of them tossed its mane, and droplets sprayed up and caught the light—a flash of rainbow.

"Caltrey," Kiela said.

"Excuse me?"

"It's an island."

"I've never heard of it."

"I'd be surprised if you had," Kiela said. "It's tiny and remote. Far to the north. It doesn't fall on any of the shipping lanes. The locals herd merhorses to aid with their fishing."

Curious, Caz lifted himself up between the crates and perched on one to look out across the ocean. "Why do you know about it? Oh, don't tell me—you read about it."

"Actually, no. It's where I was born." She heard a hitch in her voice, and she swallowed hard. She hadn't thought about Caltrey in years—she didn't know why just thinking of returning would make her feel so jumbled.

Her parents had left as soon as they could afford it, to seek a better life in the capital city—they'd wanted to experience life in Alyssium, and they'd wanted Kiela to have the kind of opportunities they, growing up on a remote island, never had. She'd been barely nine years old at the time, but she still remembered the island with its cliffs and farms and gardens. The sole village on the island, also called Caltrey, was three cobblestone streets wide with a mill by a waterfall and a school that was housed in an old barn. She remembered the way it looked at sunset, with the island's winged cats perched on the rooftops, and the way it smelled at dawn of fresh-baked bread. In spring, wildflowers sprouted everywhere—the roofs, the cliffs, the fields. In winter, snow blanketed everything in thick white fluff. She used to drink hot milk with chocolate mixed in and watch the snow fall on the sea—

"Uh, Kiela?" Caz prodded.

"I think . . . I have a house there." She knew her parents hadn't sold it. So far from the heart of the empire, it wouldn't have sold for much, and Kiela's father had wanted to hold on to it, in case they decided to retire there after they'd had their fill of city life, though Kiela's mother had loved the city too much to ever want to return. *I suppose that means I inherited it.* Certainly there was no one else who could have. She had no other family. "If no one has moved in. And if it hasn't fallen down. It's small. Just a cottage. But . . ." It was beautiful. At least it was beautiful in her mind, preserved in her memory as lovely and fragile as a soap bubble. Now, it was probably infested with bats, mice, and bears, and the roof had most likely caved in. "I just never expected to go back there." *At least not without them.*

"Is it nice?"

"Very. I think. It could have changed." *I've changed.* She'd lost her magenta freckles and the blue pigtails years ago, and she'd gained an advanced degree in library studies and a host of antisocial tendencies.

"Okay then," Caz said. "Let's go to your island."

Catching the wind, she steered the boat north.

"Just to be clear—they don't have goats, do they?"

"I am sure there are no animals anywhere on Caltrey that eat plants," Kiela said, as they picked up speed. The boat bounced over the waves.

"Excellent! Wait, are you just saying that to make me feel better?"

"Yes," she said.

Grumbling, he squished himself back between the crates of spellbooks as they sailed northward, toward their future and her past.

CHAPTER TWO

As the sun stained the horizon orange, Kiela sailed toward a little cove on the island of Caltrey. It was just a mile east of the village and its harbor, tucked behind a veil of rocks and trees. She aimed the boat between the rocks.

"You're going to crash," Caz observed.

"I'm not going to crash," Kiela said. "I'm going to dock."

Inside the cove, there used to be a wooden dock that belonged to her family's cottage. She remembered she used to squat on the end and watch the fish dance in the water. At low tide, she'd be able to see crabs scuttling over the rocks, and at high tide, merbabies would swim around the dock posts, before they were called out to sea by their parents—a sighting that locals said was good luck. She wasn't, of course, entirely certain the dock would still be standing, but she supposed she could drop anchor and they could wade to shore. Or she could just beach the boat, provided she could avoid slicing the hull on the rocks.

One hand on the rudder, she guided the sailboat around the rocks and into the cove. Caz clambered up the mast, using his tendrils to climb, for a better view. With the light so low in the sky, the cove was coated in shadows. The water looked near black, and the trees, with the rocky cliffs behind them, cast even more shadows. It was silent, except for the lapping of the waves on the rocky shore and the call of an unseen bird from one of the pine trees. But despite the shadows, it didn't feel unwelcoming. As they drifted deeper into the cove, it felt as if the shadows were embracing them, in the same way that a thick nest of blankets did on a chilly night.

Kiela spotted the old dock, right where it was supposed to be. It was more rickety than she remembered, though. About a third of the slats were missing, like the smile of an old man who'd lost some of his teeth. Luckily the posts were there, sturdy but coated in seaweed.

Using the pole, she sidled the boat up next to the dock and tossed a line around a post. Yanking on the line, she dragged them closer and tied a bowline knot. She remembered her mother teaching her how to make this exact knot on this very same dock. It felt both like just yesterday and a lifetime ago. She shook her head to chase the memory away. Clambering over the crates, Kiela pulled the sail down and wrapped it tight against the boom.

Caz was perched on one of the book crates. "I am *not* walking on that."

"You'd rather swim?"

"I'd rather stay on the boat," he said.

Kiela sighed and rubbed her eyes. She'd never felt this bone-marrow-deep tired before. Even when she stayed up all night with her books, it was never like this. Between the stress of their escape and the effort of their night-and-all-day sail, she felt like a book so well read that its pages curled and spine cracked. "I can carry you."

He was quiet for a moment, then he said, "That's undignified."

"You think the shrubbery is going to mock you?"

If he'd had eyes, she expected he would have rolled them at her. "Fine. Carry me. But only if you tell no one."

"Who am I going to tell? I don't know anyone here and don't want to." She scooped him up, careful to gather all the soil that clung to his exposed roots. It felt like holding a very plump and very leafy toddler. His tendrils draped over her shoulders, and he grumbled as she adjusted her grip. "We're going to lay low, keep to ourselves, and avoid trouble," she said. "With luck, none of the locals will even know we're here."

Kiela tapped the nearest slat of wood with her toes. It seemed sound enough. Cautiously, she shifted her weight and was pleased when the dock held. Caz's leaves flattened around her back. She carried him carefully as she stepped from slat to slat, testing each one before she trusted it. At last, she reached the shore.

He climbed down from her arms to the ground. Shaking out his leaves, he groomed himself with a tendril. He looked a bit like a cat licking his fur. "We won't ever speak of that again."

"Of course," she agreed.

She looked up at the knot of greenery in front of them. There used to be a path, with stairs carved into the rocks, but all she could see was a tangle of vines cascading down the hill. Frowning at it, she paced in front of the green. The stone steps should still be there, if she could find— Ah, there!

Kicking away a few vines, Kiela uncovered the first step. "Found it."

"Found what?" Caz asked.

"The way home." She felt the word vibrate through her.

Step by step, she climbed, with Caz behind her, clearing the steps as best she could. Some, she was only able to uncover a few inches, but it was enough. By the time she reached the top, the sun was completely down.

Bathed in the silvery gray of twilight, the cottage waited for them. She wanted to feel as if they'd made it—she was home, they were safe, and everything would be easy from now on. But the cottage was nearly as enveloped in vines as the stairs. She couldn't tell where the walls ended and the green began. Her former home looked one gulp away from being swallowed entirely.

"It's nice," Caz said.

"Now who's lying," Kiela said.

"It has a roof. And walls."

He was right about that. It could be worse.

An owl hooted much too close, and Kiela jumped. Caz skittered behind her. She forced herself to breathe and calm down. It didn't look as if anyone was living in the house, which was good. She could have come back to find squatters. Or new owners, if the locals had decided there were no more living relatives who might return to claim it. She couldn't vouch for how many mice, birds, or other critters had taken up residence inside.

She wished they'd arrived earlier so it wouldn't look so dark in there.

"Should we go in?" Caz asked.

Yes. Maybe. No. She wanted to retreat to the boat, sail back to Alyssium, and sequester herself in her nice, warm, safe cubicle deep within the stacks of books, where she knew what to expect out of every night and every day. If she went into this house, what would she find? And if she didn't, what would happen then? She hated not knowing which was the right choice.

Have I made a terrible mistake coming here?

The owl hooted again.

"We go in," Kiela said.

They approached the front door. It felt like walking up to the mouth of a slumbering beast. It was ajar, with dead leaves clogging the entranceway. She nudged them out of her way with her foot and leaned against the door to push it open farther. It squeaked loudly, as if it hadn't been moved in years, which was entirely possible.

Stepping inside, Kiela waited for her eyes to adjust. The last gasps of day shed a grayish light through the few windows that weren't blocked by vines. It was enough to see shapes: chairs, she guessed, and a table. She matched the shadows to her memories and was surprised to find that it felt familiar, like a half-remembered old tale. The wood-burning stove was . . . ahh, yes, *there,* squatting like a hulking creature, with a chimney rising from its back. A daybed used to be in the front corner—that's where she used to sleep—and her parents' bedroom budded off the back. A kitchen area with a sink and a window that overlooked the back garden should be to her left, beyond the table. She couldn't see that in the darkness, though, and it made her feel like she'd walked into a surreal kind of dream, with pieces of memories overlaid by shadows. She wondered how Caz felt about this place. "If you'd rather, we could spend the night in the boat, and explore this in the morning," she offered.

"Sleep on the boat?" Caz sounded appalled. "With fish under us?"

"You really have a thing about fish," she said. "I had no idea."

"You hear stories," he said darkly.

"Do you? Do you really?" She navigated across the room, leaves crunching underfoot, and found the daybed, exactly where she remembered it. It seemed smaller, though. And dustier. Lifting the quilt, she shook it, and twigs, leaves, and dust flew into the air. She coughed.

Setting the quilt aside in a heap, she pushed her hands against the mattress. It hadn't disintegrated, which was a plus. She supposed it would hold her, and under where the quilt had lain, it wasn't that dusty, at least in comparison. It wasn't as if, after sailing through the night and all day, she was particularly clean anyway.

"Hey, there's a hole in the floor," Caz said, pleased. "I can root here for the night."

Could she sleep here? After their escape and long sail, she should be able to sleep anywhere. *If mice or raccoons or whatever murder me in the night, at least I'll get some rest.* Gingerly, she lay down on the little bed. It creaked but didn't collapse. The quilt was the velvety soft of worn cotton, and the mattress cradled her as she sank into it. It smelled like dust and a little like roses. She felt her neck and shoulders begin to unknot.

Outside, the owl hooted softly.

As dawn pried its fingers into the vine-covered cottage, Kiela opened her eyes. And screamed when she saw a man standing in the doorway with a scythe in his hands. She tried to jump to her feet, but the little daybed couldn't handle the quick movement. It toppled over, and she spilled onto the floor.

The man rushed forward.

Kiela screamed again.

He backpedaled. Leaned his scythe against the wall. Held up his hands, palms out. "Sorry. Very sorry. I didn't mean to startle you." He had a deep voice, soothing. She'd never seen him before, which wasn't a surprise since she hadn't been here in ages. He wasn't what she'd call handsome, but he didn't look like a murderer either. Not that she knew what that would look like. He was tall, which wasn't an argument for or against murderer. He must have had to duck through the doorframe. He also appeared stronger than the average library-goer. Judging by his arms, he looked as if he could pick up one of her book crates one-handed. Or crush her throat with his pinkie. None of that was at all reassuring.

She got to her feet and scanned the cottage quickly. She didn't see the spider plant anywhere, and she felt panic rise up from her stomach. "Caz? Caz, are you okay? Did he hurt you?"

Hands still out, the man said in the same soft, deep tone, "I didn't hurt anyone. Or see anyone else. There was only you here when I came in."

Her heart was thumping wildly in her rib cage, even though he hadn't made any threatening moves beyond coming into the place where she was sleeping and scaring her half to death. It was terrifying enough that he was large, male, and here. *And I don't see Caz.* "Why are you here?" she demanded, trying (and failing) to keep the shake out of her voice. "Who are you? What do you want?"

Mildly, he said, "I had planned to ask you the same questions. This house has been abandoned for years, but that doesn't mean it isn't someone's home."

"It's mine," Kiela said. "My home. It was. Is."

"Ah," he said.

He waited for her to explain further.

"My name is Kiela Orobidan. My parents lived here, and my

mother's parents before them. I was born here. We moved away when I was eight. Nine. But they never sold their cottage. It's mine."

"Ah."

He wasn't going to say more than that?

She saw a hint of movement out of the corner of her eye and glanced up at the rafters. Caz was there, draped around one of the cobweb-choked beams. He waved a tendril at her, and she exhaled. *He's okay. Just hiding.* She wished she could have done that. "And you are?"

"Larran Maver. I live at the base of the cliff, near town. Noticed your boat in the cove and came to see who was using the old Orobidan cottage. Around here, we like to keep an eye out for each other."

Outer islanders care for our own. She'd heard that dozens of times as a kid. This far away from the cities and the larger islands, they didn't have much choice, but it was also a point of pride.

She supposed it was a reasonable explanation for why he was here. He couldn't have known she'd be asleep on a dusty old daybed. She still didn't like the way he filled the entire doorway, blocking the exit. "You mean you're nosy."

He smiled, and the expression transformed him from ordinary into stunningly handsome. It was like the sun coming out from behind the clouds over a stormy sea. She found herself smiling back without meaning to. As soon as she realized she was doing it, she frowned. "Sure," Larran said, "that's one word for it. We prefer neighborly, but 'nosy' is probably just as accurate."

Still could be a murderer, she reminded herself. There was no law that said dangerous men couldn't also be handsome. On the other hand, he hadn't moved any closer since she'd screamed. In fact, in retrospect, he'd looked almost as spooked as she felt.

She was suddenly very aware that her hair was matted on one side, and her mouth tasted like peanuts. This wasn't how she wanted to meet the neighbors. In fact, she'd been hoping to not meet them at all. It would have been simpler if she could've stayed unnoticed. Fewer variables; fewer problems. She wished he'd leave.

"What brings you back to Caltrey?" he asked.

Kiela considered a half-dozen answers, but she settled on the one that was simplest and required the least amount of reliving recent traumatic events. "I'd had enough of the city."

"Ah."

Miraculously, he seemed to find that answer both reasonable and sufficient.

"Would you like help . . ." He looked around the cottage, as if cataloging all the myriad things she could possibly need help with, which was, at a rough estimate, everything. ". . . settling in?"

Absolutely not. The last thing she wanted him to do was stay and help. The entire point of coming to Caltrey was to hide away in a place where she knew no one and no one knew her, and she and Caz and the books would be safe. "Thanks, but we—*I* have it covered."

He raised his eyebrows as if he didn't believe her, but he didn't argue or try to convince her otherwise, which she appreciated. "Well, if you change your mind, I'm just through the woods, down by the shore." He waved toward the northwest. "It's the merhorse farm with the yellow house near the water. Drop by any time."

She had absolutely zero intention of ever doing that, but she thanked him. Best not to be rude to their new neighbor. Especially if it got him to leave faster.

He left, taking his scythe, and she watched him out the window, through a hole in the ivy, as he strolled away. A few minutes later, the green had swallowed him entirely.

CHAPTER THREE

Caz climbed down from the rafters. When he reached the floor, Kiela scooped him up, and he let her. He patted her back with one of his tendrils. When her heart had calmed down enough, she lowered him back to the floor.

"Sorry," she said.

"It's fine. I was so startled that I nearly lost half my soil ball."

She examined him. He still seemed as leafy as ever. "Are you okay?"

"Fine. I can get more. Lots of nutrients in the earth here. It's much richer than in Alyssium. You should eat something. And perhaps bathe."

"Ouch."

"I can't help what I smell."

"You don't even have a nose." Or ears. Or eyes. Or a mouth. He was a dog-size pot-less plant who defied all natural laws. She wished she'd been able to study the spell that had created him. It had to have been fascinatingly complex. All she knew was he'd begun as a single spider plant seed. She'd never asked what other ingredients were involved. It seemed too personal a question.

"Now who's being insulting," Caz said.

"Sorry." Subtly, she sniffed her own armpits. She smelled like the sea and sweat. A fresh shirt would help. She should have packed more than a few changes of clothes.

"At least he seems friendly," Caz said. "Until he comes back to murder us in our sleep."

Kiela glanced at the door again. "I don't think he plans to do that." *I hope.* After the initial scare, he'd taken pains not to startle her. Most likely, he was just nosy and intrusive rather than actively dangerous. *It's not his fault he's tall and ten times stronger than me.* He probably had no idea how he looked, unexpected in the dark. He hadn't been trying to loom over her.

"That was a large blade he carried."

Indeed it was. Very alarming. Cityfolk didn't carry that kind of equipment around, at least not usually. To be fair, she didn't really know what most people carried around, since she hadn't spent any time out on the streets or canals in years. Maybe scythes were in fashion. Who knew? Most likely, though, Larran carried it for practical reasons. Whatever paths used to lead to the cottage had been swallowed by the forest years ago. It wouldn't have been easy for him to reach the house without the scythe. "He must use it to hack through the overgrowth," Kiela said.

Caz shuddered. "Yeah, that's what I'm afraid of."

"I'd never let anyone hurt you," Kiela said stoutly.

"That's a nice sentiment, but what would you do? Scream? Throw books at them?"

Fair point, though she'd never throw a book. With luck, he wouldn't come back, and it wouldn't be an issue. Instead of replying, she chose to look around the cottage. Now that it was daylight, she could see it was . . . "unkempt" was the kindest adjective she could think of. Run-down. Derelict. Disheveled. Neglected.

Unloved.

Barely remembered.

Abandoned for years.

Alone.

Just like me.

With Caz scouting through the cottage, she reminded herself that she wasn't alone. And she hadn't been abandoned, at least not deliberately. Her family had moved to the capital city to follow their dreams and to give her the opportunity to pursue hers. They hadn't intended to leave her—they'd died from an illness that no one could have predicted or prevented. After that, she had chosen voluntarily to throw herself into her work at the library. As for finding herself without family or friends beyond a self-aware spider plant . . . that had merely happened over time.

Like the dust, the dirt, the leaves, and the cobwebs sneaking in here, over time. Okay, yes, she was a lot like this cottage. She could admit to the aptness of the metaphor.

"It can be cleaned up," Kiela said. "Made homelike."

She'd start by finding a safe place to store the spellbooks. Perhaps in her parents' bedroom. For now, the books could stay in the crates, but she'd make sure the back room was sealed against leaks and drafts before she set up shelves. And she'd have to ensure they were kept safe from prying eyes as well. It would not do for anyone to discover them. What if they tried to take them from her? What if they were afraid of the emperor's wrath and tried to destroy them? Or worse, what if they *weren't* afraid and tried to use them? She was fully aware that having the books was an enormous responsibility. Many were the only copies that existed, which made them irreplaceable and priceless, and all were original works, which meant they had none of the errors that occurred in copying. Given the destruction she'd witnessed, she might possess the last of the greatest treasure of the Crescent Islands Empire. The books had to be protected, first and foremost.

She had to prioritize what was most important, after all.

And it would be nice if no one noticed that she'd kind of, sort of, stolen them.

Hauling the crates of boxes up the stone steps, Kiela regretted shooing away their new friendly, muscly neighbor. He could have carried a lot of books, though he probably would have asked why she had so many, where she'd gotten them, and were they all hers. Really, it was best if she did this herself.

She'd liberated some excess line from the boat and looped it around the crates. The wheels helped on the dock, which miraculously held, but when she reached the stone steps . . . After some contemplation, she had a solution. Not a *good* solution, but a serviceable one:

Her parents' bedroom door, which was already off its hinges, would act as a ramp.

After fetching the door and laying it over the bottom few steps, she put her plan into action. Shoving with all her might, she rolled the first crate up the ramp/door, rested it (very precariously) on the steps, hurriedly moved the door to cover the next set of steps, and repeated the procedure until she reached level ground in front of the cottage. And then she did it again for the next crate. By the time she'd finished transporting all the crates, she was soaked in sweat, and all her muscles felt wobbly. Her back was screaming at her, as were her calves, and her head throbbed. She missed the library lift.

In retrospect, it might have been easier to unpack the crates and carry the books in stacks up the steps. It would have required a lot of trips, but perhaps it would have spared the door. And her back, calves, and head. Of course, she didn't think of that until after the task was complete and after she'd also hauled up the sack of provisions and supplies she'd brought.

Kiela stumbled inside to see that Caz had been busy as well. Using his tendrils, he'd swept everywhere he could reach. All the twigs, leaves, and other debris were piled in one corner, the cobwebs were gone from the rafters, and the dust . . . well, it was mostly all over him.

"Now we both need baths," Kiela said.

His leaves drooped.

"But it was worth it," she added quickly. The front room wasn't clean yet, but it was vastly improved. She could see the wood grain of the floor, as well as the color of the chairs—a deep earth brown.

Acorns and flowers had been carved into the chair backs, and the woven seats were frayed but still whole. The daybed, stripped of the dusty quilt and no longer overwhelmed by leaves and branches, looked almost like a place one could lie down, rather than a nest for an enormous mouse. "You made phenomenal progress."

He perked back up.

Kiela crossed to the kitchen sink. It had a pump that used to draw from a well. Theoretically, it should still work. If it didn't, she remembered a stream in the forest that fed into the waterfall near the village, and there was a bucket for bailing out water in the boat. She could use that if she needed to. She didn't, though, relish the idea of hauling water the entire way to the cottage every time she wanted to bathe or not die of dehydration. Looking out the window over the sink, she tried to see the forest, but the glass was laced with vines. All she could see was green, pierced by slivers of sunlight.

"Are you going to work for us?" she asked the pump. It was made of cast iron, and it curved over a brass basin. An old kitchen towel hung from a rack on the side of the sink, and the counter was bare except for a few jars and a glass pitcher. She remembered her mother used to put fresh flowers in that pitcher.

Behind her, Caz asked, "Are you talking to an inanimate object? Because that's odd."

"Says the talking plant."

"Ouch."

Steeling herself, she raised and lowered the handle. No water. Not even a trickle or a drip or a hint that it was doing anything. She raised and lowered it again. And again.

At last, she heard a distant gurgle.

She pumped harder, and it squeaked with the effort. After five more pumps, a blast of brownish water spurted out of the faucet and splashed into the sink. Surprised, she jumped back.

"That's it," Caz said to the pump, "you can do it!"

Kiela pumped again. Soon, the water flowed clear and cold. She cupped her hands and drank it. It was sweeter and crisper than any water she'd tasted in Alyssium.

She found one of her mother's old dish towels that had been left behind, rinsed out the dust, and then used it to wash as much of herself as she could. She shivered as the cold water touched her skin, but she gritted her teeth and washed off all the grime and sweat. Half the towel was black when she finished, and she realized it was soot from the burning city.

For an instant, Kiela could only stare at it.

Until this moment, she hadn't let herself truly think about it: the loss of the library, her home, her life. The loss of all those homes and lives. And the books . . . She knew she should care more about the people of Alyssium than the books, but the spellbooks had been her family, the library had been her home, and her work had been her life.

Her eyes felt hot, and her throat clogged.

But she shook her head. There wasn't time to wallow. Or grieve. She had to figure out what she was doing, how they were going to live. She had to make this into a place where they could hole up for as long as necessary—and where the precious knowledge they'd rescued could be preserved. But without the library, without its stacks and its order and its peace and its historical, cultural, and political importance . . . What was the point? Who was she with all of it gone? What kind of future did she have?

Caz jumped into the sink. "More water, please."

She pumped water onto him and, using another towel, helped wash the dirt, grime, and soot from each of his leaves. When he climbed out, his soil ball was saturated. He dripped dirty water over the counter, which then trickled onto the wood floor.

"What's first?" Caz asked. Then he asked: "Are you okay?"

Kiela nodded, unable to speak, then shook her head. "The library . . ."

He laid a leaf on her hand. "I know."

"Everything we worked for. Believed in. Cared about."

"We'll be all right. We'll make it all right. Kiela, you can't break down on me now. You're all I've got."

She sucked in air and steadied herself. They only had each other and so, like Larran had said, they had to look out for each other.

But where to begin?

"We have to make this our home," Kiela said.

After she'd dragged the crates of books into the back bedroom, Kiela surveyed the house. First step was to see what they had. Next step was to figure out what they'd need.

"Pull everything out," she said. "We'll take stock."

That was what they did whenever a fresh donation of books and manuscripts arrived at the library. First they'd sort through the collection. Spread it all out, see what they had, catalog it, and then proceed as appropriate.

And so Kiela and Caz dug in. Together, they rooted through the house and dragged out everything in a cabinet or closet or drawer into the center of the main room.

She was pleasantly surprised at how much remained. Her parents had abandoned a heap of old Caltreyan clothes. Selecting one of the island dresses, Kiela shook it out. Dust plumed in the air. The skirt was a quilt of blue—sky blue, sapphire blue, sea blue—all stitched together with silvery thread and hemmed with silver ribbon, and the bodice was a soft white blouse. Not at all a city style, but it was perfect for a picnic in a garden or a stroll on a shore. With a few repairs, she could wear a lot of her mother's abandoned clothes, and she could use her father's for . . . She wasn't sure what, but they were nice to have. She'd find a use for them. If nothing else, she could chop the fabric up into cleaning rags. Or perhaps learn to quilt? There was a moth-eaten blanket in one closet, in addition to the old quilts on the daybed and her parents' bed. Each quilt had its own pattern—one was comprised of colors of the sunset and sewn in strips like rays of light, while another was the brown and pale green of a spring garden with pieces cut like petals and sewn like abstract flowers. *We left so many beautiful things behind.* She'd had no idea. She'd been too little to help much with the packing, though she remembered she'd tried. Carrying an armful of clothes into the kitchen, Kiela dumped them into the sink to soak in water. She planned to use the excess line from the boat to hang them out in the sun to dry. *They'll be even more beautiful once they're clean.*

The kitchen cabinet produced more treasures: a few plates, bowls, and cups. Each bowl was painted with pictures of strawberries and raspberries, and the plates were painted with tomatoes and asparagus. The teacups bore delicate pictures of flowers. In one drawer, she found a decent knife with a carved antler handle. In another, she found a somewhat warped but still usable pot, as well as a frying pan and a teakettle. One chest held a stack of slightly yellowed yet serviceable papers—useful to a librarian normally, but less vital right now. Of greater interest was the bucket behind the door. And in a closet, miraculously: a broom and a shovel, as well as a full set of garden tools (hoe, trowel, clippers, and a set of leather gardening gloves with only a few holes in them). She also found a pantry closet full of empty glass canning jars and bottles that had once been used to store fruits, vegetables, and herbs. Her parents hadn't planned to garden or can in the city, and so they'd left all their equipment behind. She hadn't even begun to explore the yard that used to hold their garden—it was so overgrown that the fences were swallowed in vines. But perhaps she could clear it, plant a few vegetables, and see if anything edible had survived their abandonment . . .

Kiela began to feel a shred of hope.

This was a good place.

It could be made whole again.

And so can we.

Kiela scrubbed the blanket and the clothes as best she could and then strung up a line between the corner of the house and a tree—there was an old plant-basket hook on the corner of the house, which worked nicely to secure the clothesline. She spread the wet clothes out on the line and admired how much better they looked already. The blues and the greens had brightened from the wash. She then stuffed the quilt from the daybed into a bucket of water and left that to soak.

Together, she and Caz cleaned the kitchen. They swept the near-petrified mouse droppings out of the cabinets, washed the plates and glasses and utensils, and scrubbed the privy until the copper bathtub shone and the walls were a cheerful white again. She found sprigs of lavender in the front herb bed, wrapped their stems with a ribbon, and hung them above the privy washbasin. Once the day-bed quilt was clean, she washed an armload of faded but usable towels.

At midday, they took a break, and Kiela ate some of the peaches and pecans she'd brought from the library—at least she'd been clever enough to stash them in the boat, though she wished she'd packed more—while Caz rooted himself in a sunny spot where the floorboards were broken enough to expose the earth beneath. When she finished, she screwed the lid back on the peach jar and stored it in a cabinet. She then stepped back and allowed herself to think about the one thing that their search hadn't produced:

Food.

She had a finite amount of it from the city, enough for a few days if she stretched it. She'd need more very soon. She'd never had to worry about the possibility of hunger before. All her meals had been provided by the library kitchens, delivered via the chutes, and Kiela was only just beginning to realize that what she had right here was all she had.

That was . . . unsettling. She felt a bit like she was standing on the very top rung of a library ladder with the safety rope unclipped.

Yes, she could reclaim the garden, but it would take time. Also, seeds. And maybe some clue how to garden? She'd never planted anything before. The same went for the ocean. She knew there were fish and crabs out in the cove, but she didn't know how to fish or . . . crab? Was that what it was called? She didn't even know what the verb was, much less how to do it. And as for wild berries, yes, she could gather whatever she found, as well as nuts and mushrooms, but how was she to know what was edible or what wasn't? If she accidentally poisoned herself . . .

She'd need medicine. If she hurt herself. If she became sick.

She'd also need soap to keep herself clean. Paste to keep her teeth healthy.

But before any of that, she needed food. Fruit, vegetables, bread, milk, cheese, meat. *At least enough to last until we're self-sufficient,* she thought. Once she figured out how to garden and fish and had the basics for hygiene and medicine, she wouldn't need outside supplies. A little voice inside her whispered that it wouldn't be that simple, but she resolutely pushed it away. *I just need enough to get by for now.*

One trip into the village.

She'd use the coin she had to purchase the bare essentials, and then they'd hole up here and not bother anyone, and no one would have any reason to bother them.

Looking at what they had and didn't have, Kiela didn't see any way around it. It was foolish to think she could build a life here just from what they found and what they brought. Besides, the fantasy of living here unnoticed had already been broken when their neighbor had discovered her sleeping.

No, there was no denying it.

She was going to have to talk to people.

CHAPTER FOUR

Kiela put off her trip to the village until sundown, by which time it was, of course, far too late to go anywhere and she was far too exhausted from all the work they'd done anyway. After eating half a jar of peaches and several fistfuls of pecans, she collapsed into the daybed and slept far more soundly than she ever had in the library. She didn't even hear the owl outside.

At dawn, she woke to a tickle on her cheek.

"Don't scream," Caz said in her ear, "but he's back."

Her eyes popped open, and she shivered. She should have grabbed an extra blanket. She'd grown too used to the always-the-same warmth of the library. She'd forgotten it was cooler on Caltrey in the mornings, even in summer. "What?"

"Who," Caz corrected. "Him."

Him . . . Wait, did he mean their neighbor? Larran? Why was he back? She thought her scream had been enough of a hint that she didn't like impromptu visitors, especially while she was asleep. Couldn't he just leave them alone?

Sitting up, she peered out the window. It was still coated with grime. *We'll have to clean that,* she thought, though she knew they had other priorities, such as food. Her stomach grumbled in agreement. Through the streaks of dirt, she saw their tall and broad neighbor striding away toward the path he and his scythe had created. It looked as if he'd come, seen they weren't awake, and then left.

"At least he didn't let himself in this time," she said. Why had he come? Couldn't he just stay in his own house and she'd stay in hers? Did she need to put up a fence or a large "Keep Out, No Trespassing" sign? She waited until he was out of sight before she got out of bed and padded to the door.

On the front step, before the mostly broken door, was a basket with several glazed cinnamon raisin buns, as well as three chicken eggs and a wedge of cheese. "Okay, well, that's nice," she said.

Fine. He was a nice, friendly neighbor who didn't understand property lines.

She scooped up the basket and scurried back into the house, closing the door behind her. Sitting on a recently cleaned chair, she bit into one of the buns. Sugary sweetness exploded in her mouth, and she sighed through the bread. Closing her eyes, she savored every morsel. It was light, fluffy, sweet, and perfect. Had he made this? How? She added "baking" to the growing list of useful skills she didn't possess.

Eagerly, she picked up the wedge of cheese and bit into it. Sharp, woody flavor filled her mouth, and she swayed a bit as she shoved more into her mouth. Cheese in the city was typically soft and bland, intended to be spread or melted, a side note to the main dish, but this . . . It demanded to be devoured.

After she'd polished off half the wedge, Kiela discovered a note in the basket:

Welcome home, it said.

She felt her stomach clench.

Home.

Was this home?

Kiela placed the note down and stared at the words. She couldn't name all the emotions that the simple two-word note made her feel. Hopeful? Terrified? Sad? *At least I'm not still hungry.*

She contemplated the eggs. If she could start a fire in the

wood-burning stove, then she could cook them and have protein inside her. It would be easier to face the village with protein.

How hard could it be to start a fire?

The revolutionaries hadn't had any trouble doing it.

Remembering the smell of the smoke in the library, Kiela squatted in front of the stove without doing anything for a very long minute, then she shook herself and took the fire-starter off the little hook by the hearth.

"Um, do you know what you're doing?" Caz asked.

"Theoretically."

"I'm not sure I'm comfortable with that."

Kiela wasn't sure she was either. "Do you want to light it?"

"Definitely not."

She'd need fire to cook, and eventually they'd need it to warm the house. Winters this far north could be extremely cold. She remembered how beautiful the snow was, but she also remembered how the cold would seep down your throat and numb your fingertips. She'd nearly lost a toe to frostbite once. Snug inside the library, Kiela hadn't had to think about that day in a long time, but she remembered how her father had blown on her toes to warm them and wrapped her in multiple sweaters. Her mother had scolded her for staying out so long and then had given her a book to read until they'd judged her recovered enough to play outside again. Previously frostbitten toes were more prone to frostbite, they'd said. She had to be careful.

She shook herself out of the memory. It wasn't anywhere near winter, but still . . . This was a skill she thought she could master easily enough. There was already wood inside, as well as plenty of dried leaves that could serve as kindling. They must have blown down the chimney.

"Stay back," Kiela warned, and Caz retreated to the far side of the room.

She struck the fire-starter. Happily, a spark jumped at her very first strike.

Easy, she thought. *I can do this.*

She lit the kindling, then closed the door of the stove. Stepping back, she listened in satisfaction as the fire within spread and crackled. She held her palm above the stovetop. It wasn't hot yet, but it would be soon.

Wrinkling her nose, Kiela tried to ignore the scent of burning dust. It occurred to her that they should have cleaned out the inside of the stove before lighting a fire. It had just seemed that with the wood already in there . . . Oh, well, it would burn away. She just had to wait it out.

She turned back to the cabinets to locate the pan they'd found yesterday. Setting it on the stove, she left it alone to heat up. While she waited, she pumped water to wash her face, and she dressed in one of the sets of clothes that she'd brought from the city. It was a beige tunic-like outfit, with soft pants, perfect for scuttling around the library. Looking down at herself, she wasn't certain it was town-appropriate. Or attractive. But then, who was she trying to impress? Certainly not her neighbor. She was hoping not to see him again. Even if the cinnamon bun had been delicious.

"Kiela?" Caz said.

"Hmm?"

"There's smoke."

"It's the dust burning off," Kiela said. But there did seem to be a haze in the room. A rather thick haze. Smoke was billowing out of the stove. She coughed as she inhaled a breath full of it, and instantly she was back in the canals, with the library burning above her and bodies in the water—

She shut off the memory and ran to the sink. Pumping water, she filled a jar.

Caz scuttled to the front of the house and pulled open the door with his tendrils. The smoke rolled outside, but all that Kiela could think was, *Save the books! I have to save the books!*

Kiela knelt in front of the stove and reached to open the door—

She stopped an inch from the handle as heat hit her palm.

Searching frantically, she located a kitchen towel and used it to yank open the stove door.

Smoke poured out into her face, and she fell backward, coughing. She made herself lean forward and tossed water onto the fire. It sizzled and more smoke billowed.

Kiela ran back to the sink for more water.

Jar after jar.

At last, every ember was out.

Kiela stumbled out of the house. Hands on her knees, she tried to get a full, fresh breath. In her mind, she heard the screams from the city, and she imagined the books were screaming. *That's past,* she told herself. *Not now. You're okay. That's over.*

Wasn't it? Or was she going to feel this way every time she smelled smoke?

Beside her, Caz was shaking so hard that his leaves rustled. "That smell . . . I can't . . ."

She laid her hand on one of his tendrils, and he wrapped a leaf around her wrist. They clung to each other like that for a long moment until her lungs felt full of fresh air.

"We can't let that happen again," Caz said fervently.

Kiela wasn't certain if he was talking about the stove or the city. "It'll air out now, if we leave the doors and windows open."

"Maybe stick to cold food from now on?" he suggested.

"Until I figure out how to harvest, fish, hunt, or any of that, I am going to have to go into the village if I want any kind of food, hot or cold." A house full of smoke seemed like a hint that she should go now, before she messed anything else up in her attempts to be self-sufficient.

Caz ruffled his leaves. "You're going to leave me here?"

"Only because I thought you wouldn't want to come with me. Do you?" Of course she didn't want to go alone, but was it wise for him to come? She didn't know what the villagers would be like, in particular how they'd react to a talking spider plant. Caz was . . . highly unusual. He was the result of a reckless librarian experimenting with an incomplete spell that she didn't have permission to use. The librarian had been caught and punished—harshly, in Kiela's opinion. Wanting to make an example of her, the emperor had ordered one of his sorcerers to transform her into wood. She'd been displayed amid other statues in the library's famed North Reading Room. Afterward, alone, Caz had wandered the stacks until he'd found Kiela.

She still didn't know why he'd chosen her, but he'd announced that he was her new assistant, replacing a boy with continually grubby hands who would not stop snacking on honey treats near the books—and that was that.

"Are there any goats in the village?" Caz asked.

"I don't know."

"Rabbits?" He shuddered. "Other herbivores?"

"Possibly?"

"Then I have an idea: How about you leave me here?"

Kiela smiled. "Good idea." Then her smile faded. "Stay safe, Caz."

"Come back soon," he told her.

She fully intended to.

Bringing a sack (slightly worn but with a charming acorn-shaped button) she'd found, Kiela headed down the trail that her new neighbor, Larran, had sliced through the greenery. It was a perfect day: blue sky peeking between the trees, birds warbling to one another, a breeze from the sea that carried the fresh scent of salty air. Within the walls of the library, she'd forgotten the wonder of a summer breeze. She loved the way it caressed her cheeks, and the way the smells of the earth, the trees, and the sea filled her mouth, nose, and throat. By the time she'd walked a quarter of a mile, she'd convinced herself that this was an excellent idea, everything was going to be fine, and she shouldn't worry.

But then the trail through the woods ended, and her path opened onto a cliff, and every single worry came crashing back into her like the waves on the rocks far below.

Ahead of her was the expanse of ocean, broad and blue and beautiful and intimidating. Below, at the base of the cliffs, was the village. Just as intimidating in its own picturesque way. A waterfall tumbled beside the village, and the mill's waterwheel turned in the force of its fall. Catching the sunlight, the spray looked like a cascade of diamonds. She flashed back to being six years old, at the top of these cliffs, with her father beside her. He took her hand and helped her down the wind-battered stairs—

Ah yes, there were supposed to be stairs. She remembered now. Searching, she spotted them, behind a row of wild roses, and she also saw what had to be Larran's house, beyond the base of the stairs on a rocky beach. She wondered if she'd been unfair to him. It wasn't his fault she liked her privacy. Maybe now that he'd welcomed her, he'd give her some space.

A boat with a white sail floated just off the shore, and she saw the silhouette of a man standing on its bow. Larran? Possibly. Around him, in the water, were merhorses. The horse-fish were pawing at the waves as the man raised his arm in the air—some kind of signal.

In a herd, the merhorses galloped toward deeper water.

Shielding her eyes from the sun, Kiela watched them as they swam farther out, toward the local fisherfolk in their boats. The fisherfolk greeted them with happy shouts and cheers that traveled over the water. Her parents hadn't wanted this life for themselves or for her, but standing on the rose-framed cliff, looking over the sparkling ocean, she wondered what was so bad about it.

Gathering her courage, she picked her way down the wooden steps. Wind whipped her blue hair into her face and then vertically into the air, but she didn't dare let go of the railing to push the strands behind her ears or to twist them into a braid like she would have in the library. She just let them blow, wild and free.

Halfway down, the wind pulling at her hair, she felt unglued, like a book whose pages had scattered on the floor. She couldn't shake the sense that if she released the railing, she'd fly into the air like a bird . . . *Which would be ridiculous,* she told herself firmly.

The stairs twisted as they clung to the curve of the cliff, but none of the steps broke beneath her feet, and by the time she reached the bottom, her heart wasn't hammering quite so hard, and she was able to take normal-size breaths. Glancing up, she wondered how she was going to climb up it again without either panicking or having delusions of flight. She reminded herself that she'd climbed bookshelf ladders and the flimsy spiral stairs in the library all the time without blinking an eye. *But there wasn't wind between the shelves,* she thought.

Patting her hair, she tried to tame the flyaway strands, but they stayed a wild halo of blue. Inside the library, lit by lamps, her hair usually was a respectably staid shade of night-sky blue, but out here in the sunlight, it was an unruly sapphire.

Giving up on it, Kiela walked toward the village. It was strange overlaying the reality in front of her on top of her memories. In some respects, not much had changed: there was the mill, the school, the colorful houses along the cobblestone streets. But while memory was fuzzy, the details of the reality in front of her were sharp.

The bright-colored paint was peeling off the walls, and the roofs had been patched and repatched. Several of the houses had their windows boarded up, and there was clear evidence of storm damage that hadn't been fixed: collapsed porches, churned-up cobblestones, broken trees that should have been hauled away. Only the thick storm shutters on doors and windows looked new, and many of them were rough and unpainted. Kiela frowned. She'd always thought of Caltrey as a prosperous, albeit tiny, village. But there were signs everywhere that the village had fallen on hard times. Children, playing in the street, looked thin. Their clothes flapped flag-like as they ran barefoot past her, rolling a hoop over the cobblestones with a stick.

Looking up, Kiela saw the winged cats on the rooftops, sunning themselves, but they too seemed thinner and rougher. One eyed her as it licked its fur. Its green-and-yellow feathers looked battered as if it had flown through a storm. Maybe it had. But why? She remembered those cats as always plump and pampered.

Seated on his front step, an old man watched her as she walked by. She tried to smile at him, but she was feeling such a jumble that she wasn't sure what her face looked like. She hoped it wasn't a grimace.

He grunted back at her, neither friendly nor unfriendly.

Kiela remembered the way to the grocer's: up two streets, and then a right at the fountain, which was now dry. She remembered how much she used to love the statue of the mermaid at the center of the fountain. As a child, she'd felt as if the smiling mermaid were inviting her into the heart of town. Now, though, one of the mermaid's arms had broken off, and she gazed out at the harbor with an expression that Kiela thought was more wistful than welcoming.

Staring at the fountain, she heard the faint sound of a harp. Someone, somewhere, was playing a complex tumble of notes that ran as pure as the fountain used to.

Following the harp music, she passed the dry fountain, expecting to find the grocer's just around the corner, but in place of the shop she remembered with its wilty lettuce and oversalted lentil loaves, Kiela found a bakery. More accurately, she smelled it.

Unlike the rest of the village, which was a shabby shadow of what it should have been, the bakery was glorious. Scents of fresh bread and honey and cinnamon poured out of its open door and windows, and the islanders . . .

Everyone was here.

Or at least everyone who wasn't working on the sea or on their farm or orchard. It looked to be mostly older islanders deep into their retirement, with faces worn from wind, sun, and time. And if she were being honest, it was less than a dozen people, but it *felt* like everyone. Six times the number of people she'd wanted to see.

I could come back later . . .

No. You're already here. Buy what you need, and then you can leave.

Taking a deep breath, she approached the bakery. Outside on the cobblestones, tables with mismatched chairs were clustered in front of an open door and a wide window with a counter. One woman with crevasse-deep wrinkles and black-and-white-streaked hair had a lap harp on her knees. Like one of the librarians who'd worked on the fifth floor, she had two sets of arms. Very useful for shelving books and, apparently, just as useful for playing the cross-strung harp. She was plucking at the two sets of strings, creating both melody and harmony, an old sailor's song that Kiela vaguely recognized. The falling notes of the harmony were the waves crashing on the sand, while the melody sang of the sailor's love for the sea.

An elderly centaur woman was beside her, seated with her horse hindquarters on a broad bench. She wore a wide red dress and a matching red hat with a brim. Visible through the gaps in the dress, her horse body blended seamlessly with her human torso, black horse hair matching equally dark skin. Her woman's head sported black hair that narrowed into a vertical strip running down her spine, exactly like a mane on a horse's neck. She was drinking tea from a misshapen mug, blowing on it before she sipped. She lowered her drink when she saw Kiela and stared openly. She nudged her companion, who paused her harp-playing to stare too.

Kiela stared back.

She'd never seen the multi-armed harpist before, but the centaur lady looked familiar. Kiela couldn't say how she knew her. All her memories of Caltrey focused on her parents. *I must have known other villagers, though. Maybe her?*

Several other men and women, mostly retired fisherfolk and farmers, were seated at tables, eating their breakfasts and chatting about the weather, the tea, their neighbors, and the sea. On the ground, an older bald man with silver scales instead of skin was playing a game with black and white stones with a boy who had tiny goat horns poking out of his hair.

All of them stopped and stared as Kiela approached the bakery. Without the harp music, the loudest sounds were the caws of seagulls, the clang of the buoy bells in the harbor, and the whispers of the strangers who wouldn't stop staring at her.

This was a terrible idea. She should have come at a different time. Or not come at all. Or searched harder for the grocer's. She wondered what had happened to the man and woman who had run the local grocery store. As she recalled, they weren't the nicest people, but they did sell the essentials. Had they moved their shop elsewhere? *I should look for it.* But the wonderful smell kept her rooted in place. It was exactly like the delicious cinnamon bun that Larran had left for her.

"I'm . . . ah . . . looking to buy some provisions?" Kiela's voice came out far too shaky and high, curling up at the end as if she was asking permission.

A woman bustled out of the bakery. She had an apron tied around her waist and a smudge of flour on her cheek. Like the boy playing on the ground, her body was covered in soft tawny fur, and she had dainty antlers poking out of her hair, though hers were more deerlike than goat. The baker flicked a dish towel at her other customers. "Hey, you lot, quit staring, you're making her uncomfortable. Can't you see she's about ready to flee? Where are your manners? Haven't you ever seen a new customer before?"

"Nope," the boy with goat horns—son? Nephew? No relation?— said.

The baker smiled broadly at Kiela. "Welcome to Caltrey and to the best—"

"And only," the harpist chimed in. Balancing her harp on her knee with one hand, she held up her teacup with one of her other three hands, and the centaur clinked the cup with her mug. They chortled like two old friends with a hundred in-jokes.

The baker ignored both of them. "—bakery on the entire island." Throwing her arms open wide, she said, "I'm the owner and head baker, Bryn, and your first cinnamon bun is on the house!"

"I ate one for breakfast," Kiela said. "It was the most delicious thing I've ever tasted."

Bryn beamed at her. "Ah, I like her already. Anyone with a taste for sugar and cinnamon is automatically someone I want to know."

Gesturing with her tea, the centaur woman cried, "Ooh, I know her!"

"You think you know everyone," her many-armed friend said.

"She's the little girl up the hill, the one who always had her nose in a book. Binna Orobidan's girl!" She whooped like she'd won a prize by identifying her. To Kiela, she said, "You look just like your mother."

Kiela startled at the sound of her mother's name. She knew she should have expected it—there were bound to be people on Caltrey who remembered her, and Kiela knew she did look similar, with the same sky-blue skin and jewel-blue hair. Same eye shape too. Her father's nose, or so people had said. But still, it felt like lightning through her heart. "You knew my mother?"

"Binna and that dreamer husband of hers left for the south. City-bound." The centaur flapped her hand as if this was utter foolishness. "Whatever happened to them? Are they here too?"

"I'm sorry, but no," Kiela said. "They died."

"Ah, what a pity. My condolences."

One of the other islanders called, "Why'd you come back?" Unlike the centaur, her tone wasn't friendly, and she was glowering so hard that her eyes vanished into wrinkles.

Taking a breath, Kiela went with the same line that had worked so well with Larran. "I'd had enough of the city."

That won a few scattered nods, especially from the centaur.

The old man on the ground playing the game snorted, though. "We don't need cityfolk here. Mark my words: she'll just bring trouble."

The four-armed woman whacked him on the top of his head with a napkin.

"Ow."

"Didn't you hear Eadie? She's not cityfolk."

The centaur, Eadie, said loudly, "She's Binna's girl. Just look at her."

Everyone stared again, and it took every ounce of Kiela's courage to stay standing in one spot and not pivot and race back to the steps and the overgrown cottage that was both familiar and unfamiliar—and, she reminded herself, currently smoke-filled, because she was incapable of getting a fire going well enough to feed herself. "I'm just looking to purchase a few supplies, and then I'll be on my way."

"On your way? You aren't staying?" Bryn asked. She looked disappointed. "But you just arrived—you haven't even tried a fish pastry. It's my own recipe—the secret is to caramelize the onion and don't skimp on the garlic."

That wasn't what Kiela had meant to say. She'd meant "on my way" as in back to the cottage where she could hide from all these staring, overly interested eyes. "I'm staying in the house. My family's house. I only meant I'm not staying here, in town, in this spot."

"You *did* come home," Eadie said smugly. "Everyone always does."

"Her parents didn't," the grumpy man said, which earned him another whack from the harpist. But a few of the others nodded with him, as if that was the expected fate of anyone who left Caltrey. She felt the urge to defend her parents and their choices. They'd only wanted a better life for their family. What was so wrong about that?

Bryn stepped forward and made shooing motions with her hands, as if scattering chickens in front of her. "That's enough, all of you—you're going to frighten her off." Coming up to Kiela, the friendly baker hooked her arm through hers, which made Kiela want to flee even more. "Come with me, and I'll get you set up with whatever you need."

Guiding her inside, Bryn pointed to a flour-dusted stool and insisted Kiela make herself at home. Kiela perched awkwardly and wished she'd had a better option than coming to town. While Bryn bustled behind a counter filled with buns, rolls, and loaves, Kiela glanced out the open door and wondered if all the customers were gossiping about her. *Probably.* The harp music had started again, but she could hear voices murmuring beneath it.

"They don't mean any harm," Bryn said. "Don't mind them."

How could she not mind? But Kiela said, "It's fine."

"Hmm, if you'd rather be offended, that's okay too. We Caltreyans can be a lot: nosy, pushy, and opinionated—and that's just me. Now, what do you need?"

Everything, she wanted to say.

She needed her library back. She needed her parents, even though it had been so many years. She needed to feel safe again. And she needed to have a purpose again. She needed to be needed—and to be wanted.

But what came out of her mouth was: "Food. Seeds. And maybe a chicken?"

CHAPTER FIVE

Bryn squeezed icing onto a cinnamon bun and handed it to Kiela.

"I can't afford—"

"A welcome present," Bryn said. Kiela thought of the basket from Larran with the same buns in them, as well as the same words in his note. If cinnamon buns were the traditional welcome on Caltrey, she liked it. "Or, if you prefer, a good-luck present for your new start."

A new start. The bite of cinnamon bun hardened into cement in her throat, and she swallowed hard. *Is that what this is?* She suddenly felt as if her head were spinning, and she was glad she was already sitting. She'd liked her life; she hadn't planned to leave it. *How do I start over?*

The baker brushed the flour off her furry cheek before climbing on her own stool. "If you don't mind me asking," Bryn said, "why uproot yourself and make such a change? And all the way from Alyssium—is it as grand and glorious as they say? I've never even been there—I'm originally from the southern isles, left home after a family issue went bad, came straight to Caltrey, and never looked back." She chattered so fast that her words tumbled over one another like a stream over rocks, and then when she finished, she waited expectantly, even eagerly, for Kiela to answer.

Not thrilled to be the focus of anyone's attention, Kiela squirmed on her stool. She *did* mind Bryn asking, and she had no idea how to answer. She doubted that news of the revolution had reached this far north, so she'd have to explain all of that. She knew how that would go: lots of intense questions about her escape, and it wasn't an experience she wanted to relive. And assuming she was able to choke out the story, she'd be admitting she was a librarian—what if they figured out she took the books? What if they guessed she hadn't had permission to take them? What if they thought she'd stolen them? What if they contacted an imperial investigator? Kiela felt a chill thinking about them. Imperial investigators were called in whenever there was a suspicion about the mishandling of magic, and they had near limitless authority to punish offenders. What if they had her arrested and the books impounded? Or worse, destroyed? Illegal possession of spellbooks was a crime with very, very serious consequences. If she were arrested, what would happen to Caz?

Bryn asked with sympathy in her voice, "Was it a lover?"

"No!" Kiela realized she'd answered that too vehemently, and she felt herself blush. "I mean, it wasn't anyone. There isn't anyone. It was just . . . time to leave."

Bryn nodded sagely. "Ah, you don't like talking about yourself—I understand, and I won't ask any more questions."

The muscles in Kiela's shoulders unknotted, at least a little. "Thanks."

"Do you like talking about other people?" Bryn asked. "I know just about everything about anyone. I can tell you all their secrets as an apology for my trying to pry into yours."

Kiela laughed in spite of herself. "No, thank you. I don't need to know."

"Hmm . . . All right then. I think I know what you do need."

I highly doubt that.

"What you need is a savory pastry."

Well, maybe . . . Her stomach let out a gurgle, and Kiela felt herself blush. She polished off the rest of the cinnamon bun.

Bryn bustled behind the counter. "Starting over is difficult work. You need fuel. Protein. Salt. Nourishing fat." Humming to herself, she pulled out another pastry, arranged it on a dish, and sprinkled sea salt on top.

As she worked, Kiela noticed that the array of baked goods was decidedly different from what was available in the city. If this were Alyssium, at least half the items would have been baked with jam and sugar-drenched fruit: cherry tarts, raspberry swirls, apple turnovers. But Bryn's bakery had none of that. Lots of sugar and cinnamon and whatever it was she was preparing for Kiela. But no splash of color from any kind of fruit. She wondered why. Jam was such an integral part of every bakery that Kiela had ever visited.

"It's my own recipe," Bryn said, carrying it over to Kiela. "Go on, try it—my treat."

"You aren't going to stay in business if you keep offering free food."

"You'll upset me if you refuse." She paused. "Unless you don't want it, or are allergic to seafood, or aren't in the mood for more food, and if so, I absolutely would not want—"

Kiela bit into the pastry and was surprised by the burst of salt that prickled her tongue, the garlic that filled her sinuses, and the wonderful sweetness of . . . "What is that?" she asked as she chewed.

"It's a kind of fish that used to be plentiful around Caltrey, the silver swift fish. I've been working on ways to highlight the flavor. Do you like it?"

She'd tasted swift fish before, and it never tasted like *this*. The fish itself melted into the butter of the pastry, and when she swallowed . . . she felt as if she were inhaling the bright vividness of the sea itself. "It's incredible."

With a modest shrug, Bryn said, "It's ingredients and a recipe. Anyone could do it."

"But you chose to do it." She took another bite, and it was just as good as the first.

"Glad you like it," Bryn said. "We so seldom have new arrivals that I have forgotten how to make a new friend without scaring her off. I've known everyone on Caltrey for ages. Know everything about them, and I mean *everything*: who snores, who eats with their mouth open, whose feet smell . . . but I'd hoped . . . that is, I believe that a proper pastry can make up for a wealth of social blunders."

A new friend. The words were such a surprise that Kiela nearly dropped the fish pastry, which would have been tragic. *I'm not looking for a friend. I have Caz. And my books.*

Traitorously, a part of her whispered, *But I would like one.*

"I would like to know one thing about Caltrey," Kiela found herself saying. "What's changed here? I don't remember it being so . . ." She searched for a word that wouldn't be offensive.

"Desperate?" Bryn supplied.

It wasn't the word that Kiela would have chosen, but it would do. She nodded.

Bryn sighed. "Politics in the capital."

Kiela felt a prickle on her scalp. "Oh?"

"It used to be that the emperor would send his sorcerers on a regular rotation to tend to the outer islands, and they'd cast spells that balanced out whatever nonsense they'd done in the capital city to throw the weather out of whack, but then they stopped coming. Fish began to get scarce, and the merhorses—you'll notice our local herd has dwindled, which makes the fishing even worse. All our weather patterns have changed, due to city-magic nonsense, and without a sorcerer to correct for that, our farms don't produce what they used to." Pausing her breathless speed for a moment, Bryn nodded at the shelves of baked goods, and Kiela noticed for the first time that not only were they lacking in jam, they were only half full. She would have guessed the other half had been bought already, but perhaps not. "It's not that we're starving, but everyone worries that if the sorcerers in the south don't decide to pay attention to the empire's citizens again . . ."

Kiela had heard a little about that, but she hadn't paid much attention since it wasn't library-related. Over time, the emperor had withdrawn his sorcerers from the other islands and canceled their circuits of the outlying farms and villages. *A waste of magic,* he'd called it. There had been arguments—she'd read some of the discourse in the pamphlets written by the revolutionaries. The empire was hoarding magic, and the outer islands, whose economies had become dependent on the renewal of particular spells and on reliable weather patterns, were suffering because of it. She hadn't thought of what that meant on a practical day-to-day level.

While the elite used magic to build their palaces and fuel their lavish lives, ordinary people suffered. That was the crux of the argument for the revolution. The world and its resources belonged to everyone, they said—which included everything kept locked up inside the Great Library. All that knowledge, the power to make lives better, was shelved away. Reserved for use by only the wealthy, when it should belong to everyone. *And that's why I never really believed they'd hurt the library—and why I don't understand why they did.* They knew books were power.

Kiela wondered what Bryn would say if she knew that a sliver of that power was currently sitting in crates in a run-down cottage beyond the cliffs.

She also wondered what the emperor would say.

Or would have said, before recent events.

She remembered early in the revolution, a man—really, a boy; he couldn't have been more than seventeen years old—had tried to liberate one of the spellbooks from the first floor of the Great Library. He'd said in his trial that he'd wanted to use it to end a drought on one of the eastern islands. As his punishment, he'd been forced to drink water until his body convulsed. She didn't know if he'd survived or not. She did know that his image had been printed in the revolutionaries' pamphlets the following week.

"That's why some of the villagers aren't so happy to see you," Bryn said. "They blame all cityfolk for the emperor's new policies, but don't you worry—they'll warm up to you once they open their eyes and realize you're just another islander like them and not a Big Bad City Dweller who kept magic locked up away from them."

That was . . . uncomfortably close to Kiela's job description. She wanted to protest that it wasn't a librarian's choice who accessed the books, but it was easier to nod and agree.

"Now," Bryn said with another of her enormous smiles, "what can I help you with?"

Kiela climbed the stairs up the cliff with a sack full of supplies, including a loaf of bread, a bag of sugar, a pot of honey, several bars of soap, and several packets of seeds. Also, she had a chicken under her arm. She hadn't actually meant to buy a chicken—she'd been thinking of the eggs that her new neighbor Larran had left her and how nice it would be to have a regular supply of them when the word had come out of her mouth, and Bryn had insisted on it.

Thinking of the baker, Kiela smiled. The woman was a force to be reckoned with. Kiela didn't know if the village had a mayor, but if so, they were clearly overshadowed by Bryn. Or at least overwhelmed by the flow of her words. She'd cajoled everyone until they'd produced everything that Kiela thought she needed: flour, sugar, salt, butter, seeds for her upcoming garden, as well as soap and candles. Also a loaf of Bryn's bread. And, of course, the chicken. Kiela had used up the vast majority of the coin she'd brought with her to Caltrey, but she felt, with Bryn bargaining for her, that she'd gotten a good price. Even on the chicken.

The hen squirmed a bit under Kiela's arm as she climbed, but once they were halfway up, the hen settled down, as if realizing she'd be in peril if Kiela dropped her, which at least showed some modicum of common sense.

She'd been gone longer than she'd intended—Bryn liked to talk, especially at high speeds, and it felt as if everyone in the village who was on shore wanted to meet the daughter of the nice, young, and foolish couple who'd left for the capital—but she thought that Caz would be proud of her. And she was looking forward to *not* having to talk to anyone but the spider plant for a nice long while.

As she made her way through the thick forest growth, following the trail hacked clear by the farmer, Kiela thought she heard voices ahead. *Must be birds,* she thought. Certainly no one was at the cottage besides Caz, and he didn't have a history of talking to himself.

Closer, though, it sounded like words, not birdsong.

My imagination? She'd been part of more conversations today than in the past . . . well, in a very long time. The voices were still ringing in her head.

Except that sounded like Caz. And Larran?

He couldn't be back again, could he? So soon? She'd just finished talking with people! Lots of people! She wanted to burrow into her house and not have to worry about what she'd say and what he'd say and all of that back-and-forth talking nonsense.

Stepping out of the woods, Kiela saw Larran up on her roof. He had a tool belt strapped around his waist, he was shirtless, and he was streaked with soot. Her brain caught on the shirtless detail for a moment, and she stared with her mouth open. She'd never seen quite so many muscles, and they all seemed to be in use as he worked on her chimney. *No wonder I shrieked when he appeared so unexpectedly. He's huge.* In close quarters . . . those were a *lot* of muscles.

Belatedly, she realized that Caz was perched on the roof with him, his tendrils sprawled on either side of the ridgepole to keep himself balanced. He was telling Larran about the time Kiela had accidentally lost her balance while at the top of one of the library ladders and instead of falling backward and merely injuring herself like a good little librarian, she'd grabbed the nearest books and somehow succeeded in knocking over the entire bookshelf. It had fallen onto the next and the next, cascading into the most humiliating moment of her professional life.

"Caz," Kiela said sternly.

"What? It was funny."

In hindsight, yes. Hilarious. But was that really the best anecdote to choose to tell their new neighbor? Especially since she'd
been so careful to dance around the fact that she was a librarian in
her very recent conversations with the other villagers?

How much did Larran know? Had he seen the crates? *Calm
down,* she told herself. Caz wouldn't have been foolish enough to
have allowed that. He was even more of a worrier than she was.
Still, it was a risk, having a stranger anywhere near the spellbooks.

Scowling at both of them, Kiela snapped, "What are you doing
up there?"

"Your chimney was clogged," Larran said. "Thought I'd fix it."

And who had asked him to do that? *Not me. And it's* my *chimney.* Of course, it had needed fixing, and she'd had no idea how to
fix it. But still. He hadn't known that.

"You shouldn't start a fire in a stove with a clogged chimney.
You'll get a lot of smoke."

She'd noticed that. Between clenched teeth, she said, "Thanks."

Caz said, "I tried to tell her."

"You didn't," Kiela said. "You know less about chimneys than I
do." At that moment, the chicken let out a squawk and, with a con-
certed effort, spurted out of Kiela's arm. "No!" She'd nearly gotten
it all the way home!

Dropping her sack, she chased after the chicken.

The hen dodged left as she grabbed for it. She felt feathers as
the chicken slid through her grasp. It dashed by with an indignant
squawk.

She was aware of Larran and Caz both watching her as she zig-
zagged across the yard after the chicken. She lunged forward as it
turned right—again, she nearly caught it. And then with a burst of
speed, it plunged into the brambles.

Kiela skidded to a stop.

Panting, she stared at the greenery. "That went well."

"If you leave out feed, it'll come back," Larran suggested.

Yay, more advice. "Great. Thanks. I'll do that." Catching her breath, she straightened and returned to her sack, which thankfully didn't have anything within it that could escape. Although what she really wanted to do was to tell him to go away, she had to ask: "What do chickens eat?"

He gawked at her. "You bought a chicken without knowing how to feed it?"

"I lit a fire in a stove without knowing the chimney was clogged," Kiela pointed out. "I think it's safe to assume I don't know what I'm doing."

He laughed, a very nice laugh. She appreciated that it didn't feel like he was laughing *at* her. "Corn, oats, beans, but only if they're cooked," he said. "Any kind of fruit. Whatever scraps you have from your meals. They'll eat just about anything."

She wanted to ask what to do if the chicken didn't like her cooking and preferred whatever it found in the wild, but she decided she'd already looked ridiculous enough in front of him for one day. "Well, as soon as you're done . . ."

He patted the chimney as if it were a well-behaved pet. "Just about done now. Let's try to light the stove. If it works, I'll cook us those eggs."

"You mean, the eggs you gave me?"

He smiled. "Yes."

"As a gift. Those eggs."

"Yes, I'll cook them."

"And eat them," she said. He wanted to eat the eggs he'd given her as a gift, which made it not quite a gift anymore, didn't it? "Fine. You fixed my chimney. A few scrambled eggs are better payment than coin."

Confused, he frowned. "I didn't ask for any payment."

And I didn't ask you to fix my chimney. "Let's get this over with." She didn't want to owe him for this unasked-for favor.

He finished up as she went inside. After a day of cleaning, it didn't look overly terrible, especially given the years of neglect. Caz had made additional progress in her absence as well. She noted that the quilt was back on the daybed and that pockets of dirt were piled neatly in various spots around the room. *Caz made himself at home.* That was a good thing.

Also a good thing: it no longer smelled like smoke.

Peeking into the back bedroom, Kiela noted that the crates were still covered by the tarp. They didn't look as if they'd been disturbed. Reassured, she returned to the front room and eyed her nemesis, the wood-burning stove. "Ready to dance again?"

"Are you talking to the stove?" Larran asked as he came inside, ducking through the doorway.

"Were you talking to a plant?" she countered.

Caz entered, walking on his tendrils. "Hey."

Opening the stove, she saw it had been cleaned out. Fresh wood was inside, as well as wood shavings ready to be tinder. No piles of dust and no leaves. She wondered if this was due to Caz or to Larran. Regardless, it was done. She told herself to be grateful, not annoyed. Taking the fire-starter off its hook, she knelt in front of the stove. *You can do this,* she told herself. She wished she didn't have an audience.

On the other hand, if the cottage filled with smoke again, this time it wouldn't be her fault. She struck the fire-starter and sparks flew onto the kindling.

"Blow on it," Larran suggested.

Kiela blew on the tiny flames, certain she was going to blow them out, but no, they grew larger and the flames spread, dancing onto the other tinder and curling onto the logs. Sitting back, pleased, she shut the stove door.

As they waited for the stove to heat, Larran helped himself to a glass of water from the sink. She watched him drink it while trying not to look like she was watching him. Now that he was inside, he seemed even taller than he had before. He was a lot of person, filling her space, and she had no idea what to say to him. She felt as if she'd used up all her words in the village. *When all this talking is over, I'm not going to speak for a week.*

Of course, she could thank him for fixing her chimney. That

was an obvious thing she could say. She knew she *should* be grateful, even if it had been unsolicited help. "Thank you for fixing my chimney," she said at the same time as he said, "What did you think of the village?"

And then they paused awkwardly, and she said, "It was very nice," at the same time as he said, "You're welcome. It's what your parents would have done for me." And then: "You knew my parents?" she asked as he said, "I'm glad you liked it."

Caz slid between them and held up his leaves. "Gah, stop! This is painful. Don't either of you know how to have a conversation? Let the plant teach you. First *you* talk, then *you* talk, then *you* . . ."

Kiela blushed, and Larran laughed. It really was such a nice, warm laugh. She wished she could forget she was annoyed at him. But he'd invaded her privacy—a dangerous thing when she had stolen spellbooks just a room away.

"You don't remember me, do you?" he said. She realized she must have been staring again, thinking about his laugh. "I was about ten when you moved away. I watched your family sail off from that tree over there." He pointed out the window at a curved tree trunk that bent out over the cove.

"Glad you didn't fall off," she said.

"I have a good grip."

"That's useful," Kiela said, and then winced inwardly. First she chased a chicken around the yard, and now she was conversing like she'd never had supper with a person before. She really, really should have practiced talking to people more in the library.

She tried to think of the last time she'd had a meal with anyone but Caz, and she came up with nothing. *Huh, that's rather sad.* She'd never thought of her life in the library as sad before, and she wasn't sure she liked that point of view. *I was happy there, without anyone.* There was no reason for her to need to be making friends left and right here.

"You were kind to me when others . . . weren't," he said. "Your parents as well."

Kiela blinked at him. She had no memory of being kind or un-kind to him. "I'm sorry. I don't—"

He smiled. "It was a long time ago. Suffice it to say, I owe your family." He turned toward the stove. "I think it's hot enough." Cracking the eggs, he whisked them and poured them into the pan. As she watched, he mixed in scallions that he produced from a pants pocket, as well as a tomato.

Caz scooted forward. "You had a tomato in there?"

Larran shrugged. "You never know when you'll need one."

"I think you really do know," Caz said. "How many tomato emer-gencies do you encounter?"

"Actually, I'd forgotten it was in my pocket until now. I'd har-vested it right before I saw all the smoke billowing up from your house. I didn't want to take the time to put it in my kitchen." He sounded a bit sheepish. "I thought you might be in danger."

He'd rushed here to save her. Very neighborly indeed.

In a few minutes, he had it all assembled: egg, scallions, and to-mato, on toast that he'd sliced and tossed on the hot stove while she was busy marveling at the fact that someone had come to save her. When the Great Library burned, the place where she'd spent over a decade of her life, no one had tried to help her, no one checked on her, no one warned her. If Caz hadn't been alert, she wouldn't have even noticed that the other librarians had fled. Not one of them had said, "You should come with us. Or at least save yourself." But this man who had known her for all of five minutes . . . or since childhood, if that was true . . . he'd rushed here, not knowing if he'd have to pull her from a burning fire. She stared at him, unsure what to think of him, as he placed her plate, heaped with food, on one side of the table.

"One second . . ." He ducked out the back door to the garden and returned a moment later with a fistful of daisies. He plopped them into a canning jar, filled it with water, and set it on the table as a centerpiece. From one of the kitchen drawers, he produced nap-kins decorated with little blue flowers. He laid mismatched forks and knives on the napkins and then sat on the other side of the table. "Hope you like it."

She stared at the daisies then at the eggs, while he began to eat. Belatedly, she cut herself a wedge of toast with omelet and lifted it into her mouth. It was nearly-but-not-quite hot enough to burn her tongue. She tasted the sharpness of the onion, the smoothness of the egg—somehow he'd managed to make it light and creamy, unlike the rubbery eggs she'd eaten in the library—and the tang of the tomato. He knew both how to fix chimneys and cook.

They ate in silence for a moment.

Kiela tried to think of what to talk about. "You said you herd merhorses?"

He smiled, and his smile lit up his face. "I do. I can show them to you sometime. You could even ride one, if you'd like."

Half of her wanted to say no. *I'm not here to make friends.* She was here to lie low in a safe place, as unobtrusive as possible in case the chaos from the capital city spilled outward. She was here to hide until it all passed by. Besides, she wasn't even sure she liked him, despite the fact he'd been helpful and friendly and was a good cook. How did he make the eggs so cloudlike? Regardless, he didn't seem to understand the concept of keeping a polite distance and waiting to be invited.

On the other hand, what harm could it do? They were a very long way from Alyssium, and she'd always wanted to see a merhorse up close. "Thank you. Maybe sometime."

"Great," he said.

"That wasn't a yes."

"Oh. Uh—okay?"

Taking a breath, she told herself to quit being ornery. It was nice of him to invite her. Just because she was tired was not an excuse to be rude. "Sorry. I just . . . Never mind."

He ate another bite and then gestured at the stove. "You know, the next time you need help with anything, you should just ask."

Any goodwill she might have felt drained away. "And the next time you want to help with anything, you should 'just ask,'" she snapped.

He blinked.

She pointed her fork at him. "I didn't ask you to come over and tromp around on my roof. I didn't want you here. Especially when I wasn't home."

He reeled back. "I . . . I was just trying to help."

Caz chimed in. "He did fix it. And *I* was here."

She knew that. It was just . . . Ugh, if he didn't understand, she didn't know how to explain it to him. "You invaded my privacy. Multiple times." She waved her hand at the stove, the eggs, the daisies, the napkins.

"Ah." It was a syllable stuffed with hurt and confusion.

Kiela squeezed her eyes shut. She reminded herself that her chimney was fixed, the eggs were delicious, and the crates were undisturbed. No harm had been done. Yet. He had to understand, though, that this wasn't acceptable. "I don't want you to get the impression that it's okay to come over whenever you want. We aren't friends."

"Ah."

She opened her eyes. He was staring at his plate, clearly unsure what to say, and she was torn between wanting to take all the words back and being glad she'd spoken up. He had to know he couldn't keep dropping by, poking his nose wherever he wanted. It wasn't safe, not with the secrets she was keeping. She couldn't afford uninvited visitors.

They fell into another even-more-awkward silence.

Caz spoke first. "So, do merhorses eat plants?"

CHAPTER SIX

At dawn, Kiela tackled the garden. It was key to her being able to stay here. The food she'd bought in the village wouldn't last long, and she didn't have enough coin leftover to buy much more—and after yesterday, she didn't expect (or want) any more gifts from her overly friendly neighbor. She had to make this work.

Standing in the backyard, she put her hands on her hips and surveyed the tangle of green. The sun had warmed the air and now heated her shoulders and the back of her hair. She'd tied her hair back from her face with a ribbon, and she'd dressed in one of her mother's old dresses, an earth-colored patchwork of soft browns and greens with lots of pockets for holding trowels and clippers and extra garden gloves. Her boots had been her mother's as well, sturdy leather boots, softened with age, that could handle the dirt. The earth beneath the soles of her boots felt soft as a quilt, like it wanted her to lie down and be engulfed by the garden. Caz sat beside her, his leaves curled around his soil, as if nervous the vines would envelop him too. Vines had crept over the fence and swallowed whatever had previously grown here. Weeds had sprouted and taken over every inch of soil. Everywhere she looked was a riot of green.

Choked by vines, a tree bent over the right fence. A few of its limbs were leafless, and a bird with orange-and-green feathers perched on it. Puffing its chest out, it trilled a descending melody. Across the garden, another bird answered with a coo-like call. Elsewhere in the woods beyond the garden, more birds chirped and sang.

A breeze whisked across the garden, and the leaves shimmered in the sunlight as they fluttered. She inhaled the heavy scent of green, growing things—she could smell a hint of honey within the breeze, and she didn't know which flowers it came from. Prickly bushes with pale flowers filled one corner, and shoots with balls of purple flowers towered over another. She breathed in again and thought the nobles in Alyssium would have paid fistfuls of money to smell as light and lovely as the air on Caltrey. Just breathing it in made her feel like she was waking up after a night of perfect, deep sleep. She'd never felt quite so aware of the taste and feel of the air, or of the sounds of the birds and the gentle rustle of leaves. It made her feel like she could tackle any challenge—if only she knew exactly how.

"Any idea where to start?" Kiela asked Caz.

"How am I supposed to know?"

"Well, I feel like you might be an expert on vegetation."

He was quiet for a moment. "That is true."

"So, tell me what's a weed and what isn't," Kiela said.

"There's no such thing as a weed," Caz said. "That's a cruel term made up by people who label some plants as 'unwanted' and some as 'valuable,' as if the worth of a living thing is measured by how useful it is to another living thing. As if a plant can't have its own intrinsic worth." He was so worked up that he raised his leaves high and shook them. It was the longest, most passionate speech she'd ever heard the spider plant make.

In her soothing librarian voice, Kiela said, "All right. From here on, the word 'weed' is banned in this garden."

He lowered his leaves, pleased.

"How about you tell me which plants are which, and we'll . . . organize them. So that they all have the chance to thrive. We can designate areas for different kinds of plants and transplant the rest outside the fence. Like at the library." She walked toward the east side of the garden. "Here's the Nonfiction section. Vegetables only here."

"New Studies and Treaties," Caz said, designating an area at the front of the Nonfiction section. "Your seeds can go here. And in the back, Histories—that's the old growth."

"In the front of the cottage, Fiction. That'll be all the flowers."

"What about the berries?"

"Journals of Scientific Papers," she decided, because of the way the brambles both supported and strangled one another. "Along the far fence."

They planned it out, giving each type of plant a corresponding book designation. Kiela hauled the gardening equipment out of the house. Caz held the smaller tools, the trowel and clippers, with his tendrils, and she wielded the hoe and shovel. Focusing on the front section, they set to work.

By the time the sun reached midday, they'd cleared a five-by-five-foot area in New Studies, which wasn't much in the grand scheme of the overwhelming overgrowth, but it was enough, she judged, to plant some of the seeds she'd bought.

Caz coaxed her through the technique: a hole for each seed, then water, then soil on top, then more water. She spaced them out according to his directions and then sat back, satisfied. It was an excellent start. And it wasn't so different from organizing a bookshelf. A bit dirtier, but she'd gotten just as sweaty hauling books from shelf to shelf. The birds continued to sing to one another, and the breeze cooled the sweat on her neck. Her lungs felt full of the sweet-as-honey air, and the ache in her muscles was a good kind of ache.

"You know they won't sprout instantly," he cautioned. "It'll be weeks."

That punctured her mood.

Yes, she knew intellectually it would take time before there was anything to harvest, but she hadn't thought through the implications. It was indeed a problem, especially since she'd lost the chicken. She'd counted on the hen to lay eggs until the garden began to produce. She'd also hoped that some of the old growth (corralled into Histories) would be edible. Unfortunately, the vast majority of the vegetation was what some, not her, would call "weeds."

"I don't have that kind of time." She needed to produce food quickly if she was going to be able to live here. After the incident with the chimney, she wasn't about to ask Larran for handouts— that would completely undo the point she'd been trying to make, which she wasn't sure he'd even understood to begin with—and she'd seen that the villagers didn't have extra to spare. *I won't beg.*

Kiela poured water on Caz's soil ball and ate two more cinnamon buns, as well as the rest of the cheese that Larran had left for her. She was proud of the progress they'd made, but what was she going to do in the short term?

I could work.

If there were any jobs.

There certainly weren't any librarian jobs. She hadn't even seen a bookshop. She thought of Bryn and wondered if she needed any help in the bakery. Not that Kiela knew anything about baking. If Bryn did need an assistant, wouldn't she have hired one of the locals already? The fact was there might not be any jobs to be had. Besides, any village job would take Kiela away from the spellbooks for too long, and she needed to be nearby to watch over them—that had to remain her first priority. She'd taken on that responsibility when she'd taken the books, and she wasn't about to abandon it. She had to take care of the books.

She wondered, though . . . *Could the books help take care of me?*

"I have an idea," she told Caz. A terrible, terrifying, wonderful idea. "Come on."

Kiela went inside, washed the dirt off her hands and then dried them thoroughly, before heading to the back bedroom where the crates sat quietly. She threw off the tarp. She knew precisely what they'd packed into each crate, and she had a loose idea of which book she needed.

"Have a question you can't answer," she said, parroting one of her father's favorite sayings, "what do you do?"

"Look in a book," Caz answered. "But Kiela . . . Spellbooks?"

She pried off the top of the fourth crate. "I know."

"It's not permitted."

She thought of the librarian who'd been turned to wood, and felt her heart thump hard in her chest. Her palms began to sweat. But she steeled herself. "By whom?" she said to Caz. The emperor had been tossed out a window. He wasn't going to object. Or know. "Who will notice? More accurately, who will notice and care?" The ones who'd made the laws had been overthrown. Most likely, by now, they were all dead. A new government had been installed, and she'd read their pamphlets. "Magic belongs to the people now. I'm people. And we're very far from Alyssium."

She lifted out the spellbook on plantwork.

Sitting cross-legged on the floor, Kiela flipped the pages. She inhaled the familiar dusty scent of beloved old books and instantly felt like she was heading in the right direction. She'd read every book in these crates, and she knew there was a useful spell for plant growth somewhere.

On the use of roses for defensive purposes, she read.

Not that.

For aid in childbirth. The list of ingredients included chamomile and stinging nettles. A fertility spell followed, requiring sea urchin and seahorse eggs. She kept looking, wishing this grimoire had a table of contents. Maybe that could be her project while she was on Caltrey, creating indices for the volumes she'd rescued—after, of course, she figured out how to stave off starvation. If she did index all the books, maybe this transgression would be forgiven? Or maybe it wouldn't need to be? Surely, no one would begrudge her keeping herself alive. Especially if no one ever found out what she'd done.

A few more pages and she had it: a spell for the accelerated growth of plants. It had been created by the sorcerer Laiken in the last century. Laiken was renowned for his greenhouses—they dominated half of the island of Belde and were said to include every species to grow anywhere in the Crescent Islands. One entire room was devoted to poisonous plants, another to varieties of orchids, and one was said to be full of ferns that grew so lush you couldn't see more than a few inches in any direction. There was even whispered to be one section of the greenhouse full of plants that didn't exist anywhere else, plants created entirely by magic. Like Caz.

She skimmed the ingredient list:

Water (easy)
Blood (unpleasant but easy)
Duckweed (she wasn't certain what that was, but Caz should know)
Elder-bush leaves (again, she'd ask Caz)
Rosebuds from a beach rose

The instructions were to mix the ingredients into a paste and add a teaspoon to the soil above each seed and then say the words, pronouncing them as precisely as possible.

Every spell was written in the First Language, a long-dead ancient tongue. According to all that Kiela had read on the subject, the First Language was the language of Creation, comprised of words that tapped into the core essence of existence. Utter the right syllables, in conjunction with the correct ingredients, and you could alter the shape of that existence.

A spell from one of these books had altered Caz from an ordinary houseplant to what he'd become. Other spells, more advanced than this one, had created the canals, shaped the mountains, and tamed the sea. But this was what she needed now.

"Are any of those shrubs outside elder bushes?" Kiela asked.

"Elderberry is a fast-growing deciduous shrub with little white flowers and dark berries," Caz said. "And yes, I've seen several. Follow me."

With Caz's help, she identified and plucked the elder leaves from a bush in their garden, and then she dumped them in a bowl in the kitchen. Sunlight streamed between the vines over the window as she worked. First ingredient, done.

"Duckweed?" she asked.

"A fast-growing aquatic plant."

Well, she knew where there was water. On a mission now, she led the way down the stone steps back to the cove. Walking out on the dock, straddling the broken slats, Kiela peered into the water beside the library boat. Gentle waves lapped at the posts of the dock. Shaded by trees that clung to the sides of the cove, the air was cooler, and it smelled of salt and seaweed, rather than flowers and honey. She loved both smells. She wondered what it would feel like to dip herself into the water . . . but she had a task to complete. She called to Caz, who was back on shore, "What does it look like?"

"Small, lentil-like beads of green that float just on or below the surface," he recited from memory. "Usually found in still or slow-moving fresh water."

Kiela raised her eyebrows. "Fresh water?"

"Oh. Yes. Sorry. I should have thought of that earlier. Back up the steps?"

"Back up the steps," she agreed.

A hint of movement from within the water caught her eye.

Beneath the surface, a merbaby swam around the posts of the dock, weaving in and out as if it were a game. It was a little boy, with seaweed hair and a pale green fish tail laced with silver strands. He swam gracefully, the water curving around him, the sea grasses brushing his belly. Ripples flowed above him.

She hadn't seen a merbaby in years, not since she was a child. They didn't live in the canals of the capital city; too polluted. Waving at him, Kiela smiled. Bubbles rose through the water and then popped on the surface, sounding like giggles, as the baby waved back with his webbed hand and then flipped his tail fin and swam toward deeper waters.

A miracle, she thought.

Standing, she looked toward the jetty and saw a mermaid, half out of the water on one of the rocks, keeping watch. Kiela waved at her as well, and she thought she saw the mermaid smile before she ducked beneath the surface.

It was said if you weren't welcome on an island, the merfolk would foul the water near your home and refuse to swim close to shore. The sighting of a merbaby . . . She knew it was only superstition that they predicted good fortune, but it made her feel as if her luck was turning. *I'm doing the sensible thing. It'll be all right. I'll be careful.*

"Let's find that duckweed," she said.

Climbing back up the steps, Kiela led the way, feeling full of energy and hope—and a sense that she was on the right track at last. She had memories of a quiet pool in the woods, where she'd retreat with her books, hiding from chores that needed to be done around the house. She remembered the sound of her parents after sunset, calling her to come home. The fireflies would flicker around her as it became too dark to read, but still she'd stay, to watch the fireflies over the water and listen to the birds and the squirrels settle in for the night and the night hunters, the owls and the cats, begin to wake. Once, she'd even glimpsed a unicorn sipping from the pond, but it could have been only a white deer and a trick of the twilight. Another afternoon, her father had come with her, avoiding his chores too. They'd read books side by side, and her mother hadn't said a word when they'd returned. A week later, her mother had been the one to join her by the pond, arriving with lunch in a basket and presenting Kiela with a new unread book, a rare treasure on the island.

Kiela hadn't thought about those memories in years. After her parents had died, it hurt too much to think about them. But now . . . to her surprise, it didn't hurt. Or rather, it did, but it was a sweeter ache than it used to be.

She found the pond closer to the house than she'd remembered. Her memory had said it was deep within the woods, but it wasn't. Only a stone's throw.

Staring at it, she realized that she'd never truly hidden from her parents. They'd always known exactly where she was and how to find her. But they'd chosen to let her come here. They'd given her those afternoons of peace as a gift, joining her when they could.

"Kiela?" Caz said, interrupting her thoughts. "Duckweed."

She blinked at the water and at the tiny, lentil-like plant floating over half the pond.

"Are you all right?" Caz asked.

"Somehow I didn't expect this to feel quite so much like coming home." She'd made the library her home and, after her parents' death, hadn't looked back. She hadn't ever considered visiting Caltrey. She hadn't missed it. But now . . . She suddenly found that she wanted to stay. She wanted to make this work.

Even if that meant taking risks that she previously never dreamed she'd take. *Times have changed. The world has changed. I can change too.*

Kneeling, she scooped up a handful of duckweed and slid it into her sack.

She knew where to find the rosebuds: on the bushes on the cliff above the village. Following the trail through the forest, she and Caz emerged into the sunlight. Everything looked just as picturesque as the day before, but this time, she found herself appreciating it more. She didn't look on the village with trepidation. Instead she admired the bright colors of the houses and the blue beyond, dotted with boats.

From this distance and height, the village didn't look run-down. You couldn't see the too-thin children or the peeling paint or the storm damage. You saw a picture, framed by the sea. Kiela gathered the rosebuds while watching the merhorses frolicking by the shore. On the cliff, the breeze tasted like both the garden and the cove: honey-sweet mixed with salty-fresh.

As soon as they had all the ingredients, they returned to the cottage. She mixed them in a bowl, mashing them with a pestle she'd found in the utensil drawer. With Caz working the pump, she added water, and she used a knife to nick the tip of her index finger. She squeezed in a drop of blood. Following the instructions, she mixed it all into a paste.

"Do you really think you can do this?" Caz asked.

Today, after the merbaby, she felt as if she could do anything. "Yes. I don't see why not. It's ingredients and a recipe," she repeated Bryn's words. "Anyone could do it." She wasn't trying to create a canal or craft a palace, after all. "It's just about being the one to choose to do it."

"You're a librarian, not a sorcerer."

"Is there a difference?"

"They've trained."

"And I've read," Kiela said.

"If it's so simple, why all the laws to keep spells out of the hands of people?"

She'd never questioned the laws before, or really thought about them much. She'd had a job, to maintain the spellbooks in her area's collection, and she'd never considered how they were used or weren't used by the library's patrons. "Because knowledge is power, and the powerful want—*wanted*—to keep it all to themselves." Their greed had brought about their downfall.

"Not because it's dangerous?"

"Of course knowledge is dangerous." Kiela felt herself grinning. She'd never done anything the least bit dangerous before. It felt like a deep breath of sea air. *Maybe the taste of the breeze is going to my head.* "But ignorance is even more dangerous. In this case, ignorance means failure, and failure means no food, no way to stay here, and nowhere else to go."

Caz accepted that and followed her out to the garden, where they'd planted the seeds. She sat next to them cross-legged and laid the spellbook open on one of her father's old (but now clean) shirts to protect it from the dirt.

Using a spoon, she scooped a teaspoon of the paste onto each of the mounds where she'd planted a seed. She then read from the book:

> Rywy cryf chi dor
> Rywy cajon rhoi i
> Rywy gobai tremadon se hia . . .

She pronounced the words precisely and carefully, drawing on her knowledge from her studies. There was scholarly debate over the inflection on certain words, and she had followed all the discourse. She knew which syllables to stress and which to swallow, and she knew how long to stretch the vowels and which required a guttural sound. This was a magic made from the music of words, and she spoke the syllables to the seeds with every bit of conviction that this was right and that this would work.

When she finished, she closed the spellbook and waited.

"Did it work?" Caz asked.

Side by side, they stared at the earth, willing the little seeds to sprout and grow. "It'll work," Kiela said. "I know it will." She'd seen the merbaby in the cove. If that wasn't a sign that she was supposed to be here and thrive here, then . . .

It was *a sign,* she thought. *And they will grow.*

From within the house, she heard Larran call, "Anyone home?"

CHAPTER SEVEN

"I came to apologize," Larran said.

Oh! That was nice! But wait, no, he couldn't be here right now. Kiela had left the spellbooks piled on the bed, and who knew what was happening with the in-progress spell in the garden . . . He really had to go away. "You didn't need to do that."

Standing on the front step, he hadn't crossed over the threshold, but he also wasn't showing any signs of wanting to leave. Glancing behind her, out the back door to the garden, she saw Caz hide the spellbook beneath her father's shirt. *I can't let him come in.*

"I did. I mean, I do," he said. "I . . . pushed too hard. With the chimney. With the eggs. I didn't ask what you wanted." He was blushing. "I'm not really good with people."

You and me both, she thought. "I'm sorry I snapped at you." She wanted to add: *Now, leave.* But she couldn't figure out how to phrase it politely.

"I'm sorry I caused you to," he said. "And I promise I won't show up uninvited again."

He looked so earnest and so obliviously unaware of the fact that he was already in violation of that promise that she couldn't help but laugh.

"Other than right now," he clarified. "Allow me to make it up to you . . ." He took a step forward, as if to walk through the doorway, and Kiela wedged herself diagonally, leaning her shoulder against one side of the doorframe while her feet were in the opposite corner, as if that were a casual and normal way to stand. He halted.

"If you'd like to make it up to me . . ." She paused, hoping a brilliant idea would come to her. What could she propose? A walk in the woods? A trip into town? A visit to the bakery? What would interest him enough that he'd abandon his idea to come into her house, where he could see the spellbooks and discover she'd cast a spell in the garden . . . "Your merhorses!"

He looked confused, and she was suddenly aware of how ridiculous it was for her to think she could block the doorway if he decided he wanted to walk through. He towered over her without even trying. If he wanted to, he could have scooped her up one-handed and set her aside, but thankfully, he stayed put on her front step. "My merhorses?" he repeated.

"You offered to let me ride one," Kiela said.

Wait—was that what she wanted to do? She'd never done such a thing. She'd seen it, when she was a kid, and she'd begged her parents to let her try. *When you're older,* they'd always said, but by that time, they'd moved to the city, where there were no merhorses or merfolk or anything but minnows and trash in the canals.

Caz piped up behind her. "You did! You said it. Before. I heard you."

"I didn't think you wanted . . ." Larran began, and then he shook his head. "Yes, that's a wonderful idea. The ocean's warm today. Perfect weather for it. I just didn't think you'd be interested."

"Of course I am!" She smiled brightly at him, and it felt so fake that she thought her cheeks might crack. She hoped he couldn't tell that under normal circumstances she would never voluntarily suggest any kind of extended social activity. If he'd shown up just an hour later, after she'd had time to hide all the evidence . . .

Cheerfully, Caz shooed her outside. "Great! It's settled. Have fun, you two." Shoving with his tendrils, he shut the door firmly behind her.

"If you want to change your clothes . . ." Larran suggested.

"Nope, I'm fine as is."

"Your skirt will get wet. Likely, all of you will—"

"I'll dry," she said quickly. "I'm not made of sugar."

Larran smiled at her, and Kiela looked up at him and hoped this wasn't a mistake.

He led the way toward the path through the forest, and she glanced back to see Caz plastered against the window, filling the panes with his leaves, as he watched to ensure they left. She then followed Larran through the green, to the cliffs. The wind had picked up, and it blew her blue hair into her face. She pushed the strands back behind her ears. Waiting for her at the top of the wooden stairs, Larran held out his hand.

She blinked at it. "I'm fine."

He blushed, lowering his hand. "Ah. Of course."

Just because she'd lived most of her life in the city didn't mean she was incapable of doing anything for herself. The sooner he learned that, the better they'd get along.

Of course, he'd be more impressed with my ability to be independent if I hadn't almost burned down my house, lost my one and only chicken, and violated imperial law all within twenty-four hours. At least he didn't know about the last one. She intended to keep it that way.

Kiela followed him down the stairs, holding on to the railing as the wind picked and pulled at her hair and her clothes. The sea was choppier than it had been when she'd gathered the rosebuds. White crests rose and disappeared. She heard waves crash against the rocks as if they wanted to shatter them.

He hadn't said anything since they'd started down, and she wondered if he was regretting agreeing to this. And fixing her chimney. And gifting her eggs, cheese, and cinnamon buns. He'd only stopped by to apologize; he couldn't have anticipated a brief courtesy call turning into an outing in which he'd have to spend time with her. Why had he said yes? *He can't have been charmed by my friendliness,* Kiela thought. She hadn't encouraged any of it.

Perhaps it had to do with whatever had happened when they were children. She wondered again what she'd done back then to make him feel he had to try so hard to be nice to her now. Or what her parents had done. But instead she asked, "How do you ride a merhorse?"

Turning his head, he smiled back at her, and she knew she'd asked the right question. "First, you need to earn one's trust . . ." He went on to describe the different merhorses in his herd and which treats they preferred. "Sian, she's the golden mare, is fond of tomatoes. I discovered that when the apple trees on Caltrey sickened and wouldn't produce anymore. You might want to start with her. She can be fast, but she won't play tricks."

"Tricks?" Kiela asked.

"A few of them like to submerge with riders on them," Larran said. "Merhorses have a sense of humor, you see, but it's not quite a human sense of humor."

Maybe she should have stayed back at the cottage and found a different way to distract him from the spellwork in the garden. The merhorse herders had always looked so gloriously wild and free when she used to watch them as a child. Now it was beginning to sound a bit more reckless. She wasn't used to taking risks.

That's a good enough reason to do it. Her life seemed to be all about taking risks lately, starting the second she'd taken the lift down to the canals. *Maybe that's who I need to be now if I want to thrive here—a person who takes risks.*

He led her past his house, a sweet yellow cottage squeezed between the cliffs and the sea. It had a porch that wrapped around the front, as well as a balcony on the roof. Rocks served as a buffer between his porch and the waves. He paused to remove his boots and socks, and she did the same, leaving them safe on the sand. She used the ribbons on her skirt to hike it up above her knees.

Following Larran, she climbed barefoot over the stones that jutted out into the sea.

Spray flew into the air as the waves crashed against the boulders. He straddled two rocks, put his fingers in his mouth, and whistled. The whistle pierced the wind.

In answer, several merhorses neighed.

Kiela watched the herd swim toward the shore. There were at least a dozen of the half-fish half-horse animals, and each was as beautiful as the sea itself. Water sprayed from the manes, and Kiela couldn't tell what was horse and what was ocean.

Closer, she could see how sleek and perfect they were. They weren't like some of the illustrations in the library's illuminated manuscripts, half a horse stuck unceremoniously to half a fish. Instead, they were one cohesive creature. The horse head and neck, with forelegs, flowed into a sleek dolphin-like body that narrowed into a gorgeous mermaid-like tail covered in shimmering scales. Their coloration varied from pale to jewel tones—shades of blue, green, purple, and red. One was as golden as the sun.

Kneeling, Larran snapped his fingers. "Sian, to me!"

He beckoned to Kiela to come closer as one of the mares separated herself from the rest and swam forward, her hooves pawing at the waves as her tail propelled her toward the rocks. She was a rich gold with black streaks in her mane, and her eyes were a fathomless blue.

"Aren't you a beauty," Kiela cooed.

The horse-fish tossed her mane as if she understood her.

From one of his pockets, Larran produced a tomato. This time, he didn't have the excuse that he was rushing to her smoke-filled house. He simply had a tomato in his pocket. She wondered if they ever ended up squished. He handed it to Kiela.

"Hand flat," he said softly. "Offer it to her."

Squatting next to him, Kiela held the tomato out flat on her palm. Water from the wet rocks soaked into the hem of her skirt, but she ignored it—she'd dry, eventually.

Sian swam forward and then treaded water a few feet too far away.

"You're new, that's all," Larran said, still soft. "She's being cautious, but not as wary as she could be. If she was with foal, she'd never have come this close. But she isn't. None of them are."

There was a note in his voice that sounded . . . sad? Worried? She wanted to ask more questions. Were they supposed to be with foal? If so, why weren't they? But before she could form the words on her lips, Sian stretched out her neck and swam closer.

Kiela held still, marveling to be so close to such a beautiful creature. They were one of the wonders of the Northern Sea. No one knew how they were created, whether by a deliberate spell or by accidental magic, but the stories claimed they'd suddenly appeared one season, while a group of island fisherfolk were trying and failing to catch any fish. Day after day, the fisherfolk had been returning with empty nets. Their families were starving, and their villages were dying. But then one day, the merhorses appeared and drove the fish directly into their nets.

From then on, there was a relationship between the islanders and the merhorses. Herders like Larran would care for the herds, ensuring they were healthy, helping them with the often-dangerous birthing of foals, feeding them when the winter drove the fish too deep for the horse-fish to dive. In return, the merhorses would aid the fisherfolk in their boats during the spring, summer, and fall.

"The key," Larran said, so close to her ear that she felt the warmth of his breath, "is to not be afraid. She won't let you drown. You need to trust."

What if this time the merhorse decided she didn't like her rider? What if that nonhuman sense of humor that Larran had mentioned caused her to dunk Kiela? To think it funny if she panicked, flailed, and drowned? *Larran wouldn't have agreed to this if he didn't think it would be okay.*

She didn't know if she trusted Sian.

But part of her wanted to trust Larran. She just didn't know if it was the sensible part or the new reckless part. She thought of what she'd done in the garden with the seeds and the spell. Even knowing how dangerous it was, she didn't regret the attempt. *I'll try again. And again. Until it works.* It was worth the risk.

"How do I mount?" Kiela asked.

"Like this." And then his strong arms were around her waist, lifting her onto the back of the horse-fish. He lowered her gently, as if she were a precious thing he didn't dare break. She felt the warmth of his skin through her shirt, and then she felt the cold of the waves as her legs dipped into the ocean. She hiked her skirt up to her thighs, but it was already soaked.

He held her a moment longer, allowing the merhorse to become accustomed to her.

"How do I steer?" she asked.

"You don't," he said. "She steers. You ride."

He then released her. Instinctively, she leaned forward and grabbed onto Sian's mane as the merhorse lunged away from the rocks. Sea spray and wind spattered Kiela's face.

The merhorse picked up speed, jumping through the waves like a dolphin. Kiela clung to her mane, feeling as if she were holding on to seaweed, slippery but soft. She let out a shriek as Sian leaped over the top of a large cresting wave, and then she laughed as they sailed down the other side.

She'd never felt anything like this. It was terrifying. And wonderful.

She felt as if her blood had become the wind, and her breath had become the sea spray. She tasted salt, and she tasted freedom. Both were glorious.

They galloped away from the island into the wide blue.

Beside her, Kiela saw Larran on a purple merhorse. He had the widest smile on his face, and she knew she was seeing him in his element. This was where he belonged. This was what he loved. She could see it as plainly as she could read words on a page. He'd allowed her into his world with this ride. It was a gift, as much as the cinnamon buns and the chimney repair.

It was easy to be annoyed with him for the way he'd overstepped. But maybe, after this, she could forgive him. At least a little. Maybe he was just as awkward with people as she was, in his own way.

The men and women on the fishing boats raised their hands in greeting as Kiela and Larran rode by. Larran waved back. She didn't dare release the mane, but she smiled as they passed.

Soon, they were beyond the last of the boats. Only blue was around them. Waves swelled gently, and the horse-fish slowed. They swam side by side, and Kiela caught her breath. On their sail in the library boat, she and Caz had been surrounded by as much blue, but somehow this was different. She felt a part of it, linked to the sea.

Her dress was soaked, and her skin was saturated. She had goose bumps all over from the chill of the wind, but she didn't care. She didn't want this to ever end.

"You like it?" he asked, almost shyly.

Kiela turned to him with a smile that felt like a laugh. "Oh, yes!"

"Not everyone does."

"I guess I'm not everyone."

He smiled. "You're not."

It was the first time such a sentiment felt like a compliment.

At a leisurely pace, they rode in companionable silence back toward shore. Halfway there, she remembered the question she wanted to ask: "Why hasn't Sian foaled?"

"None of them have," he said with a sigh. "Not for five years."

Five years? "Not one in five years?"

"A merhorse doesn't foal easily. They aren't as fertile as other creatures, and their birthing . . . It's difficult, and often fatal for the foal. Sometimes for the mother as well. It used to be the sorcerers would visit twice a year, once to help them conceive and once to help with the birthing. We'd have new foals every single year, at least five or six. Sian's herd . . . It used to be triple in size."

As Bryn had said, the herd was dwindling, which meant the fisherfolk would catch less, which meant the islanders would have less to eat and less to trade. Kiela thought of how run-down the village had looked and the hint of desperation, of flat-out poverty, she'd seen in the people. Behind the friendly smiles, there was a lot of struggling going on. It might not have been visible to Kiela as a child—and indeed, it might not have been true when she was a child, since the emperor had only just begun to tighten the laws and withdraw the sorcerers—but it was clear now.

She rode the rest of the way deep in thought.

When they reached the rocks, Larran helped her dismount. She thanked Sian and also Larran. "That was magnificent," she said sincerely.

He smiled, again a bit shyly. "I'll take you whenever you want."

"I'd love that."

"If you'd like to join me for a meal . . . and to dry off . . ."

Her blouse stuck to her skin, her blue hair was plastered to her neck, and she hadn't eaten since breakfast. But there was an idea that had dug its talons into her mind and wouldn't let go. "I have to check on my garden. And Caz. There's a lot to be done around the house."

Larran's smile dipped, and for an instant, she wished she'd said yes. "I understand."

She wanted to tell him that it wasn't him. Not this time. She wasn't just making up excuses to leave. Pulling on her socks and boots over her wet feet, she said, "Another time?"

He brightened. "Another time," he agreed.

With a wave to the merhorse, Kiela hurried up the cliff stairs. She wrung out her wet blue hair as she walked back through the greenery. The villagers needed help; she needed a way to earn a living. There could be a way for them to make one another's lives better.

Seeing the cottage, Kiela picked up her pace. "Caz?" she called.

The spider plant bounded out the front door, using his tendrils to propel himself. "Kiela! Come see!"

"See what?"

But he didn't answer. Instead, he led the way through the house, out the back door to the garden. She dripped seawater in a trail but didn't pause to mop it up. His leaves were vibrating with excitement.

In the New Studies and Treaties section, a dozen new tomato plants grew tall, unfurling fresh leaves and unfolding blossoms. The blossoms swelled into fruit that shifted from green to a deep, brilliant red as she watched. The plump tomatoes became so heavy that the plants drooped onto the ground, but that didn't seem to slow their growth at all. Mouth dropped open, Kiela stared at them. When she was able to get her voice to function again, she shouted, "It worked!"

Caz cheered with his leaves. "You did it!"

"*We* did it," she corrected. She plucked a tomato off the vine and bit into it. Juice dribbled down her chin and, laughing, she caught the drips in her palm. It was the sweetest, most delicious tomato she'd ever eaten.

"Hooray for the human not starving!" Caz said.

She swallowed the bite of tomato. "It's more than that," she said, wanting to shout and dance and sing. She settled for waving the tomato in the air. "I know how we can do better than just survive! I know how we can live here."

"How?" he asked.

"In exchange for bread and soap and the things we need that we can't grow, we're going to give magic to the people of Caltrey." There would be challenges, of course. Risks, definitely. If the ex-emperor's people heard about this, if they guessed what she was doing, there could be trouble. She thought of the librarian who'd been turned to wood and the young thief who'd suffered so horrifically for his crime. She had zero proof that the laws had been changed.

Besides, no matter who was in charge, the powerful always wanted to keep power for themselves. But the islanders of Caltrey . . . the fisherfolk, the farmers, the merhorses, even the winged cats . . . *And me. I need this. We all need this.*

Caz rustled his leaves at her. "Say again? We're going to what now?"

Kiela smiled broadly at him. "We're going to open a spellshop."

CHAPTER EIGHT

"Nope," Caz said.

Kiela blinked at him. "Nope? What do you mean?"

"It's a terrible idea," Caz said. "I am assuming you threw it out there to soften me up for your real idea, which I won't like but will at least be better than *that*." He crossed his leaves like a professor preparing to listen to a student's wildly incorrect theories. All he needed was a pair of wire-rimmed glasses perched on his root ball to complete the look.

"That is my real idea," Kiela said.

"A spellshop. An illegal spellshop. A shop so illegal that the emperor himself—"

"He splatted," Kiela interrupted before he could wind himself up into a full-blown rant. "You don't know what's changed since we left. Laws could've been rewritten." She held up a hand. "Or not, I know. But we aren't in Alyssium anymore, and it's unlikely that anyone official would have ever heard of Caltrey, much less show up here. Besides"—she plowed on before Caz could argue back—"I'm not saying we should call it a spellshop."

"Good," he said, "because 'Kiela and Caz's Really Illegal Spellshop that Will Likely Get You Killed or Cursed' would look ridiculous on a sign. You must as well just invite an imperial investigator in for tea."

"That part will be hidden, a shop within a shop," Kiela said. "And we don't have to admit we're selling spells at all. We'll call them 'remedies.'" She was sure she could extract a few useful spells from the wealth of arcane knowledge in her possession. She already had the quick-plant-growth spell, though it wasn't ideal—it looked an awful lot like magic, plus it was more of a one-time emergency-use spell. She was certain she could find another equally useful spell that wasn't so flashy, with a bit of research. If there was anything in the world she was good at, it was research.

Caz snorted.

"On the surface, the shop will sell . . ." Looking for inspiration, she scanned the cottage. She doubted anyone would buy cobwebs or old chipped plates or . . . Her eyes landed on the pantry with its rows and rows of glass jars that her parents had left behind when they'd abandoned their island lives and moved to the city. They'd used them to preserve fruits and vegetables, as well as nine-year-old Kiela's favorite: "Jam."

"Jam?" Caz squeaked.

Kiela hurried across the room to the jars. She picked one up and blew on its top. Dust plumed up in a mini-cloud. Yes, this would do nicely. Clean them up, fill them with jam, wrap a ribbon around them, and they'd make lovely merchandise. She'd already noticed the lack of jam and fruit items in the bakery, which meant there was a market for it. "We'll sell jam. Raspberry jam. Blackberry jam. Blueberry jam. Apple and berry jam." She'd seen lots of berry bushes in the garden—they'd begun to corral the brambles into the Journals of Scientific Papers section, near the back fence. She didn't know what kind of berries they were, but surely they were something that could be jam-ified.

"Jam," he repeated. "You want us to build a new life based on . . . jam?"

She pulled out the jars, counting them as she went.

"Do you even like jam?" he asked.

Twenty, twenty-five, thirty . . . Ooh, there were smaller ones on the third shelf, easily several dozen of them. Her parents had canned lots of food. Everyone on the island did. It was a way of life here: grow as much as you can in the summer, harvest in the fall, and preserve for the winter. She could offer a discount to anyone who returned a jar when they finished so that she wouldn't run out of them. "Of course. Who doesn't like jam?"

"I don't."

"You're a plant. I imagine the bulk of our customers will be non-plants."

"It makes my leaves sticky."

"Then maybe don't put your leaves in the jam?" She lined the jars up on the counter, filled the sink with water, and began to wash them.

"Jam? Really?"

"We don't need to make a fortune from the jam—it just needs to sell well enough to serve as a cover for our real product."

"This is a terrible idea."

Kiela held up a clean jar. Streaming between the vines over the window, the sun hit the glass and sparkled all over the kitchen. "This will work," she promised. All she had to do was coax the brambles into producing ripened berries, teach herself how to make jam, and package it all up. Also, turn part of her cottage into a shop. And learn more usable spells. Okay, it was a lot.

Maybe she was fooling herself. She didn't really know anything about running a shop or magic or jam . . . *But I do know books*—and that meant there was nothing she couldn't know, eventually. That was a magic in and of itself. Drying her hands so she wouldn't drip on anything, she searched the kitchen shelves.

Joining her, Caz climbed up onto the third shelf. "Now what are you looking for?"

"A cookbook."

"Oh!" He very much approved of that, she could hear in his voice. If there was a book involved, that automatically made any course of action much more sensible. Without complaint, he pulled himself up onto a shelf within the closet. He squeezed his leaves between jars, searching for a cookbook, and then hopped root-ball-first to the next shelf. She looked through the cabinets beneath the sink.

After a few minutes of searching . . . "Aha!" Caz cried.

And then: "Oops."

She turned around to see one of the glass jars tumbling from the top shelf. Caz stretched out his leaves—the jar landed in a net of leaves with a plop. Kiela rescued it and set it beside the sink. "What did you find?" she asked.

He pulled out a dusty and battered book with his tendrils.

She took it and gently brushed the dust off with the dry towel. Sitting on the floor cross-legged, she flipped through it. It was exactly what she hoped it would be: her parents' recipe book. Look, there was the potato soup that her father had loved. Oh my, it had a lot of butter. And here was the muffin recipe. She twisted the book to see her mother's handwritten notes in the margin, doubling the cinnamon in her father's recipe. Two pages later, she found a peach pie recipe in her mother's handwriting with a note from her father that read, *Delicious*. And a wet drop landed on the ingredient list.

Quickly, Caz swiped it away with a leaf.

Kiela leaned backward and wiped her eyes. She hadn't even realized she'd started crying. Awkwardly, Caz patted her back with a tendril.

"It's the dust," Kiela explained.

"Of course."

She kept going until she found it: a recipe for raspberry jam. Like the pie, this one was in her mother's handwriting with notes from her father in the margins. Hers eyes blurred again as they filled with more tears.

"Your parents left this for you," Caz said. "They would've wanted you to do this."

Kiela let out a hiccup-laugh that was half a sob. "No, they really wouldn't have." They'd left this island with dreams of a better life for all three of them, and their plans for her future had never included her coming back, especially without them. She touched the berry-stained recipe and traced the loops of the letters. "But they did like jam."

The recipe called for two ingredients: berries and sugar.

Kiela had bought some sugar from the bakery and had enough for a trial batch at least, but the berries . . . She put her hands on her hips as she contemplated the brambles in the backyard. Untidy, the branches had knotted themselves into a leafy morass of prickles. She'd trimmed them yesterday but hadn't truly tamed them yet. They sprawled across the far corner of the garden so thickly intertwined that she couldn't tell where one plant began and one ended. A few pale raspberries were growing tucked here and there beneath the leaves, but she didn't see any ripe ones.

"More magic?" Caz asked.

"Did we save the extra duckweed?"

He sighed heavily. "Yes, and we have a few rosebuds left too."

She considered the brambles while Caz trotted back into the house to retrieve the spell ingredients. Maybe if she did just a small poultice this time . . . They didn't need the bush to grow from a seed, the way they did with the tomatoes; they just needed it to hurry its cycle and produce ripe berries. So, a touch of magic?

"I hope you know what you're doing," Caz said as he returned.

"I absolutely do not know what I'm doing. I thought that was clear?"

Plopping on the ground between what looked like a celery stalk and a squash vine, Kiela combined the ingredients into a paste. She consulted the spellbook to refresh her memory of the words—she did *not* want to accidentally drop a syllable or two. She'd heard stories of what happened to sorcerers who slurred or stumbled over their spells. There were sorcerers who'd transformed themselves into trees, their houses into solid stone, their meals into poison . . . The storm that destroyed the island of Virand was said to be caused by a weather spell gone awry. A few years ago, one of the emperor's sorcerers had tried to enchant a songbird and instead had sprouted feathers herself. She was said to molt every spring, and her feathers were worth a fortune. Kiela had seen one once, in the hat of a library patron—brighter than peacock blue, with a shaft that looked to be made of gold. At any rate, Kiela didn't want to sprout feathers or bark, so she took great care as she dropped a dollop of paste at the base of a raspberry bush and chanted the words.

"That should do it," she said.

"It took a bit of time with the—whoa!"

Caz scrambled back as the brambles exploded into a burst of growth. Kiela grabbed the spellbook, clutched it to her chest, and retreated across the garden. The raspberry bushes slammed into the fence and flowed over it into the forest. Green burst from the branches as new leaves unfurled from the slender brown stalks, and flowers popped into bloom up and down the stalks. The white petals opened and then broke apart before raining down on the lawn, while the hearts of the tiny blossoms swelled and hardened into pale berries. A few seconds later, the berries darkened into red.

And then there was silence.

A bird chirped.

Kiela gawked at the bushes. She had no idea how far into the woods they'd penetrated, but they'd swallowed the back fence. Now, with the berries ripened, they seemed to be done with their unnatural growth, but she still couldn't bring herself to move closer.

"I think . . ." She swallowed. Her throat felt very dry. ". . . less magic next time?"

"Next time?" Caz repeated.

"Well, it worked."

She gathered up her courage and approached the berries. At least the brambles hadn't grown toward the house. They could have devoured the entire garden. Yeah, she really couldn't sell this spell in their shop. It was absolutely not subtle magic. On the plus side, though . . . *This will make a lot of jam,* she thought.

She picked a raspberry, stared at it a moment, and then popped it into her mouth. For an instant, it felt smooth and tasteless, and then she squashed it. Sharp sweetness exploded gloriously over her tongue. It was so overwhelmingly *raspberry* that it felt as if it invaded her skull and displaced every thought—there was only flavor. Powerful, intoxicating flavor. She'd forgotten what a freshly picked berry tasted like.

On Alyssium, the fruit was imported. There wasn't space on the city island for gardens or orchards or berry patches. The emperor had had his greenhouses, filled with delicacies, but a librarian . . . She hadn't tasted a just-ripened raspberry since her childhood.

It tasted like a bite of sunshine.

Caz poked her ankle. "Are you poisoned?"

"I'm in ecstasy," she corrected.

"Huh," Caz said. "You really think this will work?"

Kiela opened her eyes and again surveyed the wealth of berries before her, a glorious chaos of ruby-red riches, enough to create many jars of jam. "I think it's perfect."

Following her parents' recipe, Kiela chopped up a bowlful of raspberries and sprinkled a half cup of sugar over them. Her fingers were stained wine red by the end, and she washed them while the sugar soaked into the berries. Her mother had written *two hours,* and her father had scrawled *Overnight,* but Kiela wasn't patient enough for that. Two hours would be fine.

She used the time to assess the extent of the damage the spelled bushes had caused. Tromping around the fence, she squeezed be-tween trees, ducked under vines, and waded through underbrush until she reached the back of her garden.

The raspberry bushes had invaded the forest by about fifteen feet, which she supposed could have been worse. At least brambles hadn't overwhelmed any trees—they'd simply filled all the space in between the trunks. Everywhere, the bushes were thick and about as high as her shoulder, and they were covered in beautiful red berries. Finding a couple buckets in the house, Kiela returned and picked as many as she could reach. Every dozen berries, she'd pop one in her mouth instead of the bucket, but she still had three full buckets, as well as arms covered in tiny scratches, by the time the berry-sugar concoction had finished macerating.

With Caz reading the recipe, she lit the stove and set the berries to boiling. She'd have to stir continuously until they thickened. She found a wooden spoon in her parents' drawers. *My drawers now. My home.* She wasn't sure it felt like hers, though.

As she stirred, she imagined her parents in this very kitchen. She could picture them: dancing around the table, her mother laughing, her father singing off-key. They'd been happy together. Kiela felt an ache just behind her sternum as she thought of them. Her father had once told her he hoped she found someone who made her smile. Just that. No fireworks like in tales and ballads. He didn't wish her the shiver of romance or the endless ache of desire. "You should marry your best friend," he told her. All those grand emotions, he said . . . they're fun, but eventually they fade. They always fade. What was better, he'd said, was companionship. He'd wanted her to find someone who would be there for her, who'd laugh with her through the years. Every time she'd visit for dinner in the city, her parents would ask her if she'd met anyone, if she was making friends, if she was lonely, and she'd always said, *Of course I'm not lonely.*

She had her classmates. She had the other librarians. She had her parents. And she had her books. If everyone living failed her, whenever they did, she had all the immortal voices caught in pages. Her father had clucked his tongue and said, "But can a book be kind to you?"

Yes, she answered him now as she lifted the spoon out of the boiling jam.

Her parents' book had gifted her with this, a way forward.

"To see if it's done," Caz said, "you're supposed to spoon a bit onto a plate and drag your finger through it to see if it's runny or not." Perched on the counter, he peered into the pot. "And you're supposed to skim off that froth."

She dutifully skimmed off the whitish, cloudy foam and dumped it in the sink. Testing the jam, she dropped a spoonful onto the counter. Caz pulled a leaf through it, and it ran across the surface. "Almost," he said.

She got a jar ready.

The jam began to bubble. Quickly, she returned to stirring it, and the mixture settled down. It felt thicker than before, which had to be correct, didn't it? The wooden spoon was stained a deep berry red. She doubted it would ever recover its original shade. *Oh well. It's now my jam spoon.*

"You're supposed to seal it with wax," Caz said, reading. "I don't think we have any wax. But you melt the wax in a double-boiler pan, whatever that is, and after the jam is in the jar, you pour in the liquid wax. It hardens and seals in the jam. It'll last months that way."

"I'll buy some extra candles when I buy more sugar," Kiela said.

"With what money?" Caz asked.

Not having an answer to that, she tried the jam again. This time, it smeared as she dragged it with her finger. Popping her finger into her mouth, she tasted it—sweet raspberry so intense that she could almost hear her father's voice as he spread jam on toast. And *ow,* hot! But richly sweet.

"Good?" he asked.

"It tastes like a memory."

"Great." Then: "Is that good?"

She smiled at him. "Very good."

Carefully, Kiela poured the hot jam into the jar. "And as for how we're going to pay for supplies . . ." She lifted the jar up to the window, holding the warm glass with a towel. In the sunlight, the jam sparkled like crushed rubies. "I have an idea."

CHAPTER NINE

As soon as the jar cooled, Kiela covered it with a square of cloth cut from one of her father's old shirts and tied a string around it to secure it. She surveyed her work. *Pretty enough,* she thought. It would be better with a ribbon, but that could be a later embellishment.

"You think the baker will go for it?" Caz asked anxiously.

"I think she'll recognize that a raspberry croissant would be amazing." Or a raspberry donut. Or a raspberry tart. Kiela hadn't seen anything like that in Bryn's bakery—perhaps there was a berry shortage on the island. It seemed likely, given all the other troubles they'd been having. Larran had mentioned the apple orchards failing; it was logical that other crops had failed as well. Certainly from what she'd seen, there was a distinct lack of jam on Caltrey, which meant that their little shop might be very welcome.

"You don't think she'll ask where you'll get enough berries?"

Kiela peeked out the back window at the riot of berry bushes. With the sun shining on the leaves, they looked like they held a thousand shades of green, cradling the jewellike berries. She could smell the rich scent of the raspberries even from inside. It filled the house, joining with the scent of lavender—she'd filled pitchers with clippings of lavender and positioned them around the house, like her mother used to: on the table, the shelves, and the kitchen countertop.

Drying herbs hung from the rafters. "I'll tell her my family's garden, left untended, has run wild and flourished."

He bobbed a tendril in agreement. "Plausible. If you're sure this is a good idea . . ."

"I'll be careful," she promised.

"I'll have the other jars clean by the time you return," he promised back.

Tucking the jar into a basket, Kiela headed for the door. Halfway out, she stopped and looked back at the spider plant perched on the edge of the sink. He'd wrapped a tendril around the pump and was about to fill the sink with water. Sunlight spilled through the window onto him, the pump, and the pitcher of lavender beside him. "Caz? Are you ever lonely?"

"How can I be?"

She thought he'd finish with, *I have you.*

But he said, "I have books."

Smiling, Kiela headed for the path through the woods. She listened to the birds, the familiar coos and trills. She could parse a few out—there was the two-note call of the charmed warbler, the cascade of the crested parrot, and the . . . Wait, was that a chicken?

Yes, it was. *My chicken,* she thought, stopping midway down the trail. Peering through the green, she realized there was no way to identify where exactly the wretched bird was and certainly no way to reach the hen before she scuttled away through the underbrush. *At least she sounds happy.*

Kiela continued on.

She expected that this time, when she emerged from the forest, she wouldn't be quite so stunned by the view—after all, she'd seen it already. But when she stepped out from the canopy of green, the blue smacked into her, and she stopped and just stared.

It was the vastness of the blue that was so breathtaking, as well as the variation: the bleached blue-white of the sky near the sun, the deeper blue of the sky near the horizon, the slate blue of the clouds, the black-blue and green-blue and fathomless blue of the sea, all contrasted against the pale sand of the shore, the bright colors of the houses, and the dark green of the trees. Far below, at the base of the cliffs, she saw the waves crash in foaming white and then caress the sand. It was high tide, and it reached nearly to the base of the stairs. She plucked a few rosebuds as she passed the bushes and began to pick her way down the steps.

By the time she reached the base of the cliff, the water was lapping at the bottom step. Reaching down, Kiela slipped off her shoes and waded across the beach. The seawater was chilled today, and it nipped at her ankles with each wave like a playful puppy. Sand wiggled between her toes.

Climbing up to the cobblestone streets, she glanced back toward Larran's house, perched beyond the reach of high tide, and she thought she saw movement through one of the windows. For an instant, she was tempted to reverse direction, knock on his door, and show him the jam she'd made without any help from anyone except Caz, her parents, and the author of the spellbook. But she had a task to perform and no time for a chat with her overfriendly neighbor. She wanted to be back up the stairs before the sun set.

The winged cats of Caltrey basked on the roofs and in the street. She wondered if there was a spell that would help them thrive. A spell for cat-appropriate food. She didn't think they'd eat jam. One cat with gray-striped fur and orange wings raised his head as she passed and then washed his front paw.

She passed a fisherman with a tackle box in his left hand and a net over his right shoulder, and he glared at her as if she was trespassing. She tensed and then reminded herself it was a public street, she belonged here, and she had a destination. Glancing back over her shoulder, she expected to see him watching her suspiciously, but he wasn't. He shooed away one of the cats who was lounging on a doorstep and went inside one of the houses without a backward glance. Maybe the look had been unfriendly only in her imagination. Maybe he'd been scowling because she'd looked unfriendly. What had her face been doing when she passed him?

Had she smiled? Had it been a weird smile? She practiced smiling and wished she had a mirror. She couldn't tell if she was curving her lips too much or . . .

Ahead was the fountain and beyond it the bakery. Kiela dropped her face into a neutral expression and hoped that none of the bakery customers had seen her smiling inanely at no one as she walked through the streets.

She nodded at Eadie, the centaur woman, who was seated in the same bench as last time and had another cup of tea in front of her. The boy with goat horns was here again too, cross-legged on the street, absorbed in peeling potatoes. The skins were piling up next to him. Everyone else from the other day—the multi-armed woman, the grumpy man with scales, the older woman with more wrinkles than a raisin—was absent, thankfully.

"Hello, Binna's girl!" Eadie called. "How's the cottage holding up?"

"Surprisingly sound," Kiela said. "I thought it would be full of mice or badgers by now, but the only unwanted residents I've met so far have been spiders."

"You want to keep at least a few to catch the spring flies."

"Um, thanks? I will?" She didn't say that Caz despised spiders, due to the number of times the library spiders had tried to spin webs between his leaves.

"Once you're all settled in, I'd love to stop by and see the old place," Eadie hinted.

Kiela tensed. She hadn't thought about the possibility of other neighbors stopping by her home . . . but then, if she intended to turn it into a shop, she supposed she was going to have to get used to the idea of welcoming customers. Oh my, she hadn't thought about that aspect of her plan. If it was to succeed, she was going to have to interact with any number of people. She swallowed and hoped that Eadie couldn't tell that her hands had started to lightly shake. "That would be very nice," she said. "Once I'm all set up."

And then she fled inside the bakery.

She exhaled once she was safely within. The scents of bread and cinnamon curled around her, and it was impossible to feel anxious. Being in the bakery felt like sitting by the nicest fireplace in the nicest reading room of the library. It was warm and welcoming, like the baker herself.

Bryn smiled broadly at Kiela. "It's the cinnamon rolls that drew you back so soon, isn't it? Either that or my sunny personality, but I vote cinnamon rolls—no one can resist the allure of butter, sugar, and cinnamon."

Now that Kiela was here, her idea didn't feel quite so grand and sparkling. Who was she to start a business, especially one with a possibly slightly (or very) forbidden side? She didn't know anything about jam or shops or this island or people or really anything but her section of the library. Who was she to think she could transform her parents' home into a store and welcome in neighbors—strangers—and sell to them? Her throat felt clogged as she searched for the words that she'd been so sure would be easy to say.

"Hmm, if it were cinnamon rolls, you'd look happier to be here," Bryn said. "Is something wrong? Is it the cottage? An issue with your roof, your stove, your water? Once, after a storm, I had holes in my roof—I live above the bakery—holes as big as my fist and so much rain came through that I expected to find a fish in my bed. Reinforced the roof since then, of course. You have leaks? If so, you'll want to get them patched up before the next storm."

Kiela shook her head and wondered why all the words had fled her. She hadn't had any problem talking to the baker when she'd been asking for seeds and such, but now, with so much more at stake . . . It had seemed such a shiny, lovely idea before, but what if Bryn thought it was nonsense? What if there was no jam in her bakery simply because she didn't like jam? What if no one on Caltrey liked jam? What if Caz was right that this was all a terrible idea? Instead of speaking, Kiela pulled the jar of raspberry jam out of her basket and held it out.

"Ah, lovely!" Bryn took the jar, removed the cloth from the top, and sniffed. "Raspberry! You have raspberries? My crop has been measly for the last three years."

"They grew, left wild . . ." *Stop being ridiculous,* she told herself. *Pull yourself together, Kiela.* "I had an idea, to start a shop, to sell jams and . . . little remedies, to help with plants and such . . . But mostly jam. There are a lot of berry bushes behind the house, and I have a recipe . . ." She felt her cheeks blushing red and wished she'd practiced this on her walk into town. Why was it so difficult to ask for help?

While Kiela was stammering all of this, Bryn was already busy smearing a spread of the jam onto one of her pastries. "Eadie!" she hollered through the window. "Come and try this!"

Eadie trotted up to the window, and Bryn handed her the pastry.

The centaur bit into the pastry, her eyes closed, and she let out a little moan.

Bryn turned back to Kiela. "If you have more, I'll buy it."

Kiela felt her knees wobble, and she let out a little laugh. She sank into the nearest stool. "Yes, that's . . ." She took a deep breath. "I'd like to open a jam shop. I have berries and jars, but I lack a supply of sugar, as well as wax to seal the jars. I was hoping, in exchange for a cut of my product, that you could provide the sugar and wax." She took another breath, encouraged by what she saw in Bryn's eyes. "I came here to ask if you'd like to be business partners."

Slathering another pastry with jam, Bryn handed it out the window to the boy with horns. He stuffed it in his mouth in one bite. "Chew *before* you swallow," she told him. To Kiela, she said, "You just met me. I could be a terrible business partner. You don't even know a single one of my flaws."

Jam on his cheek, the boy piped up. "You're bossy. And you talk a lot."

"Hush, you," Bryn said. Then: "He's right. Admittedly, Eadie can talk circles around me"—from outside, Eadie called, "I heard that and agree!"—"but I do like to talk. When I was a kid, I heard a story about a hermit who held so many words inside that eventually he burst from the pressure of all the unsaid thoughts. Years later, they found his bones scattered and thousands of words burned into the stone walls of his cave. Ever since, I've been afraid to hold too many words inside."

"That . . . is not actually possible." Kiela might not be a trained sorcerer, but she knew that wasn't how magic worked. "Accidents can happen when you work magic, but you can't just have magic happen accidentally—spells have to be cast, with very specific words and ingredients. It has to be done deliberately."

Bryn gave a little snort, halfway between disbelief and interest. "No one deliberately causes the magic storms, and yet they happen, loudly, often."

"Yes, but magic storms are caused by the buildup of improperly balanced spell residue," Kiela said, unable to keep herself from sounding like one of the scholars who visited the library. "And they don't recoil on the sorcerer." She forced herself to stop talking. *I shouldn't be revealing I know so much about magic.*

Unbothered by Kiela spewing out magical knowledge, Bryn shrugged. "Facts didn't matter at the time. I was five. The story stuck, as well as the one about the fish that ate a boat."

"Okay, that one could be true." All sorts of creatures lived in the sea. Those books were on the second floor of the east wing. Kiela's specialty was natural sciences, but her collection didn't include the ocean, except for where it impacted the land. She'd once gotten into a nearly heated argument with the librarian on the second floor about those volumes that could have been shelved in either section. A scholar had shushed them. It had been quite embarrassing.

"I am a mess of nerves on a boat, which is an inconvenient phobia when you live on an island. You should have seen me when I first arrived. Kissed the ground and got a mouth full of sand. That was the main reason why I set up my bakery—knew I'd never make it as a fisherman. Also, I love to bake."

Kiela took a steadying breath. "Would you love to bake with jam?"

Bryn grinned. "I haven't scared you off yet?"

She shook her head. An assertive business partner who talked a lot sounded ideal to her; less need for Kiela to fill the silence. And selling jam had nothing to do with boats. She didn't see what the problem was. "You get fifty percent."

"That's terrible negotiating," Bryn said. "Offer me ten percent."

"Um, ten percent?"

"That's much too low. Why are you insulting me with such a low offer?"

"Forty?" Kiela said.

"Okay, you are not good at this at all. Fair is twenty, plus I supply the sugar and wax, and you provide the berries, as well as the labor of making and canning the jam."

Kiela smiled. "Twenty. And once my shop is open, you recommend it to your customers and neighbors."

Bryn nodded. "I'll spread the word and tell everyone it's worth the climb. In return, you need to tell me how you convinced Larran to take you on a ride on one of his merhorses, because my nephew Tobin—he's the smart-mouthed one who somehow managed to get jam in his eyebrow fur—has been drooling over those horse-fish for years with no luck."

She hadn't known that was a coveted invite. "I . . . He just asked me."

"Hmm . . ." Bryn studied her so long that Kiela patted her hair to make sure it wasn't sticking up. "Perhaps Tobin would have more luck if he tried being less annoying."

From out the window, Tobin called, "I heard that!"

Bryn grinned. "Why don't you help your mother with the nets?"

"Because that's work, and she won't pay!"

"How about I pay you then?" Bryn offered. "You help Kiela here carry a bag of sugar up the cliff steps, and you can eat the very first raspberry croissant I bake."

"I don't need—" Kiela began.

"Hush," Bryn said. "Let the boy be useful. It'll make him feel important, and as an added bonus, it will make your climb easier." Louder, she called out the window, "Deal?"

He whooped and shouted, "Deal!"

Bryn ducked through a door, dipping her head so her antlers didn't scrape the top of the doorframe, and returned a half minute later with a sack of sugar slung under one arm and a jar of wax in her other hand. Kiela took the wax, and Tobin darted in to take the bag of sugar. It was nearly half his size, but he hefted it up without complaint.

"I'll be back when I've made more," Kiela promised.

After saying goodbye to Bryn and Eadie, she followed the boy with the sugar out of the bakery and through the streets. He was, she quickly discovered, as fond of talking as his aunt, but he preferred questions. "Where are you from?" "Did you come by boat?" "Have you ever seen a kraken?" "Have you met the emperor?" "What's the palace like?" "Is it true the streets of Alyssium are made of flowers?" "Do you know any nobles?" "Have you ever been in the palace?" "Do you know any sorcerers?"

Not really wanting to answer any of that, but especially the last question, she redirected it back at him. "Do you?"

And he was off.

He hadn't seen a sorcerer since he was a kid, he said (despite still being a kid), but back in his youth, he remembered one who dressed all in purple—Tobin seemed to feel it very important that she understood how very much purple: purple cloak, purple pants, purple socks, purple belt—who would visit on her regular rotation once a season. Everything was better then, he said his parents said, because the magic was all spread out across all the islands. Fewer storms. Better crops. More fish. She'd stopped coming about three years ago, maybe four, because he hadn't learned to skip rocks yet. Since then, everything had gotten worse. Everything was unbalanced, and that's why he had to eat kelp porridge, even though it tasted like slime mold. He concluded with: "If you need a jam taster, I volunteer. Are you really going to sell jam?"

"And remedies," she said.

"For what?"

For asking too many questions, she thought, but she said, "I'm still figuring it out."

At the top of the cliff stairs, he dropped the sugar bag on the ground and stretched his arms. Kiela looked back at the village and the sea beyond it. The sun was dipping low, enough so it looked as if it were about to drip into the water.

"Whoa, what is *that*?" Tobin asked.

She turned to see Caz propelling himself toward them with his usual method: reaching out with his tendrils and then flinging his bare root ball forward. Seen at a distance, he looked a bit like a very hairy, very green dog with a very dirty belly. Closer . . . he just looked like a pot-less spider plant about the size of a dog. "*Who,*" Kiela corrected. "He's my friend, Caz."

"Wow, he's awesome. Is he a plant?"

"*Chlorophytum comosum,*" Caz said, reaching them. "And you are— Goat horns? Are you a goat?" All of his leaves began to shake, and he waved his tendrils in the air. "Kiela, did you bring a plant-eater back with you?"

Before Kiela could explain, Tobin had his hands up in surrender. "I am totally not a plant eater at all. You can ask my mom. I never, ever eat my vegetables. Except candied carrots, because those are delicious. But I would never, ever eat a talking chlorophy . . . what?"

"Spider plant," Caz said, lowering his tendrils slightly. His leaves continued to tremble. "Are there others like you who eat plants?"

"No one on Caltrey will eat you," Tobin promised. "Not even a nibble." He knelt down to see Caz better. "Sorry for scaring you. I've just never seen anyone like you. My name's Tobin."

"Well, I've never seen anyone like you either, Tobin. I apologize if I was rude."

Kiela grinned at both of them and then asked Caz, "Is anything wrong? I thought you were going to stay at the cottage."

"I just got worried about you," Caz said. "I didn't know you were making us friends."

Delighted, Tobin cried, "I'm friends with a spider plant!" He jumped to his feet. "I can't wait to tell Aunt Bryn!"

"You can head back," Kiela told him. "We can take it from here. Thanks for your help."

He hesitated. "You're sure? You won't tell Aunt Bryn that I was unhelpful?"

"You were very helpful." She *did* appreciate not having to haul the sugar up the stairs by herself, while carrying the wax. Plus he hadn't been terrible company. His relentless chatter reminded her of a bird excited for spring. Maybe it was going to be okay, talking with people more than she used to. And maybe Caz would feel more comfortable here, now that he'd met a boy with goat horns and hadn't been eaten. "If I do need a jam taster, I'll let you know. You can head on home."

"Nice to meet you, Caz."

"You too, Tobin."

Waving at both of them, he scurried down the stairs twice as fast as she ever went. She waited to make sure he reached the bottom safely, and then she lifted her eyes to watch the sunset. Golden, the sun oozed like molten jam into the sea.

And then, with Caz by her side, she headed home, carrying sugar, wax, and hope.

CHAPTER TEN

The cottage didn't look very much like a shop.

Kiela chewed on her lower lip as she contemplated it. It was clean: the wood floor had been scrubbed first by Caz, then by Kiela. It was scuffed and scratched but beautiful as only old wood can be. She'd trimmed back the vines over the windows, plus cleaned the glass, so that the sunlight could shine in freely. He'd dusted the rafters with his leaves, and she'd washed the sink, the counter, the shelves, and the table. All the jars were sparkling, ready for jam. But no matter how clean and pretty the cottage was, it didn't look like a shop.

She thought of her favorite bookshop in Alyssium, the cozy one with inviting rows of shelves. Had it burned? No, she wasn't going to think about that. Instead, she focused on what she'd loved about it: the way it welcomed you in. That's what she wanted her shop to do. Customers had to feel comfortable to browse, even if all she sold was a single flavor of jam.

"I think we need to separate the shop from the rest of the cottage." She paced a line halfway down the front room. "The front door opens onto the shop . . . So we need a wall here, to split it from the kitchen. The wall can be covered in shelves. Or it could be a bookshelf that doubles as a wall, except it wouldn't be for books. A jam shelf."

Caz climbed onto the table. "I have many surprising skills—for example, I play the harp—but construction is not one of them." He waved his leaves. "I'm too floppy to wield a hammer."

"I don't think we have a hammer. Or wood, though there is a forest right on the other side of the garden. But I have no idea how to make boards out of a tree. I imagine it's quite a bit of work . . . You can play the harp?"

He demonstrated plucking imaginary strings. "A small one."

"Where in the world did you learn to play the harp? And when?"

"I had a life before I met you."

"You literally did not," Kiela said.

"There were a few weeks before I met you, thank you very much."

"During which you learned to play the harp?" she asked, incredulous. As far as she knew, he'd spent the days wandering the library, which, while an amazing wonder of the world, was not known for its musical instruments. Any attempt at music was likely to be hushed by a patron who wanted to focus on a text.

"The janitor from the east wing taught me in his spare time," Caz said. "You shouldn't underestimate my musical ability just because I'm a plant."

"It has nothing to do with— Okay, we're straying," Kiela said. "Jam shop. We need wood, a hammer, nails, and a book about how to build shelves." She didn't think she'd packed any books like that. In fact, she wasn't entirely sure where in the library there would have been books like that. Perhaps second floor, west wing, near Art History? "And we also need shelves for the books, ideally hidden shelves, but I suppose that's not an immediate need. They can stay in the crates for now." She wondered if any of the spellbooks had spells for construction. The spun-sugar-like palace in Alyssium, as well as its arching bridges, had been built by magic . . . Slowly, she turned to face the bedroom, with all its untapped knowledge.

Following her gaze, Caz said, "Do you really want the cottage to grow like the raspberry bushes? You don't think that would lead to a whole lot of questions we can't answer? Bad enough to have extra berries. Someone like Larran would definitely notice if we sprouted a few towers and turrets."

Of course he was right. Hammer and nails and a bit of effort, that's what they needed. Luckily, she knew someone who had plenty of tools—she'd witnessed him fixing a chimney, after all. "Larran has a hammer."

"You're proposing visiting him again?"

She thought back to the merhorse ride. She hadn't realized until Bryn's reaction that it had been a special privilege. Surely if he liked her enough to let her ride, he'd let her borrow a few tools. "I'll trade him some tomatoes for use of them," she decided. The merhorse Sian would like that.

"Yesterday town, and today Larran. Before long, you'll be throwing parties."

Kiela shuddered dramatically. She'd only ever been to one party that she'd enjoyed: after she'd won her job at the Great Library of Alyssium, all the junior librarians had been invited into the North Reading Room and told that, to celebrate, they could spend three hours reading whatever they wanted and then they could take a slice of cake with them when they left whenever they wanted and without a word to anyone. That had been bliss. "No parties. Want to come with me? You haven't gotten to see much of the island, and he already knows about you." Besides, if Caz came, she wouldn't have to do all the talking. As she'd just witnessed at Bryn's bakery, she wasn't very good at asking for help.

He considered it. "What do merhorses eat?"

"Exclusively tomatoes," Kiela said. "Never anything green."

"You don't actually know that."

"Larran won't feed you to his merhorses. You know, the original name for a merhorse was 'hippocampus,' but that fell out of favor because it's the same word as a part of the brain. Also, it sounds too much like hippopotamus, which isn't a similar animal at all." She had never seen a hippopotamus, though she'd read about them.

"Did you know that hippopotami secrete a red oil that keeps their skin dry and protects them from the sun?"

"I don't think that's relevant."

"No, but it's interesting."

He considered the matter a moment longer. "All right. I'll come."

She picked a half-dozen tomatoes, wondered if that would be enough, and then, after fetching an old-but-sturdy basket, gathered a half-dozen more. If wood and nails were more expensive than a dozen tomatoes, then she could offer him jam when it was ready. *I wish I could offer a spell to help his merhorses.* She remembered the sadness in his voice when he talked about the lack of foals . . . But she couldn't promise that before she knew if it was possible. It was bound to be a much more complex spell than accelerated plant growth.

Jam shelves first. Magic later.

Before she could reconsider embarking on yet another social encounter, she strode out the door. Caz kept pace beside her. He seemed to enjoy the stroll through the woods—she knew this because he kept muttering words like "marvelous" and "delightful" and "bucolic." When they emerged into the light, she lifted her face to feel the full morning sun. The breeze off the sea tasted as fresh as an iced tea, and the waves broke in tiny crests, as if they were playing with one another. In the distance, she saw the merhorses leaping through the waves. As they went down the cliff stairs, she hoped Larran was home and not out with his herd.

As Caz hopped from rock to rock close to the cliff, Kiela walked down the beach toward the little yellow house. Shielding her eyes from the sun with her hand, she watched the merhorses play in the waves off the shore. She hoped she could find a spell that could help them thrive again. The emperor had been beyond selfish to recall his sorcerers from the outer islands. Tobin and the revolutionaries were right—the world had become unbalanced, and it wasn't fair. Against all of that, her idea of a jam shop that offered a few little homespun remedies seemed very small. Why bother when the world's problems were so large?

Because it's what I can do.

And maybe . . . I can find a way to help.

At the very least, she could supply her friendly neighbor with tomatoes.

She spotted Larran at the end of the stone pier, combing tangles out of the mane of one of his merhorses. Caz took a look at the water bashing up against the rocks and volunteered, "I'll wait for you here."

Kiela didn't blame him, given his fear of plant-eating sea creatures, but why was *she* nervous? She'd talked with Larran several times already and had found him annoyingly nice. Was it because now she knew he didn't let just anyone ride his merhorses? She wasn't sure how she felt about that. She wasn't used to anyone spending any extra attention on her.

Seeing her, Larran waved. "Be careful!" he called. The wind tried to swallow his voice, but he boomed through it. "The ocean's freezing today! You don't want to fall in!"

Carrying the basket of tomatoes, she walked, slowly and carefully, out on the stone pier. She was wearing shoes with a rough sole, which was far more practical for scampering over rocks and up and down stairs than the soft slipper-like shoes she'd always worn in the library, as well as a pair of pants she'd brought with her and a blouse that had been her mother's, embroidered with apple blossoms on the sleeves. She'd found herself wearing more and more of her mother's old clothes—they fit the weather better, with the morning chill and the afternoon sun and the sea breeze. And they fit the person Kiela was becoming better. Every time she put on an island blouse or skirt or pair of shoes, she felt more like a Caltreyan and less like a citygirl. She'd looked in a mirror this morning and seen it wasn't just the clothes that made her different either: a sprinkle of magenta freckles had developed across the bridge of her nose. She'd had the freckles when she was a child, and the sun in the garden had coaxed them out. She liked seeing them again.

As she approached the end of the pier, the merhorse Larran was combing reared back and snorted. Kiela recognized the beautiful gold skin and metallic gold scales. "Hi, Sian, remember me?"

Sian's nostrils flared, and her deep blue eyes fixed on the basket.

"If you wait just a moment, I have a treat for—" Kiela told the merhorse.

But the merhorse didn't want to wait any fraction of a moment. Smelling the tomatoes, she lunged out of the water toward the basket. Sea foam sprayed around her as her neck shot forward. Startled, Kiela took a step backward—onto the slick edge of a rock.

Her foot slipped.

She lost her balance.

And for an instant, it felt as if the world froze—she saw the sky, Larran's horrified face, the wild horse-fish . . . As she fell backward, Sian's teeth clamped down hard on the fabric of her shirt. She was yanked forward. The basket flew into the air, and the dozen tomatoes arched up into the cresting waves. She tumbled onto the back of the merhorse and then over, into the water.

Cold wet ocean swallowed her, and she dunked under. Sputtering, she clawed up to the surface. It was far colder than the other day, biting cold. Caz was shrieking from the shore, and Larran was shouting her name, about to dive in after her—

And she saw Sian chasing the bobbing tomatoes in the waves.

Kiela began to laugh.

"She, um, my fault," she gasped out.

Larran knelt on the rocks and held out his hand. She took it and clambered out. Immediately, she began to shiver as her wet clothes clung to her. *Gah, he wasn't joking about the temperature—why is it so freezing?* She wrapped her arms around her chest. It hadn't been anywhere near this cold the other day.

"I don't know what got into—" Larran began.

"My fault," Kiela repeated. "I knew she liked—"

"That's no excuse for her—"

"She must have smelled them," Kiela said. "I should have left the basket on the shore."

"She's been trained," Larran said, "by me. This is my fault more than yours—"

No, it was her carelessness and clumsiness that was at fault. He couldn't have predicted she'd bring Sian's favorite treat within smelling distance. "I don't think you can really blame yourself for—"

"Of course I'm to blame. She's my—"

Caz bounded along the jetty, his tendrils waving in the air. "Kiela, Kiela, I thought it had eaten you! Are you okay? Are you in one piece? Count your legs. Do you have two legs? Fingers? Did you lose a finger? Are you losing blood? Oh seeds, she's going to faint from blood loss, hit her head, and drown in the sea all because of shelving!"

"Deep breath, Caz. I'm fine." She held up her hands and waved her fingers. "All ten."

"You look bluer than usual," he said. "Are you cold? Do you have hypothermia?"

She laughed. "I swear I'm fine." But she was shivering, and her toes and fingers were so cold that she felt like she'd been burned. *Maybe I'm not so fine.*

Larran laid his hand on her shoulder. "Let's get you inside and warm. You need to get out of those wet clothes." She shivered beneath his touch, and he released her.

She'd been immersed in the water when they'd rode the merhorses and hadn't felt anywhere near this chilled. Granted, it was cooler today, and there was more wind, but that didn't explain why the sea was quite so frigid. Its temperature must have plummeted dozens of degrees. Her teeth were chattering hard, and she couldn't seem to stop them. "Dry clothes would be nice. I didn't bring any with me, though. Just tomatoes."

All three of them glanced at the water, where Sian was merrily bobbing through the waves, polishing off the last of the dozen tomatoes.

"You can borrow some of mine," Larran said.

He held out his hand to help her along the stone pier, but she didn't take it. She didn't want to let go of hugging her arms. The wind was slicing through her. Caz hopped along next to her, and she could feel the worry radiating off his leaves. "Really, I'm fine," she told him through chattering teeth.

"You screamed," he said.

"I was startled, due to falling into the water unexpectedly." They didn't have to make such a fuss about it. Now that the moment was over, she was more than a little embarrassed. It would be nice if they could move on and forget that it had happened, but maybe after she got a little warmer . . . Eesh, why had it been so icy?

Larran led her inside his house. "One minute," he said, ducking into the back room.

While Caz swung himself up onto a chair, Kiela, despite her shivering, looked around with interest. It was all warm honey-colored wood: the floor, the high ceiling, the walls, the table. In one corner was a wood-burning stove on a hearth made of white quartz. On every surface, he'd placed a seashell. A clamshell by the sink. A conch on the table. A spiral-shaped one that she couldn't name was on the mantel. She could tell each had been chosen with care.

Larran emerged with a stack of clothes, as well as a towel. "You can change in there, if you like." He blushed as he gestured toward his bedroom.

Gratefully, she took the clothes and towel and scurried into his room, shutting the door behind her. His bedroom had a four-poster bed in the same honey-colored wood. It was piled with quilts, slightly mussed, as if he'd straightened them quickly when he realized she might see them disheveled. Another shell sat on his nightstand, this one with a candle in it. Except for the rumpled, very-inviting-looking quilts on the bed, everything else was as neat as the library. His boots were tucked side by side next to the closet, and there wasn't a hint of dust anywhere.

Peeling off her wet clothes, Kiela listened to Larran and Caz through the door.

"That was terrifying," Caz said. "I nearly lost my root ball, I was so upset."

"She'll be fine once she's warmed up," Larran said soothingly. "It wasn't a bad fall. She didn't hit any of the rocks, and she wasn't under for more than a second."

"I saw your face. You were terrified too."

She heard shuffling noises—Larran, walking around—and then a creak—perhaps a cabinet door or the wood-burning stove? Shaking out one of his shirts, Kiela held it up. It was twice the size of her, but at least it was dry. She pulled it on. It was soft as a lamb, smelled like pine trees and ocean air, and draped down to her knees.

Larran replied something to Caz, but she missed what it was—he'd moved too far from the door. She buttoned the shirt.

Caz replied, "She's all I have. She took me in when—"

The rest of his words were swallowed by running water from the sink, but she knew the story, though she wouldn't have said "took me in." She'd been happy to have his help and honored that he'd chosen to assist her. She'd never had a competent assistant before who didn't make her want to stick her fingers in her ears and say, *For pity's sake, stop talking.* Plus he treasured books as much as she did, which had to be unusual for a plant.

"She was just as kind when she was young," Larran said.

"Oh? Tell me about Kiela as a child, and don't leave anything embarrassing out."

And that's my cue to return, Kiela thought. She left his pants—they'd never have fit, and the shirt was long enough to cover everything that needed to be covered—and padded back out barefoot, holding her wet clothes. "Do you have anywhere I can hang these to dry?"

"Yes, by the stove—" Larran began as he turned around. His voice died mid-sentence as he stared at her.

Self-conscious, she tugged at the hem of his shirt. "I know. I look ridiculous. But I'm dry."

"Ahh . . ." Larran said.

Caz snorted. "I don't think 'ridiculous' is what he's thinking."

Larran quickly turned away. "You can hang your wet clothes by the stove. They'll dry fast."

Huh, she thought. Was he . . . interested?

No, definitely not. She looked ridiculous, and the plant had no idea what he was talking about. *And now we're all embarrassed. Fun.* She spread her wet pants and blouse out on a rack near the stove. It must have been where he dried his clothes after a day with the merhorses. The stove smelled like burning pine, a woodsy almost-cinnamon-like scent.

"What I came to ask—" she began at the same time he said, "Can I get you something to eat—"

Caz flopped sideways. "Ugh, you two."

For the first time ever, she wished that Caz wasn't here. If she were alone with Larran inside his house, what would he say? What would she say? What would she do? She thought of how she'd just been in his bedroom, and she felt a blush heating her cheeks and neck. *It's better that Caz is here.* If she were alone with Larran, it would most likely be ten times more awkward than it already was, and even if he were interested, he'd quickly change his mind.

"You should sit near the fire, warm yourself up," Larran said to Kiela. He repositioned one of his chairs next to the stove and then retrieved one of the quilts from his bed. He moved to wrap it around her as Kiela reached to take it.

She froze, and he stopped—their faces an inch from each other's.

He has nice eyes, she thought inanely.

His breath smelled nice too, a little mint and a little cinnamon, and she found herself blushing. She didn't usually notice other people's breath, but then she wasn't usually quite so . . . My, they were really nice eyes.

He retreated. "Sorry."

She cleared her throat and then wrapped the quilt around her shoulders. It fell over her legs, and now she felt swaddled in the scent of him. *Change the subject.* "Why was the ocean so much colder today?"

"Same reason as the wheat stalks withering, the orchards sickening, the rain becoming erratic, and the fish becoming scarce—the magic is unbalanced, too concentrated in some areas and absent in others. At least that's how I understand it. I'm not a scholar."

Suddenly, she itched to get back to her library books. Somewhere in there were all the answers she could ever want. She remembered packing several about weather manipulation . . . Had the sorcerers caused all of this: the shrinking merhorse herds, the drastic fluctuations in ocean temperature, the gradual starvation of Caltrey? And if so, was there a way to reverse it?

There was silence for a moment, but it wasn't a terrible, awkward silence—it was just the quiet of two people, plus a plant, thinking about what had been said.

Finally, Larran said, "I do apologize for Sian's behavior. She knows better than that."

"I'm the one who brought the tomatoes," Kiela said. "I'm sorry. They were for you."

"Oh? For me?" He seemed surprised. And pleased.

Belatedly, she realized she should have led with saying they were intended as payment, for her borrowing tools and supplies. "Well, they were for you and Sian, but not all at once. And they weren't a gift."

"Oh?" This was a different "oh." Curious and a little wary.

"You see, I need to build jam shelves."

"You need shelves for jam?" Larran asked. "Why jam?"

"Exactly what I've been wanting to know," Caz said.

Because she had the raspberry bushes. Because the recipe was in her parents' cookbook. Because jam made people happy. You couldn't eat jam and be sad. It was fundamentally impossible. Besides, it reminded her of tea with her parents, and it was a good memory—the three of them around the hearth in their tiny apartment in Alyssium, her mother reading aloud from a book, her father making comments that would make her laugh, and all of them having tea with jam on slightly stale bread that her parents had bought in the market in exchange for a bit of her father's work with mending nets. It was a taste that came with near-forgotten emotions. But she didn't say any of that. She simply said, "It's nice."

"Okay," he said. And didn't ask any more questions.

She liked him all the better for that.

CHAPTER ELEVEN

Kiela stirred the vat of boiling sugar and raspberries while Larran hammered together the frame for the bookshelf. It would run half the length of the room, from floor to rafters, partitioning the tiny shop in front from the kitchen and living area. She'd already scooted her daybed into the back room, cramming it between her parents' bed and the crates of forbidden books. She'd neaten that room up later, when no one but Caz was here. At least she'd already cleaned, dusted, and hung lavender from the rafters. She'd also washed and rehung the lace curtains over the windows. So it would just be a matter of what to do with the daybed. The practical thing would be to claim her parents' bed as hers. The big bed had lots of extra room for her and—her eyes slid to Larran . . . *Don't be ridiculous,* she scolded herself. Lots of extra room for her and whatever stack of books she wanted to read late into the night.

As he worked, he was singing softly, a sea lullaby that she vaguely remembered from when she was little. He had a pleasant voice, soft and kind of furry.

She hadn't meant for Larran to build the shelves for her. In fact, after the chimney incident, she'd been determined to do it herself, and if he'd insisted, she would've . . . Well, he *hadn't* insisted. He'd simply mentioned that raspberry jam was his favorite, and Caz had negotiated for his labor. She'd been outmaneuvered by a plant.

Oddly, she didn't mind as much as she thought she would.

He didn't seem to feel the need to fill the silence with chatter, which was nice. Caz was acting as his assistant, passing him nails as he needed them and checking to ensure the angles were ninety degrees and the boards were straight. The spider plant had found a marble lost between the floorboards and was using it to ensure all the boards were level.

"What's that song?" she asked when Larran reached the final note.

"An old herder lullaby. We sing it to the mares to calm them when they're about to foal. Usually works better if you can keep a tune. Sorry—didn't realize I was singing loudly."

"It was pretty." She'd heard it before—but where and when? She hummed the melody, trying to remember the words. *The sea was a cradle and . . .* something, something *. . . the stars will watch over you . . .* "I think I knew it once."

"You did. I remember you singing it."

Kiela snorted. "You're remembering wrong. Couldn't have been me. I never sing where anyone can hear me, due to the fact that I sound like a chicken attempting to warble."

Caz stifled a laugh, which came out like a snort. He'd heard her sing before, once and only once, at an official ceremony for new library inductees, and she knew he could verify she lacked any semblance of pitch. Singing hadn't been optional, but the cream-puff-and-chocolate desserts had been worth it.

"You didn't know I was there," Larran said.

Pausing as she stirred the jam, Kiela twisted around to look at Larran. He'd framed the top and sides of the shelf-wall and was marking off where each shelf would be. It would blend in pleasantly with the rest of the cottage. "You spied on me when we were kids?"

He blushed. "Not exactly and not intentionally. You were in your family's cove with my foal . . ."

Wait, wait, wait—she remembered a baby merhorse in the cove. It had been there for a few months one summer, and she'd helped take care of it. She remembered bottle-feeding it. "Why was a foal in our cove?" She wasn't sure she'd ever questioned it, but in retrospect, it was odd. It should've been with its mother or its herd, or at least its herder. "You said it was yours?"

"I've wanted to be a herder for as long as I can remember. Used to hang out near the Caltreyan herd all the time. Another nail, Caz?" The spider plant extended a tendril holding a nail, and Larran hammered it into place before continuing. "There was a mare that died giving birth, and the foal wasn't expected to live. So I took responsibility for it. My parents, though . . . They owned the only grocery store in town, do you remember it? Near the fountain?"

Checking the jam again, Kiela said, "Yes." No one had liked the grocer's. She remembered her parents used to grumble about the overpriced spices and the way the man behind the counter would lean his thumb on the scale to overcharge for a cut of meat. Her mother had once bought a bag of flour that had turned out to be infested with ants. But there had been no other option on the tiny island.

"They wanted me to inherit the family business, but I had other dreams. Your parents were kind enough to allow me to raise the foal in secret in their cove. One morning my father . . . Well, suffice it to say, I was late to the cove. I remember being terrified that the foal wouldn't make it. When they're that young and fragile, they need regular care. But when I finally made it, you were already there, making sure the foal was fed and safe. You were singing to it."

He'd said before that her parents had been kind to him and that she had been too—*This is what he meant.* She'd been kind to his foal. No wonder she didn't remember. She'd had no idea it was his. "Anyone would have helped care for it."

He hammered in another nail and said quietly, "Not my parents."

She hadn't known that the foal was there in secret. "But what did your parents expect—"

Larran stepped back from the shelves. "For the wall, the back of the shelves, do you care if the wood matches? I have enough scraps, I think, but it'll be a patchwork of colors."

"That's fine." If they arranged it in a pattern, it would look intentionally artistic. "What do you mean your parents wouldn't have? You said they wanted you to stay in the family business, but surely they wouldn't have let a foal die?"

Larran didn't answer. "I'll be back with more wood."

He ducked out the door. She wanted to follow him and continue the conversation—he couldn't have meant that his parents would rather let a foal die than see him choose his own future? Unless that's exactly what he meant.

Her gaze followed him as he disappeared into the greenery, and then she looked down at the jam, unsure why her eyes felt suddenly hot and watery.

Thick, gooey bubbles roiled in the pot. It was time to pour the jam into the glass jars, which she, following her parents' instructions, had heated so they wouldn't shatter from the sudden heat. She retrieved the oven mitts. She'd found them in one of the drawers—they were a faded gingham but still sturdy. "Caz, can you hold the jars steady while I pour?"

Climbing along the rafters, he swung himself over to the kitchen counter and landed with a plop. "Do not—and I repeat, do *not*— pour hot jam on me."

"I'll be careful," she promised. She wondered when Larran would come back inside. There were so many other questions she wanted to ask him and so many parts of his story that he'd jumped over. What had happened to his parents? What about their store? How had he become a herder despite them? "What do you think it was that he wasn't saying?"

"I think he was saying everything very clearly," Caz said. "His parents weren't nice people. Yours were."

"Oh." Yes, they were.

Before returning to Caltrey, she hadn't thought much about how lucky she'd been to have them, only how unlucky she'd been to lose them. Glancing out through the door again, Kiela wondered if that was why Larran tried so hard to be kind. Was all of this— the cinnamon buns, fixing the chimney, the ride on the merhorse, the warm clothes after she fell into the water, the help with the shelves—a thank-you for feeding a foal as a kid? If so, after he'd said thank you enough . . . would that be it?

A day ago, she would have wanted that to be it. Now?

Now, he's making me shelves.

Lifting up the pot, she poured the jam into the waiting jars.

By the time she'd finished pouring her first batch of jam into jars, Larran had returned with a stack of wood slats over his shoulder. He dumped them just outside the door.

"If you're done with the stove, I can fry us some fish," he offered.

"You brought wood and fish?"

Coming inside, he produced a wrapped fillet from one of his pockets, and she tried not to think about what his pocket must now smell like. "It's from Sian, an apology fish. She had a string of them laid out on the stone pier when I got back. She knows she behaved badly."

An apology fish. She smiled. "I didn't know merhorses were so intelligent."

"They're more like dolphins than, say, cod or tuna. Highly intelligent. How else did their ancestors know it'd be good for them and us if they worked with humans?"

"Symbiosis is often just instinct paired with evolution, like honeybees and flowers or crocodiles and plovers, not actual intelligence." When he looked at her blankly, she added, "Plovers peck food out from between the crocodiles' teeth. The bird gets fed, and the croc doesn't suffer from toothaches. But it's not as if the birds choose dentistry." He was still looking at her blankly, and she realized she'd strayed from the normal communication pattern. "Fish for lunch would be lovely. Please thank Sian for me."

He smiled and then retrieved the frying pan. Placing the raw fish on a plate, he began looking through the cabinets as if he lived here.

She felt her warm, fuzzy feelings dissipate like bubbles in the air.

It was suddenly all too familiar, too friendly, too . . . *Too much.* She'd just wanted to build shelves; she hadn't wanted to share memories and confidences. It was nice she'd been kind to him as a kid, but she hadn't chosen to—she'd helped a foal and hadn't even known he'd been watching her. He'd embroiled her in his emotions without her consent.

She told herself not to let it bother her. She'd liked talking to him. And she'd said yes to his fish. Use of her kitchen went along with that yes. It wasn't such a grievous invasion of personal space to open a kitchen cabinet. But what if he decided it was also okay to barge into her bedroom and start pawing through the crates of forbidden books?

In as pleasantly polite a tone as she could, she asked, "Can I help you find something?"

He froze. "Uh, sorry. Salt and pepper?"

Caz climbed onto one of the kitchen shelves and plucked the little bags of salt and pepper out from behind the sugar. He passed them silently, reproachfully to Larran.

"I'm used to living on my own," Larran said, blushing. "I didn't intend . . . I'm sorry. This is your kitchen, not mine. I overstepped. I don't know why I keep . . . I won't do it again."

Kiela exhaled. That was a nice apology, and it wasn't a problem that he'd looked for salt and pepper—it was just that with the books in the other room . . . "I'm used to my own space too." It hadn't been much, her nook in the library with her bed and her cookplate and her desk, but it had been all hers and no other librarian would dream of making themselves at home in it. "Use whatever you need. But could you please just ask first?"

"Always, from now on."

He turned back to the fish.

And now it's awkward again, she thought. Had she overreacted? *No, he overstepped.* They'd been doing well there for a while, though, and it had been nice. It was a pity they couldn't return to that. She dumped raspberries into a bowl and added sugar. While they soaked in the sugar, she set a pot of water on the opposite side of the wood-burning stove from Larran and put a bowl with a chunk of wax on top of it—according to her parents' recipe book, that was the best way to melt the wax, in a double boiler. She wondered if he was regretting the fish. *Probably calculating how soon until he can leave.* "Am I your foal?"

"What?"

"Never mind." If he was only trying so hard to be nice because he felt he owed her . . . "It's just . . . I can pay you for the wood and the nails and the work and the fish. Once the shop is open, I can pay you back. This can be a business transaction. It doesn't have to be a favor you think you owe me because once upon a time I was nice to a baby horse-fish."

The fish seasoned, he laid the fillets in the pan. They stood side by side at the stove, him watching the fish sizzle and her watching the wax melt. "That's how I knew you're a good person. That's not why . . ." He trailed off, as if unsure how he wanted to finish the sentence.

Caz jumped onto the floor and landed with a plop. Loudly, he said, "Kiela, how about coming outside with me and sorting through the wood? We can make a pattern for the back of the shelves, like you said."

"Uh, okay?" Kiela followed the plant outside.

Larran had brought a stack of wood, the boards all different widths and shades, and laid them on the grass between the roses and the herb border. She and Caz began to sort the wood by color. It was rather intriguing how many shades there were. If they alternated shades in a rainbowlike pattern, from reddish to pale tan to brown . . .

"You should consider that he might be being nice because he's a nice person," Caz said.

"He's being nice because he thinks he owes me, because I took care of his foal, and because he sees me as his new foal, as someone who needs taking care of." Yes, she needed help with the shelves, but that didn't make her helpless. She'd figured out how to make jam. Really tasty jam, in fact, though it was a shame she didn't have access to lemon juice. A little citrus would sharpen the flavor and add a—

"Or maybe he likes you."

At that, all thought of lemon juice vanished. She peered in through the open kitchen door. Sunlight cast Larran in a pool of light. He was singing again as he cooked the fish. At least he didn't seem overly annoyed at her being prickly. Or maybe he just had a short attention span. "Do you think I should let him barge in wherever he wants"—she lowered her voice—"and open any crate he wants to open?"

"Obviously not," Caz said. "But he is one of the few people we know here. I just think he's trying really hard to be friendly. You could try too."

"I *was* trying and then—"

"He wanted salt?"

"Yes, but that's not—"

"*And* pepper?"

"He can't like me," Kiela said. "I'm unlikable."

"This is a ridiculous conversation that I regret beginning," Caz said. "You are not unlikable. I chose to be your assistant, out of all the librarians in the Great Library. I am a very picky plant with impeccable taste."

She couldn't help but grin.

"Accept that he's trying, albeit in a sometimes clumsy way, to be friends."

Her grin faded. "I'm not certain it's safe to make friends, given the secret we're hiding. We can have business partners, we can have neighbors, and we can have customers, but friends? I'm not sure that's wise, even if they do seem nice." She thought of Bryn and the boy Tobin.

Caz didn't reply, and she knew he was picking his words carefully.

Frowning at the wood as if it were at fault for the bramble of emotions she was feeling, she laid out the boards and organized them until they made a pleasing pattern, and hoped this uncomfortable conversation was finished.

"You're going to have to trust people if you want us to build a life here," Caz said at last.

That . . . could be true. But she didn't like it. She'd wanted to do this all alone . . . *I already haven't done it alone.* She hadn't even lasted twenty-four hours before she'd trooped down to the center of town for seeds and bread. She wasn't the hardened survive-on-her-own type, perhaps due more to a lack of experience than temperament, but still . . . "I know. I'll try."

"Thank you," Caz said. "You know, plants aren't nearly as emotionally exhausting as humans. You should try to be more plant."

She laughed. "Good advice. All I need is some chlorophyll."

"Excellent. You'd look great in green."

She laid the last board in place and then walked back into the cottage and breathed in the scent of freshly cooked fish. "Smells delicious," she said—a peace offering.

"Hope it tastes the way it smells," Larran said, with a tentative smile.

Kiela smiled back, and suddenly they were both smiling at each other. Just a whole lot of smiling all around—she wasn't quite sure what to do or say next, or at what point she should stop smiling. She wondered if her smile looked nice or awkward. She'd meant to be nice. Since he was smiling back, that probably meant she'd done it right.

Sighing, Caz scooted past her, muttering under his breath, "You are both ridiculous." But at least the atmosphere in the cottage had changed from uncomfortably awkward to companionably awkward.

While Larran finished with the fish, Kiela poured the melted wax onto the jam in each jar, a half inch thick. Caz held the jars steady for her. When the wax cooled, it would solidify, making an airtight seal that would preserve the jam for at least a year.

She took out plates from the cabinet, and Larran served the fish.

They ate in silence for a moment—it was just as wonderful as it smelled. Light, flaky, and buttery. He'd sprinkled some other herb on it. "Rosemary?" Kiela guessed.

"I've an herb border up a ways from my house. If you'd like any clippings, let me know. They transplant well. Don't need much care either, though it looks like you have a green thumb." He nodded toward the back door that led to the garden. "Your berries have done well."

"A decade or so of neglect suited them." She hoped he didn't ask more questions than that. She wondered if he'd noticed how much they'd grown since he'd been on her roof. She changed the subject. "How did you learn how to cook fish and build shelves and all of that?"

"Mostly taught myself how to build and fix stuff," he said with a shrug. "Hit my thumb a bunch of times while I was working on my own house." He showed her his thumbnail. It was warped on one side. "It never fully recovered. As to cooking . . . that was thanks to the herder who took me on as an apprentice when I was thirteen. He could fillet a fish in thirty seconds flat and make it into a feast fit for an emperor. He never measured anything, just tossed in herbs and spices by instinct."

Kiela heard a familiar note in his voice. "You miss him."

"He was lost in a storm three years ago, one of the first of the real bad magic storms to hit Caltrey after the sorcerers stopped their regular circuits," Larran said. "When it hit, we hadn't had one like that in . . . I'd never seen one like that. No one had. He underestimated how bad it would be when he went out with the herd. Thought he'd be able to handle it . . ." He cleared his throat as if the memories had lodged there.

She looked down at her fish. "I'm sorry." He'd had loss in his life too. From the tone of his voice, she guessed the herder was like a father figure to him. She wondered what other thoughts and feelings lived behind Larran's friendly smile.

"It's his herd that I inherited. Amarin—she's the one with teal scales—was the last foal he helped birth. Now *that* was a wild night." He went on to spin a tale of a mare in the moonlight, the magic of a traveling sorcerer, and a breech birth that ended in a miracle: a healthy foal and mother.

She finished her fish and cleaned the dishes, while he brought in the wood she'd chosen for the back of the shelves. Together, they assembled her new jam-shelf wall—she held the wood steady, Caz supplied the nails, and Larran hammered.

"If it were possible to find some sort of homemade remedy that would help with merhorse births . . ." Kiela began. "A natural one, not spellcraft."

Larran stopped hammering. "That would change everything. But there isn't an herb or medicine that can help. Only magic works—they're magical creatures, created by some forgotten spell. No one knows how or why they came to be, but they can't reproduce with the ease of other creatures."

She resolved to look for solutions anyway. There had to be some way to disguise it as not-magic. Maybe if she whispered the syllables? Except Larran would know it had to be magic . . . And when the other islanders heard about a new foal . . . It wasn't the same as overenthusiastic raspberry brambles that could have grown naturally.

"What kinds of things did the sorcerers used to do?" Caz asked. "You know, back when they used to come to the outer islands?"

Larran continued with assembling the wall as he answered. "It varied. Sometimes they'd calm the seas. Or they'd strengthen the soil. Coax the rain to fall or not fall. One used to shift currents—we miss that one sorely. Another specialized in orchards—a lot of our island trees aren't native to the area, and they require specially magicked soil to thrive. He knew spells that would heal storm-damaged trees, eliminate disease, and double production. Used to result in the most incredible golden apples . . ."

He waxed on about the miracles of the sorcerers, while Kiela made mental notes of all that the island had lost. Beside her, she knew Caz was doing the same.

After measuring the next board, Larran took it out to saw a chunk off the end. Kiela and Caz followed. Each of them held an end steady across two rocks while Larran sawed. He carried it back inside and fit it next to the prior board. "I haven't shared this plan with anyone yet, but as soon as the next trade ship arrives, I intend to travel to Alyssium and make an appeal directly to the emperor at his court."

Caz yelped, "You can't!"

"Really, you can't," Kiela echoed. He didn't know what he'd be walking into! She heard the screams echoing in her head, she smelled the smoke, and she pictured the flames encasing the library.

"I have to," Larran said. "I can't sit by and do nothing. Someone has to tell the emperor what's happening in the outer islands and plead our case."

Kiela shook her head vehemently. "It's *not* a good time to visit Alyssium. There's unrest." That was a mild way to put it. She didn't know if the city still stood or not. It could have all fallen to ashes by now. "It's not safe."

"It isn't safe here," Larran said grimly. "Any day another magic storm could hit and wipe us out. And if it doesn't, then it will be the slow decay of the sea and land. I've heard that there's a general audience where anyone can present an appeal to the magistrates— I'll make my case there, and I'll repeat it day after day until I'm heard, if I have to."

"But right now . . ." She didn't know how to warn him without risking revealing the secret of the spellbooks. In addition to that, she didn't want to say the words that would make all of what happened real. She didn't want to explain that she and Caz had fled—that they were fugitives. And thieves. The words stuck in her throat. They'd burned the North Reading Room. They'd thrown the emperor out a window, to his death. Countless others had died. "You don't want to go there now."

"I don't want to watch my herd, my home, my island slowly die."

Neither do I. Kiela laid her hand on top of Larran's as he steadied the next nail. "Just don't leave without talking to me first, okay? Will you promise me that much?" She'd find the words to explain by then. He looked at her hand, touching his.

She wondered if she'd stepped too far, but she didn't remove her hand. He was staring at his hand as if he hadn't heard her words. "Larran?"

"I'll talk to you first," he promised.

Good, she thought.

"But I *am* going."

Not if I can stop you.

CHAPTER TWELVE

"First, we need to catalog what we have," Kiela said to Caz after Larran left. That was step one to identifying spells that would make appropriate "remedies."

Caz rustled his leaves in excitement. "Ooh, I missed this!"

She'd missed it too. Granted, it hadn't been that long in sheer number of days since she'd processed any books, but Caltrey felt like a world and several lifetimes away from the Great Library of Alyssium. When they'd docked in the overgrown cove, she hadn't known that she'd ever feel like a librarian again.

"Do we have paper?" Caz asked. "Please tell me you packed paper. Or pencils? Do we have any pencils? I read once about a scholar who'd been imprisoned and had to write on his walls in his own blood."

On her parents' bed, Kiela opened her bag of personal items. She unpacked a set of pencils, the finest graphite in Alyssium, each sharpened carefully by her with a slim whittling knife that she kept exclusively for that purpose. Untying the ribbon around the set, she laid it out open on the bed. Caz danced above the pencils, so excited that he shed bits of soil on the quilt. She then took out one of her precious blank notebooks. "No need to use blood."

"You're a hero," Caz told her solemnly.

She never traveled anywhere without a notebook, so it wasn't a surprise she'd packed a few. She wished she'd packed a crate of them. She doubted that paper was readily accessible on Caltrey—there was the bakery, the mill, the fish market, the yarn and fiber store, and perhaps a shop for furniture? But she hadn't seen a stationery store. Opening the notebook, she stroked the smooth, crisp, blank page. There was something so very beautiful about a notebook without a single note in it. It felt like touching pure potential.

"You write, or I write?" Caz asked. He was petting one of the pencils with a leaf.

It was obvious how much he wanted to do it himself. "You can write," she offered.

Shivering in delight, Caz said, "I love you. You know that, don't you? You are the best friend anyone could ever ask for."

It wasn't clear whether he was talking to Kiela or the pencil, but she grinned. "Same to you, Caz. Also, you have exceptional penmanship." She wondered if that had been part of the original spell that created him or if that talent was inherent in who the spider plant was. It felt rude to ask.

"I'm blushing. You just can't tell because of the chlorophyll."

She laughed.

And then they got down to work.

Starting with the first crate, Kiela unloaded the books one by one. For each, she read aloud the title, author, publisher, island of origin, and year of publication, and Caz noted the information down in tiny, precise letters and numbers. They also awarded each volume a designation for topic: weather, vegetation, animals, stars, sea, etc., and a sub-designation for whether it was a practical spellbook, a scholarly study, or a historical record, as well as the secret librarian-only designation for "mostly bullshit." Caz switched leaves often, and they paused only for Kiela to resharpen the pencil, careful to preserve as much of the graphite as possible—these too were a limited resource that she wasn't certain she'd be able to renew. She wondered if you could use berries to make an ink that would last.

The pencils should last for a while, but if she was going to think long term . . . *First things first,* she reminded herself. She couldn't afford the kind of tangents she loved to indulge in while she was at the library—here, whether or not she could afford to eat was dependent on how efficient they were at their research. She'd tackle the ink problem if and only if it became necessary. When they finished the first crate, they moved on to the second.

She was pleased to see that they had saved a great number of books on a healthy array of subjects, including a few she'd forgotten she'd chosen, and she was grateful for each one. So much knowledge, preserved. Even better: so much knowledge, at her fingertips.

After every book was recorded and categorized by topic (and piled throughout the room and on every inch of both her parents' bed and her daybed, first by topic and then alphabetically by author), Kiela and Caz surveyed their treasure trove.

"Where do we begin?" he asked, wonder in his voice.

This wasn't her usual indexing project, where she prepared a list based on a researcher's specifications. Normally, a scholar or a sorcerer would come into the library, request all information on one specific line of inquiry, and she'd search her volumes and present them with a complete index of where to locate each mention. Normally, the deadline was "by the next symposium," and the only stakes were the patron's academic reputation. Normally, her research wasn't directly tied to whether or not she'd have food.

That added a flavor of urgency to the whole endeavor.

For their shop, she wanted practical spells with obtainable ingredients that could be dismissed as remedies by the casual eye, and she wanted them for an array of uses from plants to weather to (if it was possible) the merhorses. *Start small,* she cautioned herself. She didn't even know if she could find a single appropriate spell. Right now, it was all just a wild idea.

A wild idea that has to succeed. She didn't have a Plan B.

"I'd like to know everything about everything," Kiela said, "but I suppose that isn't a reasonable research parameter." She chewed on her lip as she contemplated how to narrow it down. Choose wrong, and they could waste hours and hours in the fruitless pursuit of minutiae. She didn't have that kind of time to waste. *Fruitless,* she thought, turning the word over in her head. She thought of their success with the tomato plant. "Let's start with fruit."

Caz turned to a fresh page in the notebook and dutifully wrote *Fruit* as the title.

"Larran talked about the orchards," Kiela said. "If we can find a way to restore the fruit trees to full health, that will have a lasting effect on the island. Much more impactful than a single-season tomato bush and much less thorny than a lot of berry brambles."

If it works, it could even keep him from thinking he had to go to Alyssium. Maybe. She didn't know if healing an orchard or two would be enough, but it would be a start.

"So we focus on trees." He added the word *Trees* beside *Fruit.*

They turned to the veritable mountain of books on vegetation.

"We need space to do this properly," Caz said.

Kiela agreed.

Keeping the books in careful order, she returned the unrelated volumes to the crates—Caz noted which crate held which books. Until she had proper shelves and humidity control devices established in the cottage (which could be, she admitted to herself, a while away—those contraptions were expensive), as well as some kind of security system or at least a mechanism for hidden shelves, they were safest stored away in the crates. While she hated to make any book less accessible, it was for the best. *Necessities first,* she reminded herself yet again. She wasn't trying to establish her own library; she was trying to create a jam shop, with a secret side business. And besides, there wasn't much humidity on Caltrey; the books should be fine without fancy climate devices. She whispered an apology to the unchosen books as she closed up the crates and hid them beneath quilts.

She divvied up the remaining books, and the two of them dove in. As the evening deepened into night, Kiela brought in candles within lanterns. Every so often, one or the other would share what they'd found, and they'd swap books or Caz would add to the notes in the notebook. Otherwise, they read in companionable silence.

It was the most pleasant few hours she'd had since they'd fled Alyssium. She hadn't realized how badly she'd missed this: sinking into the solace of words, letting the authors steer her toward answers or, at least, better questions. The books in her stack were written by scholars and sorcerers and, in the case of one heavily illustrated volume, a naturalist, and they each had a different perspective of how magic could be used to influence the natural world.

By the end of the night, they had a list of potential spells to try, with the tree-healing spell as the one with the most potential so far. None were momentous enough to keep Larran from going to Alyssium, but perhaps one would work for the shop? Or maybe another book would hold all the answers? Kiela wanted to keep going, but she'd reread the same paragraph three times and still wasn't sure which verb paired with which noun—it was time to sleep.

She pulled on her sleep clothes and cleaned her teeth. Ignoring her daybed, she wrapped herself in a quilt and crawled onto her parents' bed between the spellbooks. Caz extinguished the candles in the lanterns and curled up on a pillow.

With the moonlight spilling into the room and across the crates of precious books, they slept, and for the first time since fleeing the library, Kiela didn't dream of fire. Instead her dreams were filled with apple trees.

At dawn, Kiela untangled herself from the quilt, stretched between the books, and opened her eyes to see Caz looming over her, perched on top of one of the stacks. "Are you ready to do magic today?" he asked.

She let out a shriek.

Startled, he tumbled off the books and landed in a *poof* of loose soil.

"Oops," Kiela said. "Sorry. Are you okay?"

He rolled upright and dusted himself off with his leaves. Collecting his dignity (and lost dirt) around him, he said, "I've been reviewing the list of spells we compiled, and I recommend we begin with the third variant of Ylindar's spell for strengthening deciduous trees."

Sitting up, she reached for the notebook with their preliminary index and located the reference. She'd remembered reading that—Ylindar had been from an island with a dry climate, very little rainfall, where deciduous trees had a difficult time due to the inhospitable soil. "That's in her third compendium." Her mouth felt woolly, and her eyes were sticky. She was fairly certain her hair poked out at all angles, but she didn't care. There was magic to do!

Caz nudged the relevant spellbook toward her, and she flipped through the pages to the one he'd noted. It was one of the handwritten spellbooks, which was unfortunate because Ylindar liked to swoop her letters, making them tricky to read. "All the ingredients are local," Caz said, pointing at the list with the tip of a leaf. "Except—"

"Mola sap," she read.

"But according to Venik . . ." He flipped through another book.

She glanced at it. "Have you been up all night reading?"

"I have excellent night vision."

"Still not entirely sure how you have any vision, given your lack of eyes," Kiela commented, but she read the passage he was pointing to. "'In some instances, pine sap serves as a reasonable substitute for mola sap.'"

He read over her shoulder. "That's clear enough, but how do we know if this qualifies as one of the 'some instances'?"

"Experimentation?" she suggested.

"Careful experimentation," he said. "And I don't know how I have vision either, which could be a problem if I ever become farsighted. No one has invented glasses for eyeless plants."

"If the need ever arises, we'll figure it out," Kiela promised.

"Thank you. I worry about that." He shuddered, and every single leaf shook. "I can't lose books; I'd lose *me*."

One of the librarians in the south tower had been a fixture in the Great Library for so long that it was said he'd been born in the stacks and had pledged his skeleton would become a bookshelf ladder after his death. He'd lost his sight when he was in his eighties, but it hadn't slowed him at all—he'd had a cadre of assistants who would read to him incessantly. "If that ever happened, I'd read to you. You won't ever lose books. That's not on the list of things to worry about."

"You have a list?"

"Of course. First: What if the shop fails and we can't support ourselves, and I starve? Second: What if the books are discovered and stolen or damaged? Third: What if we're arrested for possession of library property and transformed into statues, skunks, or salad? Fourth: What if the shop fails, we can't support ourselves, and we freeze over the winter due to lack of firewood? What if the roof caves in? What if a storm sweeps us out to sea? What if a sea monster attacks? What if I contract a terrible, incurable disease? What if you get bugs? What if our spells backfire and we accidentally create a violent tree monster who—"

"Okay, stop!" Caz cried. "Is there any chance of us creating a violent tree monster?"

"Not with acorns and honey," Kiela said. "Those spells are much more advanced."

Returning to the book, she skimmed the rest of the ingredients. Most of the items she knew they could find nearby: an acorn cap, a pine cone, a stick with two prongs, a shard of eggshell (it didn't specify what kind of egg, but she hadn't disposed of the chicken egg's shell from the other day—that would have to do), a variety of leaves that Caz could help her identify. It also called for a blast of easterly wind. Happily, that tended to be the predominant wind direction on Caltrey—she wasn't even sure why she knew that. Her parents? A fisherman? Someone must have told her, or else it was just a stray fact she remembered. She did remember facts better than most people.

While Kiela pulled on clothes, Caz began gathering ingredients. She joined him a few minutes later, and they scurried about the house and yard until they had the full list. Unlike the prior spell, this one called for the ingredients to be clumped around the pine cone, with honey (substituted for mola sap) as the congealing agent. "Is the wind today easterly?" Kiela asked.

Caz held up his leaves to test the direction. "There's no wind."

"What if I blow on it?" Kiela asked.

"Could work. Just position yourself correctly."

She turned so that her breath would be coming from the east and hoped this counted as an easterly wind. Carefully she blew as hard as she could on the sticky pine cone mess.

"Now, we bury it between the roots of a tree," Caz instructed.

She fetched a garden trowel, and they chose a gnarled tree that grew in the far corner of the garden, well out of sight from the front of the house. It had several bare branches. Her heart was beating faster as she dug. If this worked . . . *It might not work on the first try,* she cautioned herself. After all, they'd taken a few liberties with the ingredients, and the spell itself . . . Kiela wasn't one hundred percent sure if the third syllable was a "fah" sound or a "tah." And as for the last syllable . . . She pointed to it. "Ray-sa or ray-va?"

He peered at it. "Ray-va."

"You're certain?"

"It's a minor spell from a minor sorcerer," Caz said. "If it fails, the results shouldn't be catastrophic. Most likely, if it fails, it simply won't work."

She agreed with that assessment.

From her reading last night, it was clear that the most common result from failed spells was absolutely nothing. At worst, they'd have just buried a weirdly sticky pine cone, and the worms in the soil would eventually digest it, enriching the soil but at a far less magical rate.

Kneeling next to the buried pine cone, Kiela ran through the words in her mind, silently practicing the way they rose and fell as if they were a line of music. It was far different to read a spell as a scholar than it was to try to enact one. She needed perfection. When she felt comfortable in the rhythm of the spell, she recited the words out loud, and then she sat back cross-legged. This spell was supposed to strengthen the roots. She wasn't sure if the results would even be visible, which was one of the aspects that had appealed to her about it—the less her "remedies" looked like magic, the safer they'd all be. It would be nice if the results were measurable, though, so she could know that it—

The soil erupted upward like a fountain, and a knot of brown the size of a fist punched through the ground. Shrieking, Caz skittered across the garden. Kiela stared transfixed.

As suddenly as it had happened, it stopped, and the knob of brown sat there.

That . . . was not what was supposed to happen.

Kiela leaned forward for a better look, and the brown peeled off to reveal a tender green.

"What is it?" Caz called from behind a tomato plant.

"I don't— Oh, it's not done yet." As she spoke, the ball sprouted dozens of needles. "I think it's a cactus?" Slowly, she stuck a fingertip toward it. She touched the plant between its needles. Its flesh felt springy and cool, clearly a living plant and not one she'd ever seen before. She remembered the author of the spellbook, Ylindar— she'd had trouble with deciduous trees on her rainless island, but perhaps she had an abundance of cacti? "Do you think it was the honey, the breath, or the pronunciation?"

"I think it was a disaster."

"It's not a disaster," Kiela pointed out. "It's a succulent."

"No one needs a succulent."

"Hey, weren't you the one lecturing me about how a plant's value isn't dependent on its usefulness?" It was kind of beautiful, in a bulbous, pointy way. She was irrationally a bit proud of it—they'd created something that didn't exist before. She wondered if it was a specific type of cactus, or if they'd invented a new species.

"Back to the books," Caz instructed.

"But the cactus—"

"Gah!" He tossed his tendrils in the air. "Never mind the cactus! Books!" Grumbling about how they had no business attempting magic of any sort, Caz trundled himself back into the cottage, and Kiela followed, glancing back several times at the innocent and un-expected and strangely lovely addition to their garden.

Breath, several scholars concurred, was a key ingredient in spells that summoned new life. It was, she thought, a likely ingredient in the spell that had created Caz, but she didn't say that out loud—she wasn't certain if he was sensitive about his creation or not. At any rate, the substitution of breath for breeze was most likely responsi-ble for the new cactus in their garden. "Looks like we need actual wind," Kiela said.

"And we should have used pine tree sap instead of honey," Caz said, showing a passage he found in another book. "'When work-ing with plants, one must bind the ingredients with a plant-based substance, not one produced by either insects or mammals.'"

"Makes sense," Kiela said.

"Also, I found a copy of the same spell but in neater writing."

She examined the syllables. *Really, that was supposed to be a "fa"?* If she ever met Ylindar, she was going to suggest the sorcerer work on her handwriting skills. "So basically we did everything wrong." Perhaps they should have done a bit more research before jumping into spellcasting, but at least they hadn't done any harm. "Ready to try again?"

"Let's pick a tree somewhere out in the woods, in case we create more cacti."

"You don't like cacti?" she asked.

"I support all plants," Caz said loftily. "But I do know whatever *that* is, it's not native to this area. More of it will draw a lot more attention than overabundant raspberries."

Fair point. "How about the willow tree by the pond where we found the duckweed?" She remembered it had looked spindly, with sparse leaves on its limp branches.

Caz agreed, and they gathered a fresh supply of ingredients, using sap from an oozing pine tree to bind the elements together. Checking the wind, Kiela held the pine cone up so that the easterly breeze hit it, and then she wrapped it in a cloth in case the wind direction shifted.

"Attempt number two," she said.

Together, while the late-morning sun streamed through the leaves and the squirrels rustled in the branches, Kiela and Caz strolled into the woods.

It wasn't far to the pond, but it was far enough that no one would blame them for any abnormalities—*Hopefully.* As they picked their way between the ferns and overgrowth, the birds chattered overhead. She listened for the squawk of an errant hen, but she only heard the familiar calls of the songbirds, trilling and cooing and warbling. She heard a trickle of water before she saw the pond, fed by a stream, and she followed it until the forest opened.

Last time she'd been focused on the pond itself, with its light spread of duckweed, but this time she climbed around the pond and over a mossy fallen tree to reach the willow. It was a great old tree, with bending branches that swept the surface of the water with gentle kisses. Its ancient trunk was twisted, frozen middance, and the old bark looked as if it had been stretched too far and cracked from the strain. In its day, it must have been a magnificent sight. She could see the shadow of the tree it had been, echoed in the graceful drooping branches. Once, those branches would have been thick with teardrop leaves, and they would have rustled in the wind as if they were singing. She thought of Larran singing the old lullaby. Her mother could have sung that to her too, but she had no memory of it. She wondered if the old willow remembered.

Suddenly, Kiela wanted this spell to work as much as she'd ever wanted anything. It felt important that the tree's leaves sing in the wind again. Kneeling at the willow's knobby roots, she used the trowel to dig a hole and placed the sticky pine cone in it. She folded the soil over the pine cone as she said the words, correctly and precisely and intensely.

Side by side, Kiela and Caz watched the soil.

"Odds that it'll be another cactus?" Caz whispered.

"Eighty-twenty," she whispered back. She wasn't sure why they were whispering, but it felt appropriate.

"Eighty it will be a cactus?"

"Eighty it won't," Kiela said. She believed it would work this time. And if it didn't . . . there were plenty more ways it could fail other than producing another cactus. Some outcomes were potentially even more dramatic. She began to wonder if any of this was wise. "It's not doing anything yet."

Both of them stared so intently at the roots that Kiela almost missed the moment when the leaves above began to tremble. She heard them first, a whistle and then a rustle. She looked up to see a cascade of green as branches waterfalled from the trunk of the willow. Beside her, Caz let out a gasp as the tree healed: the branches softened into supple strands instead of brittle whips, leaves popped out as thick as fur, the bark shifted to a younger, greener shade. In front of them, the roots thickened.

"It worked," Kiela breathed. It wasn't any more subtle than the plant-growth spell, but wow. As an added benefit, it didn't force the tree out of season. If they could adapt it to be less showy . . . Of course, that all depended on whether this was a one-time miracle or whether the spell was replicable . . .

Caz did a little dance next to her. "Let's make more!"

She grinned at him as she stood up and brushed the dirt off her knees. "Absolutely," she said. She laid her hand on the trunk and thought she could feel the fresh life flooding through the tree. "It's beautiful."

As she marveled at the reborn tree, Kiela thought she heard a soft voice repeat in a whisper, "Beautiful." Listening, she heard nothing further. *It must have been the wind.*

CHAPTER THIRTEEN

The apple orchard was a boneyard.

Every tree was a skeleton, with bare limbs that twisted like arthritic fingers. Several had shriveled leaves that looked pasted onto them, and a few had the rare apple, not yet ripe, hanging lonely on its branch, hardly a harvest. Kiela halted at the fence around the orchard and felt a lump in her throat.

"This shouldn't have happened," Caz said.

Kiela nodded. It was a crime, to allow these trees to wither. "It's not the right soil for them," she said. "They were only kept healthy with magic. Withdraw the magic . . ."

"Good thing we're here then."

Were all the orchards on the island like this one? She remembered there used to be hundreds of fruit trees across all of Caltrey. Apples, cherries, peaches, pears, plums. As she climbed over the fence, she said, "We have to fix this. All of this."

"Our first goal has to be to keep you fed, especially through the winter," Caz reminded her. "Selling spells in addition to jam is a good idea, if and only if we can figure out how not to get executed for it. You need to eat."

She strode to the nearest tree and began to dig a hole for the first pine cone. He was right, of course, but she couldn't help but want to fix all of this. They still had a couple hours until sunset, thanks to it being summer, but still, there was no time to waste. "Fine. We sell remedies—not spells, *remedies*—for a fee. But whenever we have extra time and extra ingredients, we come out here and heal more trees for free."

"Do you really think that just rebranding the spells will solve the problem? We write 'Not at all illegal magic' on the label and hope that people believe what they read?"

"It'll work because people will want to believe it's true," Kiela said. "They need this to work." *If we can make it work.* The willow tree could have been a one-off. "Okay, here goes."

Kneeling by the roots of the apple tree, Kiela recited the spell.

"How long do you think—"

A second later, the tree was bathed in white blossoms like a sudden snowfall. She breathed in the fresh, heady scent of apple blossoms and watched as the petals peeled back and the heart of the flower swelled into a green orb the size of a baby's fist. Leaves cloaked the tree, and the roots stretched, causing the earth around it to buckle. Half a minute later, it was finished: a perfectly healthy tree, with fruit ready to ripen in the fall. The light and heady scent of apple blossoms filled the breeze.

"It worked!" Kiela said. "Same spell, same result. Proof of concept!"

"Excellent!" Caz punched the air with one tendril. "Except that it looks like magic, and I don't think we can assume the revolutionaries won and changed all the laws, as much as I want that to have happened. So, how do we make it look less like magic?"

That was the trick.

If she was going to convince the islanders that these were harmless remedies, not illegal spells, then they couldn't look so spectacular. There was no imperial investigator stationed on an island this small and remote, and so long as no one became suspicious enough to summon one . . . Well, they just had to make sure no one became suspicious. She and Caz had brought a bucket of pine cones, along with as many of the other ingredients as they could collect in a few hours.

It was time to experiment. "First, fewer ingredients . . ." Kiela replicated the concoction but used the smallest pine cone and only a fraction of the other ingredients. "I'm cutting everything to a fifth of the amount."

Caz took notes.

First result: unimpressive.

Only a few new leaves and a handful of fruit, but they popped out just as quickly; too quickly to be mistaken for anything but a spell.

For the second experiment, she returned to the full recipe but substituted a scraping of oak bark for the fern fronds—according to one book, fern fronds added oomph to nature spells, whereas oak was used for slow-reaction spells. (The actual language of the book was denser than that, but once Kiela boiled it down to its meaning, that was what ten pages of text equaled.) This time, when she planted the pine cone, it didn't react immediately. And then all of a sudden, blossoms popped into bloom all over the branches, but instead of hardening into apples, the petals burst from the tree and flew into the air as butterflies. Kiela tilted her head and squinted at the sun as the butterflies scattered across the orchard.

"Test three?"

She continued adjusting the ingredients.

The third tree shrank to half its size.

With the addition of apple blossoms to the spell, the fourth tree transformed into a red-apple-colored bird with a tail of white blossoms and flew over Kiela's head to disappear into the forest. It trilled joyfully as it flew.

"Oh dear," Kiela said.

"Do you think anyone will notice?"

"The other birds will." Maybe it would stick to the forest. She hoped it found things it wanted to eat. What did an apple bird eat? If it had stuck around, they could have tried to help . . . But it hadn't. She turned back to the orchard and consoled herself with the thought that it was unlikely that anyone would connect the bird to her and Caz. "Maybe it'll be happier as a bird."

The fifth tree, whose pine cone had been wrapped in debris from an abandoned bird nest, began to sing a wordless melody. As the branches crooned, Kiela joined Caz by the side of the orchard. *I didn't want a literal singing tree.* "Original recipe seems best," she said.

"It's a nice tune," Caz said.

"Mmm." Definitely an irrelevant detail. It shouldn't be singing at all, though he was right that the tree had chosen a pleasant melody. Perhaps with luck, passersby would think it was a trick of the wind. A lot of luck.

Sitting on a rock near Caz, she ran through the different variations she'd read in the various books last night. She'd committed several to memory, as well as taken notes. "Maybe we need to use the recommended ingredients but vary the words."

"Maybe we need to read a lot more books and take multiple years' worth of classes," Caz said. "Do you think that bird will be all right?" It still hadn't returned from the forest.

"It'll probably become friends with my chicken."

Taking the notebook from Caz, she studied the notes they'd made so far. He was right that one day of reading and another of experimenting wasn't a replacement for the rigorous training that an actual sorcerer underwent. *I'm not trying to be a sorcerer, though. All I need is to perfect this one minor spell.* She wasn't trying to change the world. Just heal a tree. It should be doable.

Giving the notebook back to Caz, she looked out at the view. Beyond the orchard was the sea. She knew there was a fence to keep anyone away from the cliff, but from where they were, she couldn't see it—it looked as if the orchard melted into the sea. Sun glinted on the water, like diamonds strewn out onto satiny blue. Far in the distance, she saw the scaled back of a sea serpent rise and fall.

They *did* have a spell that healed trees. Couldn't they just stick with that?

Not if our secret is immediately discovered.

There had to be a way to slow the effects of the spell.

Most sorcerers wanted their magic to be as showy as possible, to prove their worth. She'd once witnessed four sorcerers work together to create a spectacular light display over the city, to celebrate the anniversary of the emperor's ascension to the throne. They'd been raised up on a dais lit by hundreds of candles, and their voices had been amplified to echo the spell through the city. Fire had danced in the night sky, drawn by their words. The display had begun as ribbons of light, but then the dance became more complex. It formed the shape of a sea serpent with the moon behind it, and then a lion racing between the stars, before it split into a thousand birds and then burst into flowers. She remembered later one of the other librarians saying the true magic wasn't filling the sky with fire—it was extinguishing it later. For that, the sorcerers had embedded spells within the highest towers of the city. As the show drew to its end, the spells released and quenched the sky with rain. It had smelled like lilacs.

"What if I say the words *before* the pine cone is buried? All the same elements will be there so it shouldn't change the outcome, but it could change the timing." As she spoke, she was already assembling another sticky pine cone.

Caz frowned at the orchard. "The spell was written in a specific order . . ."

"It was also written with specific ingredients, and we varied that. One more experiment, Caz, and if it doesn't work, we just sell jam." She noticed that the singing tree had switched from an aria to a lullaby. Perhaps it would be silent soon. At least it was on pitch.

"Do it," Caz said. "But if you start sprouting leaves . . ."

She faked a smile. "Then we'll be plants together."

"It would solve the food problem if you had chlorophyll."

She finished preparing the pine cone and wondered if she was making a terrible mistake. If she activated the spell while she held it, would it turn on her? As much as she loved and respected Caz, she did not want to become anything other than a person.

On the other hand, if this worked and she proved she could enchant the pine cones before she sold them, then no one would witness her speaking the First Language, which would go a very long way toward convincing islanders this wasn't a true spell.

"Kiela . . . you know this is a risk," Caz said.

"Everything we've done from the moment those fires began has been a risk." Speaking the words directly to the pine cone, she recited the spell. And then she held her breath.

She didn't feel any different.

"No leaves," Caz reported.

Holding out her arm, she checked for any bark, leaves, or blossoms, but her arm looked the same shade of blue as always, if a little dry from being out in the sun all afternoon. She felt the same. Still blood in her veins, not chlorophyll. And she didn't feel the urge to sing, which was nice. "All right, let's see if the magic works at all."

Kiela picked another apple tree and buried the pine cone between its roots. She stepped back without speaking and waited. Slowly, from the roots up, the tree came back to life. Leaves unfurled from the branches, the trunk thickened, and buds appeared. A few minutes later, the buds opened into blossoms.

"What if you wait longer between the spell and the burying?" Caz asked.

By sunset they had it: a slow-release spell to heal trees, encapsulated in a sticky pine cone.

Kiela and Caz spent the next day making jam, assembling pine cones, and preparing their shop for opening day. She positioned the jam jars on the new shelves, changed her mind and repositioned them, and then repositioned them again until Caz at last said, "It's ready."

All of the pine cones had been wrapped neatly in strips of cotton from clothes that were too shabby to be worn, and they were in a basket behind the shelves, ready to be offered to prospective customers. In total, they had several dozen jars of raspberry jam and an equal number of enchanted pine cones. Everything suspicious was hidden in the back bedroom, with quilts artfully arranged over the crates to make them look like extra tables. She'd added vases of daisies and roses on top to complete the effect, on the off chance that someone wandered back there before she could stop them. The bedroom door would be closed while the shop was open, though, and she and Caz had no intention of leaving any stranger alone in the cottage.

It was all as ready for tomorrow as they could make it.

She just hoped this wasn't all a mistake.

Shortly after dawn the following day, Kiela ventured into the village to let the baker know that her jam shop was ready to open. She'd expected that Bryn would spread the word, and Kiela and Caz would see their first visitor later in the afternoon.

To her surprise, Bryn, despite the line of customers waiting for their early-morning pastries, turned the sign on the door to "Closed" and shooed everyone out. She left Tobin with a tray of muffins and strict instructions to sell them, not eat them. She then ordered Kiela to hurry back to the shop ahead of her. "Open it up," Bryn said. "I'll recruit your first customer and be there quicker than a serpent can sink a ship."

"That can't be a real saying," Kiela objected.

"Knew a sailor who said it all the time," Bryn said. "Admittedly, it was cuter when she said it. Go on, scoot. Get ready to hawk your wares."

Thus ordered, Kiela scooted. It had all happened so quickly that she felt as if she'd been spun in a circle three times fast.

As she bounded up the stairs on the cliff, she wondered if she was more excited or more nervous, and she decided there should be a name for an emotion that was both equally: "excivous" or "nercited." Glancing behind her, she saw Larran's house—the merhorse herder was on his porch, his back to the cliffs, looking out at the sea—and she hesitated.

I wish he was my first customer.

She shook herself, not certain where the thought had come from. It didn't matter who was first. What mattered was making the shop a success. Impressing Bryn and whoever the baker brought with her was all Kiela should be focusing on.

This has to work.

She didn't really have any kind of backup plan.

Jogging through the greenery, Kiela let the bird calls buoy her. She felt as if the forest was cheering her on. She burst out of the woods in front of the cottage—and a chicken, *the* chicken, *her* chicken, lifted its head and clucked at her.

She skidded to a halt.

She looked at the chicken.

The chicken looked at her.

And then it darted into the woods again.

Kiela sighed. But as she crossed the yard to the door, she spotted, nestled in a clump of grasses, an egg. She scooped it up. The shell was warm, clearly just laid. Feeling as if it was a good-luck sign, she carried it into the cottage and called to Caz as she placed the egg in a dish so it wouldn't roll away, "Customers are coming!"

He scurried out from the back bedroom and climbed onto the kitchen counter, which afforded a line of sight into the front. "What should I do? Should I welcome them? Or should I hide? Is a sentient spider plant a plus or a minus for a business?"

"You are always a plus," Kiela told him firmly.

It was one thing to not risk Caz in town, but the cottage was their home. If the islanders couldn't handle Caz, then she didn't want their business. Or their friendship. It wasn't as if talking plants were unheard-of. It was only on the outer islands, where there were fewer sorcerers to (legally) create them, that they were rare. She re-adjusted one of the jars on the shelf and then turned with a bright smile on her face as she heard voices approach the shop.

Bryn was coming up the path, followed by the centaur, Eadie. The baker had removed her apron and was dressed in teal pants and a white blouse, which complemented her tawny fur. A leaf had gotten stuck on one of her antlers.

Beside her, Eadie trotted on her four hooves while gesturing ani-matedly with her human arms. She wore a cloud-white top over her human half and a silvery-gray skirt over her horse hindquarters, and she'd braided silver ribbons into her black mane. The ribbons draped across her horse body down to her hooves. She had a wide, friendly smile, and Kiela told her heart to quit hammering. Both Bryn and Eadie had been nice before; there was no reason to think they wouldn't be happy shoppers now. Clearly, they'd both made an effort to dress up, as if this were an event, not an errand.

Giving herself a silent pep talk, Kiela met them at the door. "Welcome! Thank you for coming to Kiela and Caz's Jam Shop."

"Who's—" Eadie began.

"Hello!" Caz called. He waved his leaves.

Eadie blinked, stared, and then blinked again.

"Ah, so you're the one that Tobin has been chattering on about," Bryn said. "Pleasure to meet you, Caz. Welcome to Caltrey! It's so nice to have new residents. We haven't had new islanders since . . . well, I can't have been the most recent arrival, but certainly there haven't been many, unless you count newborns. How do you like our lovely island so far?"

"Very plant-friendly," Caz said.

Kiela stepped away from the door so her two customers could come inside.

"Oh, isn't this lovely!" Bryn said. Gushing, she admired the shelves with their alternating wood grain, the flowers that Kiela had put in vases and extra glasses, and the rafters with drying herbs hanging from them. "Every detail is charming. Ooh, I love the painted flowers on the chairs—I once wanted to be an artist, and I borrowed my sister's paints and decided the stairs would look prettier with flowers. Let's say that painting is not my strength, and my mother was not pleased, nor was my sister, or really anyone, and I haven't painted since. Luckily, I'm far better at baking."

Eadie clopped in halfway, with the back half of her horse self still outside. It occurred to Kiela that she should have made the shop larger or the door wider or . . . "It *is* charming," Eadie said, pleased. "Don't work yourself into a lather, Binna's girl. I'm used to not fitting everywhere. One suggestion—and you can take or leave it—you could use your front window for window service like Bryn does at her bakery, to accommodate Caltrey's larger residents. Ivor in particular has difficulty with ordinary-size doorways."

Bryn tapped her delicate antlers. "He's a twelve-prong."

"I love that idea," Kiela said. Perhaps she could add a counter to the outside of the window. She wished Larran had left his hammer. Not that she knew how to make a counter, but how hard could it be? He had left some wood behind . . .

"So much beautiful jam," Bryn said, examining the jars. "Eadie, look how they sparkle, packed with so many berries—you can see how rich they must taste."

"I wanted to preserve the berries while they were at their peak ripeness," Kiela said. "I plan to make other flavors soon, as well as experiment with adding various spices and herbs. I think cinnamon and cloves would work well with cherry, for example."

Eadie snorted. "If you can find a healthy cherry tree, more power to you. Remember the lovely cherry tree beside my house, Bryn?"

"Yes, it used to sag with so much fruit the branches would touch the ground, and—"

"And we'd stuff our faces and spit out the seeds on Fenerer's yard," Eadie said. "Only when he wasn't watching, of course. Such a wonderful tree. Joy and petty revenge in every branch."

That was a perfect intro to their other offering . . .

Caz heard it too. He hopped off the counter and waddled

himself into the shop. "To special customers, we're also offering a special remedy that improves the health of trees."

Both Bryn and Eadie looked at him.

Kiela held her breath—this was it, the moment that it could either all work or all fall apart. If they didn't accept the fiction of a "remedy" . . .

"What sort of remedy?" Eadie asked.

"A family recipe," Caz lied. Kiela felt her eyes go wide. Luckily, neither the baker nor the centaur was looking at her. He continued with blithe confidence. "Handed down through the generations, plant to plant."

"Ooh," Eadie said. "And it works?"

"Plants know what plants need," he said in a lofty tone.

That was absolutely brilliant. Kiela wished she'd thought of it. *Nice work, Caz.* She ducked behind the shelves and pulled out one of the wrapped pine cones. "Simply bury it between the roots of the tree. Don't delay, though, or it will lose its potency."

Eadie accepted the package. "Just bury it? No . . . anything else?"

She guesses, Kiela thought. She hoped it wasn't obvious the way her heart was hammering against her rib cage. She rubbed her suddenly sweaty palms on her shirt and wondered when it had become so hot in here. "That's all."

"And what do I owe you for this remedy?" Eadie asked.

She looked at Caz, who shrugged his leaves. "It's the first one we've sold . . . How about this: try it, and if it works, then pay us what you think it's worth to you?"

Eadie considered the wrapped pine cone, the sentient spider plant, and Kiela. "Fair enough," she said. Beside her, Bryn was beaming at both of them.

Kiela felt the muscles in her shoulder unknot, though her heart continued to race. She smiled at the centaur. *Our first sale.* "Can I also interest you in some jam?"

"Absolutely," Eadie said.

"I'd like a few jars as well," Bryn said. "There's a pastry recipe that would be perfect with it, spread with a layer of goat cheese, which adds the nicest flavor."

Caz rustled his leaves and groaned, "Ugh, goats."

As Kiela negotiated payment, Bryn launched into an anecdote about an overfriendly goat who loved to eat buttons—everyone who passed by had to watch their coats and their sweaters because he'd pluck off any button he could reach. Even Caz laughed as she described the lengths one islander went to to retrieve her buttons . . .

CHAPTER FOURTEEN

Kiela was reading another spellbook when their next customer arrived. She was so engrossed in the theories of the effects of enchantment on the taste of garlic, written by a scholar who was both a sorcerer and a cook at one of Alyssium's top restaurants, that she didn't hear the footsteps of the customer shuffling into the shop or his irritated "Is anyone here? What kind of shop doesn't have a shopkeeper?" But she *did* hear him shriek, "What is *that*?" and the thump of soil hitting the wood floor. She burst out of the bedroom to see Caz racing out the back door to the safety of the garden.

She pivoted to chase after her friend. "Caz, are you—"

"Oughta have a warning on your shop, if you're going to allow unnatural creatures in it," their customer said. She turned back to see a man who looked familiar—where had she seen him before? *Ah yes,* she remembered, *the unfriendly man by the bakery.* He'd been playing a game with stones with Tobin. Standing, he was much larger than she'd thought he was the first time she'd seen him. The top of his bald head nearly brushed the rafters of the cottage shop, which made her feel as if he were looming over her. He had scales instead of skin and was wearing the beige work clothes of a dockworker.

"I'm sorry you were startled," Kiela said, with a worried glance at the garden door, "though it seems you both startled each other."

"Looked like a plant," he said, still scowling. She wondered if that was his permanent expression.

"He *is* a plant, a spider plant—*Chlorophytum,* an evergreen perennial flowering plant related to the asparagus," Kiela said in her best don't-let-the-patron-see-your-clenched-teeth librarian tone. Hoping to forestall any unfortunate misunderstandings, she added, "He's inedible."

The man snorted.

"His name is Caz, and I'm Kiela. Welcome to our jam shop!"

"Fenerer," he said.

She'd heard that name before. *Where and when?* He hadn't introduced himself when she'd first visited the bakery. "Nice to meet you. As you can see, our initial offering is raspberry jam." She picked an apron off the back of one of the chairs and wrapped it around her waist, hoping it made her look more like an official shopkeeper.

Fenerer shifted his scowl to the shelves. "Just raspberry?"

"We'll have more choices in the future."

He grunted.

"Do you have a preferred flavor?" she tried. "We can take that into account when we produce the next batch. Blueberry? Cherry?" She suddenly remembered where she'd heard his name: Bryn and Eadie. They'd said they spat cherry pits onto his yard when he wasn't looking.

"Lemon. But you won't ever have that. Citrus doesn't grow on Caltrey unless you have one of those fancy glass greenhouses, and nobody here can afford one of those. Especially just selling jam. You ever think about selling more than jam? Can't imagine this shop will last."

She gritted her teeth and reminded herself that she'd handled grumpy sorcerers, rude scholars, and condescending students before. Granted, she hadn't handled them *well.* The one month she'd been assigned to work at the circulation desk, she'd accidentally reduced a particularly rude researcher to tears when she'd mentioned that his dissertation topic had been disproven fifteen years prior, and she'd been reported three times for delivering the wrong tome to unpleasant sorcerers who'd interrupted her reading without even an apology. But the difference was that back then she'd been hoping to be transferred back into the stacks, and now she wanted the shop to work. "Thanks for your concern. Would you like any jam?"

"No," he said.

Then why did you come to a jam shop? she wanted to ask. "Well, then, I'm sorry I can't be of assistance." She wasn't going to mention the remedies to this man—she'd decided that already. If he thought Caz was unnatural . . . well, to be fair, Caz *was* unnatural, but that didn't mean he needed to come with a warning.

Fenerer grunted again. He was a man of many noises, she was discovering. This one was a grunt that sounded halfway between disapproval and disbelief. And with that last utterance, he left.

Kiela waited, watching as he walked into the greenery without a glance backward, before she scurried into the back garden. She scanned the plants: the flourishing tomato, the sickly stalks of who-knows-what, the chaotic overabundance of raspberry bushes—and she spotted Caz in the back corner, crooning to a spot near the fence.

"Caz? He's gone. Sorry he was unpleasant. I think he was just being nosy. And judgmental. He didn't even buy any jam."

"Kiela, you have to come see this." Caz beckoned with several of his leaves. He didn't sound upset. In fact, he sounded more excited.

Kiela crossed the garden, carefully stepping between the plants. Once the shop was closed for the day, she thought she'd bring the naturalist's plant book outside and try to identify any plants that Caz couldn't. She thought one might be an onion . . . and a nearby vine was either a squash, a pumpkin, or a watermelon.

She reached Caz—

And a round green shape darted out around him and dashed to the other side of the garden. Kiela spun as it ran on . . . feet? Or was it needles? Roots? "Is that—"

"Our new cactus," Caz said. "Apparently, it's ambulatory."

"That's . . ." She wasn't sure if it was good or bad or what. ". . . interesting?"

"I'm trying to make friends with it." He flared his leaves out like a peacock would spread its feathers. She supposed it was meant to be a welcoming display? Or something?

She decided not to ask. "Great. Um, do you need my help?"

He waved a leaf at her and began to stalk the cactus across the garden. "All good. You can go back in. Just . . . you know, watch where you step."

Keeping an eye out for the running cactus, Kiela returned inside and removed the apron. She left it on a hook by the kitchen counter in case another customer came, and then she sliced up a tomato and ate it while she thought about whether or not the grumpy man was right—was it foolish to think she could make this shop work? Shaking off the doubt, she returned to the bedroom for her book. This time, she brought it out to the kitchen table, but she kept a dish towel nearby to toss over it in case of another visitor.

She'd just sunk into the next chapter, which analyzed three different approaches to soil rejuvenation in kitchen gardens, when she heard footsteps outside. She tossed the towel over the book, grabbed her apron, and hurried around the shelf-wall.

It wasn't, thankfully, the grumpy man again, but it was another stranger, which shouldn't have been a surprise since she only knew a handful of islanders so far. Everyone here was, by definition, a stranger, except for Bryn, Eadie, Larran, and Tobin. Her newest customer was an older woman. Like Kiela, she had blue skin, but hers was mottled with patches of green. She walked with a cane that was carved into a spiral like a unicorn's horn.

"Welcome," Kiela said as she entered.

Her name, Kiela learned, was Halio, and she spoke in a near whisper. She liked the shop, she liked the shelves of jam, and she liked Kiela's blue hair. She splurged on three jars of raspberry jam, offering a carton of eggs and a wedge of sharp cheese in exchange.

She was in every way the opposite of Fenerer. Taking a risk, Kiela said, "If you're interested, we also offer home remedies. We have one prepared now that strengthens trees."

"Don't have any sick trees," Halio whispered. "But . . ."

Kiela leaned closer.

"No reason to think you would . . . Never mind."

"It doesn't hurt to ask," Kiela said. "Questions are the heart of a functioning society." She wondered if she'd read that somewhere or had just invented it. She rather liked it. The empire had squelched questions about magic—restricting access to answers to the elite— and look what had happened. Imagine how glorious the empire could have been if everyone with a question had been welcomed into the stacks of the Great Library of Alyssium.

"I have a spring . . . *Had* a spring . . . It used to flow so beautifully, the freshest water, but it doesn't run anymore . . . But you said you help sick trees, not failed springs. Forgive me."

"Have you checked upstream?" Kiela asked.

Halio shook her head. "There's no upstream. My mother's mother conjured our spring from the bare rock, back when she settled on Caltrey."

"Your grandmother was a sorcerer?"

"Oh, no," Halio said. "But back then . . . Well, things were different. All this was before your time. It used to be we weren't so dependent on those imperial sorcerers. We took care of our own. Minor magics, yes. Nothing as flashy as sorcerer spells, but they did the job. Kept everything healthy and balanced."

"What happened to all that knowledge?" Kiela asked. "Why didn't your grandmother pass the spell down?" She thought of the recipe book she'd found in the cottage kitchen. What a shame that those homegrown spells hadn't been recorded and preserved and treasured like her parents' recipes. Someone should have done that work. If she'd been here . . . Would she have thought to gather it, like a scholar recording oral history? Or would she not have guessed it was necessary? How much knowledge had been lost because no one wrote it down?

"We didn't think we'd need it," Halio said. "The emperor's sorcerers always came, with spells so much grander than our homespun ones. The older generation was happy to leave the spellcraft for the experts, and the experts were eager to insist their way was best. And then some fluffed-up bureaucrats in the capital with no knowledge of the outer islands or how the world's interconnected codified that into law, and well, where does that leave us now?"

Kiela had to lean in close to catch all the words, and she didn't realize that Halio had asked a question, not just a rhetorical one, until the older woman was staring at her expectantly. "It leaves us with finding our own way again, and taking care of one another."

Halio smiled. "And it leaves us with jam."

Bidding her farewell, Halio hobbled out of the cottage and away through the greenery. Kiela watched for a moment and then scurried into the back room to search for books about fixing formerly magical springs.

At sundown, Caz finally came in from the garden and flopped down on the hole in the kitchen floor. He sank his roots into the soil and sighed. "It's still running amok."

"Is it hurting anything?" Kiela asked.

"It tore a few leaves with its needles at first and impaled a tomato—that was funny, juice everywhere—but it's gotten the hang of steering around now," Caz said.

"Is it upset?"

"Not at all."

"How can you tell?"

"It's started shouting '*Wheeee!*' as it rolls."

Oh. Oh, wow. "Are you saying it talks? Is it like you?" Had she and Caz accidentally made a sentient being? If so . . . was that okay? What kind of responsibility did they have toward the cactus? Should they offer to educate it? What did it need, and what did it want?

"It just says '*Wheeee.*' I'm exhausted. What did I miss here?"

Kiela told him about the two customers and how radically different they were, and she told him how she'd been researching the creation of wells and springs by magical means. "It's really fascinating." She fetched the book she'd been reading. "According to the sorcerer Lunia Wheelan, the water is either coaxed from beneath the bedrock or it's collected from—"

A knock sounded at the door. "Kiela? Caz?"

Caz let out an "Eep! It's Larran."

Quickly, Kiela scooped all the books into the back bedroom, tossed a quilt over them, and shut the door. She hurried back to the front of the cottage, slightly out of breath, as he ducked through the doorway. "Larran! Hi. Um, welcome to our shop."

"Did I catch you at a bad time?" he asked.

"Just . . . cleaning up." She turned to the sink to gesture at the dishes—and it was empty. She'd already washed the dishes and glasses she'd used during the day. She felt herself begin to blush. "Would you like to buy some jam?"

"Uh . . . I didn't . . . That is, I didn't think to bring anything with me to buy jam. I just came by to check on how your first day went."

"Good! I think." Actually, she had no idea how many customers were considered good, but she had sold a few jars of jam, which was a nice start? "I had some customers. Oh, that reminds me—one of my customers suggested that I make a counter for the window, so I can sell from there and not make the larger islanders feel uncomfortable trying to fit inside the shop."

"I can make you a counter," Larran said happily. He gestured to the tool belt around his waist. "I brought my tools just in case any of the shelves needed a fix."

"I didn't . . . I wasn't asking a favor. I mean, I was about to, but . . ." She collected herself. "Caz and I have created a remedy for healing trees. It's an old plant tradition kind of thing. Anyway, I would be happy to give you one in exchange for your assistance with building a counter for the front window." There, she said that without tripping over too many of the words. What was it about Larran that made everything come out so tangled?

"Healing trees?" Larran said, eyes wide.

Caz lifted a few of his roots out of his soil and waved them in the air. "It strengthens their roots. Old family recipe."

"You have a family?" Larran asked the plant.

Oops. Had they told Larran how Caz was made? She didn't remember telling him that story. Maybe Caz had told him?

But Larran backpedaled. "Sorry, that was rude. Of course you could have a family."

"We're estranged," Caz said loftily. "Kiela is the only family I need now."

We need to make sure our stories are straight if we're going to stay here. Neither of them had much experience with lying. It didn't come up much when you avoided talking to people. *Maybe it would be simpler if we talked less.*

Larran didn't seem interested in talking less, though. In fact, the herder seemed to be in a chatty mood. While he began work on her new counter, he told her about the antics of his merhorse herd. One of the mares, Amarin, had spotted a harbor seal today and decided to make it her pet. The seal, though, hadn't been interested in playing with a massive horse-fish. It tried to beach itself on a buoy, and Amarin kept bringing it little gifts in an attempt to either play with it or woo it: a bit of driftwood, a clam, a strip of kelp, a feather from a seagull. At last, she found a ball that had drifted out to sea.

While he talked, Kiela thought about which books to look through for the solution to rejuvenating the magical spring. She'd narrowed it down to three to research after Larran left. Kiela held the wood steady while he nailed it into position on the windowsill.

"What Amarin didn't know was that the boy Tobin—Bryn's

nephew, have you met him?—left the ball for her to find," Larran said. "He's a good kid."

Caz agreed. "He doesn't eat plants. Not even vegetables."

"He wants a ride on a merhorse," Kiela said.

"Does he?" Larran considered that.

With Kiela's help, he sawed support pieces, angled slices to attach to both the cottage and the shelf.

"Are there many magical springs on Caltrey?" she asked.

He blinked at the change in subject. "Sorry?"

"A customer was talking about hers. It's not running anymore. I was curious if that was common." She knew her water was from an ordinary well, dug long before her parents had been born, but she hadn't thought about how the rest of the island got fresh water. She thought of the waterfall that powered the mill. Had that been magically created, or was that just plain gravity?

"There are a few. The fountain in the center of town, for example—it was created with magic, but it's dry now. I suppose the spell simply ran down after time. I tried to fix it once, but there's nothing mechanically wrong with it. Its water source just isn't there anymore."

"Huh," Kiela said.

She wondered if the sorcerer had drawn from an existing source or had squeezed water out of rock. It couldn't be as hard to restart an existing spell as to begin one from scratch. Maybe *that* was the angle she should come at this with . . .

Larran hammered the last nail into the counter and patted the shelf hard. "Nice and solid. Happy to help with anything else."

"Oh, no, that's fine. Let me get you that remedy." She ducked inside and plucked a wrapped pine cone out of the basket. Thinking about an entirely different set of books she could read for restarting old spells, she brought the remedy out to him. "Thanks for stopping by."

"Uh, okay. If you'd like . . ."

"You just need to bury it between the roots of the tree, that's all."

"Sunset should be pretty today, if you . . ."

"Oh, and you should do it soon," Kiela said. "I don't know how long the remedy will stay potent. We haven't tested that, though I would think it would last. Better to just bury it now." She wondered if there had ever been a study for how long a spell stayed potent before its effectiveness wore off. But that was a tangent. She wanted to focus first on techniques for restarting stalled spells, especially water spells—that had to be much easier than creating an enchantment from scratch. Plus there should be minimal risk of mistakes, which was a plus. She thought of the cactus running around in the garden.

Larran was staring at her, she noticed, and she realized he'd spoken again and she didn't have any idea what he'd said. "Hope you have a good night," Kiela said, and hoped that was a reasonable response to his words.

"Good night, Kiela," Larran said.

She went back inside as he trudged toward the trail. The books she needed were in the third crate . . . As she passed Caz, he let out a dramatic sigh.

She paused. "What's wrong?"

"You are hopeless," he said.

CHAPTER FIFTEEN

Kiela didn't intend to stay up late reading, but the water-magic texts were tricky—the answers always seemed just a few pages away, as elusive as a shadow. By the time she woke, the sun was streaming through the windows. She padded into the kitchen to help herself to a glass of water. As she primed the pump, Caz burst in from the back garden. His tendrils were flailing high above his root ball.

"Are you okay?" Kiela asked. "Is it the cactus? What happened?"

"It's . . . we, uh . . . you have to come see. We have visitors. Lots of visitors." He punctuated each sentence with another wave of his tendrils. She hadn't seen him this worked up since . . . *Since the library burned,* she thought.

Leaving the sink, she hurried out the back door into the garden. Caz hopped behind her and bumped into her ankles as she halted abruptly and stared.

In every direction she looked in the garden, there were . . . oh my goodness, was that a *bear*? Or not a bear exactly, because it wasn't made of flesh and fur. It was . . . the idea of a bear, shaped from a cloud. Vast as a boulder but as insubstantial as mist, it hovered a foot off the ground above the daisies. Its shape wavered, wisps of cloud stirred by the air.

As soon as she saw one, she spotted another and another, cloud-smoke-wispy creatures that looked like bears of various sizes.

Beneath the pumpkin leaves: a tiny one like a puff of clouds.

Within the raspberry brambles: a tall and broad bear, made of smoke.

On the roof: the largest yet, spilled across the shingles, wider than her arms could reach, so large it obscured her view of the chimney, but soft and weightless.

Each of the bears had eyes that glowed like embers of a fire, flickering with an intensity that was both wild and beautiful.

"Forest spirits," she breathed.

She'd read about them, in scholar Cypavia's *Examinations of the Function of Forest Spirits in Fact and Fiction,* and she knew they weren't technically spirits. Originally, their species was from the flying islands in the far western reaches of the empire. When their kind first floated down to the islands in the sea, they hid in the forests and were mistaken for ghosts. Later, when their connection to the trees was discovered, they became known colloquially as forest spirits or tree spirits.

She wished she had Cypavia's books with her here. The scholar had studied them for decades, embedding herself in their most secluded forests, working to untangle the myths from the facts. On occasion, she could be coaxed to emerge from the trees to give a lecture at the University of Alyssium, and it was said those lectures were absolutely fascinating, especially given how animated she'd be about her topic. Kiela had been tempted to attend one once, but the idea of squeezing herself into the crowded audience . . . She *had* listened to a secondhand description of the talk, though, and it was indeed riveting.

Fact: they were neither ghosts nor spirits. A more accurate name for them was cloud bears. Or, given their function, tree guardians.

Fact: they acted as guardians of the forests and were fiercely protective of the trees.

Fact: they were shy, solitary creatures. *Solitary?* she wondered, as she spotted several more, tucked into the corners of her garden and visible over the top of the fence.

Fact: they did not punish trespassers. They did not kidnap innocent children who strayed from the path. They did not destroy villages whose inhabitants ventured too far into the forest with their axes and saws . . . except for when they did.

Some of the stories about cloud bears were true. If you were a danger to their trees, they would sweep over your home, as silent as the fog, and when the mist cleared, you would be gone, never to be heard from again.

Kiela was thinking all of this as she stared at the creatures, and her heart began to beat faster, her palms began to sweat, and she was acutely aware that she and Caz were surrounded. What if they were here to punish *her*? She had cast a spell that caused the raspberries to spread into the forest. She had tried and failed with several apple trees before her eventual success. What if the cloud bears had decided she and her illegal magic were a danger to their protected forest?

Caz tucked himself behind her ankles. "What do we do?"

"I don't know," she whispered back.

"What do they want?" he asked.

She didn't know that either. "I've never heard of them gathering like this. It's extraordinary." She tried to think positively. She and Caz had mastered the spell at the end. Maybe she could explain that? Did the cloud bears understand speech?

"Oh, yay," he whispered, "we can take notes. Publish a paper. Posthumously. It'll make us famous, but oops, we'll be dead, attacked by rampaging tree spirits. What a pity."

"They don't seem hostile." They were merely watching, silently, with their fiery eyes, from everywhere. Twisting around, she glanced behind her and saw, beside the sprawling immense bear, yet another one on the roof of the cottage, half-hidden behind the chimney and perched on a branch that hung over the kitchen. The cactus, she noticed, was huddled in a corner of the garden, beside a basket, doing its best impression of a lifeless rock. Occasionally, though, a few of its needles trembled.

Kiela took a step forward.

The shadow-clouds shifted, as if blown by a breeze.

She stopped.

Raising her voice, she asked, "Can we help you?"

It seemed to be the right question to ask.

A whisper of a breeze swept through the garden, but Kiela didn't feel its breath on her face. She waited, and a few seconds later, a cloud bear about the size of a cat inched forward from behind one of her plants. It was holding a leaf in its wisp-like paws. Laying it on the ground at Kiela's feet, it looked up at her with its flickering-flame eyes and then it scurried back behind the plant.

Kiela picked up the leaf. It was long and slender, supple and green.

"Willow," Caz identified.

Another tree guardian scooted forward—this one even smaller, the size of a rabbit. The little cloud bear laid a tiny branch covered with apple blossoms at her feet and then retreated. Kiela picked that up as well.

"Apple tree," Caz supplied.

A third cloud bear swept toward her at the speed of wind, and this one was *not* small. It loomed over her, so large that she couldn't breathe. Everything in her screamed to run. It could envelop her in its mist, swallow her whole. But it merely dropped a shriveled branch at her feet that was covered in dead leaves. This time, the cloud bear didn't retreat. It sat in front of her and looked down at her with ember eyes.

"Sycamore," Caz said. "I think. Why—"

"I can guess," Kiela said. She knelt and picked up the twig with the dead leaves. "You want us to fix your tree, like we did the willow and the apple trees?"

The windless breeze echoed through the garden again, and all the cloud bears crept forward until all she could see in every direction was a kind of waiting fog, with eyes. It was, to say the least, disconcerting. Caz scooted closer to her until his root ball pressed against her foot. She felt stray bits of soil drop into her shoe.

Softly, she whispered to Caz, "It's okay. I think they just want our help." Louder, she said to the bears, "Wait here—I'm going to get the spells . . ."

"Remedies," Caz murmured.

". . . and then you can show us where the sick trees are, okay?"

She had no idea if that was okay with the tree guardians or not, but they didn't move as she and Caz went inside to retrieve the basket of pine cones. She had no idea how many sick trees there were in the forest, but judging by the number of tree spirits in her yard . . .

"We were going to sell those," Caz said mournfully, trailing after her. "That was the plan, so you can eat and not get as sick as the trees."

"I know, but they need our help."

Caz humphed. "Did anyone help us when we needed help? Did anyone tell us to evacuate when the library was breeched? Did anyone check to see if we were okay? If the smoke had reached our floor? Did anyone care that we were in danger?"

Kiela thought for a moment. "Larran came when he saw smoke. He fixed our chimney."

Another snort. "Larran thinks you're the answer to every question he's ever had."

"He . . . what?" That was absurd. "He doesn't ask me questions." He mostly talked about his merhorses, which she didn't mind, but . . . "What in the world do you mean by that?"

"If you have to ask . . ."

"I do have to ask, obviously," Kiela said. "Because you aren't making sense."

Outside, she heard the wind pick up—or *was* it the wind? She glanced out the window over the kitchen sink, and it was crowded with cloud bears, their ember eyes staring in at her and Caz.

She shot Caz a look. "We'll continue this later," she told him.

Carrying the basket of pine cones, Kiela scooted out into the garden. "We'll help as many of you as we can," she said to the forest spirits. "Who's first?"

A midsize bear led the way. Around them, the others streaked between the trees like scraps of mist at dawn after a rainfall. They clung between the leaves and then dissipated, until Kiela wasn't certain she'd seen them at all. It was as beautiful as a meteor shower.

The sun fell through the leaves, filtered through the green, reminding Kiela of the North Reading Room in the Great Library with its stained-glass windows that cast patterns on the tables. The forest was hushed just like the library as well, but it was the hush of focused attention, not of sleepiness—a heightened silence that flooded everything. She and Caz didn't speak.

She couldn't stop thinking about what Caz had said about Larran. Why had he said that? It didn't make sense. She didn't have any answers. She had *access* to answers, but that wasn't the same, and, besides, Larran didn't know about the spellbooks. Wait, no—Caz hadn't said Larran thought she *had* the answers.

He said Larran thinks I am the answer.

She turned those words over in her head.

I am the answer.

She shook her head.

Nope, still doesn't make sense.

A cloud bear hovered on top of a fallen log, waiting for them to catch up, and the other tree spirits streamed on either side. She kept catching glimpses of them between the ferns—eyes watching her. It should have been unsettling, but now that they were between the trees, there was something oddly comforting about it. They were deep into the forest, climbing over mossy rocks and logs, far from anything familiar and so very different from the city she'd been living in, yet it felt as familiar as a childhood dream.

She tried to keep track of their path: left beside the tree with a triple trunk, straight by a boulder made of pink quartz, across a stream that trickled over mossy stones, but after a while she fell into a kind of meditation.

Everything felt soft and alive, and she felt as if she were welcomed within.

As they crossed the forest, though, she began to notice hints of decay: a stunted tree, a bare grove, a trickle of water that had once been a river. When the cloud bear in the lead stopped, she should have been ready for what they'd find.

A dying tree.

She knew that would be where they were being led, but what she hadn't guessed was the vastness of the tree. It was enormous, with a trunk wider than her arms could possibly reach and mottled bark that looked like a painting. Its thick limbs spread above them, like open arms that wanted to embrace the sky. Only a few leaves clung to its branches, the rest were bare.

A rabbit-size cloud bear danced around the roots and then curled as if in need of comforting between two enormous exposed roots that threaded through the mossy ground, while a massive seven-foot cloud bear hovered nearby, in a patch of ferns. The tree had to be at least two hundred years old.

"It's old," Caz said. "Do you think the spell will work?"

"There is a bristlecone pine tree that's nearly five thousand years old." Kiela laid her palm on the trunk. "A cypress on the island of Illirna is reported to be as old as the island itself, which is said to be two thousand years old. A fig tree on the island of Oteg has been worshipped by the islanders for over a thousand years. And an olive tree that's said to be as old as time itself. They'd consider this tree a child."

"Very nice, but what if the remedy fails because the tree has reached the end of its natural life?" He kept his voice low. "Do you have any idea where in the forest we are?"

She shrugged, unconcerned. "It's an island. Walk far enough, and we'll reach the shore." Tilting her head back, she looked up at the stripes of blue sky between the bare branches.

"If they let us go," he said darkly.

"They haven't threatened us," Kiela whispered back. "Don't assume the worst."

"Oh? You haven't read the *Tales of Nivve,* collected by the scholar Idya Warne, have you? In one, there was a child lured into a forest by tree spirits, and he walked out as only bones." He dropped his voice even lower. "He'd been stripped of all his flesh."

She dug through the pine cone basket, searching for the largest one. "I am certain scholar Cypavia would say that was metaphorical. Bones can't walk. Also how did Idya Warne know that the forest spirits were to blame? Are they even solid enough to hurt? And why would they want to?" Glancing at the cloud bears that were drifting between the bushes, she added, "I don't think we should be having this conversation now anyway." It was a bit too late for doubts about the wisdom of following incorporeal creatures into the woods.

Kiela pulled out the trowel and knelt between two of the great roots. As she stabbed the mossy ground with the tip of the trowel, a keening noise rustled through the bushes around her.

"In another tale," Caz whispered, "the spirits swallowed an entire village because they objected to them chopping down trees to build their houses and fill their fireplaces."

"I feel like this book is anti-tree propaganda," Kiela said. "Whom did the scholar credit as the author, and did he own a lumber mill?"

She peeled a square of moss back and dug into the soft earth.

The keening grew louder.

Looking up, Kiela said, "I have to bury the remedy between the roots. It won't work otherwise." She'd recited the spell to plenty of pine cones—all the ones in the basket, in fact—but the spell only activated after it had been buried. She was positive it was necessary. "I'm sorry for harming the moss." She wondered if any of the tree guardians belonged to the moss and if they'd be offended. Gently, she pushed more of it aside, hoping its roots would stay intact and it could regrow over the spot where she was digging.

The tiniest cloud bear drew closer, and she let it inspect the start of her hole.

When it withdrew, she asked, "May I proceed?"

The bear inclined its head.

So it can understand me, even if it can't speak. She'd suspected as much, though it was unclear earlier whether it had understood her words or simply the act of bringing the basket of pine cones outside. She wondered how intelligent they were and what they thought of the islanders. Did they share Caltrey willingly? Her parents hadn't talked much about the history of the island, but she knew people had lived here for many generations. The villagers and fisherfolk weren't newcomers, but to a several-centuries-old tree, perhaps they were.

She wondered if anyone had studied the forest spirits of Caltrey. Cypavia had worked primarily on the islands to the west, both those on the sea and in the air. Kiela didn't think anyone had studied these particular cloud bears.

If they haven't, she thought, *I could.*

After she grew her jam shop. After she proved she could feed herself. After she healed the forest. And helped the island. And figured out what Caz meant when he'd said Larran thought she was the answer . . .

Kiela buried the pine cone.

She thought about leaving it to do its work—she'd already said the spell once when they'd assembled the remedy. But would it be enough? This was an exceptionally large and old tree.

It couldn't hurt to say it again.

She chanted the words to the spell out loud. After testing so many pine cones, she had the phrases seared into her mind, and she was confident that she pronounced each of the ancient syllables correctly. While she chanted, it felt as if the forest stilled—the birds were silent, the breeze died, and the tree spirits were motion-less around her.

As she said the last syllable, Kiela rocked backward and exhaled.

"Uh, Kiela?" Caz whispered.

All the cloud bears had drawn closer, blurring into a fog that crept around her, Caz, and the sycamore tree. She couldn't see the forest in any direction, only the dying tree before her. She looked up at its branches, and then she felt the roots convulse beneath her knees as magic flooded the old tree.

It looked like a wave of green light, beginning with the roots and pulsing through the trunk until it split at the branches. It chased down every limb. Every branch it touched burst into life: leaves budded and then unfurled, and the most glorious scent of *green* and *life* and *spring* and *summer* all wrapped together filled Kiela's nose, mouth, and body. She felt as if she were breathing in the es-sence of the forest, alive and full of growth. Leaves layered over one another so fast that the sky disappeared and the sun vanished into a glow of green.

Pressing itself against the trunk of the sycamore, the rabbit-size cloud bear wept tears as bright as diamonds. Its tears rolled down the bark, and where they touched the soil, delicate white flowers bloomed. She'd never seen flowers like it: they were clusters of pet-als that glowed with the soft, white light of the full moon.

"Wow," Caz said. "Just a suggestion, but if you want to stay in-conspicuous, don't say the spell twice."

"Yeah," Kiela agreed.

A breeze-like whisper swept through the tree spirits, and they drifted apart to create a clear path away from the sycamore tree. Kiela stood up and picked up the basket. Clearly, the tree spirits wanted to lead them to the next—

A unicorn stepped onto the path.

Kiela gasped.

Caz breathed, "Whoa."

It was like moonlit water, so bright that tears sprang into Kiela's eyes as she looked at it. Shaped like a dreamer's idea of a horse, the unicorn was slender and graceful—closer to a line drawing than an in-the-flesh creature. Its neck curved like a wave, with its mane as the sea foam. The longer Kiela looked at it, the more she saw that it wasn't as white as the moon, it was iridescent, like mother-of-pearl, with purples and reds and blues that swirled through its silvery white hide. Its horn was a slender spiral of gold.

It regarded them with ocean-blue eyes.

And then the forest spirits flooded toward it, and the unicorn disappeared from view.

Kiela found she was shaking. Seeing a unicorn . . . Well, it simply didn't happen, not to ordinary librarians or ordinary island shop-keepers. It happened in tales. Or to children, who later believed they'd dreamed it. It was a gift.

"I think we should heal more trees," Kiela breathed.

Beside her, Caz was quivering. "Yes, absolutely."

As the setting sun tinted the sky rose and orange, Kiela and Caz stag-gered back to the cottage. They'd crisscrossed the forest and used every pine cone in the basket. They didn't see the unicorn again, but they saw wonders all the same:

Birds with plumage that draped behind them like a grand cloak.

Cobweb-like moss that sparkled with twinkling lights.

A rainbow waterfall that poured down a white quartz cliff.

Countless creatures that Kiela had only read about, like the shy bird-foxes who could fit in the palm of your hand or the tiny golden monkeys who guarded ruby-red fruit or the squirrels with emerald tails.

She felt dazed and drained, and all she wanted to do was flop onto her bed. Maybe eat something first; ideally anything that didn't need to be cooked or prepared. Maybe just raspberry jam. And then she'd sleep.

The cloud bears left them at the clearing in front of their cottage, and even after all the spectacular wonders she'd seen since dawn, Kiela thought it was a magical sight: their home, tucked between the bushes and trees, covered in ivy and flowers, with the sign she'd painted, "Kiela and Caz's Jam Shop," over the door and the new counter that Larran had built under the window. She wondered if they'd missed any customers today, and decided that next time they went traipsing off into the forest with magical beings, she'd leave a "come back tomorrow" note on the door.

She opened the front door, and they both went inside. Caz scooted himself out through the back door to the garden. "I'm going to check on the cactus," he told her.

"Mmm," she said. It was the most conversation she felt she could manage.

Going from lantern to lantern, she lit a few candles, and then she sank into a chair. She thought about not standing up again. She could sleep sitting, couldn't she? No, she had to eat, and then she could drag herself to bed.

Caz hopped back inside. "You have to come see!"

"Unless it's as good as a unicorn, I'm not moving," Kiela said.

"Just come," Caz said.

She pried herself off the chair and shuffled out to the garden. All around the garden, the tree guardians had left gifts: nuts, mushrooms, wild edible roots, as well as the ingredients needed to replenish her basket of remedies (pine cones, leaves, even a chunk of pine sap) and then some. There was also a tiny mountain of blueberries that she could use for another flavor of jam. And best of all, next to the house was a bush whose branches had been woven together to form an enclosure—a homemade chicken coop.

Within the coop was her errant chicken.

The hen clucked at her once and then settled placidly onto a nest of grasses and hay.

CHAPTER SIXTEEN

The next day, Kiela checked the garden before she opened the front door to the shop. She fed the chicken, located the wandering cactus (it was busy chasing a bit of dandelion fluff), and picked a couple tomatoes for breakfast.

There were no tree spirits that she could see. *But that doesn't mean they aren't there.* "Good morning," she called to the garden and to the forest beyond.

She waited for an answer. After a few seconds, she heard the whisper of a breeze that wasn't a breeze. Smiling, she returned inside. While she ate a bit of Bryn's bread (with jam) for breakfast, Kiela considered the bucket of blueberries. She'd make more jam today, she decided. And open the shop properly, without disappearing into the forest to frolic with a unicorn.

Did I really see one?

It felt like a dream today, but the blueberries were real, the remedy basket was empty (though they had a full supply of fresh ingredients, thanks to the cloud bears), and the chicken was in the backyard. She wondered if it would harm the garden to have a chicken wandering through it. How much could one hen eat? Did they eat tomatoes? What about raspberries? She thought they just ate worms and . . . She didn't know. What had Larran said to feed them? Scraps from her food?

Thinking about Larran again, she rinsed the blueberries and then poured them into a bowl with a heap of sugar. She left them to macerate while she opened the window with the counter and flipped the sign on the front door to "Open."

Had he ever seen a unicorn? She wondered what he'd say if she told him about what she and Caz had seen and what they'd done. She could picture him listening and smiling before talking about his merhorses. Or maybe not. *More likely, he'd be appalled,* she thought. What they'd done was indisputably spellwork—unicorn-approved but very, very illegal, unless the revolutionaries had changed the laws and decommissioned the imperial investigators already, which of course she had no way to find out without exposing herself and risking losing the books, the shop, the cottage, and even her life.

I can't tell him.

But she could bring him some blueberry jam. And a jar for Bryn too. Kiela was eager to visit the bakery again, which was funny because she'd never sought out people to talk to before, but after a day that felt so dreamlike, she wanted to hear real voices and see real people. *Am I becoming an extrovert?* That seemed unlikely. It was more that her brush with so much enchantment made her want to reach out and touch something solid.

A trip into town, stopping at Larran's on the way, she decided. It would be good for her. She could bring her new flavor to Bryn, buy a loaf of bread, and see actual people. Sitting at the table, she began sorting the ingredients to make more sticky pine cone remedies.

Caz waddled into the kitchen. "Morning, Kiela. So, yesterday . . ."

"Not a dream," she confirmed. She waved at the piles of raw ingredients as proof. They had everything they needed for several dozen more tree remedies, and they hadn't had to gather any of it themselves.

He pulled himself up onto the table by his tendrils and began sorting leaves with her. They'd just finished organizing everything when she heard a voice at the front window.

"Hellooo? Are you open, dear?"

Kiela wiped the excess sap from her fingers and scooted around the shelf-wall. "Eadie, hello, welcome. Nice to see you again." She was surprised to discover she meant that.

Beaming at her, the centaur leaned against the counter. She was wearing a wide-brimmed purple hat on her human head and a white-with-purple-flowers dress draped over her horse torso and hindquarters. Her mane was braided with purple ribbon. "You took my advice."

"It was good advice," Kiela said. "Larran helped me build it."

Eadie grinned at her. "Ahh, he did, did he?"

Kiela felt herself blush, though she wasn't sure why. It was a perfectly neighborly thing for him to do, plus she'd paid him with a pine cone remedy. She wondered which tree he'd used it on, if it had worked for him, and what he had thought of it. And what he thought of her.

"Glad to hear he's spending time with you," Eadie said. "He's had quite a lot of tragedy and loss in his life, that one has. Very bad, and none of it his fault. It would be good for him to find some happiness."

She wasn't certain that she was his happiness, and that wasn't a conversation she wanted to have with Eadie. Not so subtly, she changed the subject. "How did your remedy work?"

Her grin transformed into a genuine smile. "Beautifully! That's why I'm here. I came to pay you what it's worth to me." She pulled out a pouch and spilled a heap of silver on the counter.

Kiela's eyes widened. It was as much as she was paid in a month at the Great Library. Vastly more than any outer islander was paid in a month. "It isn't worth *that* much."

"It is to me," Eadie said firmly. "My grandfather planted that tree when our family first arrived here. He'd fled his home island with my pregnant grandmother—there had been an uprising, a whole mess. It was a harrowing journey, according to the family stories. Half their boat was eaten by a sea serpent, and they capsized twice in storms, yet they still managed to drift their way to the shores of Caltrey. He'd brought the pit of a cherry from his home and planted it in the finest patch of soil he could find, his way of claiming Caltrey as our new home. By the time I was born, it was a fine tree, producing fistfuls of fruit every summer, and he babied it like it was one of the family. He'd convince every traveling sorcerer to come and cast strength spells on it so it would survive the winters. He passed away before the sorcerers quit coming to Caltrey, and so he didn't have to see his beloved cherry tree fall prey to the new string of magic storms. It would have broken his heart. It broke mine seeing the tree dying. It felt like losing him all over again. But you . . . you gave the tree back to me. You gave me back my grandfather's soul, and that's worth all the silver in the world."

Kiela felt tears pricking her eyes. "I'll take three pieces of silver. You have to keep the rest."

"Five pieces. You shouldn't argue with a woman with hooves."

Below, Caz bumped against Kiela's ankle. "Say yes."

"Five, okay," Kiela said.

"And I'd also like to buy more."

She thought of the merbaby she'd seen—he had brought them luck. *This shop is going to work. We're making a life for us.* "We're currently out, but we'll be making more. If you'd like to stop by tomorrow, I should have them ready. Or I could bring a few to you in town after I finish the next batch of jam. I'm planning to stop by the bakery later this afternoon. Will you be there?"

"That would be perfect. I'll prepay, and you can bring me five more this afternoon." Leaving a smaller but still impressive stack of silver on the counter, the centaur trotted away from the shop and back into the greenery.

"I love it here," Caz said fervently.

In high spirits, Kiela headed out after she'd finished a batch of blueberry jam and she and Caz had made a dozen more pine cones.

She took two jars of jam (one for Bryn and one for Larran), as well as the five remedies for Eadie.

Kiela sang as she walked down the trail through the greenery. She knew she wasn't quite in tune, but the birds didn't seem to mind. One of them she recognized: a bird with red feathers and a tail of white apple blossoms. It flew above her, singing joyfully. She wondered what would happen if the blossom-bird decided to follow her into town. Would anyone guess he was supposed to be an apple tree? Would they suspect she was responsible?

She decided not to worry about that. It was a beautiful afternoon, the bird seemed happy, and she was in a wonderful mood. As she stepped out of the greenery, Kiela inhaled the sea breeze. Ahead of her the sky was a lovely quilt of purple-and-blue clouds, and the sea was dancing with white waves, quite lively.

She gripped the railing firmly as she made her way down the stairs—she was happy, but not giddy enough to be careless, and falling down the cliff would put an end to her excellent day quite rapidly, especially since the wind seemed extra-enthusiastic today. It danced around her as if it wanted her to waltz with it, never mind gravity. Holding on tight, she made it to the bottom safely enough.

Glancing toward Larran's house, Kiela scanned the beach and the jetty for the herder. She spotted him out on the waves, riding one of his merhorses. Oddly, there were no boats out on the water beyond him—perhaps the herd had already finished helping the fisherfolk for the day? It seemed early for that to be done. *Bakery first, then Larran's house,* she decided. Maybe he'd be back to shore by then.

She turned toward the village and walked into town. It looked . . . She couldn't put her finger on what was different at first, but then she began to notice details: there were no carts or wheelbarrows or any- thing in the streets, the flower boxes were empty of pots, and shut- ters were pulled closed over the windows. Additionally, she heard a steady bell ringing in the harbor. It wasn't marking out the time, and it didn't cease.

Seagulls circled overhead, far more of them than she'd seen before—an uncomfortable number of them, in fact. Perhaps the fishing boats had docked, and the gulls wanted a share of the catch? Craning her neck, Kiela looked to see the docks between the streets and glimpsed fishermen and women spilling a net onto the street. A few crabs skittered out, and then her view was obscured by a woman hauling a crate cross the street.

Kiela continued on past the dry fountain to the bakery, expecting to see the usual crowd of customers at the tables and by the counter, but instead it was empty. No tables. No chairs. And the window with the counter was shut. *Huh, where is everyone?* At least the bakery door was open so she knew that Bryn at least hadn't—

A man strode out of the bakery with a stubby loaf of bread clutched in his hands. *I know him.* He was Fenerer, the man with scales who'd come to her shop, grumped at her, and failed to buy any jam. Seeing her, he halted. "You, citygirl."

She couldn't help glancing behind her, even though it was obvious he was talking to her. One of the winged cats, gray-furred with maroon wings, eyed them from a nearby roof. All the cats seemed on edge. Maybe because of all the seagulls? Or maybe they didn't like Fenerer either? She wished she'd arrived just a few minutes later. And she wished the harbor bell would quit tolling.

"You can't come here and cause trouble," he barked at her. "This is a peaceful island. You need to go back to where you came from."

"I'm from Caltrey," Kiela said in a small voice.

He snorted. "You left. You came back with all sorts of unnatural ideas. Bringing trouble to our island. We don't need that. We have enough troubles on our own, without strangers coming in and making things worse."

She glanced right and left. There was no one nearby to interrupt this unpleasant conversation, and he was blocking her way to the bakery. She didn't want to just turn around. "I'm not causing trouble."

"You think I don't know about the orchard?" Fenerer barked.

"All the oddness. One of the trees . . . It won't stop singing. Singing! An apple tree. Unnatural."

She felt herself grow cold. Had he seen her and Caz working magic? What could she say to convince him he'd imagined it? Pretend it wasn't her? Say it was just a game?

He wagged his finger at her. "You're the only new arrival we've had, the only thing that's changed on this island in weeks. It had to be you."

He didn't see me, she thought, relief flooding through her. *He's guessing.* "I don't know what you're talking about. I haven't been near any orchards. I live in my family's cottage in the forest beyond the cliff. You've been there, remember? My shop?" She heard her voice squeak, and she wondered if he could hear that she was lying. She'd never been a good liar. It was part of what had gotten her assigned to the third floor of the library with the less-flashy books on nature spells, instead of a section more popular with scholars, such as palace construction or canal construction or fire magic. When directly asked what she thought of their research, she often answered honestly before realizing they'd merely wanted her to praise their brilliance.

"You can't fool me. I know—"

Behind her, Kiela heard the clop of hooves on cobblestones. Eadie's voice rang out, "Kiela, is this old snot bothering you? Don't you mind him. He hasn't been the same since the day he drove his precious boat into a rock."

Fenerer's scowl depended. "There was an unexpectedly strong storm."

"Yours was the only ship foolish enough to be out after the harbor alarm sounded," Eadie countered. "But enough about that, what are you doing in town today?" She directed the question at Kiela.

Why shouldn't I be? And what was a harbor alarm? There had never been such a thing when she was a child, or had she simply not known about it? "I tried a new flavor of jam, and I thought you might like to try it—a gift. Blueberry." She drew the jam she'd intended for Larran out of her basket and held it out to Eadie. *Please don't mention the remedies.* She didn't want to hand Eadie the pine cones in front of Fenerer. That would only give him more fuel to suspect her.

Eadie accepted the jar and held it up to the light. The deep blue-purple glowed like a jewel in the bit of sunlight that slipped between the clouds. "Ah, lovely. I'll enjoy this. You know"—she addressed Fenerer—"your disposition might sweeten if you tried some jam with that bread."

He grunted, "Humph," before stalking off down the street.

Kiela felt her chest loosen, and she could breathe again. "Thanks."

"Don't let that old grump get to you," Eadie said quietly. "Not all of us think the way he does. Most of us don't. Now, is this really what you came to give me?"

She glanced down the street, waiting until Fenerer turned out of sight, before she drew out the five pine cones, wrapped in cloth. "Maybe don't bury them when anyone is looking? Just to avoid misunderstandings."

"Of course," Eadie agreed. "We don't want any misunderstandings. Now you'd better go on and finish your business with Bryn. Not a day for dallying." She gestured toward the sky, and Kiela noticed that the wind had picked up. Overhead, one of the gulls was flying into the wind and making no progress—it looked as if it were hovering stationary above the roofs. Most of the cats had cleared off. The roofs looked bereft without them.

Thanking Eadie again, Kiela scooted inside.

Once again, the scent of warm bread enveloped her like a hug. She stood for a moment and breathed it in before raising her voice to call, "Bryn? Hello?"

The baker bustled out of the back room. She wasn't wearing her apron, but instead was in sturdy brown pants, a plain shirt, and waterproof boots. "Ahh, Kiela! Surprised to see you here on such a day. What are you doing in town?"

That distracted her from offering the blueberry jam. Eadie had said it wasn't a day for dallying. Why not? And where had the winged cats gone? "What do you mean, 'such a day'?" Kiela asked.

"Storm's coming, about to blow in from the southwest. The fisherfolk have already pulled their boats in and are securing them—don't you hear the harbor alarm bell?"

Oh. That was what that was. "I hadn't realized . . ."

"When the sky starts looking blue and purple, the harbormaster rings the bell, and that's the sign to stay home. It'll blow in quick and blow out quick, but there's no way to guess how badly it'll pummel us in the meantime. I'm about to close up the shop, since there's no point in being open when everyone's just going to hole up in their homes, which you should be doing too."

"Right. Okay. Yes, I will." She pulled the jar of blueberry jam out of her basket and placed it on the counter beside a vase of daisies and a roll of ribbon. "I wanted to give you this, a new flavor for you to try."

"I'm sure it's delicious, but it's not worth risking your safety." Bryn frowned at her. "Why don't you stay here? I've an extra bed upstairs—you can wait out the storm in town and head home afterward."

She shook her head. How could she stay when Caz was by himself back at the cottage? If a storm hit hard, he'd worry himself sick. She knew the spider plant—he had an impressive imagination. He'd concoct all sorts of disasters that could have befallen her and convince himself that she'd washed out to sea. "I'll hurry home," Kiela promised.

"Take these," Bryn said, scooping several cinnamon rolls into a bag and handing it to her. Kiela reached into her pocket for a coin, but Bryn stopped her. "A gift for a gift, and besides, they'll just go stale if no one comes to buy them. You're doing me a favor by taking them—I hate to see a baked good go to waste."

"Thanks," Kiela said.

Taking the rolls, she headed outside. Behind her, Bryn began to close up the shop, securing the door with a second, heavier door. As Kiela hurried through the street, she noticed that in addition to shutters, more than a few windows were boarded up with thick planks. *Caz won't know to do that,* she thought. *He doesn't know a storm is coming.* But he would notice the wind and stay inside. Hopefully, he'd coax the cactus and the hen in with him.

She didn't see a single cat.

The wind was blowing harder now, whipping between the buildings. Her hair blew into her face, and she kept pushing it back so she could see, but the wind lifted it and twirled it until it danced on her head. She hugged the bag of rolls to her as she broke into a run.

How did I fail to realize the pretty blue-and-purple clouds were storm clouds? She'd been so cocooned within the library that she didn't know the signs of an impending storm. Even if she hadn't known what the bell signified, she should have been aware of the shape and color of the clouds.

She realized the bell had stopped ringing. Good? No, bad. Very bad.

The rain swept in as a sheet of water. It pelted the cobblestones, and Kiela broke into a run toward the shore. The waves were crashing harder than before, no longer dancing but fighting in spurts of froth that slammed down onto the pebbles and sand.

Rain soaked her clothes, and it obscured her view of the cliff. She couldn't see up to the top. Climbing the stairs—she could barely make them out, and the wind was causing them to sway, pulling them away from the rocks.

I can't climb that.

She'd be blown off the steps. Or washed off.

Back to the bakery? Kiela turned—

Fast and rising, water swept down the streets and spilled onto the beach to meet the crashing waves. Much more sensible to go to

Larran's house. It was closer. She had no more blueberry jam, and the cinnamon rolls had to be a soggy mess by now, but maybe he wouldn't mind a visitor anyway. As the waves smashed down, she pushed against the wind, heading toward the warm glow of lanterns visible through the seams of his shuttered windows.

CHAPTER SEVENTEEN

Kiela pounded on the door as the storm lashed at her. Behind her, over the water, she heard a crash, and she jumped. She looked over her shoulder and saw the sky had deepened into a purple-red, with streaks of lightning inside it—*A magic storm,* she thought. Of course. She should have known, given how fast it had swept in.

"Larran!" she called.

He wasn't going to hear her over the crash of the waves, the crack of the thunder, and the thud of the rain on his roof. She shivered hard.

Shaking the door handle, she shouted again, "Larran! Please, let me in!"

I should have stayed in the bakery. Or with Caz in the cottage. Was he okay? He had to be so worried. And scared. She wiped the rain from her eyes with the back of her hand and then she pounded on the door and shook the handle again.

Kiela heard a roar behind her. She turned—

The storm clouds had twisted into the shape of a sea serpent. Lightning sparked from its eyes and skittered down its rain-slick back. She stared at it, frozen. Her heart pounded hard in her throat, and she was fully aware of how small, how breakable, how utterly fragile she was in the face of *that.*

Her arm was yanked backward.

She stumbled inside the house. With an *oof,* she smacked directly into Larran. He wrapped one arm around her and slammed the door shut with the other.

"Uh," she said.

He was really quite tall. She somehow kept forgetting that. It made her feel like she'd found shelter beneath a strong oak tree. Pressed up against him, she had to tilt her head back to see his face. He was looking down at her, clearly worried. "Kiela?"

It occurred to her that she was making his shirt very wet. Like a startled deer, she sprang backward out of his arms. "Sorry. I . . ."

"What are you doing here? There's a storm—"

"I didn't bring you jam," Kiela burst out.

Why did I say that? Yes, she'd meant to bring jam, but that wasn't the most important detail or really any kind of explanation for why she was here, soaking wet and shivering.

"You're soaked again," he said.

"I don't mean to make it a habit." Her teeth chattered together. "May I—"

"Yes, let me find you a shirt."

She noticed he was blushing. Without another word, he strode into his bedroom. She followed him and watched him lay a shirt on the bed. He carefully didn't look at her in her wet clothes as he slid past her back into the front room. *I must look like a drowned rat.*

He closed the door.

She changed quickly and reemerged to hang her wet clothes by his hearth. Outside, the wind had been joined by an eerie howl, as if a wolf pack hunted within the clouds. "Are there storms like this often?"

"Yes. More and more, over the past few years."

The shutters shook. She wondered if the waves ever reached the house. She decided not to ask about that—it wasn't as if she had other options. It was stay here, or venture back toward town and hope not to be swept out to sea on the way. *Safer to stay here.* "It's the unbalanced magic, isn't it?"

He nodded. "The emperor's sorcerers could defuse the storms, if they chose to. Either they haven't noticed how bad it is because the storms hit too far from where they are, or they simply don't care."

The wind shook the shutters as if it wanted to pry them off and reach inside the house.

He got a funny look on his face, his eyes focused on her head. Kiela automatically patted her hair. It was soaked, of course, but—oh, there was something stuck. It felt like a wet ribbon. She pulled it out and dangled a strip of seaweed in the air.

"That kind is edible," Larran said.

"I carry my own salad," Kiela said.

He laughed, even though she didn't think that was particularly funny. He had a nice laugh, warm and furry. Not sure what to do with the piece of seaweed, she dropped it into his kitchen sink and then moved closer to the woodstove. Last time she was here and soaked through, Caz was with her. This time it was just her and Larran. And the storm. "Caz must be so worried," Kiela said.

"He'll be okay," Larran said. "Your cottage is sturdy, and it's tucked back behind the cove, which offers some protection."

"How bad do these storms get?" she asked.

He hesitated. "It varies."

Very bad, she translated.

"But they can be beautiful. Come see." Beckoning to her, he removed one of the slats covering a smaller window above the larger, shuttered one. "It's safer not to unblock the whole window, but you can stand on the chair."

Kiela stepped up onto the chair. As she leaned forward to peer out the slit of window, she wobbled, and he wrapped an arm around her waist to steady her. She tensed.

"Sorry," he said, withdrawing. "I . . ."

"No, it's okay. Thanks." She stared down at him. On the chair, she was taller than he was. His eyes looking up at her . . . They were warm brown, flecked with green and amber with a hint of blue and even purple. The more she stared, the more colors she saw, until she realized she was staring and blinked, blushing. She forced herself to look out the window at the storm instead.

The storm held as many colors as Larran's eyes, all swirling over the sea, purple chasing blue, black streaking through like the inverse of lightning. Shapes formed and then dissipated—the face of a lion that roared so wide its jaw split apart and then re-formed as a bird diving toward the sea. It vanished in a spray of waves that crashed against the rocks.

"Are *we* safe?" Kiela asked.

She was aware of how close he stood, also looking out at the storm. She felt the heat of his skin, smelled the faint cinnamon scent that she'd come to associate with him, listened to the steadiness of his breath. "Nothing's safe," he said.

She had the sense that he wasn't talking just about the weather, but she didn't know what he meant. Eadie had mentioned tragedies, plural. Kiela knew he'd lost his mentor in a storm, and she had guessed his parents were gone. She studied him again and wondered what to ask that would make him say what he was thinking. "Will your merhorses be all right out there?"

He looked startled—and pleased—that she'd asked about them. "They're more suited to this than anyone. See?" He tapped the window, and she bent to follow his finger and see where he was looking. "They dive down to protect themselves from the excess magic."

Out in the wild waves, the merhorses leapt as if they were dancing with the lightning. They arched their bodies out of the water into the rain, leaping over one another, and then diving deep within the waves the second before purple lightning skittered over the sea. Kiela realized that her cheek was next to Larran's. If she turned her head just a little . . . if he did . . . Their lips were so close.

She wondered why she was having these thoughts. Because he'd been nice to her? Was that a good enough reason? Or was it the only reason that was good enough? He cared. He'd cared from the very first morning when he'd delivered cinnamon rolls to her doorstep.

If she turned her head . . . If she kissed him . . .

Would he kiss her back?

Or would he pull away?

Would she surprise him, or was he thinking it too? Was he as aware as she was of how close they were, of how sweet he smelled, of how warm he was?

Would he want her to kiss him? Or, worse than pulling away, would he merely tolerate her lips on his because he was kind, and he wouldn't want to hurt her feelings? He'd be kind, she was sure, no matter what, and she wouldn't know if he—

Larran pressed closer to the window. "Is that a boat?"

Beside him, Kiela peered out. "Where? I don't see—" She spotted it, a white craft being tossed like a ball from wave to wave. "Who would be out there in this?"

"Someone foolish," he said.

"Or desperate." She thought of how she and Caz had fled Alyssium. "Is it a fishing boat? Someone from Caltrey?" As she said it, she knew it wasn't. The fisherfolk were all aware of the weather. Bryn had been shocked she hadn't noticed the clouds—everyone else had known to haul in the boats, board up the windows, and seek shelter.

"Looks smaller. Sleeker. It's not one of ours."

Its sails were flapping uselessly against its mast. A wave reached up like an arm and wrapped itself around the hull, and the boat disappeared from view. Kiela gasped. Like that, it was gone. No, wait—it had surfaced again, but it was listing to the side.

Larran pushed away from the window and strode toward the door.

"Where are you going?" Kiela said, nearly a shout.

"They aren't going to make it to shore. Whoever's on that ship is going to drown."

She jumped off the chair. "That doesn't mean you should join them!"

"I can help." He grabbed a coat and pulled it on.

"But—" The storm would swallow him! He couldn't go! "How will you even reach them? The waves! The wind!" And the lightning and the rocks and— "You don't even know if there's anyone alive on that boat."

"I can do this," Larran said. "I've ridden a merhorse in a storm before."

This was a terrible idea. She didn't know what to say to make him see that. *I can't stop him.* "Let me help. How can I help?"

"You've ridden a merhorse once and that was on a perfect day. Stay here."

"And just wait? But what if—"

He pulled the door open, and the storm rushed in as if it had been waiting for an invitation. Everything in the house blew. Seashells clattered onto the floor. Lanterns rattled as they shook, and the nearest candle was snuffed out. "Watch for me. Listen for me. I'll knock—don't open the door until you hear me knock."

And then he was gone.

She shut the door and rushed back to the chair by the window. Pressing her face against the glass, she strained to see—there he was, leaning into the wind at a deep tilt as he walked toward the stone jetty. "No, no, this is a terrible, terrible idea," she murmured.

His arm was flung up to shield his face against the wind. Leaning forward until his entire body was tilted, he fought against the storm, taking step after step. Kiela squeezed her hands into fists. She could imagine how it felt—the rain and the wind pushing against him. *Don't fall,* she thought. *Please don't fall.* And:

Come back to me.

Three-quarters of the way out onto the rocks, he halted. *What's wrong?* She wanted to rush out to him, but she knew that would be a mistake. If she went out there, he'd worry about her, not about himself, and it would make the situation twice as dangerous.

Kiela saw the sea shoot up before him, and she clutched the edge of the window, willing herself not to scream. But the wave didn't fold over him and sweep him away. Instead, out of the foam burst a merhorse. She saw the mare silhouetted against the stormy sky, her head flung back, her mane flowing like a waterfall.

Larran leaped off the rocks.

The horse-fish twisted in the air, and he grabbed her mane, swinging himself onto her back. She thundered away from the jetty, toward the floundering ship, deeper into the maelstrom. The cloud serpent had been joined by two more, and they fought, snapping their jaws with every crack of thunder, twisting and writhing as they tore one another apart.

Rain smashed into the window, and Kiela flinched back.

When she pressed forward again, she couldn't see him. "Larran!"

Her voice was instantly swallowed by a crack of thunder so loud that it shook the walls. She felt wetness on her cheeks. Not rain. Tears. She hadn't noticed when she started crying, but at some point she had. She ignored the tears and searched the sea. Where was—

There.

Carrying Larran, the merhorse leapt out of the waves. They were halfway to the ship. Above, the sky twisted as if it were being strangled. It bled rain.

He reached the ship.

It was listing on its side, water pouring over it. Another wave, and she lost sight of him again. She held her breath, exhaled in a sob, and then held her breath again.

A minute passed.

Another.

She didn't see him.

He's drowned. I lost him. And I never— She didn't know how to end that thought. She didn't know what she could have had, what they could have had, but whatever could have been had been swallowed by the angry sea and sky.

And then she saw movement, away from the ship: the golden merhorse was swimming through the wild waves with two figures on its back, one riding tall and the other limp. She watched, unable to move, unable to help, unable to do anything but shake and not breathe then breathe again, as they reached the jetty. She watched as Larran climbed off the merhorse and lifted the storm's victim into his arms. Step by step, he walked over the rocks. His foot slipped once—he caught himself—he continued on, cradling the stranger against him.

He reached the shore.

And he kept going, fighting the wind and the rain.

Kiela rushed to the door and flung it open before he could knock. He stumbled inside. She helped him carry the woman—the survivor was a woman, slight and pale and very cold, with flame-red hair—to his bed. She was breathing, so quietly that Kiela could barely hear her and then only because her breath had a whistle-like hiss.

While Larran secured the door, Kiela pulled the unconscious woman's wet tunic off and dressed her as quickly as she could in warm layers. Coming back into the bedroom, Larran piled quilts onto her and tucked them around her.

He then shed his own shirt and pants and dressed in dry clothes. He was shaking hard, and she saw a scrape on his calf. Blood, watery from the rain and sea, had flowed down to his ankle. Kiela worked quickly, washing out the wound and then wrapping it with bandages she found in a kitchen drawer.

Neither of them spoke.

He didn't seem to have the strength left for speaking. She didn't know what to say. She felt as though a thousand words were jumbled just behind her lips, battling to come out. At last, she said, "I'm glad you didn't die."

"Me too," he said.

They both fell silent again. Outside, the unnatural storm wept and raged.

CHAPTER EIGHTEEN

"You saved her life," Kiela said.

She'd never seen anything that heroic. Or idiotic.

He hovered over the rescued woman, adding yet another quilt and then removing it and instead tucking the quilts she already had around her tighter. "She isn't awake yet."

"You could have died."

"She would have died," he pointed out. "Still could. Why isn't she awake?"

Leaning over her, Kiela felt the woman's forehead. Her skin had warmed from chilled-as-a-fish cold to tucked-into-bed toasty. She had pink in her previously pale cheeks and was breathing easily. Really, it was nothing short of miraculous that she was breathing at all. "I don't think she has a fever."

"She could develop one," Larran said. "She could have internal injuries."

Kiela kept picturing the moment when he'd disappeared from view, the waves too high for her to see beyond. She'd felt as if she'd drowned in that instant. She'd never felt so helpless. She knew she was going to be reliving that in her nightmares again and again. *No one ever drowns in a library.* And then she thought: *No, they just burn.* "Is there a healer on the island?"

Not taking his eyes off the rescued woman, Larran nodded. "Ivor.

As soon as the storm ends, I'll take her to him. Or have him come here. She shouldn't be moved if she has internal injuries. There's no way to know if she does, until she wakes. If she wakes." He began to pace back and forth, between the bed and the window, alternating between checking on the woman and checking on the storm.

Kiela watched him fret. "Do you know her?"

He shook his head. "She's not from Caltrey."

"You know everyone on Caltrey?" She hadn't known everyone in the library, though she supposed not all of them left their stacks, so she'd had no opportunity. She'd at least been able to recognize by sight the ones on her floor and . . . Okay, fine, she didn't know even a quarter of the librarians. It hadn't seemed necessary.

"It's a small island. Plus, her fire hair is recognizable."

"Not in Alyssium. It's fashionable." Nobles liked to have sorcerers spell their hair different colors. She'd seen hair that boasted all the colors of the rainbow, hair that gleamed silver as metal, and hair that sparkled as if fireflies were caught between curls. Kiela knew one library patron who not only changed her hair color weekly but would have it crafted into the silhouettes of animals, as if her hair were an elaborate topiary. With just a single color . . . this woman was most likely a lesser noble. Or a shopkeeper with extra spending money who wanted to socialize with the rich. Kiela hadn't paid enough attention to fashion to know if it signified anything more, such as an allegiance to a particular family or cause, but she supposed it was possible. "She could have fled the city."

"Fled?"

Immediately Kiela wished she'd chosen a different word. She hadn't brought herself to explain to anyone why exactly she'd left. She didn't know why it was so difficult to say. After all, she hadn't caused the revolution. All she'd done was escape it. If she simply left out the detail of the rescued books . . . Somehow, though, talking about it was just as hard as talking about when her parents died. It made the loss more real. But he had to be told, especially if she was going to keep him from paying a visit to the capital to plead for sorcerous aid. *I should tell him now.* "It's not safe there. A lot of unrest. The day Caz and I left—"

Outside, the storm died. It happened in an instant, even faster than the storm had brewed, as if someone had snuffed it out like a candle flame. Larran threw open the shutters on the window, and Kiela joined him to stare out across the ocean.

The sky looked as if it had been ripped apart. Jagged slashes of yellow and orange stretched across the blue-black-purple, like wounds. As she watched, the colors faded—the garish orange faded to lemon, the yellow paled to white, and the sky around it shifted to a calm blue. Below, the ocean stilled.

The silence, after the crash of the waves and the howl of the wind, was almost as stunning in its completeness as the furor had been at its height. It was the sudden absence of a scream—almost as loud, in a way, as the scream itself.

"How . . ." she began.

"They've been like that. Like a toddler throwing a tantrum and then collapsing in exhaustion. I think the magic runs itself out." He headed for the door. "I need to fetch Ivor. Could you watch . . ." He halted, his hand on the handle. "No, you can't stay. Caz. But I can't leave her alone."

The name shot through her like a lightning bolt. "Caz!" She had to check on him. He could be hurt. He could be terrified. But the rescued woman— "You stay with her. I'll fetch Ivor on my way to Caz. If he's on the way. Where's Ivor?" She should have asked that first before she'd offered. Now that she began to think about Caz, her mind conjured up a thousand images of him, blown away by the wind, unable to keep his root ball together, his soil washed out . . . *He would've stayed inside. Safe.* Unless he'd worried about her and ventured out to find her. Unless he hadn't noticed the storm stirring until it was too late, and he was out in the garden. Unless he'd tried to help the cactus after the storm hit. Or the chicken. And they'd all been blown away by the too-strong wind. *I have to get back.*

"He's up the cliff stairs, by the waterfall," Larran said. "I'd go with you, but I don't want to leave her alone. If she wakes, she could be frightened. Confused. And if she doesn't wake . . ." He looked back toward the bedroom. "She shouldn't be alone."

"Where by the waterfall?" Kiela hadn't seen a house on the bluff.

"Call his name when you're close to the water." He shepherded her to the door. "Oh, wait." He retrieved her mostly dried clothes. She pulled on her pants, wobbling awkwardly, and then reached for the buttons of his shirt before pausing and blushing. "Keep it. Just hurry. Carefully. Don't risk yourself. But hurry as quickly and safely as you can."

"I will," she promised.

He'd already turned back to the rescued woman.

Carrying her shirt and wearing his, she ran out of the house. Outside, the beach was strewn with driftwood and seaweed. Half a dead tree lay across the pebbles, and a chunk of a roof with a weathervane still attached had crashed down beside it. Kiela climbed around both. The wind had died back completely, and the waves were lapping gently, as if in apology. Above, the sun had begun to shine, causing the wet cliffs to glisten. It was strangely beautiful in its sparkling chaos. She looked up at the stairs.

A few steps had been ripped from the cliff wall. Kiela swallowed hard and wished there were another way up. Glancing back at Larran's house, she wondered if he knew how to—

He'd already closed the door.

He has someone new to take care of now.

She immediately squelched the thought. Of course he was worried about the rescued woman—that was the kind of person he was. He was a caretaker. It was why he spent his days caring for a herd of merhorses. It was why he'd rushed to her cottage when he saw smoke and fixed her chimney. It was the way he was.

Kiela just had thought, for a moment, that it was something more with her.

Foolish, she told herself as she began to climb the stairs.

She tested each step before she put her full weight on it, and she clung to the wet rocks of the cliff. The breeze tickled her cheek, as if teasing her. Her heart beat hard and fast. She climbed as quickly as she dared and tried not to think about how far it was to fall.

Reaching one of the broken steps, Kiela lunged over it—

The next step creaked but didn't snap, and she exhaled in relief. She continued higher as the sun continued to brighten above.

By the time she reached the top, the sky was picture-perfect blue with no trace of any storm. The meadow beyond the cliff, though, was strewn with debris: leaves, branches, a fishnet. Petals from the beach roses were scattered everywhere. She looked out over the village and saw cats flying over rooftops, their colorful wings bright in the sunlight. Where had they— Ah, the attics! Several of the villagers had opened windows in their attics for the cats to shelter in. *Outer islanders care for our own.* She loved that the Caltreyans had expanded that belief to include all the village cats, both wild and tamed.

Veering around a fallen branch, Kiela jogged toward the waterfall. "Ivor? Hello, Ivor?"

Swollen with excess water, the waterfall tumbled down the cliff. It filled the air with spray, each drop sparkling in the sunlight. Shielding her eyes from the droplets, she looked for any sign of a home. She saw nothing. Larran had been clear about the directions—by the waterfall at the top of the cliff. It wasn't as if she could have misunderstood.

"Ivor!"

"I am here." A man stepped from behind the waterfall, through the spray. *He's a twelve-prong,* she remembered Bryn saying, but Kiela hadn't pictured what that would look like. He was a short, thin man with brown skin, in a brown leather cloak that draped to his ankles, and he wore his antlers like a massive crown.

For an instant, she couldn't think of what to say. It felt akin to the moment she saw the unicorn, as if he was a being of magic, created by the waterfall.

"You are the one who healed Eadie's cherry tree." He executed a bow, his antlers bobbing forward. She glanced at his feet, half expecting hooves, but his feet were human, bare, and as green as the grass he walked through.

"I gave her a remedy," Kiela said. "You're the island's healer?"

He nodded, which caused his antlers to dip again, a significant movement.

Quickly, she explained about Larran and the rescued woman. As she described the rescue, the fear rushed back in a wave. "She hasn't woken yet, and Larran is worried about internal injuries."

"He would be. He has seen it before. I will hurry to him. But you . . . When the aftermath of the storm is resolved, I would like a conversation about your remedies."

She flinched and then wished she hadn't. "Of course. I live—"

He cut her off. "I know where to find you." With his cloak flapping behind him, he trotted past her toward the stairs.

Kiela watched him go and felt shivers walk up and down her spine. Exactly what she didn't want—questions about her remedies from someone who could have the training to recognize them for what they were.

As he reached the rosebushes, she remembered the damaged stairs. She called out, "Watch the steps! A few are missing!"

"Not a concern," Ivor said without turning around. And then his cloak extended, and she saw it wasn't a cloak at all. He had wings— brown and leathery wings, like a dragon. As she stared, he glided off the cliff.

After staring for a moment, she pushed her worries about her remedies and his suspicions from her mind and ran into the forest, toward home and Caz.

CHAPTER NINETEEN

The storm had battered the trees, but as densely packed as they were, they'd held one another upright. Only a few had fallen that she could see. Leaves had been ripped from the canopy, and it looked as if the whole forest had been shaken. But she could still find the path, and in a few moments it opened onto her cottage.

Petals, leaves, and branches were everywhere—spread across the yard, tossed on the roof, leaning against the cottage. A pine tree had fallen but missed anything vital. It lay beside the cottage on the cove side.

"Caz!" she called. She skirted between the debris to the door.

The door hung open.

Why isn't it shut? Where's—

"Kiela!" Caz tumbled out of the front door, running as fast as he could on his tendrils, until he was close enough to launch himself upward and into her arms. He wrapped his leaves around her neck. "I thought you'd died."

Ignoring the dampness of his soil ball, she hugged him back, her arms around his leafiness. "I'm okay. I'm glad you're okay."

"You could have been struck by lightning, swept out to sea, crushed by a tree—I'd half written your eulogy. I said very nice things."

Kiela laughed. "Thank you, I think?"

"It was in iambic pentameter."

"That's amazing."

"I had to create different versions, to match the different ways you died."

Gently, she said, "I didn't die. I was in town when the storm blew in, and I couldn't make it back here. I took shelter at Larran's. Until he dove into the ocean to rescue a woman from a ship that capsized."

Caz pulled back from her, disentangling his leaves from her hair. "He has a real savior thing going on, doesn't he? That can't be healthy." He climbed down from her, and she dusted the soil bits off the front of Larran's shirt. She'd have to wash it before she returned it. "Sorry about the dirt, though it's entirely your fault for dying six different ways."

Kiela started to laugh again, half in relief—

"Now that you're not dead anymore, I have to tell you we have a problem," Caz said.

Her heart sank. Had the storm caused damage to the cottage? Had the roof leaked? Were the books okay? What about the garden?

Before she could ask, she heard a wail from the cottage—shrill, loud, inhuman. The hair on her neck stood up. What was *that*? "Caz? What kind of problem?"

"You won't believe it until I show you." Using his tendrils, he propelled himself back toward the cottage, and she hurried after him. She noted that the grass was flattened and smeared in a path leading to the door, as if something had been dragged through the mud.

In the cottage doorway, the cactus shivered. Its quills clicked as they rattled against one another. "Meep?" it said. Beyond it, she saw that several of the jam jars had fallen from their shelves. They'd shattered on the floor during the storm. The smear of muddy water continued through the shop.

"Glad you're okay," she told the cactus, and then she rounded the corner of the jam shelves, following the mud. To her surprise, she saw the copper bathtub from the privy was in the center of the room in front of the stove.

In it was a mermaid.

Kiela felt her jaw drop open. "Why? How?"

Her body was submerged, her silver tail flopped over the edge, and her head was in her arms with her seaweed hair draped over her. When Kiela spoke, the mermaid lifted her silvery-scaled face and wailed, a piercing sound like the cry of a seagull. Inside the tiny cottage, the wail was magnified until it rattled inside Kiela's skull.

Rushing to her side, Kiela asked, "Are you all right?" Of course she wasn't all right. She wouldn't be wailing if she was. But why was she here? Was she injured? Kiela felt a hundred questions battering inside her.

Behind her, Caz said, "She hauled herself up the stairs from the cove. I found her at the top, with her baby."

Baby? "Why—"

The mermaid pointed with a trembling webbed finger.

Lying on the hearth on top of a stack of quilts was the merbaby, the same merbaby whom Kiela had seen swimming in the cove. His pale green body was covered in jagged purple slashes that reminded her of the sky split by the storm, and tiny sparks arched over his closed eyes like stray bits of lightning.

Shedding leaves as he shook, Caz said, "He can't be in the water, not with the sparks he's giving off, but he's drying out in the air. I don't know what to do. I don't know what's wrong with him. Meep and I—we took out the tub and filled it for the mother, but—"

"He's storm sick," Kiela said. She'd read about this—if a creature born of magic absorbed too much excess magic at once, it could overwhelm them. The merbaby's tiny body hadn't been strong enough to process all the power within the magic-driven storm. Left unchecked, it would stop his heart. "There's a healer. Ivor. I'll bring him here." He should be with the rescued woman in Larran's house—

As Kiela turned to go, the mermaid's hand shot out and closed over Kiela's wrist. Her fingers were wet and hard, like they were made of shell, not flesh. "No healer."

She can speak! Kiela hadn't thought a mermaid's throat was shaped to be able to utter land-dweller words. This was remarkable. Did scholars know— *Stop, focus on the baby.* "He needs help, and I don't know how—"

"You."

Kiela shook her head. "But I don't know—"

Sloshing water out of the copper tub onto the floor, the mermaid lurched closer until her face was inches from Kiela's. Her breath smelled like the ocean, heavy with fish. Her teeth were pointed like a shark's. "You."

Tears pricked her eyes. She *wanted* to help, but how? What did the mermaid expect her to do? "Tell me what to do. I don't know how to help."

"Spell."

Kiela shook her head. "I don't—"

"Of course!" Caz said. "She needs magic! It's magic-caused, so she needs a spell to heal him. If there was a sorcerer—"

But there wasn't. There was only Kiela and her stolen spellbooks.

"You. Heal. Trees." The mermaid flinched, as if each word hurt her. "Heal. Him."

That's why she came here, to us. She thinks we can help.

But the tree spell was a single remedy, only discovered after a lot of research and experimentation. She thumbed through her memory for books that could help—did she have any on storm sickness? She knew she'd read about it, but where? Had she brought those volumes with her?

Yes.

Yes, she remembered a book. Green cover. Deckled edges. Two authors, a sorcerer and a healer, had cowritten it. She'd stored it in the third crate. "Caz, speed-research."

"Whoo!" Caz cheered.

The mermaid hissed, baring her sharklike teeth.

"Taking it seriously! I swear!"

Kiela barged into the back room and threw the quilt off the third crate. She began pulling out books and piling them on the bed. "Green cover. Two authors." He joined her and helped pull books out of the crate. "It was mostly a collection of spells for sick livestock—it was published as a veterinary companion—but there was a section on magic-infused creatures." She hoped the mermaid wouldn't be offended. Merfolk were people—classifying them as "creatures" was rude, though common in earlier texts—but knowledge was knowledge, and that was the closest bit that Kiela had.

She and Caz dug deep into the crate. The cactus darted around the room. Kiela had the sense that it wanted to help, which was a surprise, but she didn't have time to think or worry about what it meant for the cactus to be so alert and aware. She filed the oddity in her head to mull over later, when there wasn't a life at stake.

"Aha!" Caz held up a slim green book with his tendrils.

Kiela plucked it out of his leaves, dropped cross-legged onto the floor, and began to read as fast as she could. Storm sick, storm sick, storm sick . . . Yes, there was the chapter! She skimmed it quickly. There had to be a cure . . . Why write about it in a book like this if there wasn't? "We need these ingredients." She held the book up for Caz to see. The cactus scooted beside him and appeared to be peering at the book. Kiela wondered if the cactus could read. She still wasn't clear how Caz knew how to read. He'd been created with the knowledge. She guessed it was a side effect of being created by a rogue librarian. Looking at the cactus, Kiela wondered if that was the case here as well. *I suppose I'm the rogue librarian now.*

Most of the items on the list were natural and easily obtained: sap from a tree struck by lightning (she'd seen one on her journey back to the cottage), spit from a grown human (she could supply that), a feather (she hoped the chicken was still in the backyard), a handful of soil (plenty of that in the garden or even attached to Caz, though she wouldn't take that, of course) . . . but it also called for the leaves of a verisad plant. "What's a verisad plant?"

"Rare, shiny leaves, very tiny plant that grows in the shade of other plants." Caz's leaves rustled. "I haven't seen any in the garden. I don't know if it grows on Caltrey."

The cactus darted out of the bedroom with a "Meep!"

"Then we'll research substitutions." She wasn't going to let the mermaid down, not when she had all the knowledge of centuries around her. "You want to start on that? I know where to find a pine tree struck by lightning."

"On it," Caz said.

Rushing out of the bedroom, Kiela told the mermaid, "We have a plan. Just . . ." She didn't know what to tell the mermaid to do—make sure her child didn't die? "We'll be back. We need supplies."

The mermaid flopped her tail and hissed, "Go."

Kiela raced out of the cottage, skirting the broken jam jars. Where exactly had she seen the lightning-burned tree? It had been on the path to the cliff . . . She plunged into the forest without a backward glance. Around her, the birds called, and she realized this was the first time she'd heard them since the storm. She hoped they'd weathered it okay. Scanning the trees, she looked for the apple-blossom bird but saw only sparrows. She wondered if the cloud bears were okay. Was there one attached to the damaged tree? Would her pine cone spell help heal it? First, though, she needed the sap—

She found the lightning-struck tree, a third of the way down the trail. Skidding to a stop, she murmured an apology to whatever tree guardians were out there watching her. She grasped a bit of the bark and ripped it off, taking care to get some bark with char and some without. She didn't know which exactly the spell called for, but it was safest to have both.

Kiela pivoted and darted back toward the cottage. She beelined through the house, past the mermaid in the copper tub and the merbaby on the hearth, out the back door, and into the garden. Several of the plants had been flattened in the rain. Mud stuck to her shoes. The chicken was still in her muddy pen. She had survived fine. Kiela plucked a feather from the hen's back.

She squawked and ruffled her feathers.

"Sorry."

Kiela scooped up a bit of soil that was at least partially dry from being close to the house. Running inside, she dumped the dirt, the feather, and the bark into a bowl on the counter. Behind her, the mermaid splashed in agitation as the merbaby let out a weak moan. Kiela spat in the bowl and mixed. The only ingredient missing was the leaves.

"Any luck with a substitution for the verisad leaves?" Kiela called to Caz.

Emerging from the bedroom, Caz waved his tendrils in the air. "No! No luck at all! I can tell you the substitute for basil, for goat cheese, for goat hooves, for goat spit—why do so many spells involve a goat? You can use a chicken egg to substitute for a goose or swan egg so long as you are okay with the result only taking effect close to home. Apparently chickens don't like to wander and that's why? Except for our chicken, though she seems happy enough now. But no mention in any books of any viable substitute for verisad leaves, because no other spell requires it, and I can't—"

"Meep."

Kiela turned around.

In the garden doorway was the cactus, with a collection of small, shiny leaves stuck to its needles. "Caz?" Kiela asked. "Are those—"

"Oh, you beautiful genius," Caz said to the cactus. "Verisad leaves."

Kiela plucked the precious leaves off the cactus's spines and mixed them with the rest of the concoction into a paste. "You're a hero," she said to the cactus. "Thank you."

"Meep."

Carrying the paste to the hearth, Kiela knelt beside the merbaby. He'd curled into ball. His tail was wrapped tight around himself, and he was trembling. His mother had to stay in the tub to keep her skin moist, but she couldn't bring him into the water with her—the magic lightning from the storm still skittered over his body. If he submerged, it would worsen the effects. But if he didn't . . .

"It's going to be okay." She didn't know if that was true, but she had to say it. Aside from the storm sickness killing him, he'd been out of the water for far too long. His skin looked flaky and pale, and his breath wheezed as if every inhale and exhale hurt. "Caz, would you hold the spellbook open?"

The merbaby whimpered in pain, and his mother wailed again.

His outer leaves trembling, Caz held the book steady beside Kiela.

Carefully, she spooned the concoction onto the merbaby's back, along his spine as the book instructed, and then she read the spell out loud. She pronounced each word as clearly as a bell, focusing all her attention on the child.

It felt as if every breath of wind in the forest, every call of a bird in the trees, every heartbeat inside the tiny cottage was silent.

As she spoke the last syllable, the concoction sank into the merbaby's skin, leaving only a patch of brownish-green that faded as she watched. She held her breath. Slowly, very slowly, the bits of lightning vanished, and the merbaby uncoiled.

He opened his eyes and held out his arms.

The mermaid let out a cry and launched herself out of the tub. Water splashed onto the floor, the hearth, Kiela, and Caz, as she gathered her child into her arms—Caz protected the spellbook with his leaves. Flopping, she pulled herself back into the tub with the merbaby, who instantly submerged.

"Meep?" the cactus asked.

Popping back up, the merbaby laughed, a sound like waves crashing into the sand, and Kiela smiled. "He's all right," she said. "We did it."

CHAPTER TWENTY

After helping the mermaid and the merbaby down the steps to the cove, Kiela returned to the cottage to clean up from both the storm and their unexpected visitor. While the cactus mopped the floor, using its needles to hold the towel, Kiela emptied the copper tub and hauled it back behind the privy door. She rinsed the quilts and set them out to dry on a line in the garden—they had slight singe marks from the baby's sparks but no holes. She then helped Caz return the spellbooks to the crates and covered them with the quilts that the merbaby hadn't used. Once the bedroom was restored to order, she examined the broken jars in the shop. To her relief, many were still intact. It had looked worse than it was, which was excellent news, considering that the spilled bloodred raspberry jam made it look a bit like a murder scene.

As soon as the glass was picked up and the floor mopped, she collapsed into bed and didn't wake until the sun poked its way into the cottage and prodded at her closed eyelids.

The instant she was awake, she thought of the merbaby, followed by the rescued woman, and she made herself get out of bed, wash, and dress, selecting a seafoam-green skirt, a clean blouse, and her favorite boots. She wondered if there were any other storm victims and if they'd been helped. *How odd,* she thought. Usually when she woke, her first thought was to worry about her books. *This place is changing me.* She wasn't sure how she felt about that.

Both the spider plant and the cactus were already outside in the garden, cleaning up debris. Caz was using his tendrils to pick up stray twigs, while the cactus speared stray leaves with its spikes. "I'm going to check on the mermaid, then Larran, okay?" Kiela called to them. "Do either of you want to come?"

"Lots to do here, thanks."

"Meep," the cactus agreed.

Kiela waved to both of them. "Okay, have fun." She wondered if the cactus was going to learn to say more words. She had no particular feel for the developmental timescale of sentient succulents. *Ooh, that would made an excellent research paper.* If, of course, revealing the origin of the cactus wasn't a disastrous idea.

On her way out, she picked up one of the undamaged jars of jam. If the rescued woman was recovered enough, maybe she'd like some? Or perhaps the merbaby would? Did merfolk like jam? Had anyone ever written a research paper about the culinary likes and dislikes of merfolk? Certainly she'd never heard of any scholar, sorcerer, or librarian finding one in their bathtub. *That was new.* She checked the cove, but neither the mermaid nor the merbaby was there, which she took to be a good sign—they were off in the sea, which had returned to its normal state of placid indifference.

The birds were singing cheerfully as Kiela headed through the forest. She peered between the trees, looking for any sign of the forest spirits, but she didn't see any.

She wondered if the rescued woman had woken.

She wondered if Larran had recovered from his plunge into the stormy ocean.

She wondered if Ivor was still at Larran's house. She wasn't sure what she'd say if he decided to ask questions about her remedies. It would be best if she could avoid him.

Maybe she should have waited longer before she left the cottage. She could have stayed and helped Caz and the cactus clean the

garden and around the cottage. She could've made another batch
of jam to replace what broke. Or she could have studied more spellbooks.

Coming out of the forest, Kiela halted. Ahead of her, across the
open field, the waterfall tumbled over the cliff. Half of her wanted
to flee back the way she'd come. *Stop it,* she told herself. The healer
had no proof that she'd cast any spells, and besides, the best way to
avoid suspicion was to not act suspicious. It was natural for her to
check up on Larran and the rescued woman.

Resolutely not looking at the waterfall, Kiela descended the
stairs. She reminded herself to watch for broken steps—there had
been one a third of the way down.

At exactly a third of the way down, she realized that someone
had replaced all the missing steps with fresh slats of wood. Also,
the railing had been mended in spots.

It had to be because of Larran. She was certain of it. It felt like
something he'd do. But when? He'd been caring for the rescued
woman, yet he'd taken the time to come out here and fix the stairs—
For me? There was no one else who lived up beyond the cliff, except
Ivor, who'd proven he had no need of stairs. She felt herself smile.

He did this for me.

It was exactly the sort of thing he'd do, an unasked-for kindness.

She'd never met anyone so full of kindness. He'd fixed the stairs, in
the midst of his own exhaustion, simply because he knew she'd return
down them. No one had asked him to. No one else had even thought
of it. He overflowed with kindness, perhaps to a perilous degree.

Kiela kept smiling as she reached the shore and crossed the
seaweed-strewn beach toward his house. The shutters had been
thrown open to let the sunlight in, and the seaweed had been swept
from the porch. She knocked on the door.

As she waited, she thought, *I should have kissed him.* She replayed
the moment in her head where they'd been so close, and she felt
herself begin to blush.

He didn't answer the door.

She knocked again. Again, no answer.

She peeked in the window and didn't see any movement. Maybe he wasn't home? Where else would he be? What if he was sick? What if he'd collapsed? He could've had his own internal injuries from the storm. He could have weakened himself fixing the stairs.

"Larran?" she called as she opened the door.

Silence.

Stepping inside, she called his name again. She peeked into the bedroom. He wasn't there, and neither was the rescued woman. But the bed was made, the dishes were washed, and there was no sign of any disaster. Kiela set the jar of jam on the kitchen table.

Perhaps Ivor had taken his patient back to his house and Larran had accompanied them? If so, perhaps that was why he'd fixed the stairs. Not for Kiela, but for her. *It still shows his kindness, no matter who it's for.*

Oh good grief, I'm not jealous *of a nearly drowned woman, am I?* That would be absurd.

For one thing, Larran was just a neighbor who was very devoted to being neighborly. Despite the almost-kiss . . . which could have been entirely in her head anyway . . . they had no sort of relationship that would justify feeling jealous of anyone. For another, the woman was unconscious. It would make more sense for Kiela to be jealous of Sian.

She closed the door behind her as she left his house and considered what to do next. Visit Ivor behind his waterfall? Much too risky. Return home? That seemed silly, considering she'd already climbed down the cliff stairs.

She'd visit Bryn, she decided. Make sure her friend and the bakery had made it through the storm okay. And then she'd return home to help Caz and the cactus in the garden.

Decided, Kiela marched across the beach, or she tried to. It was still covered in so much driftwood that she had to climb over half of it and weave between the rest. Reaching the town, she saw the streets were not much better. Everything had been tossed around by the storm: carts, barrels, laundry, papers . . . but the worst was the fish. Dead fish had been flung into the streets and onto the roofs. On the streets, folk ran with baskets, gathering up the carcasses for either bait or stew. On the roofs, the winged cats were feasting. Everyone else was cleaning—more people than Kiela had seen on any of her visits to town—and she began to wish she'd chosen to simply slink back home.

Most ignored her, busy with their own tasks. A few waved. Others watched her with curious eyes as she dodged the chaos in the streets. She walked quicker and quicker, hoping her pace would be mistaken for purpose, not panic, until at last she saw the dry fountain and then beyond it, Bryn's bakery.

Bryn weaved between the tables, dispensing pastries and beverages to very tired, very hungry people who'd come for a break from the hard work of storm cleanup. So far as Kiela could see, the bakery looked intact, mostly. The sign had been knocked off and now leaned against the wall. A few shingles had been ripped off, but the shutters had preserved the windows. Aside from blotches of seaweed spattered on the walls, it looked undamaged. She breathed a sigh of relief. Maybe the only casualty was the rescued woman's boat.

"Kiela!" Bryn called. "How'd you like your first island storm?"

"I didn't love it," she admitted. "But the town seems okay."

"Yeah, we build our homes strong on Caltrey." Bryn slapped the wall, and a loose shingle tumbled off the roof. It landed with a smack, cracking in half.

Both of them stared at the shingle.

"Strong-ish," Bryn clarified.

"Can I help you with anything?" she offered.

Bryn shook her head. "Oh no, you have your own—"

From inside, a boy shrieked, "Bryn! It's smoking! What do I do?" The boy—her nephew, Tobin—stuck his head outside. "Never mind. I dumped water on it. All good now."

Closing her eyes, Bryn visibly counted to ten before she opened them again. "Actually, yes, if you wouldn't mind . . . If you could pour tea for everyone, I can make sure that Tobin stops flooding my oven. I'll pay you for your time."

"No need to pay me," she said, and then thought of Caz. He wouldn't have approved of her not valuing her time, but there was a storm, and Bryn was a friend. "Or you can pay me in cinnamon buns." She'd lost track of what had happened to the soggy rolls she'd carried to Larran's. *I must have left them there.*

"Deal," Bryn said, before sprinting inside.

Kiela followed her inside the bakery to the counter. She set a row of cups onto saucers on the counter, added tea leaves to a strainer for each, and then filled them with hot water from the carafe. As she poured, she heard a familiar laugh through the open window.

Larran.

She hadn't realized that she knew what his laugh sounded like, especially to recognize it instantly, but she didn't even have to look to know it was him. She *did* look, though, and she saw him position a chair for the fire-red-haired woman to sit. Kiela couldn't see the woman's face from this angle, but she did see his as he smiled at the woman.

A few seconds later, her view was obscured as other townspeople clustered around the new arrival, clamoring for her story, and Kiela listened as the tea steeped.

Her name was Radane, and she was from Alyssium.

She'd fled for her own safety, because of the violence in the city.

What violence? the townspeople asked.

"Have you not heard about the revolution?" Radane said. In her polished accent, she told them everything: the riots, the coup, the murder of the emperor, the burning of the palace and the government building . . . When the revolutionaries lost control of the revolution and the carefully constructed coup exploded into chaos, they even burned the library.

Kiela couldn't listen anymore. All she could hear was screams of people dying in the streets, the clash of weapons within the stacks, and all she could smell was the stench of smoke. As Bryn bustled out of the back room with a tray full of slightly soggy muffins, Kiela said, "I'm so sorry. I can't— I have to go."

Abandoning the half-steeped tea, Kiela bolted out of the bakery and past the customers clustering around Larran and the new arrival. She half heard Larran call her name, or perhaps she imagined it. She didn't linger to see which it was. Driven by the memory of screams and flames, she fled back to the beach, up the stairs, and into the green.

CHAPTER TWENTY-ONE

Kiela decided to bury herself in research. She'd promised Halio, her customer with the whispery voice, that she'd find a remedy for her waterless spring, but between the cloud bears, the storm, and the merbaby . . . Well, she had work to do, and the rescued woman—Radane, she reminded herself—was fine, as was Larran.

She flipped the sign on her shop door to "Open" and asked Caz to watch for customers, while she barricaded herself in the back room. Sitting on the bed, she began with the index they'd created to identify the relevant tomes.

But she kept thinking about Larran.

And Radane.

And Larran again.

And about the way she'd run out of the bakery, after offering to help Bryn, and hadn't given any kind of reason. How was she going to explain that?

Usually, when she sank into research mode, she blocked out the rest of the world. It faded away until all that existed was books. Sequestered within the library, she'd lose track of time and would work through meals, through sleep, with little awareness of whether it was day or night. But this time it was near impossible to focus. Maybe it was because the heavy scent of sea left behind by the mermaid still lingered in the air, which made her think of fleeing to

Larran's house as the rain fell. Or maybe it was because the soft cotton of the quilt reminded her of the feel of Larran's shirt after she'd changed out of her wet clothes. She thought of how close he'd been as they gazed out at the storm, how she'd almost kissed him. And then how everything had changed in an instant.

She was sorting haphazardly through books on water magic when she discovered a slim book with cramped and faded writing inside, simply titled *On Storms*. Setting aside the problem of Halio's waterless spring and the dry town fountain, Kiela picked up a notebook and began studying the work of a master sorcerer who had made it her life's mission to understand the taming of storms.

It was only after reading the book three times that Kiela conceded that it was impossible. One lone librarian-turned-shopkeeper couldn't tame a storm. It required a wind-speaker, a sorcerer who was specially trained in weather magic. Wind spells were so carefully guarded that only wind-speakers knew them. In other words, the spell wasn't written down. The book only alluded to it.

And even if she was a wind-speaker, she couldn't cast it. It was a feat that could only be accomplished by a group of sorcerers, executing the spell in unison. Even if Caz joined her, even if the cactus learned to speak, it wouldn't be enough. Such magic required a chorus.

Regretfully, Kiela set the storm book aside and returned to the smaller, more possible task of causing water to flow again. Two hours later, she'd made significant progress. She was copying the syllables for the spell, as well as a list of ingredients, into her notebook when she heard voices from the shop. Concentrating on her penmanship, she ignored them. Caz could handle this sale without her.

And then the voices came closer to the bedroom door.

Springing off the bed, she covered her books and notes with a quilt before she realized she knew the voices: Caz, of course, and Larran. She froze for only a second before rushing out the door and closing it quickly behind her.

Larran was inches in front of her, his hand already raised to knock on the bedroom door. Her speedy appearance had clearly startled him—his eyes were wide, and he forgot to lower his hand. She looked up at him and said eloquently, "Hi."

"Uh, hi? Sorry to interrupt your nap? Caz said you could help."

She glanced at Caz, and he waved his leaves. She wasn't certain what he was trying to say, but he ducked out into the garden. Perhaps to give them privacy? Or to check on Meep? Looking up at Larran again, she blurted out, "Sure, yes, maybe, probably? With what?" Kiela winced at herself for that mess of words. "Oh! I still have your shirt!" She hadn't washed it yet, but she also hadn't worn it long. Crossing to the kitchen chair where she'd left it draped over the back, she picked it up and sniffed it. It smelled a lot like Larran.

"Caz said you helped a merbaby with storm sickness."

Caz really needs to watch what he says. "Old family remedy." She immediately wished she'd thought of another excuse, since Larran had actually known her family. She didn't think either of her parents had ever dabbled in healing, nor had any contact with merfolk. Until the mermaid spoke, she didn't even know merfolk could speak to land people—according to everything she'd read, they communicated with one another in trills and songs, like whales and dolphins. "Why? Is Radane all right? Are you?"

"It's Sian. She hasn't been herself since the storm. I thought her favorite treat, tomatoes, would help. That's why I came, to see if you had more ripened tomatoes. But then Caz said—"

A whole day had passed since the storm. If Sian had been sick all this time . . . Kiela thought of the merbaby and how close he had come to dying. "Do you think she has storm sickness?"

Larran spread his hands. "I don't know. Maybe? I haven't encountered it before with one of my merhorses. Usually they dive beneath the waves for the duration of the storm, but Sian . . ."

He'd ridden her out to rescue the woman on the boat, and she'd been directly exposed to the storm. Kiela burst into motion. *I need the spell.* She could take just the page to hide the fact that it came from a spellbook, though everything in her quailed at the idea of damaging a book. *I'll copy it onto a fresh sheet.* But what about the ingredients, especially the verisad leaves? She'd used all of them for the mermaid. How was she going to find more—

Caz tumbled back in through the garden. He had a wad of leaves pressed between his tendrils. *What a brilliant plant.* She'd just need the lightning bark and soil. As she scurried back and forth assembling the ingredients, she realized Larran was watching her.

How was she going to explain all of this to him? It looked like a spell. It sounded like a spell. She didn't have time to figure out how to modify it so that it didn't. "Can Sian swim to my cove? It'll be easier to treat her there."

He shook his head. "She's on the rocks. I don't dare try to move her."

Fine. She'd have to hope that Larran was too worried to notice exactly what she was doing. "You go back to her, try to keep her comfortable. Caz and I will gather what we need and meet you there."

He agreed to that and headed for the door.

"Wait," she called. She darted out to the garden, plucked three tomatoes, and then returned and thrust them at him. "Go. Comfort her until I get there."

He took the tomatoes, and his hands brushed hers. "Do you really think you can help her?" His eyes were anxious, and she saw every bit of fear and hope he was holding inside.

She knew she should say she'd try. Any decent scholar would couch her response in qualifications. It was inaccurate to claim any kind of certainty. But looking into his eyes, all she could say was "Yes."

Clutching the concoction and a hastily scrawled copy of the spell, Kiela hurried through the woods, across the field, and down the stairs to the shore. She ran through the list of ingredients in her head, certain she hadn't forgotten anything but calmed by the repetition of the list, and then the words to the spell, silently practicing the music of the syllables.

Caz galumphed beside her, using his tendrils to catapult his soil ball forward. At the stairs, he simply wrapped his leaves around his roots and rolled from step to step. He reached the bottom before she did.

Up ahead, she spotted Larran out on the jetty with Sian—the horse-fish was slumped over the rocks, and for one horrible moment, Kiela thought they were too late. But then Sian lifted her tail for an instant before lowering it again.

"We need a way to distract Larran," Kiela said. "He'll want to hover."

"Tell him you need one more ingredient," Caz suggested. "While he's helping me find it, you can cast the spell."

"Perfect. It's a plan."

"Just make sure it's an ingredient he'd have in the kitchen, not, like, seaweed."

"I wasn't going to say seaweed."

Caz halted at the end of the jetty, and Kiela stepped onto the first rock. From the house behind them, she heard the door open and turned her head to see Radane step out onto the porch. The rescued woman wore a loose green dress that fluttered in the breeze, her hair was tied back with a white bow, and she looked fully recovered from her ordeal.

Caz asked the question that Kiela wanted to ask: "Why's she here?"

She supposed the new arrival didn't have anywhere else to stay, but still . . . It was, at the very least, inconvenient to have her here too. Also, she was certain that Larran only had one bed.

Radane smiled radiantly at them. "Oh, good day! Are you here for the laundry?"

Laundry? Did she think— Never mind. It didn't matter. "No, we—" Kiela didn't want to spend the time explaining, not when

Larran and Sian needed her. "Caz?" She turned and picked her way along the stones toward Larran, while Caz greeted Radane.

"We're neighbors," Caz told her. "We came to help Larran with his merhorse. We have an old island herbal remedy that's good with colic. Learned it from an old villager years ago."

Radane boggled at the spider plant. "You talk! What a fascinating revelation." Kneeling, she began to examine him, lifting up a tendril and peering under his leaves. "I had believed sentient plants only existed on Alyssium."

Caz recoiled. "No touchy, please."

Kiela felt prickles on her neck and hoped that Radane's reaction wasn't going to be a problem. Sentient plants weren't common outside the capital city, but there was nothing illegal about Caz existing. Unlike the cactus, Kiela was legitimately not responsible for his creation.

One problem at a time.

"Did this villager also create you?" Radane asked. "I would be honored to meet him or her."

"Sadly, my creator died in a fire."

If Radane was interested enough in Caz, it might be sufficient distraction for Kiela to get the job done. She raised her eyebrows at him, and Caz shook a tendril at her—*go,* it meant.

Kiela hurried down the jetty toward Larran and Sian. "I've brought the remedy." She emphasized the word "remedy." She wondered if she should repeat Caz's lie about the old villager.

He didn't look up. "She's weakening. Look at her eyes."

Her eyes were cloudy with flashes of light that swallowed her pupils. Her once-golden scales were a lemon yellow, laced with streaks of purple—faint, but after the merbaby, Kiela knew what to look for. Sian was definitely storm sick. *She's dying.* An uneaten tomato lay beside her on the rocks.

"I need pepper," Kiela said. It was the first kitchen item she thought of. "I didn't have any, but the remedy will be more effective with it."

Jumping to his feet, Larran shouted, "Radane, can you get the bottle of pepper? Third shelf to the left of the sink. Please, hurry!" He squatted again and stroked Sian's mane.

Well, that didn't work. And now she'd have to wait for Radane to return, or Larran would suspect she'd lied. Worse, the woman would probably come out onto the jetty, and then Kiela would have two witnesses.

"Also, rosebuds. I was in such a hurry that I forgot to gather them." She pointed to the top of the cliff, where the bushes hugged the edge. "I'll need six."

He turned back to the house to call to Radane again, but she had already gone inside. He took a breath to shout to Caz, and she interrupted him. "He doesn't have thumbs," Kiela said.

"What?"

"No opposable thumbs. It's hard for him to pick roses."

"But I've seen—"

"Also, it's against his ethics to harm other plants." That wasn't true. He'd delivered the verisad leaves to her, after all, as well as multiple other ingredients. But it sounded plausible. "He wouldn't forgive himself if he harmed a rosebush, even to save a life. Could you please—"

"Of course." He bounded down the jetty.

When he was far enough away, Kiela knelt beside Sian. The merhorse was breathing shakily, each inhalation causing her entire body to ripple. Her tail was flapping weakly against the rocks.

Quickly, Kiela smeared the remedy along Sian's spine. She hoped they'd made enough. Sian was quite a bit larger than the merbaby, and it had been longer since the storm before treatment—more time for the sickness to spread and worsen.

This has to work. She'd promised Larran.

Taking a deep breath, she unfolded the spell and softly, insistently, read the syllables.

She waited a moment.

Behind her, from the beach, she heard Larran's footsteps on the stairs as he ran up them to retrieve the rosebuds. Waves crashed against the rocks of the jetty. She kept all her focus on Sian. "Come on, you can do it," she whispered. "You'll be okay."

She read the spell again, louder this time.

The purple streaks between the scales began to pulse.

Please, let this work!

Kiela wrapped an arm around Sian's neck and spoke the words a third time, directly into Sian's ear. Her other hand shook as she held the paper with the spell. *Please, please, please.* She pronounced each word as clearly as she could.

Suddenly, the merhorse convulsed in her arms. Her back arched, and her tail slapped the rocks. Kiela heard Larran cry, "Sian!"

He was close.

How close? What did he see? What did he hear? It didn't matter. Only Sian mattered right now. Kiela stared into the merhorse's eyes. "Come on. Be okay. Please."

Like the clouds draining from the sky after the storm, the milky white cleared from Sian's eyes. They deepened back into their rich blue, and the lightning vanished. The color of her scales spread like a sunrise, the gold overwhelming the purple streaks.

Sian stuck her muzzle in Kiela's hair and snorted.

Kiela laughed and released the horse-fish, who promptly inhaled the uneaten tomato. Pushing off the rocks with her front hooves, Sian launched herself back into the waves. A smile on her face, Kiela turned to face Larran—

And saw Radane staring at her, only a few feet away.

Caz was at her feet, quivering on the rocks, unable to pull Radane's attention back to shore. Larran dove into the water. A second later, he surfaced. Sian played in the waves around him.

Holding the paper behind her back, Kiela crumpled the spell and dropped it into the sea. She stood up, hands empty. "Guess it didn't need the pepper or the rosebuds."

"Miraculous," Radane said.

"Just an old herbal remedy," Kiela said.

Joyful, Larran played with Sian in the waves, while Radane watched and Kiela tried to convince herself that she'd done the right thing, not made an irreversible mistake.

CHAPTER TWENTY-TWO

The morning after she'd saved the merhorse, Kiela resolved to have a quiet, unexciting day. She flipped the shop sign to "Open" and hoped that no customers came, which she knew wasn't exactly the entrepreneurial attitude.

"Let's make more pine cone remedies," Caz said.

They'd stored all the ingredients delivered by the forest spirits, but Kiela and Caz hadn't had time to assemble them. She thought of Eadie and how pleased she'd been with her cherry tree. And then she thought of Radane and how close she'd been standing when Kiela had cast the spell on Sian. "Maybe we should take a break from remedies. Just for a little while."

"But we've barely begun."

"I don't want to draw more suspicion."

"I really don't think that woman heard anything. The waves were loud, and your back was to her. And Larran was too far away. Besides, all he cares about is that Sian recovered. You could have stripped naked, cast the spell with blood, and he wouldn't have cared."

He could be right. Still . . . "You think he wouldn't have cared if I was naked?"

"Okay, that's not— Hey, customers!"

Ugh.

Not ugh, "yay," she corrected herself. The plan was to sell jam, not hide hermitlike with her books, so she should be happy to have customers. *I should have come up with a better plan.*

Maybe she should have established a delivery-only shop and hired Bryn's nephew to deliver the jam so she wouldn't ever have to deal with visitors. Except that she couldn't afford to hire anyone yet. First, she had to sell more jam.

Kiela opened the window with the counter as three figures emerged from the greenery. She recognized them instantly: Bryn, Eadie, and the harpist with multiple arms.

On the plus side, it wasn't Fenerer. Or Radane. Or a stranger. Or the emperor's guards come to arrest her for unauthorized magic use. She tried to be happy that it was Bryn and Eadie, but she couldn't help thinking, *So much for my no-people day.*

Quickly, Kiela scanned the shop and cottage: the bedroom door was closed, the books were under quilts, the cactus was in the back garden with the chicken, and the jam jars were neatly displayed on the shelves. She had peonies and larkspur in a pitcher on the kitchen counter and daisies in little glasses between the jam jars. Dried herbs, tied with ribbons, hung from the rafters in between copper pots. After the storm, she'd washed the gauzy curtains on the windows, and Caz and Meep had mopped the wood floor just this morning.

Caz climbed onto the shelves and plopped himself on an empty spot so he'd be eye level with the new arrivals, while Kiela checked her clothes for any jam stains or dirt. Since she'd planned to spend the day in the garden, she hadn't worn anything particularly nice. This was one of her handle-dusty-manuscripts outfits. It had a tea stain on the neckline, as well as a rip in the left elbow. Her three visitors were all neat and lovely: Bryn in a red plaid pinafore dress that was fancier than her usual bakery garb, Eadie in bright green with a matching hat, and the harpist in white pants with a yellow blouse with four sleeves for her four arms. Oh well, it was too late to change now.

Plastering a smile on her face, Kiela swung the door open wide.

"Thanks for coming to Kiela and Caz's Jam Shop. Lovely to see you all."

"Kiela! Caz!" Bryn waved cheerfully to both of them. "I think you've met Eadie. Let me introduce you to our friend Ulina."

Ulina waved with both of her right hands, as if they were connected by a string. Imagining how useful an extra pair of hands would be for shelving books, Kiela tried not to be jealous. She didn't have bookshelves right now anyway. Just jam shelves. "We almost met outside the bakery. Nice to officially meet you, Ulina."

Closer, Ulina elbowed Eadie with one of her arms. "You're right. I see it now. Just like Binna. It's the eyes. Plus the freckles."

Since she'd come to Caltrey and spent so much time outside in the garden, instead of within the library stacks, a scattering of magenta freckles had appeared on the bridge of her nose, and her hair had tinted different shades of blue, some strands lighter and some still a dark sapphire, a rainbow of blues.

"Also, the smile," Eadie said. To Kiela, she said, "You have your mother's smile."

Kiela wasn't sure how hearing that made her feel. Jumbled inside, really. She liked that her smile sparked memories—it made it feel a little like her mother was still here to be able to smile, but then her mother wouldn't have been happy to be back on Caltrey. Her mother had loved Alyssium—loved all the shops and the bustle, loved the flowers that draped from every window box. She'd been so excited to get her own window box full of flowers. She'd nursed those seeds into sprouts, and every spring, she would proudly report on every blossom that appeared. Given how much she loved flowers, Kiela wondered if she'd ever missed her island garden. "She liked to smile."

"We went to school together," Ulina said. "She always had her nose in a book, while I was always showing off how well I could walk on rooftops. I was a bit of a daredevil back in the day."

Eadie snorted. "Binna used to dare you to *not* do dangerous things, just to make sure you made it out of your childhood alive."

Kiela felt herself smile. That did sound like something her mother would do. And her mother had always loved to read. She'd taught Kiela at a very young age, and on their very first day in Alyssium, her mother had brought her to the Great Library. Without an imperial pass, they'd only been allowed in the public foyer, but Kiela had glimpsed the stacks up the spiral staircase and the reading rooms through the occasionally opened doors. She'd fallen in love with the place that day, and her mother had encouraged her. She'd been so proud when Kiela was accepted into the librarian program at the university. She'd told everyone in her book club and her gardening club and everyone at her favorite tea shop about her daughter the librarian-to-be. Kiela hadn't thought about that in years. She was surprised at how nice it was to remember. She would've expected it to hurt more. Somehow, being here in her family's old house, with people who'd known her parents . . . It was nice.

It took her an extra second to realize they were waiting for her to respond.

"Sorry, yes. She taught me to love books. Not rooftops. I mean, I'm sure rooftops are nice. To walk on." Ugh, what was she saying? "Would you like some jam?"

"Smooth," Caz murmured.

"Actually . . ." Ulina began.

Eadie jumped in. "She saw my cherry tree. It's spectacular. Completely covered in ripening fruit. I've revitalized the trees behind my house as well. They're flourishing."

Bryn nodded in agreement. "We're here to buy more of your tree remedies."

Behind her, Caz said, "Told you."

"We don't have any at the moment," Kiela said. "With the storm and all, we haven't had time . . ." She trailed off as their faces fell.

They came all this way, she thought. Dressed up nice for a visit. Climbed the cliff stairs. Bryn had probably closed her bakery to do this, or at least found a replacement to run it. She didn't know what Ulina or Eadie had given up to come here today, but they both looked deflated. She felt as if she'd told eager partygoers there was no more cake.

"But I could make some," Kiela said. "Caz could keep you company while you wait?" She glanced over her shoulder at the spider plant to see if he'd mind. Assembling the pine cones would be quicker with his help, but someone had to distract their visitors. "You could have some bread and jam, on the house, as an apology for the delay. We have both raspberry and blueberry." She still had one of Bryn's loaves. It was a reasonable offer, especially if they paid for the remedies.

All three of them perked up at that, and she felt a rush of relief. *I said the right thing. Yay.* Maybe she could handle being a shopkeeper after all.

"We'd be happy to help you, my dear," Eadie said.

"Many hands make the work go faster," Ulina said, wiggling her many fingers.

Uh-oh. If they helped, they'd witness her spellcasting. She had to say no. But how did she say no without sounding more suspicious?

On the other hand, should she say no?

If more islanders knew how to heal the trees, wouldn't that be a good thing? She thought of the forest spirits and of the orchard. She'd never intended to keep knowledge from people, the way the emperor did. She'd just wanted to protect it, but if these three women would value the knowledge . . . *Who am I to keep it from them?*

Someone who doesn't want to be transformed into anything unpleasant.

"Unless it's a family recipe?" Bryn said, noticing her hesitation. "Caz, are you comfortable sharing it? I have plenty of secret family recipes that don't leave my bakery."

That was the perfect out.

But did Kiela want to take it? She glanced at Caz for his opinion, and he shook his tendrils—he didn't know, and he was happy to leave it up to her.

In the beginning, she'd thought this would be safe enough: homespun remedies to help the people of Caltrey. She didn't think anyone beyond the island would notice or care. But now there was a woman from the capital, probably a noblewoman, who'd seen plenty of magic close up . . . It was an entirely different kettle of fish.

Wasn't it?

Maybe it wasn't.

Could she trust these three women? She hadn't known either Bryn or Eadie for long, though she liked them quite a bit, and Ulina she'd just met. They didn't owe her anything. If they knew the full "remedy," how would they react?

They'd given her no reason to distrust them—this was their home, and they just wanted to heal their trees. Both Eadie and Ulina were old enough to remember a time when homespun magic wasn't illegal. The laws were a recent development, invented by those who wanted to consolidate power. *And see where it got them.* In truth, spellcasting had simply faded out of fashion and was forgotten—it wasn't that most people believed it was wrong. Besides, it wasn't as though she was trying to work major spellcraft. Just a little remedy.

Beyond them, in the green, Kiela saw a wisp of haze.

A cloud bear?

That decided her.

She wasn't going to let a little fear keep her from doing what was right. A lot of fear . . . well, then, yes, maybe she'd reconsider. But all she had right now was a vague kind of unease. She had no way of knowing where Radane's political leanings lay—she might not care what a few islanders and a plant did to a handful of trees, or she might be so grateful for her life that she didn't want to stir up trouble. Besides which, they were a long way from the capital.

"If I teach you, you need to understand that it's just a simple plant-family remedy," Kiela said. She glanced at Caz, but he wasn't contradicting her. She hoped this was the right decision. "Nothing more."

All three women beamed at her. "Of course," Bryn said. "We understand."

Eadie added, "And we'll take you up on that bread and jam."

"Actually," Bryn said, "I also brought cheese and salami—in case we wanted to have a proper picnic." From the pockets of her pinafore dress, she produced wrapped packets, and Ulina clapped her four hands happily.

A short while later, Kiela and Caz and the three women were seated on a blanket spread out on the grass in front of the cottage. After asking Kiela if she could use her stove and kettle, Bryn had made fresh tea, while Kiela had sliced the bread and Eadie cut up the sausage and cheese. Caz had enlisted Ulina into helping carry out the baskets of ingredients. Due to her second set of arms, she could carry quite a bit at one time.

As they nibbled on the sandwiches, Kiela picked up a pine cone. "It's fairly simple. You use the sap to stick the ingredients onto the pine cone—there's an acorn cap, elderberry leaves, huckleberry leaves, shell of a chicken egg . . . Any eggshell would work, but I've only tried it with chicken shell."

"Specifically huckleberry and elderberry leaves?" Bryn asked.

"I don't recommend experimenting with the ingredients. It can have unexpected side effects." She wondered if the apple tree in the orchard had ever stopped singing. "Your neighbors might not like it."

Eadie snorted. "My neighbor doesn't like anything. He'll seize any opportunity to complain." She launched into an anecdote about her neighbor fussing over the fact that his flowers bent toward her house—which meant she could see the blossoms and not him, as if she had anything to do with the position of the sun. "He once yelled at a bird for daring to chirp by his window. Apparently it should respect the fence around his property?"

Halfway through her third story, Kiela realized which neighbor she meant: Fenerer. She swallowed her bite of sandwich—the sausage was peppery and the cheese was sharp, absolute perfection—and said, "He came by my shop the first day it opened. Told me he doesn't like jam."

Bryn shook her head. "But you have a jam shop—why come to a jam shop if you don't like jam? It's like visiting a fish market if you hate seafood or a baker if you don't like bread and then complaining that they don't offer steak and corn, which is a fine meal but—"

"He likes to complain," Ulina said. "Some people are like that. They derive joy from sapping other people's joy. The trick is not to let them. Just keep playing your own song."

"I recommend being aggressively happy in their face," Eadie said. "Makes Fenerer's scales turn bright red." She imitated him: "'Terrible weather we're having.'" And then as herself: "Yes, the rain will be great for the flowers."

"Brilliant," Bryn said, laughing.

Finishing her first sticky pine cone, Kiela showed the others what it was supposed to look like. The others compared theirs. "Caz, what's the wind today?" Kiela asked.

Caz held one of his tendrils up in the air. "It's easterly," he reported.

"Excellent." Kiela held up her completed pine cone. "It requires a breath of easterly wind. Only wind will work. Definitely don't try just blowing on it."

"You're making me very curious," Eadie said, lifting her pine cone into the air. "What happens if you deviate from the spell?"

"Remedy!" both Kiela and Caz said. Calming herself, Kiela said, "Think of it like a recipe. Like for jam. If you mix in salt instead of sugar, it won't taste the same, right?"

Bryn grinned at her. "You tried it, didn't you. Go on, tell us. What happened?"

"It didn't work," Kiela said.

"One of the trees turned into a bird," Caz said.

Kiela shot him a look.

"What? They should know if they don't want extra birds."

"Easterly wind," Kiela said firmly. "And then . . ." She hesitated. Here was the part that felt the most like a sorcerer's spell, because it *was* a sorcerer's spell. "You say a few nonsense syllables."

Bryn raised her eyebrows.

Ulina and Eadie exchanged glances.

Kiela tried not to wince. Why had she thought this was a good idea? It was not. Definitely not. But . . . *Knowledge is meant to be shared.* That was the entire point of a library. Otherwise it would be a sealed vault. "You know, the syllables are just for fun. Someone in Caz's family must have thought it would make it all look more impressive, if it sounded like they were really doing magic."

"It was my grandpa," Caz lied. "He was trying to woo my grandma. But tradition says you have to say the words or . . ." He shrugged with his tendrils.

"Or you'll dishonor his grandpa," Kiela said.

Caz nodded all of his leaves.

"So you'll teach us these nonsense words?" Eadie asked.

"Yes, but I recommend not saying them around anyone who might misunderstand," Kiela said. "Like Fenerer. He'd probably see it in the worst possible light."

"Instead of a harmless tradition to honor a grandfather," Bryn said.

"Exactly."

All the women nodded, and Kiela taught them the words syllable by syllable. She corrected their pronunciation until they had it completely perfect. Only then did they speak the words with the sticky pine cones in front of them.

Completed, they wrapped the enchanted pine cones in scraps of fabric. And then each of them reached for another pine cone to begin again. It was Bryn's turn then to regale them with a flood of anecdotes. She described various baking accidents she'd had and experiments with recipes, plus the time she'd been distracted and had in fact mixed up salt and sugar. "I didn't create a bird, but I did create the most inedible pudding that you can possibly imagine."

"Let me guess," Eadie said. "Tobin ate it anyway."

Bryn grinned. "Every last bit of it."

Hours flew, and by the time the sun was overhead, they'd created several dozen remedies and depleted the entirety of the ingredients from the forest spirits. Caz offered to gather more for their next working picnic, if they were interested in making this a regular event. Everyone loved that idea, and Bryn offered to supply the bread next time, Ulina offered to bring the cheese, and Eadie volunteered honey.

As they poured themselves a final round of tea, Eadie said, "If this is going to be a regular meeting, we should have a name. I vote we call ourselves the Pine Cone Coven."

"Yes!" Bryn said.

"I love it," Ulina said.

Kiela held up a finger. "That might cause problems."

"The Pine Cone Society?" Bryn suggested.

All of them agreed to that, and Kiela felt an unfamiliar knot of warmth. She'd never really been part of a group before. Even in school . . . Well, this was nice.

Bryn lifted her teacup. "To the Pine Cone Society."

"The Pine Cone Society," they all said, lifting their cups. Caz lifted a cup using his leaves. They clinked and then drank. Caz dumped his cup, with water not tea, onto his root ball.

Kiela smiled as she set down her cup—

And saw a bush shiver at the edge of the forest. A tree guardian? She smiled, thinking the cloud bears would be happy about the Pine Cone Society saving more trees. As she watched the bushes for a hint of cloud, she thought she saw a flash of red.

"Did you see that?" she asked.

"What?" Caz asked.

All of them turned to stare at the woods, but Kiela didn't see any other hint of motion. For an instant, she'd thought she'd seen the red of Radane's hair.

Just my imagination.

CHAPTER TWENTY-THREE

Pine Cone Coven, Kiela thought as she waved goodbye to the three women. She decided she'd call it that to herself, though it was wise to say "society" out loud. All total, they'd made forty-six more remedies. She'd wanted to gift them at least half, in thanks for their work and company, but Caz had jumped into negotiations—and somehow, in payment for her teaching them the spell, they'd agreed to supply her with a quarter of the harvest on any fruit or nut trees, or a fish a week for a month if they used the remedy on another kind of tree. She had no idea where the spider plant had learned how to handle business negotiations, but she was grateful. Also, she was going to have to learn how to cook fish.

Larran would know.

She wondered if that was a decent enough excuse to visit him . . .

She could also ask how Sian was feeling . . .

But what if Radane was there?

She wondered if that really had been her, lurking in the greenery, or if it had only been Kiela's imagination. *Maybe I'm just overly jumpy.* She'd glimpsed a bit of red—it could have been a bird. Perhaps even the apple-blossom bird with its red feathers. She headed back inside the cottage.

"The cactus wants to help next time," Caz said.

"Of course!" She was ninety-nine percent certain the Pine Cone

Coven wouldn't bat an eye at the addition of a sentient succulent. Or at least ninety percent certain. Eighty-five? "It's welcome to help whenever it wants."

"Meep," the cactus said from the garden door, before darting back out to play with the chicken—the two of them seemed to be playing some variant of tag.

"The cactus wants you to know they prefer 'they' to 'it,' 'she,' or 'he,'" Caz told Kiela.

"Ah, okay. Thanks for telling me," Kiela said. "Wait, you can understand them?" She hadn't realized the cactus could communicate, especially at such a grammatically nuanced level.

"Sure. It's a plant thing."

"How intelligent are they?" She kept her voice low, in case the cactus was insulted by the question. She didn't mean to be insulting—she just had very limited experience with this. She didn't recall any of her books mentioning the developmental speed of accidentally enhanced plant life.

"They have a working understanding of theoretical astrophysics."

Staring out at the cactus and chicken, Kiela said, "Really?"

"No. But they do like poetry."

She raised her eyebrows.

"They prefer free verse."

"Huh." She rather loved the idea of the spider plant and the cactus reciting free verse poetry to each other. She wanted to ask whether they wrote their own or drew from the masters, but her mind shifted back to that hint of red in the greenery. How much did she have to worry about the rescued woman? What would Radane think of a sentient succulent who was advanced enough to appreciate poetry? Maybe if Kiela visited Larran, she'd be able to determine whether Radane had overheard her spellcasting with Sian, whether she had been spying on her, whether she was a threat at all, or whether it was all Kiela's own paranoia. "I'm thinking of visiting Larran . . ."

Caz made a rustling sound that was suspiciously like a giggle.

". . . to check on Sian and to try to determine if Radane is a threat."

"Mmm, of course."

"And to ask him how to cook fish." She winced at herself. Okay, now it just sounded like she was making up excuses. "But first, I want to finish the spell for Halio."

"Which spell for who?"

"Remember the older woman with the dry spring? She bought some jam on our first day? I almost have the spell for her. I just need to confirm the pronunciation of line three."

"Ooh, research!" He sprinted into the bedroom.

"Cactus?" Kiela called. "Can you mind the shop? 'Meep' if anyone comes."

The cactus waddled into the cottage, followed by the chicken.

"Don't let the chicken escape," Kiela told them.

"Meep," the cactus said.

Kiela wasn't certain what that meant, but it sounded like agreement? She'd have to ask Caz if he could teach her to speak plant. She was fluent in several languages, as was any librarian in the Great Library, but flora wasn't included. She wasn't certain it was a recognized language—*Perhaps it should be.* "Thanks." She followed Caz into the bedroom, where he'd already hauled out a dissertation on the linguistics of ancient languages, including the First Language of spellwork. Joining him, she immersed herself in research until Kiela felt confident that they had the solution. Reasonably confident, at least.

"How do we test it?" Caz asked.

She only knew of one waterless spring so far, and she really didn't want to be experimenting in front of Halio when she was going to claim it was an old family remedy. If it failed, that would be hard to explain. *Wait, I do know a second one.* "The fountain in town. It's dry too. If I pick a time when everyone is out at sea . . ."

"Like right now?" He waved his leaves at the window. "It's a beautiful afternoon."

She jumped to her feet. "Like right now. Can you and the cactus—"

"Go," he said. "By the time you're done, it'll be dinnertime. You can just happen to be passing by Larran's house. Perhaps he'll invite you to share a romantic meal."

Kiela blushed. "I'm not looking for a romantic meal."

"I have read that sharing meals can be very bonding," Caz said. "The act of nourishing one another creates a tie. Like when I share my soil ball . . ." He trailed off.

Lowering her notebook, Kiela looked at her spider plant friend. She could've sworn his leaves were tinted greener, the plant equivalent of a blush. "Caz?"

"You should visit Larran."

Kiela grinned at him. "Is there something you want to tell me?"

From the other room, she heard, "Meep!"

Still grinning, she tucked the spell into a pocket and headed out, but she resolved to continue that very interesting conversation later—after the fountain and after Larran.

Kiela lucked out: there was no one by the fountain.

She checked in every direction, studying the windows of the houses for any hint of movement. She could hear voices from the direction of the bakery, as well as shouts, seagull caws, the clang of metal, and the thunk of wood from the direction of the dock, but the only one watching her was a ginger cat with dirty white wings who had squeezed himself into a window box, displacing whatever flowers used to grow there. A lone daisy bloomed limply by his hindquarters, occasionally hit when he swished his tail.

"Don't tell," she said to the cat.

With another glance down the empty street, she stepped into the basin of the fountain. Kneeling by the spout, she inserted the ball of ingredients (both Caz and the cactus had helped her harvest them from the garden and the pond—this particular remedy required aquatic freshwater plants) beside the statue of the mermaid. Carefully, she said the words, pronouncing each syllable as she and Caz had determined.

She climbed out of the basin and wondered if—

Voices came closer.

Kiela scooted down a side street. She'd check back later. Perhaps even tomorrow. It would be better not to have any suspicion thrown on her at all. If she was nowhere near town when the spell took effect, that would be best. She began walking toward the beach and Larran's house. She didn't look back. Either the spell worked and she had a new remedy for her customers, or it hadn't and no harm done. It was worth it to try, especially since she had such a perfect opportunity. *Luck is with me today.*

She hoped that luck lasted. As she walked, she considered what she was going to say to Larran. Obvious start to the conversation was to ask about Sian. It was a reasonable excuse for a visit, regardless of whether Radane was there or not. If Radane was present . . . well, it would be a short visit.

She wondered where the rescued woman was sleeping. Larran had only one bed. There was no guest room or even a daybed like she had in her cottage. Exactly how kind was he?

Kiela had read tales of people who fell in love with either their hero or their healer. *Larran was both.* If Radane was grateful . . . If she realized how much he'd risked . . . If she saw how kind he was, how sweetly awkward, how . . . *Gah, what does it say about me that I'm clearly jealous of a woman who nearly died?* Kiela wouldn't blame Radane if she fell for Larran. *All he did was fix my chimney, and I can't stop thinking about him.*

No, it wasn't the chimney that had drawn her. It was the apology afterward. Yes, that was the moment that she began to have feelings for him. His clumsy apology.

If Radane was sharing his bed . . . *I'll be fine.* She hadn't needed romance in her life before, and she didn't need it now. It was a new idea, spurred by being in a new place and trying new things, but that didn't make it a necessity. Kiela thought of her happily married parents and how irritating it used to be when they'd pressure her about her love life. She didn't have what they had—a union, a partnership. Not everyone did. Some people were solitary, and she'd done just fine on her own. She'd been content.

And I can be content here, with Larran as a very nice neighbor.

On his porch, she raised her hand to knock on the door, and it swung open. His smile lit up his face, and for an instant, she forgot it was smart to breathe.

With a laugh, Larran stepped out onto the porch, wrapped his arms around her, and swung her in a circle, lifting her off the ground. In that instant, she was surrounded entirely by him, and she was only aware of the breath in his chest, the strength in his arms, the warmth in his skin, and the smell of the sea.

"You saved my Sian," he said.

Gently lowering her, he released her, and she had to catch herself to keep from staggering. He didn't seem to notice. He took her hand and pulled her across the beach and down the jetty. Kiela had to concentrate to keep from slipping on the way, and both of them were laughing by the time they reached the end, where the merhorses were playing.

Larran put his fingers to his lips and whistled, three short and one long.

Sian broke from the herd and leapt through the waves. She looked magnificent with the sunlight on her golden scales. She tossed her mane as she reached the rocks. Rising up onto her front hooves, Sian snuffled at Kiela's hands and then her pockets.

"No tomatoes today," Kiela said. "I'm sorry."

"She's herself because of you," Larran said. "I don't know how to repay you. Again. Sian was the foal, the one you sang to. You've saved her twice."

Kiela shook her head and didn't feel like laughing anymore. "You don't need to repay me. That's not why . . ." She took a breath. "You would've done the same. Both times. If you could have."

He took her hands in his. She liked the way his hands enveloped hers, swallowing them completely. "Yes, but you—"

"*Larran! Kiela!*" From the shore, Tobin waved both his arms over his head. He was puffing as if he'd run from the bakery to the beach. "You have to come see!"

Stepping back, Larran released her. "What's wrong? Is someone hurt?"

Tobin was dancing between the driftwood and seaweed. "The fountain! It's running again! You have to come see! It's a miracle!"

Larran shook his head. "Not possible." He smiled at her. "Looks like it's a day of miracles. We have to see this." He took Kiela's hand again and led her back down the stone jetty. She glanced at Sian, who bobbed in the waves, watching them.

He's not going to finish that sentence.

She knew she was going to spend the next day, week, lifetime wondering what was going to come after *Yes, but you* . . . But what? What did he think of her? Did he think of her? Or was he merely grateful? She'd saved his beloved merhorse twice.

Her father would have said it was a sign. He'd liked to see signs and portents in the random occurrences in the world. When they'd chosen their new home in Alyssium, the flowers above the window were pink roses. He'd said that was a sign. She hadn't realized at the time that those roses were the same pink as the ones on the wild rosebushes that edged the cliff. She also remembered the time she'd lost a scarf in the canals—her father had said it was a sign that she should live at the Great Library, shielded from any wind or sea breeze. At that point, she'd already taken the library assignment and was full of doubt about leaving her parents' home. He'd been trying to say, in his own way, that it was okay for her to go.

They reached the beach and followed a very excited Tobin as he leapt like a goat over the beach and into town. Kiela heard the crowd long before she saw it, squawking like a flock of gulls, with words piling onto one another so fast that they became meaningless.

If Larran wasn't still holding her hand, she'd have pivoted and fled up the cliff stairs . . . But he was still holding her hand, even though she wasn't sure he realized he was. All his attention was on Tobin.

As they approached the fountain, he slowed.

The crowd was thick, clustered in a ring around the fountain. She couldn't even see the mermaid statue, but then Larran pushed forward, and a gap opened up.

Sparkling in the sun, water arched around the stone mermaid. Kids were dancing in the fountain, splashing and laughing. Islanders—more than she'd seen at one time—were marveling at it, repeating the same amazed phrases over and over, asking how this could happen, wondering what it meant . . .

A woman's voice rang out, harsh as a gull. "What it means is that someone on Caltrey has access to illegal magic."

Kiela felt her heart sink.

Radane stepped onto the edge of the fountain. She'd pitched her voice loud so that it carried over all the wondering and murmuring and explaining and reminiscing over the last time the fountain had run, as well as the weddings that were held by it, the proposals that had happened near it, and the festivals that occurred around it. As soon as she spoke, the murmurs shifted. "Illegal magic? But who . . ."

Kiela wanted to melt away, but Larran was still holding her hand. It was harder to breathe, as if a storm were sitting in a ring around her head. She tried to look as shocked as the people around her. She felt the bodies around her, penning her in.

"You have a rogue sorcerer on Caltrey," Radane shouted, "and it is imperative that he or she comes forward! If you do so voluntarily, I promise that the imperial guard will be lenient. If you do not . . . then you will be considered a traitor to the empire."

Out of the corner of her eye, she saw Larran scowl.

Don't say anything, she thought at him. *Don't draw her attention.*

But it was Bryn, not Larran, who shouted, "Who are you to come here and make threats? You were saved from the sea by one of us—quite a display of gratitude to now turn your suspicion on us."

"I am an imperial inspector," Radane said, "authorized to enforce the laws. And it will go more smoothly for your island if you do not hide this criminal from me."

She doesn't know it's me.

Kiela hadn't been here when the fountain began to gush. She'd been with Larran, outside of the town. Larran could vouch for her. Tobin had seen her. *I can't be a suspect. Can I?*

"I am authorized to search each of your premises, if I must, and confiscate anything contraband and levy fines as appropriate for any infractions," Radane said. "But I do not wish to disrupt the lives of innocent people. Bring me the rogue sorcerer, and no searches will occur, no fines will be levied, and I will leave your island with no reports against the people here. You will avoid the imperial eye—for it does continue to see all, even without the emperor himself. The Crescent Islands Empire will not be denied. Who is your sorcerer?"

Don't run, Kiela told herself.

She wormed her hand out of Larran's and began to inch backward through the crowd. He shot her a look, but she couldn't tear her eyes from Radane.

"I want to speak to all older villagers with knowledge of 'herbal remedies,'" Radane said, "as well as any healers known to mumble to their patients or anyone who's witnessed any unusual or unexpected activities."

Fenerer called out, "Never had any trouble until the new citygirl came."

As eyes turned on her, Kiela froze in place.

"Nonsense," Ulina said. "She's one of ours."

"You just want her cove and her woods," Bryn snapped at Fenerer. "You've wanted that land since her parents left. You should be ashamed, stooping this low out of greed."

Everyone murmured. Most of the voices agreed with Bryn. As

nice as that was, Kiela wished she had the power to disappear. Or to turn herself into an apple-blossom bird and fly away. She would have given up several books to not be here right now, obviously depending on which book—perhaps the virtually incomprehensible *Thoughts On the Ineffable Behavior of Half-Moon Caterpillars* by scholars Mimay and Liy or the insufferable *Arguments for Moss* by that puffed-up half-scholar Wilgafort or . . .

Radane scowled at her through the crowd, and Kiela thought, *This is it.*

Stepping up onto the edge of the fountain with the inspector, Bryn said to Radane, "I have a proposal. Instead of intruding on people's homes and making everyone uncomfortable, why not come into the bakery? You can interview anyone you wish there, with tea and pastries for all who volunteer to speak with you. I'm quite certain that you'll realize there's no illegal activity here. Just good people trying to live their lives as best they can."

"That's not how this works," Radane said. "But yes, I will begin my search with your bakery. You'd best hope that I find nothing that isn't regulation."

"All are welcome in my bakery," Bryn said loudly. She shot a glance through the crowd—her eyes met Kiela's, and then she looked away. Marching through the crowd, she led the inspector toward her bakery, while Kiela retreated down the street at a fast-but-hopefully-innocent walk.

When she made it to the beach, she ran.

CHAPTER TWENTY-FOUR

Kiela ran up the cliff stairs—her sides hurt, her lungs hurt, her legs hurt, and her heart hurt to think that she'd ruined everything. If she hadn't shared her spells with anyone . . . If she hadn't experimented on the apple trees . . . If she had just left the books alone . . . But she hadn't, and now she'd endangered not only herself but Caz, Larran, Bryn, Eadie, Ulina, and possibly everyone else on Caltrey, depending on how hard this inspector decided to come down on the island for harboring a "rogue sorcerer."

What else would Radane's investigation expose?

Who else have I endangered?

Panting, she reached the top of the stairs. What about Ivor? He'd said he wanted to talk to her about remedies. She'd assumed he disapproved, but what if she had it backward? He was the island healer. Perhaps he slipped in some illegal "remedies" of his own to save a patient. In Alyssium, it was universally known that no one looked too closely at what healers did so long as they kept healing the rich and powerful, but what about on an island in the outer region? Would they still look away? Radane had specifically mentioned healers, so she might not look away. As an imperial inspector, she had the authority to enforce the laws against non-approved magic use to their fullest. She could call a legion to Caltrey to comb through their houses, observe their activities, question everyone . . .

and then levy fines, make arrests, dole out punishments. She could, if she chose, strip Caltrey of every resource and call it justice.

Outside the waterfall, Kiela called, "Ivor!" She bent over, hands on her knees, and tried to catch her breath. Straightening, she shouted louder, "Ivor!"

He stepped out from behind the spray of water. Wet, his magnificent antlers gleamed. "Who needs help?"

"You do."

He blinked at her.

"There's an imperial inspector in town," she said. "You may have nothing to hide, but if you do . . . hide it." She turned without waiting for him to reply.

"Kiela, I know what you did for Larran's merhorse."

She froze.

And then he said, "It was a true kindness."

With a nod, Kiela set off toward the greenery. She held her side as she ran. Every breath felt as if it were scraping her throat. She wasn't used to running. Not much need in the Great Library. She didn't see the point unless something was chasing you.

Well, now something is.

Consequences.

Consequences were chasing her, and even though a good, upstanding citizen of the empire might choose to face those consequences . . . *I have a spider plant, a cactus, and a chicken to think of.*

And the books.

She couldn't let Radane claim the spellbooks. An imperial investigator wasn't a librarian. Radane wouldn't know how to care for them, how to protect them, how to return them safely to where they'd be guarded and valued. At best, she'd confiscate them, and they'd languish in a warehouse for illegal magic. At worst, she'd destroy them, deeming them the instrument of illegal activities. She might not believe they were library books. Or care.

It's not a risk I can take.

Stumbling onto the green in front of the cottage, Kiela collapsed

onto her hands and knees. Her voice croaked as she called, "Caz."
She tried again. Louder: "Caz!"

"Meep?"

"Get Caz, please," she told the cactus as they peered at her from
around the side of the cottage. "Tell him it's an emergency. Tell
him . . ." *Tell him it's all gone wrong. Tell him I failed. Tell him I'm
sorry.*

Before she could say any of it, Caz spurted out over the garden
wall and toward her. "What happened? Are you hurt? Oh seeds
and soil! You're dying!"

She shook her head hard. "Radane—she's an imperial inspector.
She knows there's illegal magic on Caltrey. We have to hide the
books."

"Gah!"

He bolted into the cottage, followed by the cactus. "Meep, meep,
meep!"

She got to her feet and puffed after them into the bedroom.
Throwing the quilts off the crates, she piled the research books
she'd been reading back inside and closed the lids. She then began
tugging the first crate out of the cottage.

"Where to?" Caz asked.

"Boat," Kiela said.

"How?"

"We pull it down the stairs? I guess?" As she maneuvered the first
crate to the top step, she heard the rustle of bushes near the path.
Her heart hammered inside her rib cage. "Hide," she ordered Caz
and the cactus.

There was no hiding the crate. She couldn't just drop it down the
stairs, not safely, not with water at the bottom of the steps. She had
to guide it down, but there was no time—

Larran burst out of the greenery. "Kiela?"

"Over here," she said, and then thought she should have stayed
silent. Of course, he would have seen her in a second, just standing

at the top of the steps with an enormous crate. She braced herself as he crossed to her—this wasn't going to be a pleasant conversation. She expected questions. Or a demand for an explanation. She knew he'd seen her flee—there was no way to hide that. She only hoped she had enough of a head start on Radane, that Bryn would keep her busy in the bakery for long enough—

But he didn't demand anything. He merely asked, "What do you need?"

Kiela wanted to cry. That was the most— *No, fall apart later.* "I need help with the crates. I have to hide them. Caz and I . . . We need to get the crates to our boat and then . . . somewhere." She didn't know where. Out to sea. Along the coast. She didn't know, but she'd figure it out. First, she had to get the books away from here. Maybe she could find another cove, one where no one knew to look for her. Or better yet, a cave. Yes! There were caves riddling the cliffs. She didn't know where any were, but if she searched for long enough . . . *I just have to get the books away.*

He didn't ask what was in the crates.

He didn't ask why they needed to be hidden.

He simply helped. Grabbing the crate, he muscled it down the stairs himself, while she, Caz, and the cactus dragged the second crate from the back bedroom to the top of the steps.

Larran jogged back up the steps and hefted the next crate into his arms. She saw the strain in his arms and the sweat on his forehead. She knew the crates were painfully heavy, even for him, but he didn't say a word. He didn't slow.

She went for the third crate.

The fourth.

The fifth.

By the last one, her arms were aching so badly that they shook. But she helped him carry the final crate down the steps, both of them grunting and wheezing. They positioned it onto the scow next to the others, and Kiela covered them all with the tarp.

"Kiela?" Caz called from shore. He was holding the bag of pine cone remedies in his leaves. The cactus was beneath the bag, helping support it.

"Caz, wait there. I'll carry you over the dock. Cactus—"

"I'm staying," Caz said.

Staying? Here? "You can't. If she saw you and misunderstood . . ."

"There's nothing illegal about me," Caz said. "My creation, yes. But after my creator was punished, the head librarian did the paperwork to ensure I would be protected."

"If Radane doesn't believe you—"

"Meep!"

"They want to stay with me," Caz translated.

This was a terrible idea, for both of them. She remembered how Fenerer had reacted when he'd just seen the spider plant. He hadn't paused to ask about paperwork. "It's dangerous. You don't know—"

"Meep, *meep!*"

Kiela didn't need a translation for *that*. The cactus wanted to stay with Caz, which would normally be sweet but right now was just plain reckless. If Radane saw either Caz or the cactus, she'd be convinced that Kiela, not some elderly villager with an herbal remedy, was the source of the magic—and she'd be right. Kiela tried another tack. "I need the two of you to guard the books wherever I hide them. I can't just stash them somewhere unguarded, and I can't stay with them myself. It'll be suspicious if I'm not at my shop."

"What if she comes while you're gone?" Caz argued. "Someone needs to delay and misdirect her—"

Larran spoke up. "I'll do it."

"Don't be ridiculous," Kiela said. He wasn't involved. He had no idea what was going on or what was at stake. He shouldn't have to— She suddenly realized with horror that she'd said the word "books." A second later, she realized he hadn't flinched. He hadn't asked, "What books?" Or worse, "Whose books?" Maybe . . . *No*. This wasn't his responsibility. He didn't owe anything to her, no matter what he'd said before with Sian. *I'm not his . . . anything.* He had no reason, except this was Larran, and this was what he did and who he was.

Still, though, she couldn't let him. He'd be accused of obstructing an official investigation, and he couldn't afford to be arrested—his merhorses needed him. Besides, he didn't deserve to be pulled into this mess. He was a good person, kind to a fault. Kiela shook her head. "No, I won't be responsible for ruining your life. Go home, and be innocent. You rescued her, so she should leave you alone—"

"I brought danger to you, however unintentionally, by bringing her into your life," Larran said. "Don't argue. Just go. Take Caz and . . ." He hesitated.

"Meep," the cactus said.

"Take Caz and Meep with you, and I will delay Radane, if she comes."

She half laughed and half hiccupped. "Meep is an excellent name," she told the cactus as they waddled down the dock toward the boat. Carrying the bag of pine cones, Caz followed the cactus. He kept to the middle of the boards, but he didn't falter. Both of them jumped onto the scow, and Caz climbed on top of the crates, as far from the water as possible.

Following her to the edge of the dock, Larran asked, "Where will you go?"

"Better if you don't know." Kneeling, she untied the line from the dock and then stepped onto the scow and pushed off. "What will you do if she comes before I'm back?"

"Sell jam," Larran said simply.

Caz snorted.

"Thank you," Kiela said. She wanted to say more: she was sorry for not telling him the truth, she was in awe of how kind he was, she really liked his eyes, but she couldn't find the words. Maybe she'd have another chance to say them later, when she knew how to say what she was feeling churning inside her. Reaching for the pole, she pushed her way through the cove toward the waves. He then turned and ran up the steps, two at a time, while she propelled the scow out of the cove.

Outside the shelter of the cove, waves slapped at the hull, and wind tangled her hair. She untied the silver sail and raised it. Overhead, the sky was bright, blue, and cloudless, as if it hadn't a care in the world and would never allow a storm or even a drizzle—in other words, lying. Seagulls circled above them, hoping they'd stop and fish, but Kiela ignored them.

"Where to?" Caz asked.

She should have asked Larran . . . *No, he's doing enough.* "Look for caves." She remembered visiting several caves around Caltrey with her father when she was a child. There were a few that had thousands-of-years-old paintings inside them, animated by magic— proof that there had been magic on the Crescent Islands long before the emperor and his greedy laws. Kiela's father had been fascinated by caves of Caltrey. He'd never have imagined she'd need to hide in one. She felt a sliver of anger coil inside her. She shouldn't be punished for what she'd done. Protecting the books was her actual job description, as well as her life's mission, and as for using what was in the books and sharing the knowledge they contained . . . well, that *should* be her job and her mission.

Books should *be shared with everyone who wants to open their minds and hearts to them.*

Keeping them, keeping knowledge, from people who needed it, *that* was the real crime. The words belonged to the people, all the people, not just the wealthy and powerful, even if that led to a few disasters due to magic in the hands of inexperienced spellcasters . . . Well, the current laws weren't keeping anyone safe. In fact, the status quo was only making everything worse. If it was up to her, she'd share the spells with everyone.

Of course, all that was true but unhelpful. Whether she had

the moral high ground or not, she still had to find a cave, hide the books and the plants, and then make it back to Larran before Radane came snooping around, which was definitely going to be soon, especially if Radane had indeed spied on them through the greenery. Caz's lie about an old villager with an herbal remedy wouldn't delay her for long. *She'll be coming soon.* The faster they could find a place to hide, the better.

A splash beside the boat caught her attention.

Kiela looked into the water and saw the mermaid from the cove with her merbaby swimming beside them. She couldn't help but smile as the merbaby leaped like a dolphin through the waves. He giggled as he waved his webbed hand.

Caz leaned over the edge of the crate. "Excuse me. We're in a bit of danger. Do you know a cave we can hide in? Large enough to hold the boat and everything on it, but small enough not to be noticed? You see, there's an imperial inspector on the island, and she'll take the spellbooks if she finds them and arrest us, which would mean prison or worse." He shuddered and shed a leaf.

The mermaid popped higher out of the water. "Danger?"

"Yes, danger," Caz said. "Can you help us hide?"

The mermaid disappeared under the waves.

"Meep?" the cactus said. They stabbed the lost leaf with their needles and offered it back to Caz, who let them plant it in his soil ball, even though that was hopeless.

"I don't think she understood," Caz said.

Their needles drooped. "Meep."

"Well, I doubt that merfolk have issues with imperial inspectors," he said. "They certainly don't have books underwater. She might not—"

Popping up near the prow, the mermaid ordered, "Come."

Kiela adjusted the sail, and they bounced over the waves, following the mermaid and her baby. They sailed past the orchard on the edge of the cliff, and Kiela wondered if the tree was still singing. If it was, she didn't doubt Fenerer would show the inspector and share all his suspicions. Frankly, it was sheer luck that Radane hadn't begun her search at the jam shop. *No, it's not luck,* she thought. *It's Bryn.*

She wondered what Larran would say when Radane finally came, whether she would search the cottage, and whether she'd guess what they'd removed from the bedroom—Kiela hadn't had time to reorganize the furniture. What would she make of the pile of quilts? Would she notice the boat was gone from the cove? If she discovered Kiela had come by boat, she'd demand to know where the boat was.

A good inspector would crack through Kiela's lies in a heartbeat. *I didn't hide well.*

She hadn't been trying to hide; she'd been trying to escape. And once she was here . . . well, she'd thought she was too far from Alyssium for anyone to care what she did. She'd let herself be lulled into an illusion of safety, and look where it had gotten her.

"I'm sorry," Kiela said to Caz.

"For what? You came back as quickly as you could."

"For all of this. If I hadn't touched the books . . . If we'd just left them behind . . ."

Caz shook his tendrils at her. "They'd have burned."

"Then I should have just left them hidden. I shouldn't have—"

"Meep!"

If she hadn't cast spells, then Meep wouldn't exist, the forest spirits would be treeless, the merbaby and Sian would have succumbed to storm sickness. *It wasn't all a mistake.* Ahead, the mermaid swam toward what looked like a shadow in the cliff wall. Kiela pulled the sail tighter, and they shot through the water, following her. They sped toward the rocks.

Caz rustled his leaves. "Kiela?"

She wasn't certain where the cave was, if there was a cave, but the mermaid—

"Kiela!"

"I trust her."

And there it was: the cave. It was a trick of how the cliff wall was angled, combined with the color of the rock. She'd never have seen it at all if not for the mermaid. Loosening the sail, she let the boat drift toward the opening.

They slipped inside between the silent stone. Shadows closed around them, like a mother's arms, to protect them. The lap of waves echoed within the cave. *I know this place.* It was her father's favorite.

On the ceiling and the walls, painted flowers sparkled around them in a magical light show, courtesy of a spell that had been cast thousands of years ago. Marveling, Kiela turned in a slow circle as the petals of ancient roses, lilies, daisies, and flowers twinkled in every color of the rainbow, and she felt, for a brief moment, safe.

CHAPTER TWENTY-FIVE

"You should stay here," Caz said to Kiela.

"Meep," the cactus agreed.

Kiela climbed out of the boat onto the rocks. She spotted a sliver of sunlight—the way out of the cave by foot. "I have to go back to the shop. Our only chance at dispelling suspicion is if I act unsuspicious. Wait, that's not the right word. Guiltless? Innocuous? Innocent?" She looped the line around a jagged rock, securing the boat in place.

"And then what?" Caz asked. "Keep us plants hidden forever? Never use any spells again? Let the forest spirits lose their trees? Don't save future merbabies or merhorses?"

She didn't know. How was she supposed to know what would happen next? None of this was planned. She'd known what her life and her future was: the library, day in and day out, until her skeleton was swept away with the dust.

I could go back.

Back to the library. Back . . . home? Was that home anymore? When she thought "home," she pictured a cottage, cradled by a forest, with an overflowing, barely tamed garden behind it. *Don't I want to go back to Alyssium?*

Radane being here meant the empire hadn't fallen, which could mean that the library was still there. Kiela could sail back to the capital, explain what she'd done and why. Heck, she could even be welcomed back as a hero for saving the books from the revolution.

If she left . . . She'd miss the cottage and the jam shop. She'd miss the bakery. She'd miss the cloud bears and the unicorn sightings and the mermaids. But was that enough to keep her here? This was only ever meant to be temporary.

Near the boat, the mermaid splashed her tail, and the sound echoed through the cave. Her baby cooed. He was swimming around the boat, plucking barnacles off the hull with his little fingers and showing each one to her as if it were a treasure.

"Meep?" Leaning over the edge of the boat, Meep poked a barnacle with a needle. The merbaby beached himself on the deck of the boat and attempted to pluck needles from the cactus. Waving his leaves, Caz shooed him back into the water.

I can't return with Meep. Not if the laws were unchanged. He wouldn't be welcome, and she could become the newest statue in whatever was left of the Great Library. It was only because of a lot of pulling of strings by influential librarians that Caz had been spared. There was no guarantee that Meep would meet with the same mercy. *I can't risk it.* As tempting as it was to flee back to her lovely little alcove between the stacks, it wasn't just her and Caz anymore. It was Meep too, and she couldn't leave them.

Also, what about Larran, who was waiting for her at the shop? If she just vanished and ran, what would the imperial investigator think? She'd turn her suspicion on him, as well as Bryn, Eadie, and Ulina. No, her only option was to go back to the cottage, act innocent, and hope to convince Radane that there was no illegal spellwork on Caltrey. Just nice jars of jam. *Maybe the imperial investigator has a favorite flavor.* If that failed . . . "We'll figure it out," Kiela said. "One step at a time."

"You have to promise to be careful," Caz said.

"There's just one of her," Kiela said, trying to sound brave.

"And one of you," Caz said, shaking his leaves for emphasis. "You promise me you'll run if it goes sour. Come back here and we'll sail away. Find a new island. Please, promise me. Don't take any risks."

Every single thing I've done since the library burned was a risk, she thought. But she promised anyway.

Leaving Caz, Meep, and the merfolk in the painted cave, Kiela picked her way across the island. She kept to the forest, away from the fields and the dirt roads that led to various farms and orchards. She wasn't entirely certain of the way, which was a problem given the urgency. It helped that the island was, well, an island. She knew to keep the sun behind her and the sea to either side, at least when she could see it.

When she reached the pond with the willow tree, she thought, *Almost home.*

And the thought surprised her so much that she stopped walking. When did this start to feel more like home than the library? She'd only been here a short while, whereas she'd lived in the library for years.

The willow tree whispered as a breeze blew through its leaves. She thought she saw a wisp of a cloud bear dangling from its draping branches.

Feeling braver, Kiela pushed forward through the ferns and underbrush until she reached the brambles that marked the overflow from her garden. She circled around until she reached the corner by the front—

—and stopped when she heard voices.

"If my boat had not encountered that unfortunate storm, then I would have all the proper documentation." It was Radane. She wasn't shouting, but Kiela knew that tone of voice. That was the voice of someone who was used to being obeyed.

She heard Larran reply, apologetic and polite. He couldn't allow her inside without that documentation. He was only obeying the law.

Kiela smiled. *Clever boy.*

"You do not want to obstruct me," Radane warned. "Trust me on this."

"It's not my home," Larran said. "I can't let you in. Check your laws on that. The homeowner needs to say it's all right—"

"Except in an official investigation," Radane said.

"And I'd be happy to help if you'd show me the paperwork. I'm just trying to do what's right, Radane. You wouldn't want a stranger marching into your home."

"Then where is the homeowner?" Radane demanded. "If she has nothing to hide, then why is she in hiding? Her absence alone is enough to qualify as obstruction—"

It was time to intervene. He'd kept Radane busy while the books were hidden, and that was victory enough. Kiela cast about for anything she could use to— Aha, there was a sprig of blue-black berries. She had no idea what kind they were, but it didn't matter. She broke off the tip of a branch with a cluster of berries and came around a corner. "Larran! The foraging trip was a success! I can mix these huckleberries with raspberries and— Oh, hello, Radane."

Larran broke into a relieved smile, which quickly turned into a frown. "Those aren't huckleberries. You really shouldn't mix them with anything if you don't want your customers' stomachs to, uh, rebel."

"Eeks." Kiela tossed the branch away and then smiled her best polite-librarian smile at Radane. "Would you like to try some jam that I guarantee will not cause any kind of rebellion?" She winced at herself. She shouldn't have said "rebellion" in front of Radane, but Larran had planted the word in her mind and it had just popped out. Hoping the imperial inspector didn't take offense, she pushed on. "I have raspberry and blueberry available. Larran, thank you so much for minding the shop. I really thought I'd find ingredients for a new flavor."

Radane raised both her eyebrows. "You were walking in the woods for jam ingredients?"

"It *is* a jam shop." Kiela pointed at the sign.

Larran chimed in. "You had one customer before Radane. He bought a jar of blueberry and said he hoped you'd make rhubarb jam next."

"I'll plant some rhubarb," Kiela said, trying her hardest to keep her voice level, casual, and calm. She clasped her hands behind her back so Radane wouldn't see them shaking. "Do you know anyone with seeds?" When Larran shook his head, Kiela repeated the question to Radane.

Radane was scowling. "Rhubarb is not my line of inquiry." She took a breath. "On the authority of the emperor, I demand to search the premises for contraband material."

"Okay," Kiela said.

About to launch into threats or arguments or whatever she'd planned to say, Radane halted. "I am sorry? 'Okay,' with no further objection?" She glared at Larran. "Why have you been blocking me for the past half hour if she has no objection?"

He shrugged. "If it were your house, I'd do the same. It's what good neighbors do. You didn't have permission to enter her house, and now you do."

He must have never told Radane how we met. He hadn't been so scrupulous about private property then. Kiela resisted a smirk. "Can I get you a glass of water?" she offered Radane. "Or jam on toast, though I do have to charge for that. Business, you know."

Glaring at her, Radane marched past Larran. He quickly moved out of her way to allow her inside. Larran met Kiela's eyes, and she mouthed, *Thank you.*

Kiela slipped inside, and she and Larran stood by the sink while Radane searched the cottage, beginning with every shelf in the jam shop. Finishing those shelves, she spotted the closed door to the bedroom and strode across the cottage. Kiela silently prayed to the memory of her parents that they'd taken every book, every scrap of paper, and every note with the crates. *Of course we did.* She wouldn't have been given responsibility for the entire Natural Sciences section of the Great Library if she had ever proven negligent with details. She'd never once misplaced a book or manuscript—why would she think she'd start now?

Radane rooted through the bedroom while Kiela and Larran stood in the doorway, watching as she flung Kiela's parents' quilts, looked under the mattress, and probed at each board in the floor to see if any were loose.

"What are you looking for?" Larran asked mildly.

"Hiding places," Radane said shortly.

"I have nothing to hide," Kiela said.

"Someone on this island does," Radane said, "and I will not rest until I find it."

That . . . wasn't good. "I can assure you—"

Radane stomped out of the bedroom, pushing between Kiela and Larran. She began opening every cabinet in the kitchen. She pulled out Kiela's parents' cookbook. "Aha! What is this?" She slammed it down on the table.

Kiela started forward. "Careful. That's—"

Radane flipped through the pages so fast that one ripped.

"It's my parents'!" Kiela ached to grab it out of her hands. To be that careless with a book, especially a book that had belonged to her parents, the memory of what they'd written, with love, with exhaustion, with whatever they'd felt when they'd recorded those recipes. "A cookbook. Just a cookbook."

"They appear to be spells." Radane slapped her hand on an open page.

"Those are a list of ingredients for cakes and soups."

"They could be in code."

"If they are, I don't know it," Kiela snapped. "And my parents are dead. That's my legacy you're handling. Show some care."

Radane slammed the cookbook shut. "I will be confiscating it."

Kiela's hands curled into fists, and she wanted to yell. No one took books without her permission, especially someone who did not know how to handle them properly. Outside, the wind blew a vine over the window, and a shadow momentarily crossed the kitchen. It reminded her of Caz, and she exhaled slowly.

The cookbook isn't what I need to protect, she reminded herself.

"Confiscate it if you must, but I expect it to be returned in the same condition," Kiela said. "It's brittle, and it's one of a kind. It must be treated with care."

Radane tossed her fire-red hair. "I will do what I must to fulfill my duty."

Larran asked gently, "What is it you're afraid of?"

Recoiling, Radane glared at him. "How dare you. I am an imperial inspector. When I speak, when I act, when I do my duty, I am embodying the glory and power of the empire."

"In my experience, when one of my merhorses is aggressive, tossing around his weight, acting like he's the leader of the herd when he isn't, it's out of fear." His voice was gentle, and Kiela thought this must be how he tamed his merhorses, with kindness and understanding. "I've seen young merhorses full of spitfire attack ocean waves. The water just breaks around them."

"Are you saying I'm like an aggressive fish?"

"Merhorses, or more technically 'hippocampi,' are mammals," Kiela supplied. When they both looked at her, she said, "Marine mammals. Not fish. It's how they're classified based primarily on how they breathe combined with how they bear young. Fish lay eggs."

Larran looked pleased that she knew this.

"I did some reading," she told him.

Radane pounced on that. "In this spellbook?"

"Cookbook," Kiela corrected. "And no, back when I was a kid in school. I was born here, grew up here, and went to school in the village." She left out the piece about how they'd left for Alyssium when she was nine. It wasn't a lie to omit it, and the less Radane knew about Kiela's background with spellbooks, the better. Let her think Kiela had lived here her whole life. "This cottage was my childhood home. My parents moved here when they first got married. They were born on Caltrey too. Met when they were kids on a fishing boat." She remembered that story—her father had wanted to see the stars from out on the sea, but his parents worked in an orchard. They didn't have their own boat, and they thought it silliness to borrow one for something as frivolous as stargazing, and so her mother had invited him on her parents' boat. Her mother's mother, whom Kiela remembered as a tiny, wrinkled woman with a terrible singing voice, had been a fisherman, and she'd been planning a night-fishing expedition—there was a particular kind of fish that was most active at night. Kiela's mom and dad had both been eleven years old, and her dad had always claimed that that was when he'd fallen in love, under the stars while the fish jumped in the moonlight. Kiela couldn't help but look at Larran as she remembered that story. She wondered if he ever rode his merhorse out under the night stars.

"Put another way," Larran said, "go softer, and you'll find that island folk *want* to help out. Order them about, and they'll bristle. I've known these people my whole life, and they're good people. But we've our pride. Treat us like criminals, and we'll push back."

"You don't push back against the Crescent Islands Empire," Radane said. She slid the cookbook into a pouch at her waist, with who-knew-what-else that could stain or damage the pages.

Kiela ordered her fists to unclench. *Say nothing. Do nothing. Think of Caz and Meep.*

"When the rogue sorcerer is found, your property will be returned," Radane said. "Unless it is determined that you aided the sorcerer. If you are concealing him or her, all of your property"—she gestured to the cottage, the shop, the garden—"will belong to the empire."

As Radane strode out of the cottage, Kiela felt Larran's hand on her shoulder. It was warm, heavy, and comforting, and it kept her from screaming or, worse, hurling a jar of jam at Radane's retreating figure. Neither of them spoke as the imperial inspector walked into the greenery, and Radane did not look back.

"Thank you," Kiela said.

"I couldn't save your cookbook," Larran said. "Not without making it worse."

She shook her head. "You did right. There was nothing either of us could do. Imperial investigators have virtually unlimited power." She didn't need to consult a law book to know that. Once, an entire wing of the sixth floor of the Great Library was sealed by investigator order. No one, not even the assigned librarian, was allowed in the stacks for thirteen months. When the wing was at last unsealed, it was discovered that the investigators had torn pages from one-of-a-kind, irreplaceable books and burned them in a cauldron they'd brought for that exact purpose. No one ever discovered why the books had been condemned, but librarians spoke of it in hushed whispers ever since.

Feeling as if her heart were clenched inside a fist, Kiela leaned against Larran. He wrapped his arms around her. "It's my fault she's here," Larran said.

"It's no one's fault. It's sheer bad luck."

But her being here meant that Kiela couldn't be. *We can't stay.* Everyone would be safer if she took all evidence of spellcasting far away from Caltrey. But where could she go? And when should she leave? If she left immediately, it would just cause suspicion to rain down on everyone who'd befriended her.

Like Larran.

Unsure what to do, she just stood still, within Larran's arms, looking out at the greenery, and tried not to wish that Radane's ship hadn't sunk so close to home.

CHAPTER TWENTY-SIX

Without the spellbooks safe in their crates around her, Kiela couldn't sleep. She tried valiantly, curled up in soft quilts made by her mother and her mother's mother, but she woke at every hoot of an owl, every blast of wind through the chimney, and every creak of the shutters.

She hated that she was alone. In the library, she never was. Even if she didn't speak to the other librarians, she'd hear them murmur, hear the whir of the lifts, hear the echo of distant footsteps from another floor. And always there was Caz, somewhere nearby, swinging himself between the shelves.

Lying awake in the darkness, she wished she could check on him and Meep, but she didn't dare. Radane could be lurking in the forest beyond the garden, waiting for Kiela to make a rash move like that. She had no way of knowing how suspicious the imperial investigator was, and she didn't fool herself into thinking she was safe just because Radane had walked away. Any second, she could return and have her arrested. The local police would obey her—they'd have no choice. Punishment would fall on them and all of Caltrey if they didn't comply.

The revolutionaries must have failed.

If they'd won, they would have stripped the imperial investigators of their unchecked power, and they would have eliminated the laws against non-approved spellwork. Kiela wondered how bad it must be in the capital now. She'd read enough history to know that the retaliation for a failed revolution would be swift and brutal.

She wondered which noble or general had claimed the throne after the emperor's death and then decided she didn't care. All she cared about was how far she'd have to go for her and the plants and the books to be safe. Was any place safe anymore? Even an obscure outer island like Caltrey wasn't far enough to escape the imperial reach.

Where could she go?

She didn't know the other islands or anyone on them. She didn't want to start again—where would she live? How would she eat? Where could she go where she could ensure that Caz, Meep, and the books were safe?

At some point, she must have slept, because she woke in a knot of quilts with all the same worries swirling through her mind.

The birds were barely awake, and the sun hadn't peeked through the branches, but Kiela rose anyway. The early morning had a chill bite to it, with wisps of mist and dew thick around the cottage, and she put on a woven blouse and thick skirt that was as soft as a blanket. Once the sun was out, it would warm, but for now . . . She couldn't stay in bed with her thoughts a second longer anyway. She had to go through the motions of an ordinary day, at least until she could be certain she could slip away to the painted cave.

Watching the woods for any hint of Radane, Kiela picked a basket of raspberries and wished she could stay. Oh, the things she'd do! First off, she'd begin by identifying other berries for new flavors of jam: strawberries, blackberries, boysenberries (and making sure none were poisonous). She'd buy apples from an orchard owner and try to make apple jam. Secretly or not secretly, she'd heal all the orchards on the island and restart all the magical springs. Eventually, hopefully, she'd find a way to help the merhorses bear their young again. Maybe even discover how to protect Caltrey from the worsening storms. And how to feed the winged cats. She'd spend more time with Bryn, Eadie, and Ulina. And Larran. There was so much she hadn't said to Larran. He'd helped her without even knowing what was in the crates or what he risked or why. Who did that? Who was so kind, so trusting, so selfless? Only Larran.

She was crying as she stirred sugar into the raspberries. Tears fell into the bowl, and she quickly leaned back and wiped her cheeks. She didn't want to add extra salt to the jam.

I can't stay. No matter how much I want to.

Kiela was sweeping the floor when she heard voices drift through the open window—familiar voices, talking as they approached, their words blending like bird calls. Familiar, worried voices.

Wiping her cheeks to make sure there was no evidence of her earlier tears, she hurried outside as Bryn, Eadie, and Ulina emerged from the greenery—Bryn in her baker's apron, Eadie in another splendid hat, Ulina in her many-sleeve blouse, and all of them with anxious, concerned looks on their faces, as if they didn't know what they'd find at the old cottage.

Kiela tried to gather herself to welcome them with as much cheerfulness as she could manage, but Bryn rushed forward and hugged her. "You're all right! We wanted to come yesterday, as soon as the inspector left the bakery, but—"

"I didn't think it would be wise," Eadie interrupted. "I've dealt with these types before. They see everything as suspicious. If we'd rushed here—"

Bryn cut back in. "We didn't want to make anything worse for you. But we're so sorry you had to go through it alone." She hugged Kiela again. She smelled like fresh bread and cinnamon. Kiela squeezed her back awkwardly and hoped she didn't have any raspberry on her. She'd been embraced more in these past couple days than in the prior several years. It was . . . nice. Very nice.

They were worried about me. Me, who they barely know. Me, who endangered all of them. "Is the bakery . . . Did Radane . . ." She didn't know how to ask what she wanted to ask. Did Radane find the pine cone remedies? Was Bryn in trouble? Were any of them? Where was the investigator now?

Ulina patted Kiela's back with three of her arms. "It's over now."

No, it isn't. She didn't know how to tell them that there could be worse to come. She thought of the librarian who'd created Caz, who'd most likely burned with the manuscripts and tapestries in the once-beautiful North Reading Room. She wondered if Caz had realized her fate.

Eadie snorted and rolled her eyes at Ulina. "It isn't over. And if you think it is, then you're so adorably naïve that I'm going to pinch your cheeks and offer you a candy. You know that investigator won't give up. She can't. She sailed into a storm and sank her ship. It doesn't matter that the empire caused the storms—they don't forgive mistakes. After a disaster like that, she has to produce a result. Arresting a rogue sorcerer will buy her forgiveness. She can't afford to fail."

Ulina asked, "How do you know that? You're just guessing. When she doesn't find anything, she'll leave. She's not going to manufacture—"

"She took my cookbook," Kiela said. "As evidence."

"She was very interested in mine as well," Bryn said. "Only when I pointed out that baking was my livelihood did she leave them alone."

Eadie asked, "Your remedies . . . Were they . . ."

"It was my parents' cookbook," Kiela said. "None of Caz's family remedies were in it."

"Your parents' . . ." Bryn repeated. "Oh, I'm so sorry."

Kiela told herself not to cry again. She didn't need the cookbook. She had her memories, and they'd been sharper recently than before she came to Caltrey. Losing the cookbook shouldn't feel so much like losing a piece of her past, but it did.

"And Caz?" Eadie asked. "What did she think of Caz? Investigators aren't much for nuance or for explanations. My husband and me . . . this was back a few years before he died . . . We'd latched on to this plan to market our work beyond Caltrey, to other islands . . ."

"Eadie's husband was a woodcarver, and Eadie a painter," Ulina put in. "You should see the work they created together—beautiful. I have a seagull they gifted me."

"The third island we visited, an imperial investigator was looking to make a name for himself," Eadie said. "He claimed we were smugglers. Accused us of stashing illegal mind-altering herbs within our sculptures. He confiscated them and smashed them open, and of course found nothing, but we were in no way compensated. In fact, he charged us for tax evasion because we did not complete the paperwork for the sale of goods—because he'd taken them before we could sell them. My husband wouldn't carve after that. Seeing his creations destroyed . . ." Eadie sighed heavily. "Oh, we tried to report that odious investigator, but that went nowhere."

Kiela wasn't surprised by that. Imperial investigators were nearly untouchable. "I'm sorry for what happened. And for your husband."

Eadie smiled. "Thank you, my dear. It was a while ago, but I still miss him. Sometimes I sit on my porch and have a chat with him, as if he were still there. Extra bonus: my neighbor can't stand it when I do that, but I always tell him I'm not talking to him and it's rude to butt into other people's conversations. But my point is that I don't think Radane is done yet."

"You may be right," Ulina admitted.

Kiela took a deep breath. "That's why I need to leave."

The other women drew closer to her, until Kiela realized they'd encircled her, consciously or unconsciously protecting her from anything beyond them. It felt like an embrace without being touched.

"You've only just come home," Eadie said. "You can't leave."

"Absolutely!" Bryn said, nearly a shout. A bird startled on a nearby tree, and Kiela caught a glimpse of its apple-blossom tail as it flew deeper into the forest. "You have a shop, and you've already made your mark, which means you belong here."

"You need to stay with the Pine Cone Coven," Ulina said.

"Society," Eadie corrected.

Kiela's eyes filled, and she blinked hard. "I'm not . . ."

Bryn poked her shoulder. "And what about Larran? You can't just leave him. I've seen the way he looks at you. He'll be crushed."

She felt herself blush. "He doesn't look at me in any particular way. He's just a nice person who sometimes feels sorry for me." Maybe they'd almost had a moment, or almost had a few moments, but that didn't mean they had any kind of relationship. With her responsibilities, she didn't have the luxury of that kind of sentimentality. Never mind all the mushy thoughts she'd been having lately. "He'll forget me as soon as I sail away."

"Oh, sweetie," Eadie said.

Ulina kept opening and closing her mouth, fishlike, as if she wanted to say something but didn't know which words to say. "You don't know him like we do. You should know . . ."

Eadie interrupted her. "We should have this conversation over tea. And toast with jam? Can we buy some of your raspberry jam?"

Kiela ushered them inside the cottage. "You don't need to buy it."

"As your business partner, I say you shouldn't argue when people want to give you money," Bryn told her. She softened her words with a smile as she stepped inside. Kiela backed up so that Eadie could squeeze through the door after Bryn. The shelves rattled as Eadie clip-clopped into the kitchen.

While Kiela lit the stove, Eadie filled a kettle with water. Ulina retrieved teacups from the cabinet and set them on the table. The four chairs were placed around, and in a few short minutes, the water was hot, a loaf that Bryn produced from her vast pockets was sliced and warmed, and the air smelled like pine tea, raspberries, and bread.

It was all so homey and lovely that Kiela wanted to cry again. *What's wrong with me?* She rarely ever cried. She wasn't an ups-and-downs emotions kind of person. Usually she was quiet and calm and even-keeled.

For a little bit, while the tea steeped, they chatted about inconsequential things. Bryn talked about Tobin forgetting the fountain was functional again and falling straight into it, and how all the winged cats would cluster around the fountain every morning to drink from the cold, clear water. Ulina told a story that her great-aunt had told her, about how the fountain had come to be—the man who'd commissioned it had been saved by a mermaid once, when his ship was capsized by one of the giant squids that lived out in the deep. He'd been responsible for the law that prohibited gill nets to be used on Caltrey. Before then, fisherfolk would leave nets in the water unsupervised, suspended off of jetties, and occasionally merfolk, particularly curious merbabies, would become tangled in them, leading to tragedies. The fountain was installed to celebrate the law, and his wife had cast the spell to make the water flow. Back in those days, that wasn't forbidden. "Used to be, islanders looked out for one another," Ulina said, "and the empire let us be. Better that way."

"You can't let Radane hear you say that," Kiela said. "You heard her talk about the uprising—the revolution. The fact that imperial inspectors still exist means it failed. And post-revolt, she'll come down extra hard on anyone who says anything that sounds anti-empire."

Ulina snorted. "Never been a law against being opinionated."

"Yet," Kiela said. She had no idea what laws were being passed in the wake of a failed revolution. "We can't take chances. That's why I have to go. If I stay—"

"Are you happy here?" Bryn asked. "Do you want to stay?"

"Yes," Kiela said. Her voice was a whisper.

She thought of her parents and wondered if they'd have understood why she felt that way—they'd been so excited to leave, so happy in Alyssium, so certain they were in the right place to pursue their family's dreams. Initially, she'd only come back to Caltrey because she had no other choice. She'd started the shop because she hadn't wanted to starve. But now . . . *It's more than that.* She thought of the garden and the orchard and the willow in the woods and all she'd done in such a short period of time. *It's not just that either*. It was Bryn and Eadie and Ulina and, of course, Larran. And it was the way she felt closer to her parents now in a place they'd wanted to leave than she had in a place they'd chosen for themselves.

She answered again louder, "Yes."

"Larran wants you to stay," Eadie declared.

"That boy . . ." Ulina shook her head. "He hasn't had an easy time of it. His parents . . ." She trailed off and shook her head again.

"I know they weren't kind to him," Kiela said. "He's told me as much."

Eadie snorted. "Not kind. Ha! You're sugarcoating it, Ulina. Hasn't had 'an easy time'? She should know the truth, as tragic and ugly and terrible as it is."

Ulina stirred her tea with one hand and spread jam on toast with another. "Larran's parents were dung in the form of people. Exactly the kind that should never have kids. If we'd realized sooner . . . Well, we didn't. They hid it, and poor little Larran didn't know he could trust other adults for help. How could he have known? The ones who were supposed to care for him, protect him, love him . . . If they were still here now . . ."

"Here's the long and the short of it," Eadie said. "His father was a yeller. We all knew that. We'd hear him from the street, but there wasn't a thing anyone could do about it. I remember asking him about it once—I was always the nosy type—and he said he had a right to his emotions and it was healthy to get them out. Besides, it let his family know where he stood. It was a form of love, he said. If you don't yell, how do they know you care? Healthier for all of them to let it out, rather than bottle it up."

Bryn snorted. "Self-indulgent bullcrap."

"We all considered it a different parenting style," Eadie said. "But yes, I believe you should show *more* control with the people you love, not less."

Kiela couldn't think of a single time she'd ever heard either of her parents yell. Maybe once, when she'd almost fallen off a bridge into a canal . . . But never in anger, at least not in any of her memories. They'd be disappointed sometimes, yes, but no worse than that.

"Some people are yellers," Eadie said. "It's not pleasant. Heck, I've lost my temper a few times. Also, I can be a bit too blunt, and excuse it by saying I'm just an honest person, but if I'm *truly* being honest, sometimes blunt is just mean. Honesty can be an excuse for bullying."

Ulina patted her mane. "You try. Larran's father didn't try."

"Nobody knew it wasn't just yelling," Bryn said, "or so I've been told. Everyone swears that no one knew what was happening or had a clue as to what was coming—they kept it behind closed doors, and no one ever was allowed to see how much darkness that family was hiding."

Kiela wondered if her parents had suspected. They'd allowed young Larran to use their cove, which implied they must have known things weren't right in his family. "What happened?"

"It wasn't pretty," Eadie warned. "One night, after a day of fishing when the fish weren't schooling—none of the fisherfolk came back with anything in their nets. It was dinnertime . . ." She trailed off, as if searching for the words that would make the story nicer.

Bryn cut in. "There's no gentle way to say it: he killed her."

"Larran's father knocked his mother down the stairs," Eadie said. "She hit her head. Later, he told everyone that he didn't mean it. Shouted in the street that he couldn't have helped himself, that he felt what he felt, and he didn't intend to hurt her . . ."

"A few days later, he took his boat out, and it drifted back to shore empty," Ulina said. "His body later washed up on the rocks. We don't know if it was an accident or intentional, but at age thirteen, Larran became an orphan. A merhorse herder took him in, but only a handful of years later . . . there was a sudden storm, and he drowned. Larran was the one who found him, tried to save him, but he was past saving." She sighed heavily.

"Boy has seen a lot of bad things," Eadie said. "He's worked hard to be the very opposite of his parents in every way, but he's careful with his heart. Never lets himself become close to anyone."

"Until you," Bryn said with a smile.

Kiela shook her head. He'd been through so much . . . *Poor Larran*. But surely, *she* wasn't the first person he'd cared about. She didn't even know if he did care about her. All they'd had were a few moments. He'd been kind to her because of Sian. He felt gratitude and maybe friendship. *It could have become more, if I could have stayed. But I can't.* "He doesn't . . . We're not . . ."

"You can hear it when he talks about you," Bryn said.

Kiela blinked at her. "He talks about me?"

"He comes for a cinnamon roll nearly every morning," Bryn said. "He's mentioned you every single time. Often it's a stray thought, like wondering whether you saw the sunrise, whether you like tomato sandwiches, or how you feel about merhorses, but I can tell you that he's never acted like this before."

Eadie rapped her knuckles on the table. "We're not saying you should stay because our boy is sad and needs fixing. Gah, that would be a terrible reason. Never think you need to fix a lover. You should stay because there's a chance you two could make each other happy, and that's a special thing."

"It's worth taking a risk," Ulina said.

"I can't endanger everyone," Kiela said. "Not for a relationship that may or may not exist, that may never be anything. You all could be reading into what isn't there."

"Then talk to him," Bryn said, as if it were the simplest thing in the world.

"Unless you were planning to leave immediately?" Ulina asked.

"I don't recommend that, if you want to avoid raising Radane's suspicions," Eadie said. "You don't want her chasing you. So, go talk to Larran. Bring him something from your garden—that way, no one will question your visit." She smiled. "Talk to him, and see if you've a reason to stay."

"Besides us, of course," Bryn said, refilling everyone's teacups. "Obviously, we're an excellent reason to stay, but if you need additional motivation . . ."

Ulina grinned at her. "He does have nice eyes."

The other two women nodded.

CHAPTER TWENTY-SEVEN

Carrying a basket of tomatoes, Kiela picked her way down the cliff stairs. The sea breeze was playful today, dancing through her blue hair and tickling her neck. All the pink roses were in bloom, and their scent was heavy in the air, tinged with the ever-present scent of seaweed that had been soaking in the sun. She remembered her father had hated that smell—*overcooked salad,* he'd called it—but she thought it smelled wonderful. *It smells like summer.* With the cloudless blue overhead, it was hard to believe that anything awful could ever happen here.

Like what Larran's father did.

She reached the beach and, shielding her eyes, looked out toward the end of the jetty. *Bryn, Eadie, and Ulina are wrong. He doesn't need me.* He had his merhorses. He had friends. He knew nearly every islander. She wasn't anything special to him.

Out in the waves, Larran rode on the back of a golden merhorse. Spray flew all around them, sparkling in the air. He was turned away from her, but she saw the shape of his shoulders and the muscles on his arms as he steered Sian into the breaking foam of a swell.

Kiela drew a tomato out of her basket and held it in the air. She didn't know if the merhorse could come out of the water—did they beach themselves like walruses? How much time could they spend out of the water? Did they like it? She'd have to ask Larran, after she convinced him there was nothing between them and therefore she wasn't ruining any potential future by fleeing. Or . . . maybe she should start with questions about merhorse behavior.

She heard him shout, startled, as Sian charged toward the shore.

He saw her a second later, and she couldn't help but smile—he was smiling, his hand raised in a wave, as Sian leapt through the waves to the shore. Kiela kicked off her boots and waded into the shallows. She'd worn her favorite of her mother's old island dresses, the one with the soft white bodice and a blue patchwork skirt with silver thread. She hiked her skirt up to her knees to keep the silver-ribbon hem from being soaked. Today the water was as warm as breath.

Sian plucked the tomato out of her hand and then stuck her head into the basket. Kiela laughed. "Sorry, is it okay—" she asked as Larran said, "Thank you for bringing her a treat."

"Thank *you* for—" She cut herself off and glanced at his house. "For yesterday." It was safer to not be more specific than that.

"She's not here," Larran said firmly. "We never . . . That is, she was never in my bed, except for that first night, when she was unconscious, but after she woke . . ." He repeated, "She's not here and hasn't been here for a while. I just want to be clear about that."

He hadn't welcomed her back, and she wasn't sharing his bed. He'd chosen Kiela's side, despite the fact that she'd clearly broken the law and endangered all her new friends. "Thank you," Kiela said again, as if those two words could encompass everything.

"Of course," he said, as if those two words explained everything.

They stared at each other for a moment, while the golden merhorse rooted through the basket. She huffed, snorted, and munched with so much enthusiasm that Kiela started to laugh—until Sian grabbed the basket with her teeth and tried to yank it off Kiela's arm, knocking her off-balance. Kiela yelped.

"Sian, back!" Larran barked as he lunged forward to grab Kiela before she could tip.

The horse-fish tossed her mane, whickered, and raced off into deeper water.

"I'm fine," Kiela said, regaining her balance without, thankfully, splashing into the water this time. *I should bring spare clothes every time I come to visit.* Except this could be her last visit.

He hadn't released her arms, and she didn't want him to.

Staring up into his eyes, Kiela tried to think of all the words she'd planned out on the walk through the greenery and down the cliff stairs. She was going to remind him that they hadn't known each other long, even if he did remember her from years ago, and that they didn't know each other well. She wasn't ending anything because nothing had ever begun.

"Are you all right?" he asked.

"Yes, fine, of course."

"After yesterday. Are you all right?"

He was looking into her eyes so intensely. She gazed back. "Yes."

"Is Caz all right?" he asked.

And with that, she couldn't say any of the words that she'd wanted to say. That question—the fact that he chose to ask about her best friend, the fact that he genuinely cared as he waited for her answer—it undid her.

She rose up on her tiptoes in the wet sand and kissed him.

He froze, his lips motionless and his eyes wide open, as if he hadn't expected this—how could he, when she hadn't even planned to? She nearly pulled away, but then he was kissing her back, suddenly, as if he'd snapped awake after a thunderclap.

He pulled her closer, and the seawater from his chest soaked through the fabric of her dress. She didn't care. He tasted like the ocean, and his lips were warm.

The kiss ended. But he didn't pull back. He was only an inch away, and she was still breathing his breath. He was looking at her as if she was all that existed on the entire island.

"I came to tell you that I have to leave," Kiela said.

"What?" Larran said.

She took a deep breath and took a step backward and then another step until she was out of the water and on the sand. It was easier to think when he wasn't so close. "I said I have to leave Caltrey. With Caz. And Meep. Because we can't stay."

He blinked at her as if her words were in another language. "Why?"

"Because I'm a librarian."

"Oh."

She wanted to kiss him again. It was odd how much she wanted to—she wasn't used to her lips telling her brain what to do, but she wanted to feel his body against hers, and she wanted his hands to touch her.

He frowned. "So, why?"

"Because I'm also a thief and a liar." Kiela made herself take another step backward, farther away from him, and then another toward the shore until she was standing on the pebbles beyond the touch of the waves. "The emperor was thrown from a window— not by me. I didn't have anything to do with that. I'd never even met the emperor. Saw him once, in a parade, or at least his ship— twice a year, he'd parade through the canals of Alyssium, and this was while I was at the university and usually I'd remember to stay late to study so I wouldn't have to navigate the crowds, but this one time I forgot and . . ." She took a breath. "The night the emperor was killed, there were fires. The library began to burn. Everyone else had already evacuated, but Caz and I . . . We fled when it began to burn, with as many books as we could save. The only place I could think to come was here. Home."

"Then the crates . . ."

"Spellbooks."

"Ah."

"I'm the rogue sorcerer that Radane is searching for," Kiela said. "Well, sort of. At least I read through several of the books and cobbled together a few practical spells, like the one with the pine cone that heals trees, but I'm not really a sorcerer."

He was still staring, but now she couldn't read his expression. "You're not."

"Right."

"You're a librarian."

"Yes."

"Who saved her books," Larran said.

"I like the word 'saved,' but given that I didn't actually bring them back, I think the empire might choose the word 'stole.' You see, I thought it had fallen. The empire. I thought the revolutionaries had taken control, and eventually I'd reach out and, if the Great Library had been restored . . ."

He stepped toward her, coming out of the shallows onto the sand, closing the gap between them that she'd created. "I think you were incredibly brave."

She gave a hiccup sort of laugh. "Oh, yes, I bravely ran away."

"You did." He was serious. "You saved yourself, your friend, and you came here and saved us."

She felt herself blushing and knew her cheeks had to be tinged purply. "Okay, that last bit is somewhat of an overstatement. I made jam and some sticky pine cones."

"You saved Sian's life. And I am guessing you are responsible for Meep?"

"They were an accident. But yes." She supposed all of that was good, to balance out the bad of the theft and the lawbreaking, and he didn't even know about the merbaby and the forest spirits. But none of that changed the fact that she'd endangered him, her friends, and everyone on Caltrey by exposing them to Radane's investigation. "I don't regret any of it. It can't continue, though, not now with an imperial investigator on the island."

"She'll lose interest," Larran said. "And when she leaves Caltrey, everything will return back to normal, and you don't have to be afraid—"

"The only way it returns to normal is if I leave," Kiela said. "If I stay and Radane realizes what I've done, everyone in Caltrey will be suspect. Everyone who has been kind to me will be named con-spirators. And it will be worse now—the imperials need to prove they're still in power. They'll come down hard. Fines. Worse."

Larran shook his head. "She won't."

"You don't know that. She saw me help Sian. She doesn't have proof yet, but my pine cones . . . And the fountain! Someone could have seen me. If she talks to enough people, the right people, if she asks the right questions, applies enough pressure . . . I thought it would be safe enough this far from Alyssium. I didn't think anyone who'd care would come here. But she's here, and that's that. I have to come up with an excuse that won't sound suspicious and then leave, before I make everything worse."

"You want me to let you sail off and just shrug and say 'that's that'?"

Well, yes, she did. Or at least she had wanted that. Before they kissed. Before . . . "I don't want to leave." As she said it out loud, she realized how deeply true it was. The idea of sailing away from Caltrey, of leaving her parents' cottage, of never seeing Larran and Bryn and Eadie and Ulina, even little Tobin . . . She would never have believed how attached she could become in such a short amount of time. She wanted this to be her life, here on Caltrey, in her little cottage with her garden and her jam shop, with Caz and Meep, with the mermaid and her merbaby in the cove . . . She wanted to keep helping the tree guardians. She wanted to heal the rest of the orchards. She wanted to make sure the bird she'd acci-dentally created from an apple tree was okay. She wanted to help that customer with the waterless spring. She wanted to try to make cherry jam from Eadie's cherry trees. She wanted to ride Sian again out in the waves. And she wanted to kiss Larran more. Right now, please.

He'd stepped closer to her too. "Then don't leave."

"It's not so simple."

He was inches from her, not touching, but so close that she felt as if the air were vibrating between them. She barely heard the waves crashing at their feet or the gulls overhead. She wished the rest of the world could disappear, and it could be just this stretch of beach for just this stretch of time.

"Why can't it be?"

"Because. Empire. Laws. Really terrible punishments."

He kissed her first this time, and everything melted away as his arms wrapped around her. "Stay," he said, breathing the word into her.

"You don't want me to."

He kissed her neck, light kisses that made her breath catch. "I do."

"You don't know me. Not well enough."

His hands were on her back, and she'd never felt safer. If the earth fell from beneath their feet, she felt as if he'd hold her up. "I want to know you better," he said. He kissed her ear.

"No, you don't. I'm not friendly. I like to be alone."

"You can be alone with me."

She ran her hands up his neck and tangled her fingers in his hair. "That doesn't make sense."

"Sorry. You're right."

Kiela kissed him and forgot what she was going to say back. Something about how she wasn't really alone since she had Caz. Something about how she didn't want to be alone. Something about her parents or his parents or Radane or . . . "I like books too much."

He paused mid-kiss. "What?"

"You don't know me. So I'm telling you about me. So you'll know me and why it's better if I leave. I read and I forget anything else exists. And I don't forgive anyone who isn't careful with books. I hate people who tear out pages, who bend corners, who break the spines."

"Unforgivable," he agreed.

She pulled back and frowned at him. "Are you laughing at me?"

"Yes. These aren't flaws. They're just . . . you. And I like you. Very much."

She couldn't help but ask, "You do?"

He nodded. "As much as Sian likes tomatoes."

Kiela laughed and kissed him again and again, as the waves kissed their bare feet and the sea breeze danced around them and the sun shone down—and it all felt so eternal and so ephemeral at the same time.

CHAPTER TWENTY-EIGHT

As much as Kiela wanted to endlessly kiss Larran, it simply wasn't practical. She had books and plants to protect. She cradled his cheek with her hand. "Larran . . ."

He kissed her palm.

Thinking about how to say goodbye, she felt as if someone had reached into her rib cage and yanked out all the squishy bits. *I don't want to leave.* She wished she could say she didn't have to, that it would all be okay, and that there was nothing to worry about, but she couldn't. Instead, she said, "There are more tomatoes about to ripen on the vine, if you want them."

He leaned his forehead against hers softly. "Don't leave."

"I have to check on Caz."

"I'll go with you."

She wanted that, but she shook her head. "It'll draw too much attention. Do you ever leave your herd this time of day?"

He didn't answer. Instead, he asked, "Will you come back?"

She didn't know. "I'll try."

"Did you eat lunch? You should make sure you eat. And stay hydrated. Do you want some water before you go? Or tea? I can make tea. And sandwiches."

Kiela laughed, even though she felt like crying. She gently shoved him toward the water. "Feed your merhorses. They need you."

He turned back toward her. "I need you."

"You don't need me, and frankly I'd be a little uncomfortable if you did. We just met. You like me for unfathomable reasons."

Larran smiled. "Fine. But I like you a lot."

She blushed. "I like you too."

Kiela forced herself to cross the beach to the stairs. Glancing back, she saw Larran wading into the water—a half-dozen mer-horses bobbed in the waves just off shore. *He likes me a lot.*

She climbed the stairs and walked through the greenery. She was no closer to a solution to her problems, but a piece of her still felt like singing. She didn't, though. Obviously. Even as deliriously distracted as she felt, she was aware of the need for caution. She settled for humming softly as she reached her cottage and then strolled beyond it—just a casual walk in the woods for an ordinary shopkeeper or a jam-maker in need of ingredients.

Only when she was as certain as she could be that no one was following her did she make her way back to the cave with the painted flowers.

"Caz," she whispered as she slipped in between the rocks.

She waited an instant for her eyes to adjust to the dimmer light. A little louder: "Caz? Meep?"

Why aren't they answering? She felt fear creep up from her stomach and clutch her throat. She crept deeper into the cave. The air was cool and damp on her skin, and she tasted salt with every breath. Water lapped at the walls, echoing, and as her eyes adjusted, she saw the painted flowers flickering above.

The library boat was here, a shadow in the water. But where was—

She heard a muffled shout.

Hitching up her skirt, Kiela ran through the shallows toward the sound. Ahead, she saw a figure thrashing on the rocks in the far corner of the cave. Shadows flailed on the wall.

And she heard Caz: "Hold her down! Almost got it— Meep, don't poke her!"

On the ground, wrapped in line from the boat, was the imperial investigator. Her red hair stuck out at all angles, and a wad of cloth—it looked like a ripped piece of sail—was shoved in her mouth.

"What did you do!" Kiela cried.

"Kiela! You're here! Help us!"

They couldn't tie up an imperial investigator! This was a terrible, terrible idea. "I'm so sorry." Kiela dropped to her knees and yanked the bit of sail out of Radane's mouth.

"Did the mermaid find you?" Caz asked at the same time as Radane shouted, "Release me this instant, or you'll face the full force of imperial wrath!"

Meep stabbed the cloth with their prickles to pick it up, and then they shoved it back in Radane's mouth. Her shouts became muffled.

"We can explain," Caz said to Kiela.

"Meep," Meep agreed.

He repeated his question: "Did the mermaid find you?"

"She didn't," Kiela said. "I came to check on you."

"I sent her to— Never mind. You're here now. We caught Radane"—he gestured to the bound woman with his leaves—"sneaking into the cave. She said that nasty man, Fenerer, had seen us in the boat. We must have sailed right past his house, and he saw us and told her that we were acting suspicious and where we went, so she came here and—"

Kiela shook her head. "Please tell me you didn't attack an imperial investigator."

"We didn't attack an imperial investigator," Caz said, and held up his tendrils as if swearing an oath of truth.

"Then why—"

"Because Radane is *not* an imperial investigator."

Water lapped at the walls of the cave. Kiela stared at Caz, then at Radane. But . . . She'd said she was. She'd acted like one. Granted, there was no proof, but she had been in a shipwreck and lost all her belongings, so how could she have proof? "How do you know?"

"She wasn't trying to confiscate the spellbooks; she was trying to steal them."

"Meep," the cactus agreed.

Radane thrashed and mumbled through the gag.

Again, Kiela asked, "How do you know?" If Radane sneaked into the cave and was poking around the boat . . . wasn't that the action of an investigator? What made him think she was trying to steal them rather than—

"She tried to do a spell," Caz said.

Oh.

Kiela looked at Radane. Yeah, that wasn't something an investigator would do. Certainly not an honest one. She removed the gag. "Would you like to explain yourself?" she asked politely.

Spitting bits of fuzz onto the cave floor, Radane started babbling. "You can't possibly believe that. It's a plant! You can't take its word over mine. I have been granted authority—"

"You see why we gagged her," Caz said.

"Caz prefers 'he,' and Meep is 'they,'" Kiela said. "And I haven't heard anything that says you weren't casting a spell."

Radane glared at her, which was less effectual given that she was lying on her side, squirming like a trussed-up chicken. "He and they are mistaken. I was checking to see if it truly was a spell. I didn't want to act without full knowledge."

"You confiscated my parents' cookbook without any hesitation," Kiela said. Radane would have no need to read aloud any of the spells to know these were spellbooks. The word "spell" was literally in half the titles. Plus, open any of them, and she'd see the First Language. The spellbooks didn't try to hide what they were, which was why she'd kept them in a crate hidden beneath a tarp on the boat and quilts in the cottage. Kiela asked Caz, "Which spell did she try?"

Meep scurried over to the boat and returned with a book, open to a page three-quarters of the way in. Kiela thanked them, took it, and read. "Invisibility?" She had disregarded this volume because it wasn't nature-related. Looking closer, she saw it was more of a stealth kind of spell, to dampen one's footsteps and make clothes, eyes, and skin less reflective. It had a list of ingredients, including a very rare and expensive gem. Checking the spine, she saw it was aimed at hunters. The spell was designed to make it easier to sneak up on their prey. "Among other ingredients, she'd need a ruby with no inclusions, three carats, for it to work."

"See!" Radane said. "I wasn't casting a spell. I was merely reading out loud when your monstrosities jumped me—"

Caz reached toward her neck with a tendril, and Radane flopped onto her stomach. Meep butted against her bare wrist with their prickles. Radane yelped and flinched, and Caz used the moment to seize a necklace around Radane's neck. He pulled it out of her shirt to show the ruby pendant. "Well, look at that. Exactly the specific ingredient for the spell. What a coincidence."

Radane pressed her lips together and glared so hard that Kiela was half surprised that lightning didn't spark out of her eyes.

It was a highly improbable coincidence that Radane had chosen the one book in the collection with the one spell that used the very jewel she wore around her neck—a very expensive jewel that an imperial investigator had no business wearing in the first place. "Who are you?" Kiela asked her.

"I am an imperial investigator charged with—"

Caz leaned closer to her face. "Kiela is a nice person who doesn't think about extreme solutions to any situation. It didn't occur to her that the revolutionaries would throw the emperor out a window. Or that they'd allow anyone to burn the library. Or that anyone would really come after us. Yet here you are. I would like to point out, though, that if you are who you say you are, an imperial investigator who crashed on our island, then no one knows you are here. You could have drowned in the storm."

"The islanders know—"

"But they don't like you," Caz said. "They want you to leave, and if they think you left on your own after finding nothing more suspicious than a cookbook owned by a jam-maker, do you really think they'd ask questions?"

Kiela frowned. She wasn't certain what Caz was getting at, but it sounded an awful lot like he was about to threaten Radane with something dire. "Caz—" she began. The cactus poked her in the ankle.

He loomed closer to Radane's face and spread his leaves wide. "You'll note the water here is deep. Your body wouldn't even wash to shore. If we attached a few heavy rocks—"

Radane's eyes widened.

Appalled, Kiela said, "Caz!"

"I'm just explaining options to her," Caz said.

"We can't . . ." Kiela couldn't even say the word "murder." That was much too far. They should definitely not even be having this conversation.

Caz fixed his attention back on Radane. His leaves were still puffed up, and all his tendrils were vertical. "Kiela is my best friend."

"Meep!"

"And practically Meep's mother."

Kiela startled at that. She hadn't thought of herself as anyone's mother. Certainly she'd never acted or felt motherly toward the cactus. Was she supposed to? "I don't think—"

"If it makes you feel better, Meep says they consider you more of an aunt."

Okay, that was nice, but . . . *Stay focused. Potential murder talk here.* "Caz, we are absolutely not going to—"

"*You* aren't going to," Caz said. "You're going to sail the boat back to the cottage, put away the books, and then have lunch with your nice handsome neighbor. Meep and I are going to continue our conversation with our new friend, Radane."

"I'm not leaving if you're going to . . ." Kiela swallowed.

"Kiela . . ." Caz said.

"No." She began to tug at the ropes that bound Radane. "I don't know who you are or what you want, but you aren't an imperial investigator, and we aren't murderers. So we're going to have a conversation like civilized people, and you're going to tell us why you're on Caltrey and what you want. I am not letting my best friend commit an act he can't undo and will regret."

"Kiela . . ."

"We protect each other," she told him. "You caught her. Now it's my turn." She finished loosening the knots. She met Radane's eyes. "I am—or was—a librarian at the Great Library. Caz was my assistant. We escaped the fires and came to my childhood home. Since then, we've been doing our best to set up a life here. Your story now."

Radane pushed the ropes off her ankles and then sat up.

Kiela tensed, expecting her to attack. Or bolt. It entirely depended on what kind of person Radane was, and Kiela knew nothing about her except she'd been rude and hostile . . . *We're not murdering anyone. That's* not *what librarians do.* Bit of shelving, bit of researching, bit of underhanded violence? *No.*

Radane studied them without either attacking or bolting. Or jumping for the boat and the books. Kiela began to hope she'd made the right choice.

"My name isn't Radane. It's Ravandil Etra—"

A wave crashed within the cave, rocking the boat, and splashing into them. Kiela sputtered as she spat out seawater. Radane—or whoever she was—had been drenched. Caz was shrieking and trying to climb the cave wall, and Meep darted for the boat and, using their needles as if they were climbing picks, scurried up the mast.

A herd of merhorses stampeded into the cave. Water flew around them, and they neighed like they were trumpeting. Kiela spotted Larran riding one of them, silhouetted against the light from beyond the cave, looking like a hero from an ancient tale.

"Larran? What—"

The mermaid popped up in front of the herd.

"Oh no you don't," Caz said, and Kiela turned to see that Caz had wrapped his leaves around Radane's ankles. She'd begun to flee toward the cave entrance.

Half the herd beached themselves, blocking Radane's escape on land with their hooves and powerful tails, while the others blocked the exit by sea. Larran leapt off Sian's back and swam to the cave's shore. He climbed out. Dripping wet, he confronted Radane. At the same time, Larran said, "You can't arrest her! She's innocent!" as Caz shouted, "We're not finished here!" Kiela cried, "Everyone, calm down!" while the mermaid sounded a siren-like cry, the merhorses snorted and neighed, and the cactus shrieked, "Meep, meep, meep!"

Radane put her face in her hands and sat down hard on the shore.

Caz loosened his grip.

Larran held up one hand, and the merhorses began to calm. Seawater sloshed around them, but slowly began to steady. Meep quieted.

Radane's shoulders were shaking.

Was she . . . crying?

She's laughing.

Shaking her head, Radane looked up. "I escaped the best-trained guards in the entire empire, a violent mob, and every single highly qualified bounty hunter sent to retrieve me, and I'm captured by a librarian, two plants, and a farmer?" She laughed harder.

Kiela said as patiently as if she were talking with a toddler having a tantrum, "Radane. Tell us who you are and why you're here."

Wiping her eyes, Radane sobered, straightened her shoulders, and said, "I'm Ravandil Etra L'sari, and I'm the emperor's heir. And I'm here because I want to be neither empress nor executed."

CHAPTER TWENTY-NINE

"Meep?" the cactus said.

"Exactly," Caz said.

Larran snorted. "You . . . what?"

Kiela studied her. "Unlikely. The emperor's heir is his firstborn son, Umele S'rov Vironin. Second in line is his daughter, the next eldest, Seviene Nicla Edin Lariviron, followed by his brother, his sister-in-law, their children."

"I was sixteenth," Radane said. "It wasn't ever supposed to come to me, and I don't want it. I lied about what happened in Alyssium—"

Caz muttered, "There's a surprise."

"The revolutionaries were victorious, and the generals in charge of the military, in their zeal to prove their loyalty to the cause, began executing anyone with any claim to the throne whatsoever. Whether the new government wants this or not is debatable and also immaterial, since the end result is the same. The politicians among the revolutionaries are still establishing control and cannot afford to alienate their military leaders. To put it more simply, it's an unhealthy time to be related to the former regime. Lucky me, I'm a distant cousin on my grandmother's side, and I was in training to be a wind-speaker. In fact, I had completed my third-year exams and was waiting for my first assignment on a ship—but that's all over now, because someone traced a family tree and decided that a short-lived marriage was close enough. A faction of loyalists want to use me as a figurehead so they have an excuse to throw the islands into civil war, and the revolutionaries—who have not crowned an emperor but instead installed a parliament—don't want the loyalists to have any kind of legitimacy whatsoever and are willing to turn a blind eye to any actions taken by their more bloodthirsty factions." She spat all of this out with the bitterness of someone who has been holding words inside for much too long. "I think the empire will be far better off without an emperor or empress, but no one ever asked me my opinion. They just assumed because some relative I never met was briefly married to someone . . . I didn't want to be an excuse for more bloodshed, so I fled."

Kiela stared at her. "You have a ruby because you're high-level nobility."

She nodded.

"And you spelled your hair red so you'd look like low-level nobility."

"No one glanced twice at me," Radane said. "The guards did not know my face. Just my wealth. Even guards I have known since I was a child."

"Your family owned the boat that sank?" Kiela guessed.

"One of my aunts was an imperial investigator," Radane said. "She gifted me the boat when the revolutionaries disbanded the office of investigations and confiscated their badges. The new government plans to install their own people, after they finish overhauling the laws, but it's a lot of change all at once. Everything is in chaos, but without an heir to the imperial throne, it's bureaucratic chaos, not violence in the streets."

Larran laid a wet hand on Kiela's shoulder. "Then the empire won't be after Kiela? No one will arrest her?" *I can stay?* she wondered. *I can unpack the books, make my jam, share a dinner with Larran . . .*

Radane shook her head. "Yes to the first, but the second . . . As far as I know, the laws have not been overwritten yet. What you have done here"—she gestured toward the boat with the books and the sentient succulent—"could still get you arrested, tried, and found guilty. But I am not the one who'd do it."

Using his leaves, Caz was squeezing saltwater out of his root ball. "So I was right: you were trying to steal the spellbooks for yourself."

"Only the useful ones," Radane said.

"All books are useful," Kiela and Caz said simultaneously.

"Uh-huh, definitely librarians," Radane said. "I needed spells that would help me hide. I do not wish to ever go back to that life. I want what you have. An ordinary life without the constant fear of assassination."

That . . . sounded like a very reasonable wish.

"How can we trust you?" Caz said. "You threatened to have us arrested and punished, even though the revolutionaries won—which, by the way, yay."

Radane countered, "How can I trust *you*? You threatened to murder me and hide my body."

Larran looked startled.

Caz waved his leaves at him. "Not Kiela. She has more morals than common sense." To Radane, he said, "Can you prove you are who you say you are this time?"

She spread her hands. "No. I have nothing but what I was wearing when the storm hit."

"You say you're a wind-speaker," Caz said. "Why didn't you spell the storm away?"

"A single wind-speaker cannot work such large magic," Radane said. "It requires multiple spellcasters to affect a storm. Best I can do solo is summon a pleasant breeze."

Kiela glanced at Caz. She wanted to trust Radane, but she had already lied once and taken it to an extreme—the cookbook was a particularly unforgivable line to cross. She'd caused a lot of distress in people and plants who Kiela cared about.

Bobbing in the cave, the mermaid cooed, "You are you."

"What?" Caz asked.

"You are you."

Kiela understood. *Take the librarian out of the Great Library, she's still a librarian. Take a noble out of her palace . . .* She looked at Radane. "You're still you. When a high noble bathes, how many people must be present?"

"Two," Radane said. "One to watch inward: to regulate the water temperature, supply the towels, and dry the tile so he or she doesn't slip, and one to watch outward: to ensure he or she isn't disturbed or attacked while in a vulnerable state."

"When did this tradition begin?" Kiela asked.

"After High Lord Irizinth slipped on a bar of soap, hit his head on the tile, and died of his injuries. His brother was blamed for murder and executed before the guilty soap was discovered."

Caz jumped in. "How many spring festivals must a high noble attend?"

"In an even year or an odd one?" Radane countered.

"Even, but in a year with three rains before the first bloom," Kiela said.

"Six, but everyone must be masked for the first three," Radane said, "because the third empress met her wife after three spring festivals and ever since it has been considered good luck."

"Which dessert is considered—"

Larran held up his hand. "If you and Caz know all this, how is this proof?"

"Ask me a question I would only know if I were a high noble who'd studied for her third-year exams in wind-speaking," Radane said. Wind-speaking was a study of sorcery that focused on controlling the movement of air. It had numerous applications: on ships, obviously, for filling sails, but wind-speakers were also employed as spies, for their ability to carry distant voices to their ears.

"What section of the Great Library holds the treatises on Oppeindone's experiments on wind manipulation from the third dynasty?" Kiela asked. It was a trickier question than it appeared, because the sorcerer Oppeindone had conducted a wide variety of cross-discipline experiments, and he hadn't been as organized in his writings as a librarian might wish. His treatises tended to flit from topic to topic. If she'd been his mentor, she would have spoken to him sternly about the need to focus, at least enough for the paper to match the abstract. Scientific books were not supposed to be stream-of-consciousness. That said, his work was brilliant, and any sufficiently advanced wind-speaker should have been assigned to read his original texts.

Radane stared at her for a moment.

"If you were as advanced as you say, you'd know," Caz said.

"I didn't say I was going to pass my exams," Radane complained. "We were assigned to read Oppeindone's early experiments in wind . . ." She squeezed her eyes shut. "I spoke to the librarian with the green-streaked beard. He had moss growing on his tunic and grumbled about being transferred from the west wing . . ." She opened her eyes. "He was on the second floor, north wing, by the stained-glass depiction of Empress Pergin and the building of the Alyssium canals."

"And what did Oppeindone's wind experiments prove?" Caz asked.

She glared at the plant. "I just admitted that I was not a good student. But I can tell you his notes were handwritten, near impossible to read, in a blue book that had tea stains on the cover. And I would have read it, if his handwriting hadn't been so atrocious."

Caz glanced at Kiela, who nodded. "He did have atrocious handwriting. No imperial investigator would know that." She would've heard if an investigator had requested any books from the second floor, north wing. It was rare enough that gossip about such a request would have spread, but a mere student, no matter how noble, was exactly the sort of patron who the library was designed to accommodate. "She's telling the truth, at least as far as I can tell."

"All right then," Larran said.

Caz nodded.

"Meep?"

Kiela understood that question without need of translation. "Now what?"

Together, they sailed back to Kiela's cove.

Whatever they were going to do next, they could figure it out in the comfort of the cottage with some tea and jam—after the crates of books were safely back inside. Without an actual investigator on the island, there was no need to keep them so hidden. Kiela's bedroom would do just fine.

Larran rode on the back of a brilliant teal merhorse, while the mermaid and her child dove through the waves. Meep stayed stuck to the top of the mast, while Kiela sat near the rudder. Caz stretched himself over the crates of books and watched Radane.

Radane was very carefully steering clear of any topic that made her sound like she was still a threat. "I always hated the spring festivals," she said, raising her voice to be heard over the wind. "You dance too much, you eat too much, and a lot of nobles assume that since they're 'anonymous'—even though the costumes make it blatantly obvious who is who, since they're typically designed around a play on the wearer's name and status—that the rules do not apply to them. I like to be asked before I'm kissed. And the noise! I do not mind musicians, but one at a time."

"I hid in the library for all festivals," Kiela said.

"Lucky," Radane said. "My mother would not let me. She claimed it was my duty to represent my family. One year, my younger sister, who was desperate to go to her first festival, paid me in all her birthday candy to let her masquerade as me. Later I sneaked into her room and put her candy back, because the truth was I would have paid her to go in my place. She came back saying she had a magnificent time."

"Sounds smart." Kiela wondered where Radane's mother and sister were now and if they were considered heirs. Had Radane's escape just delayed civil war? "Are you the last heir, or does it fall to another relative and then another?"

"My mother remarried after my father died, and the bloodline is on my father's side. The remarriage voids my mother's claim to the throne. So they are safe, if that is what you are asking."

"Glad to hear it." So that meant war wasn't inevitable, which was excellent—a true civil war would undoubtedly spread to the outer islands. A coup had the chance of being contained to just Alyssium. *A good reason for people to be hunting Radane.*

"I did not have a chance to say goodbye to them," Radane said. "That is the only piece of this I regret. Also, I regret taking your parents' cookbook. It felt in character, and I needed you to believe I was who I claimed to be."

"It was effective," Kiela said. She hadn't doubted that Radane was an imperial investigator when she took the precious cookbook.

"I will return it," Radane said. "It is undamaged, I promise."

"Thank you." Perhaps she could forgive her for confiscating it, though Kiela couldn't help but wonder how far Radane would have taken her act. She had frightened people, but short of taking the cookbook, she hadn't caused any real harm. If her plan was simply to disappear . . . Kiela was glad that Caz hadn't taken more extreme action.

But what were they to do with Radane now?

As they drifted into the cove, Kiela lowered the sail, and Radane poled them to the dock. Kiela tied the boat securely to the dock and then stepped out. Larran joined them, and together they carried all five crates back up to the cottage. Caz and Meep rode on one of the crates.

At Kiela's direction, they positioned them in the back room around the bed. When they'd finished, Caz and Meep scampered into the garden to plunge their roots into the soil, while Kiela made mint tea and worried about Radane.

Larran slid the final crate into place and emerged from the

bedroom. "If you'd like, I could make you bookshelves. Now that you aren't leaving."

I'm not leaving. The realization blossomed like a rose in the sunshine and completely distracted her from everything she was worrying about. She smiled at him. Bookshelves! That was the most perfect thing anyone had ever offered her. Better than jewels or a feast or a palace. He smiled back at her, and she felt as if the world were singing around her. "Yes, that would be nice."

He smiled back. "All right then."

Maybe this *was* something that could last. How often did you meet someone who offered to build you bookshelves? As Kiela watched, Larran headed outside, whistling, to fetch wood and tools.

Heaving a sigh, Radane plopped down on one of the chairs. Startled, Kiela half jumped. For almost a minute, she had forgotten that the ex–imperial investigator was here.

"While I appreciate that you did not let your talking spider plant drown me," Radane said, "I still have my little problem." She pulled out her ruby pendant and held it in the air so it caught the sunlight. "Can I buy your spellbook?"

"It belongs to the library!" Kiela said.

"It seems to belong to your bedroom."

Kiela shook her head. "I can't sell any of them. That's not how it works." She was their caretaker, not their owner. "How are you even planning to use that spell? You can't stay invisible forever. A hidden life isn't the same as an ordinary life." Besides, Radane would need to keep the ruby to cast it, which made it an insincere offer. "What you need is a way to start over, and I think—"

She heard footsteps outside.

"Hello?" Bryn's voice was bright and cheery. "Are you open? I don't mean to be one of those demanding customers who's always popping in after hours when you're trying to get a decent amount of chores done, but I'd like to buy more raspberry jam."

More jam already? Kiela came around the corner. "Hello. Yes, of course."

Leaning on the window counter, Bryn beckoned her closer and whispered, "Are you in trouble? Say the word, and we can be out of here. I'll hide you."

"No, I . . . You would hide me?" Glancing over her shoulder, Kiela saw Radane's elbow sticking out beyond the jam shelf. "I don't need help, but . . . Come in. I'm making tea." She opened the door and let Bryn inside. "Out of curiosity, why do you think I need help?"

Bryn waved her hand at the shelves, the garden, and the cottage. "Just concerned."

Understandable. She wondered if Bryn had guessed the full story and knew what was in the crates. Just the existence of the Pine Cone Coven was enough to condemn Kiela and Caz, if Radane had been a true imperial investigator.

Coming around the corner of the shop into the kitchen, Bryn saw Radane, and she halted. "Oh." She turned to Kiela. "Are you sure . . ." She let the question trail off, with her offer of help implied. "I can come back later. Or stay. Do you want me to stay? Of course you do. You offered tea. Yes, I'd love a cup of tea." Bryn sat down in a chair opposite Radane as if she were making a point.

Kiela said to Radane, "I trust Bryn."

"You're saying I should too?" Radane asked.

"You either trust us, or you keep running. It's your choice. I'll give you a copy of the invisibility spell, of course, and you can keep your pendant, but where will you run to?"

Bryn looked from Kiela to Radane and back again.

As the kettle whistled, Kiela picked up a towel to hold the handle. She poured hot water into three teacups and then distributed them on slightly chipped saucers to her two guests, who were watching each other as warily as two winged cats who didn't want to share a roof.

"I don't know where to run," Radane confessed, "or even how. My ship sank."

"You could buy another," Kiela said. "But we're already on one of the outer islands. I don't know if you'll find a better place to hide than this. Plus, no one knows where your ship went, do they? They don't know it sank, or that you survived."

"Wait—do you *want* me to stay?" Radane said. "After—" She shook her head in obvious confusion. "Why would you want me to stay?"

Because Radane said she wanted a life like this. Because Caltrey had gifted Kiela with a future that she'd never even imagined she'd want. Because this was a good place with kind people who cared about one another. Because there was a unicorn in the woods, mermaids in the coves, and the best raspberries she'd ever tasted.

Also because if Radane stayed . . . then she couldn't tell anyone outside Caltrey that Kiela, Caz, Meep, and the spellbooks were here. It was practical as well as kind.

"It's safer for me if you stay," Kiela said.

"Ahh." That clearly made sense to Radane.

Not to Bryn, though. "Why would that be?"

Kiela glanced at Radane and wondered how she was going to explain who she was, why she was here, and why she wanted to stay and hide.

"I want to leave my job as an imperial investigator," Radane said. "My employers, however, will not be happy about this. I need to disappear."

That was close enough to the truth, though it downplayed how "unhappy" her employers would be or how many people from Alyssium would like to get their hands on Radane. "You said you had a way to hide me," Kiela said to Bryn. "Would you have a way to hide her?"

Bryn sipped her tea and studied Radane. "You made a mess of my bakery."

Hunching her shoulders, Radane stared into her tea. "I'm sorry. I . . . I was not myself. I was . . . I thought I had to be the imperial investigator."

"Hmm," Bryn said.

"How can we hide her?" Kiela asked.

Taking another sip of tea, Bryn contemplated it for a minute more. She then lowered her cup and said decisively, "In plain sight. She comes to work for me at my bakery, for free until she's made up for the mess she made and then for pay after that, in plain view of everyone, until she's as familiar a sight as Tobin. She becomes an islander, and we convince as many people as possible to swear she's lived here for years."

Radane gawked at her. "People would do that?"

Bryn shrugged. "They did it for me."

Caz and Meep came inside from the garden, and the spider plant helped the cactus up onto the kitchen counter. They sat quietly listening, while Caz plucked stray leaves off Meep's needles. Meep made a soft sound like a cat purring.

"My wife's parents didn't approve of me," Bryn said. "I'm from a clan that lives . . . Well, better if I don't say names, but I'm from a forested island far from here and suffice it to say that our clans hated each other for generations. So long that no one could remember how it started, but everyone could list out every single slight and insult and wrong since then to the point where our families were poisoning the trees and rivers on one another's land. My wife . . . I met her while I was trying to stop one of my cousins from dumping waste into a lake that fed not only into my wife's family's land but also onto ours. He completely missed the metaphor about how our hatred was destroying us, but my future wife understood. We started to meet secretly of course, and in the egocentric innocence of youth, we thought if we showed our families how in love we were . . ." She sighed heavily, and then said to Kiela, "I think the rest of this requires jam to tell."

"Of course." Kiela got up and opened a fresh jar, and Bryn produced several freshly baked rolls from one of her many pockets.

Radane blinked at them. "Wait, this really is a jam shop?"

"Yes." Kiela spread raspberry jam on half a roll and bit into it. The bread was as fluffy as a cloud and tasted a bit of pepper and honey, which complemented the jam perfectly. "I used a plant-growth-acceleration spell to grow the raspberry bushes."

Her jaw dropped open. "You . . . Five crates of . . . And your priority was raspberries?"

"I was thinking of strawberries next, but I haven't seen any in my garden." Kiela turned to Bryn. "Does anyone in town have any strawberries? I could replant a few . . ."

"I'll ask around," Bryn said. "Strawberry jam would be excellent."

"I could try mixed berry too, with blueberries and raspberries." Radane gaped at her.

Bryn piled a heap of jam on a plate with a roll and handed it to Radane. "Eat something sweet. It'll make you sweeter."

"Uh, thanks."

Looking down at her own roll, Bryn didn't eat. Instead she continued her story. "You can imagine how it went when our families found out. Both my wife and I were disowned. My uncle, a man who used to give me treats and play hide-and-seek in the woods with me . . . well, he made it abundantly clear how they all felt. My wife died from her injuries at his hand, and her family blamed me. If I hadn't wooed her, they said, then my uncle wouldn't have been driven to hurt her. And so I fled. Kept going and going until I came to Caltrey. Changed my name and started a new life here. But her family had hired a professional to exact their revenge. When he found me . . . the people of Caltrey rallied around me. They swore that I wasn't the one he was looking for. I'd been born here, they said. And he believed them and left. I've lived in peace ever since."

Kiela's heart ached for her friend. "I'm so sorry." She wished she could think of other, better words to say. Bryn shouldn't have had to bear that kind of heartache and grief. She had such a giant heart.

Stretching out a tendril, Caz patted her arm. "We all are."

"Meep," the cactus said soulfully.

"Aw, thank you, but I didn't tell you for pity," Bryn said. "I tell you as proof it can be done. Islanders protect our own. They adopted me—Tobin's mother, she's my sister now, and he's my nephew. The people of Caltrey are my new family."

"I'm not one of you," Radane said.

"You could be, if you want to be." Bryn held up her hand. "Think about it before you answer. The question isn't will you be safe here; it's do you want to stay here? It's not always easy to start over and become a new person with new dreams. Do you want to start a new life here?"

Radane frowned at the jam, but she picked up a knife and spread some on the roll. She took a bite and chewed. Politely, Kiela and Bryn sipped their tea and nibbled their rolls with jam. Kiela wondered if she should make apple jam next. Caz swung himself onto the table and then sent a tendril down and helped Meep up onto the table as well. The plants waited for Radane to think.

After a little while, Radane said, "I'd like to make a life here."

Bryn nodded briskly. "Then you can start as I offered: by cleaning up the mess you made in my bakery. I'll hire you as my assistant, at least temporarily. If you like working at the bakery, you can stay. If not, I'll help you find another job in town. Regardless, I live above the bakery and have a spare room. It can be yours. If anyone comes to look for you, we'll tell them you've lived here a decade and worked at the bakery for just as long."

Radane swallowed her mouthful of jam and bread. "I was terrible to both of you. Why are you being so kind?"

Kiela thought of Larran, leaving cinnamon rolls and eggs in a basket on her step the first morning she was here, and went for the simplest and truest answer: "Because we can."

CHAPTER THIRTY

Kiela heard Larran whistling before he appeared, carrying his tools on a belt at his waist, as well as a stack of wood balanced on his shoulder. He deposited the wood just outside the cottage door, beside the rosebushes. "I'm picturing shelves all along the walls on either side of the bed. Every wall."

Kiela smiled happily. So many shelves! "It *is* a lot of books."

He laid his saw and the other tools from his belt on a nearby stump. "How did you manage . . . Never mind. Not my business."

"We started preparing when we first heard about the unrest," Kiela said, watching him organize his tools with the same care he did everything. "I only wish I could have saved more. I didn't believe it would get as bad as it did. By the way, in case it's not clear already, you really shouldn't go to Alyssium right now."

He nodded. "Got that. But the storms are—"

"Meep!" the cactus said from the cottage doorway.

"Okay, yes," he said with a laugh. "I'm not going anywhere."

Kiela, Bryn, and Radane scooted the crates and the bed out of the way to clear room for the shelves, while Larran cut the wood. Radane had never held a hammer or saw before, but she was adept at measuring. Kiela and Bryn hammered the shelves in place, and Caz, with Meep, issued instructions: floor-to-ceiling shelves, twelve inches for the bottom three, eight inches for the top. Unlike the jam shelves, these would be built into the wall. As they worked, they talked about things close to their hearts—Kiela and Caz about the library, Bryn about the bakery, Radane about the university where she'd studied, and Larran about Caltrey and the merhorses.

It took them two very pleasant days to complete the shelves: beautiful shelves of multicolored wood on every wall of the bedroom, floor to ceiling, framing the windows. They filled the cottage with the scent of fresh-cut wood. At night, Radane slept in Bryn's above-the-bakery apartment, while Larran returned to his house to care for the merhorses. And Kiela dreamed about being in the heart of the forest, with the cloud bears and the unicorn.

On the second day, Eadie and Ulina stopped by to visit. Eadie brought a basket of ruby-red cherries, and Ulina brought a spare harp for Caz to keep, a lap harp with two sets of strings that was nearly the same size as Caz. They all paused construction for a meeting of the Pine Cone Coven and to snack on the cherries that hadn't been pitted for jam, while Caz played on his new harp and Meep swayed their needles to the music.

Kiela had never been happier.

On the third day, only Radane returned at dawn. Bryn couldn't spend any more time away from the bakery, and Larran was needed with his herd out with the fishing boats.

"Bryn said I can start my bakery job tomorrow," Radane explained when she arrived. She withdrew a tattered and familiar book from a pouch. "I wanted to come bring you this."

It was her parents' cookbook.

"I was going to bring it sooner, but I wanted to repair the page that ripped."

Kiela took it and clutched it to her chest. She felt like a piece of her was slotted back into her heart. "All right." She wasn't going to say thank you since Radane had taken it against her will in the first place, but she *could* say it was all right, especially since she'd taken the extra step to try to repair it. "Caz and I were about to shelve. Would you like to join us?"

"You'll let me handle the books?"

Only if she did it carefully. Certainly not unsupervised. But yes, she would let her help, if she wanted to. She'd earned that much trust. "You can take them out of the crates and pass them to us. We'll organize them."

"Fair enough."

They set to work.

As they shelved, Kiela told Radane about her experiments with the tree and water spells, and Radane told her and Caz about which books she'd studied for her degree. There wasn't much overlap between the two, but Kiela found the conversation fascinating. She was familiar with some but not all of the books Radane had read, and Radane was fascinated by Kiela's experiments. At the university, they had not been permitted to alter any spells or even try any that hadn't been thoroughly tested by their professors—the city was considered too crowded and the spells too volatile to take any risks.

"I'd like to find a spell to help the merhorses." Kiela explained how they had difficulty with both conceiving and birthing without the aid of city sorcerers. "I haven't run across any text that addresses it directly, but there are a few avenues that look like they have potential."

Caz pulled out the books with relevant spells to show Radane. None were specific to merhorses, but they'd thought that with some study, perhaps they could be adapted? Sitting on the edge of Kiela's bed, Radane began to study one of the books. "This one is for horses. If it were combined with spellwork on pure magical creatures, it could work. Do you have Stigard's third, no wait fourth, volume on the physiology of spell-born constructs?"

Kiela consulted her notebook with the index. "Third crate."

Abandoning the shelving project, they began to pore over the various books. Kiela knew of several in their collection that had been too advanced for her—they'd required a background in spellwork that she didn't have—but Radane *did* have training.

By sundown, only a quarter of the books were shelved, but they were closer to a workable spell. "Can you ask Bryn for one more day?" Kiela asked.

Radane startled. "You want me to come back?"

"Why are you so surprised? We're making progress."

"But I . . ." She took a breath and then exhaled. "The reason that I wanted to go to the Crescent University in the first place was that I wanted to be more than my name. No one has ever needed me for what I know or what I could do before. It's always been about who I am."

"Who you were," Kiela corrected. "You're a Caltreyan now."

Radane smiled.

And she came back the next day.

By the fourth day, the shelves were complete (thanks to Larran), the books were organized (thanks to Caz), and the spell was workable (thanks to Radane). Meep gathered the ingredients, and Kiela mixed them into a paste, which she sealed in a jam jar. When Larran came to visit—he came daily, though they hadn't been alone since that day on the beach—Kiela shared the news that it was ready.

Wordless, he kissed her. She felt as if she'd been plunged into the ocean, but on a warm day. She submerged herself into the kiss, and it was as if the rest of the world had been subsumed, until Radane cleared her throat. They separated, and Kiela felt herself blush.

When they both could breathe again, Larran asked, "How can we be certain the spell won't hurt my merhorses?"

Kiela had been thinking about that. "We'll bring Ivor."

"He'll know it's a spell," Radane warned.

"I don't think he'll be shocked." Kiela looked at Larran. She wasn't going to do anything to a single mare of his herd without his approval. They were a piece of him, of his heart, and if he said no, that was it.

Larran nodded. "I trust Ivor, both with your secret and my herd."

"Are you certain?" Radane asked. "The more people who know, the more risk there is."

She wasn't certain that was true. "The more friends I have, the safer I am. The same is true for you." Isolating herself wasn't the answer, not for her, not for Caz, and not for Radane. If they were going to be safe here, they needed the whole community around them.

And it was going to start with helping the merhorses.

"Everyone needs the herd to be healthy, don't they?" Kiela said. "If the herd grows, it helps the fisherfolk. If they catch enough fish, then everyone thrives, right down to the winged cats. We look after the islanders, and the islanders will look after us." As an added benefit, it would make Larran happy. She looked at him. "Your merhorses are important to all of Caltrey, as well as to you."

As she'd hoped, he smiled. "True."

"Then let's do this," Kiela said.

Caz stayed behind with Meep to mind the jam shop, and Radane returned to town to help Bryn at the bakery, since her job had officially begun. So it was Kiela, Larran, and Ivor who walked out onto the stone jetty with the spell and the ingredients.

Ivor knew quite a bit about merhorse biology. "The reason the sorcerers are able to help, or were able to, when they chose to, is because the mares carry fertilized eggs within them through the spring and summer months. It is merely with implantation that they need magical assistance. This is why it didn't matter when the sorcerers would choose to come to Caltrey on their circuit; the mares would be ready whenever they arrived."

Kiela interrupted his lecture. "So you think this will work?"

"I have absolutely no idea," Ivor confessed. "I've never been privy to the spells they used. But I can be on hand in case anything goes wrong. I will monitor the mother-to-be and assess if she's in any physical distress."

And if the mare turns into a bird? Or a tree? Kiela, Caz, and Radane had gone over the spell multiple times. They'd cross-referenced every word and every ingredient, but Kiela wouldn't truly know until she cast it. She'd discovered there was a world of difference between studying a spell and making magic.

"I will also be able to assess if it was successful," Ivor said.

"How?" Kiela asked. If she understood the spell correctly, it would merely facilitate implantation. The merhorse wouldn't be noticeably pregnant for weeks, and she wouldn't give birth for another four months.

Ivor wiggled his fingers. "Magic."

Kiela raised her eyebrows.

"I may not know *this* spell," Ivor said, "but you were correct that I have other secrets that I wouldn't want an imperial investigator to know."

"We're all lucky that Radane decided to retire," Kiela said.

"Indeed," he agreed.

At the end of the jetty, Larran pulled off his shirt. He then jumped into the water and whistled—four short and one long— and one of the merhorses broke from the herd with a neigh. She was a pale blue mare whose scales looked like the midday sky.

"This is Marri," Larran said. "She's four years old, exactly when she should be having her first foal. She's in ideal health but has showed no signs of quickening." He cooed to the merhorse and patted her mane. She nuzzled against his neck. "There, girl. There, there."

Kiela climbed down the rocks and into the water beside Larran to stand beside the merhorse. Curious, Marri whickered at Kiela's hair.

"No treats right now," Larran said. "Later. If you behave." He clicked his tongue, and the horse-fish rolled in the waves. "I train them to do this so that Ivor can treat them for any injuries or illnesses."

Opening the pouch, Kiela handed the spell to Ivor, who had stayed up out of the waves. "Can you hold this up for me?" She'd memorized it, of course, but it was better to be safe than cocky. She unsealed the paste and smeared it onto the merhorse's stomach.

Marri shivered beneath her touch but stayed calm. She was floating on her back, with her equine forelegs in the air, and her fish tail swaying back and forth, resisting the pull of the tide and keeping her close to Kiela and Larran.

Taking a breath, Kiela chanted the words, syllable by syllable, her eyes on the paper that Ivor held out of reach of the ocean spray. She kept her hands on the merhorse, moving them in circles in the paste, covering every inch of her stomach scales. She pushed the paste into each crevice as she spoke.

Off shore, the merhorses bobbed in the waves, and Kiela felt as if they were watching her too. She tried to block it all out and speak each syllable carefully and confidently. Waves crashed against her, and she ignored them. Gulls called overhead, and she didn't hear. For the space of those minutes, it was only her, the merhorse, and the words.

And then she finished.

She stepped back. "You can release her."

Larran clucked his tongue, and Marri rolled over in the water. "Is it done?" he asked.

She looked up at Ivor. "Did it work?"

Ivor lowered his head, bowing his antlers forward, and murmured a few words—Kiela wouldn't have known them for the First Language if she hadn't been listening for the particular lilt. He was good at hiding what he did. She made a mental note to practice that kind of spellcasting with the Pine Cone Coven. As he finished, he flung a handful of what looked like sand at the merhorse.

Kiela held her breath.

The sand glowed gold.

"It worked," Ivor said confidently.

Larran put his face in his hands. His shoulders began to shake. Kneeling, Ivor laid a hand on his shoulder as Larran cried, while Kiela climbed out of the waves onto the stone jetty.

After a gulp, Larran swallowed back his tears to smile at his merhorse. "Good girl," he told her. He patted her neck. "Go on."

With a neigh, Marri raced back to her herd, who clustered around her in the deeper water, and Larran pulled himself out of the water onto the jetty.

"Congratulations," Ivor told him. He then turned to Kiela. "Call on me when you choose to repeat this. Tomorrow, I presume?"

Kiela nodded. Now that she knew it worked . . . *It worked!*

Her knees felt like jelly—or, more accurately, not-quite-set jam. She hadn't realized how tense she was. She began to shake. "Yes, as soon as I've prepared more ingredients."

With a nod to both of them, Ivor stretched his wings out and launched into the air. Kiela and Larran watched him fly back to the cliff and up toward the waterfall. Once the antlered healer was above the roses, Larran turned to Kiela. "You did the miraculous. I don't know how to thank you."

Kiela looked down at her wet patchwork dress. Once again, she hadn't considered her clothes before she'd jumped in the water with the horse-fish, though she supposed if she'd considered the logistics beyond simply the syllables and the ingredients, she would have anticipated this. "You can start by loaning me more of your clothes."

Larran wrapped his arms around her waist and drew her close. Spray flew around him as he kissed her, and she kissed him back. She felt as if she were melting. The sun warmed her sea-wet skin as he kissed her lips, her neck, her ear, her chin, and then her lips again.

He asked, breathless, "Would you like to . . ."

"Yes," she said.

"You don't know what I was going to say," Larran said. "I could have suggested a swim. Or a merhorse ride."

"Yes to whatever you want to do," Kiela said.

He kissed her again. "Yes."

She sank into his kisses. He tasted of the sea and of cinnamon.

Out in the waves, a mermaid shrieked—a siren-like scream, and Kiela and Larran broke apart. Beyond the merhorse herd, the mermaid was swimming dolphin-like toward them. She shrieked as she leaped out of the water.

"Ship!" the mermaid called.

That alone wasn't unusual. A dozen fishing boats and a half-dozen sailboats dotted the water just beyond the harbor. A few were farther out, but the waters were calm . . .

Larran stiffened beside her. "Imperial."

"What?" She didn't see anything but Caltreyan boats . . .

He pointed just left of the sun, and she saw it: one of the empire's warships, sailing straight for the harbor.

CHAPTER THIRTY-ONE

"We need to hide the books," Larran said, staring at the warship.

She loved that that was the first thing he said. "Yes."

"I'll make a false wall," Larran decided. "Hide the bookshelves."

She'd toyed with that idea as a long-term solution, but she hadn't thought they'd need it so quickly. "Can that be done before they dock?"

The answer was no. She could see it in his eyes, but he refused to say it. "I can try." He took her hand, and they hurried down the stone jetty toward the beach. "As a bonus, it will add insulation to the house, which should help in winter."

She wanted to laugh. Or cry. After Radane, she'd thought that she'd be safe, but she should have known— *Oh no, Radane!* "They aren't here for me and my little remedies." How could they be? Word hadn't spread that far that fast. No one beyond Caltrey knew or cared that she'd healed a few trees and a merbaby, and only Fenerer had been fussy about any of it. She doubted he had the contacts to summon a warship. "They're here for Radane. We need to warn her."

Together, they reached the beach.

"You warn her, and I'll start on the walls?" Larran suggested.

It would take a bit of time before the imperials sniffed out the jam shop, but Radane was right there in the village bakery, exposed.

"Remember to warn Ivor when you get to the top of the cliff," Kiela said. "Please tell Caz and Meep to hide in the forest. Insist on no heroics. If the imperials don't find what they're looking for, they might start sniffing around for a consolation prize, and that's when we'll be in danger."

Larran kissed her. "Be careful. Come to the cottage as soon as you can."

She raced toward the village while Larran took the stairs two at a time. She ran past the fountain, which bubbled and burbled, to the bakery. *Empty*—no one at the tables outside, no one behind the counter or back with the ovens. "Bryn? Radane? Tobin?"

Voices came from the direction of the dock. Leaving the bakery, she jogged through the streets toward the harbor. Ahead, a crowd had gathered to watch the sparkling imperial ship with its three masts and red sails come into the harbor. Seagulls circled above it, and waves from its wake caused every anchored and docked ship to bob in an undulating rhythm. Kiela squeezed between the crowd until she reached Radane and Bryn at the edge of the dock.

Bursting through, she grabbed Radane's hand. "What are you doing?" Kiela demanded. "You need to—I don't know . . . Hide? Come up with a cover story?" She noticed belatedly that Bryn was holding Radane's other hand, and they were standing very close together. She wondered what had transpired since they'd all built the bookshelves together. *Stay focused. She shouldn't be here.*

"It'll be okay," Bryn said. "I admit I'd thought we'd have more time to spread the story that she's been here for years, but Caltrey-ans like to—"

"It won't work," Radane said.

"You don't know that," Bryn said.

Radane shook her head. "I know that ship. Its captain—I have known him since I was eight years old. He is the man my parents wanted me to marry. As soon as he sees me, the lie will be exposed."

Releasing her hand, Bryn repeated, "Marry?"

"Neither of us wanted it," Radane said firmly. "We both agreed we were not suited for each other. But he would absolutely recognize me on sight."

Kiela felt their plan crumble around them. Radane was right—if the captain knew her, then it wouldn't matter how many townspeople swore that she'd been on the island for years. What would the imperials do when they saw Radane? Would they blame the Caltreyans for harboring her? And what would they do to Radane? *This is worse than I thought.* "What will he do?"

"It depends which side he's working for—the ones who want to kill me or the ones who want to use me." Her shoulders sagged. "I guess I am about to find out."

Closer to the dock, the ship was even more massive than it had appeared, and the white-and-gold hull gleamed in the sunlight. Kiela saw the soldier-sailors swarming over the rigging, preparing to drop anchor in the deeper water of the central harbor. She calculated they'd have a few minutes while they secured the ship and then a few more while the sailors rowed to the dock in one of the multiple dinghies attached to the sides of the warship.

"We need a new plan," Kiela said. She had magic on her shelves, didn't she? If she could just find the right book, then surely, they could read their way out of danger. She wished they had a bit more time . . .

"Let's get out of sight," Bryn suggested. "We can talk inside the bakery."

As the ship dropped anchor in the harbor, Bryn hooked her arm around Radane's, and they strolled purposefully and not-suspiciously off the dock. As the three of them headed for the bakery, questions flew around them—"Where are you going? Don't you want to see?" And "Who is it? Why are they here?" And "Is it a sorcerer? Have they finally sent one?"

In response to every question, Bryn repeated the same answer: She was going to make more baked goods. The new arrivals would be hungry, and she wanted to make sure her bakery was ready. She didn't know if it was a new sorcerer. She didn't know any more than they did, except that everyone likes baked goods so that's what she was going to make. Probably muffins, because they're quick. Yes, she'd use Kiela's jam.

Kiela listened to the gossip swirl and determined the consensus was that the emperor had at last sent his sorcerers out on circuit. They were coming to end the storms, fix the islands, and unravel the mess they'd made. So far, no one had linked the ship to their resident ex-investigator, but she was certain it was just a matter of time before the words popped out of someone's mouth and then spread.

At last, they ducked into the bakery and shut the door.

"It could be a coincidence," Bryn said as she pulled the shutters over the windows. "You don't know they're looking for you, and you were caught in a storm, blown off course—they shouldn't have any idea you're here."

"Even if it is a coincidence and they are not here for me, once they see me—" Radane shook her head. "I need that invisibility spell."

"It's not a true invisibility spell," Kiela cautioned. She'd read the description when Radane had confessed in the cave. "It's more of a stealth spell. It's supposed to make your footsteps quieter and your appearance fuzzier. I don't know if it'll stand up to direct scrutiny. Plus I can't guarantee it will work at all. We've never tried it."

Radane began to pace back and forth in front of the bakery counter. "If they suspect my presence at all, they will search for me relentlessly. You don't know how thorough imperial soldiers can be. They will turn over every rock on the island."

"It's a very poorly named spell, if anyone searching for you can still find you." Bryn positioned herself in front of Radane and caught her in her arms mid-pace. Radane sagged against her.

Kiela had an idea. "What if they didn't? Search, I mean."

Both of them looked at her.

"Your ship sank, right?" Kiela said. "What if we spread the word that you drowned with it? Larran never saved you. You never

reached Caltrey. If they believe that's true, they won't have any reason to search the island. We can hide you with a combination of the
invisibility spell and the island caves until they leave."

"I like it," Bryn said, "but too many people know she didn't
drown, and there's not enough time to spread the word to everyone. With my family, we had months to establish my new truth, but
with only a few minutes, someone could spill the truth without ever
knowing they're causing problems. But . . ." Now it was her turn to
pace, talking as she walked and waving her hand excitedly. "Why
not a smaller lie, one that it's plausible that not everyone would
know, that doesn't contradict anything? A woman was rescued. She
claimed to be an imperial investigator. All I have to do is say that
you left, after having found nothing. Who's to say it's not true? Especially if no one can find you. You could have left."

"Yes!" Radane said. "Tell everyone that I left after I failed to find
any evidence of wrongdoing. While you are spreading that, Kiela
will assist me in casting the invisibility spell." She turned hopefully
to Kiela. "If you are willing?"

"Obviously, yes," Kiela said. How was that even a question? She
thought of Larran rushing out into the storm when he spotted
the floundering ship and wondered if this was how he had felt. If
there was a way to help, she had to try. "One complication: we'll
need the spellbook to cast it, but if you're seen going up to my
cottage, then that's the first place the imperials will look. We won't
have time to perfect the spell." Every spell she'd tried had required
significant research and experimentation first—look at the singing
tree, the apple-blossom bird, and Meep. "We need to buy as much
time as possible. Is there a less visible way up the cliff?"

Bryn twisted her apron in her hands anxiously and shook her
head. "Not unless you can fly, scale vertical rocks, or swim up a
waterfall."

"What about Ivor? Could he fly us—"

Cracking a shutter open, Radane peeked out the window down

the street. "The ship is anchored," she reported. "Sails down. I cannot be here."

"You'll go in disguise, dressed as me." Bryn ducked into a back room and emerged with a pile of clothes and aprons. "Anyone who sees you will assume you're going to purchase more jam for the muffins. That's perfectly plausible, isn't it? So many muffins would require a lot of jam. I'll start baking them, act as casual and innocent as possible, while you—"

"It won't work," Radane said. "We are too dissimilar in both size and demeanor." But she began pulling on a pair of flour-dusted pants and tying an apron around her waist.

"It could work," Kiela said. Everyone was at the dock, gawking at the new arrivals. They wouldn't be watching the bakery or the cliff stairs. "You only need to pass at a distance."

Bryn pulled out a handkerchief and tied it around Radane's hair, tucking the red behind the fabric. After studying her for a moment, she piled on extra aprons to make her silhouette rounder. "Everyone's attention is on the ship. They won't look that closely at you."

"You do not know that," Radane said.

"Then I'll create a distraction," Bryn said. "I'll . . . lob muffins at them. I don't know. I'll think of something. All you need to do is make it out of town, and I'll—"

Eadie barged in through the bakery door, her horse hindquarters bashing against the doorframe. She leveled a finger at Radane. "You! Imperial investigator! You said you'd quit. Was that a lie? Did you call your people here for our Kiela? Because we won't let you— Why are you wearing so many aprons?"

Our Kiela. Kiela felt herself blush. She'd never had anyone rush to her rescue before.

Radane fixed a gaze on the centaur. "Why would anyone come for Kiela? She was born and raised in Caltrey and has never left. There is no reason she would be of any interest to anyone from the capital."

Startled at the lie, Eadie stared at her. "You didn't summon our new arrivals?"

"I did not," Radane said firmly.

"She didn't," Bryn echoed. "In fact, it would be great if word spread that after failing to find anything suspicious and announcing her retirement, the former imperial investigator left the island just this morning. Shame they missed her, but we don't know where she went."

"Ah," Eadie said. "Brilliant. I'll spread the word. What else do you need from me?"

"A distraction," Kiela said. "We have to get Radane up to my cottage without anyone knowing she's left the bakery. She's going dressed as Bryn."

Eadie looked her up and down and sniffed. "It'll hold up from a distance." She pivoted, and her hooves clattered as she clomped out of the bakery. "Ulina, we need everyone at the docks, not just the nosy masses, but every Caltreyan in the village. Our new arrivals need to be greeted with fanfare! Let's roll out a welcome worthy of the first visiting sorcerer in years."

Ulina's voice drifted in from outside. "Ooh, you think they really sent a sorcerer?"

"Honestly, no, but they should have." From the street, Eadie bellowed at the few islanders who weren't already gawking at the ship. "To the docks! Everyone, to the docks! Let's show our new sorcerer how we say 'welcome' on Caltrey!"

Bryn finished tucking in Radane's hair. She didn't look anything like Bryn close-up, Kiela thought, but with the clothes, the apron, and the handkerchief, it could work? "We'll move quickly. Pretend it's a jam emergency."

Radane let out a slightly hysterical giggle. "Jam emergency."

"Just please be careful," Bryn said. "I can't lose you before we even know what we have. It's too—" She was going to say more, but Radane kissed her. Bryn kissed her back just as urgently, the kind of kiss shared by desperate people who aren't sure they'll see each other again.

Giving them a moment, Kiela checked the street. Eadie and Ulina were herding everyone toward the dock, but she didn't know how long that would last. She waited until the tail end of the crowd was out of sight before she said, "I'm sorry, but we have to go."

"You must be careful too," Radane told Bryn. "Consider that an imperial order."

"Go," Bryn said, and her voice cracked on the word.

Kiela and Radane darted out of the bakery. They crossed the square, past the fountain, and through the empty streets. Kiela kept an eye on the houses, but she saw no one, only the winged cats on the rooftops.

A few precious minutes later, they reached the beach and climbed the cliff stairs. Radane clutched her handkerchief, keeping her bright red hair tucked in. Kiela hoped that no one was watching them. All eyes should be on the ship in the dock. After all, this was the most exciting thing to happen on Caltrey in seasons, and it would make sense for everyone to be there to observe the spectacle, especially with Eadie herding them together. Hopefully, that would buy them time to perfect the spell. If it didn't . . .

They ran across the field and through the greenery. Kiela was panting by the time they reached the cottage. She ran inside to find Larran with Caz in the bedroom, nailing planks of wood over the bookshelves. Only a quarter was finished.

This isn't going to work, she thought. The wood was too fresh, the construction too new, plus even if they could doctor the boards to seem old, there were still the windows, sunken back from the shelves, a dead giveaway that the walls were thicker than they should be. *We need another solution.* But first, she had to deal with the immediate problem of Radane. Kiela darted to the bookcase that she knew held the right spellbook. "Caz, research mode. We need to perfect the invisibility spell that uses Radane's ruby."

Larran paused mid-hammering. "Invisibility spell?"

"The captain of the ship knows me," Radane said. "If he sees me, it's over."

"So he can't see you," Larran said.

"Exactly," Kiela said. "The spell isn't the perfect solution, but it's all we have. If we cast it and stash her in a cave or someplace the soldiers have no reason to look—"

Radane stood for a moment, as if frozen.

"What's wrong?" Kiela asked.

"It's just . . ." She gulped in air. "When I escaped, there was no one to help me. I had to . . . I did it all on my own. But all of you, who have known me for only a few days . . . My family wouldn't have done this, and you don't hesitate."

"Family isn't always the people you're related to," Larran said. He added the next board in front of the shelves and began hammering it into position. "Mine . . . Anyway, how much time do we have?"

"Not enough," Radane said.

"Found it," Caz said. Using his leaves, he flipped it open. He, Radane, and Kiela crowded around the bed to read the spell. It required a ruby, which Radane had, but it also called for a snow flower, which wasn't native to Caltrey, and lightning-struck sand, which she didn't know where to find, especially on short notice.

"Well, this is a problem," Kiela said. "Do you have the other ingredients?"

"I was hoping the ruby would be enough for at least a partial effect," Radane said. "It wasn't, which is why the two plants were able to capture me."

That was a detail that Radane could have mentioned at any point between the bakery and the cottage. *Fine. It's fine. We can handle this.* Kiela asked Larran, "Do you know where lightning has struck sand?"

He spread his hands. "I don't know that there were any lightning strikes on Caltrey with the last storm. And I haven't heard of any hitting the beaches recently. It happened once—the sand turned to glass. Looked like a sculpture. Someone may have kept a shard of it, but I don't know who. If there were more time, we could ask around . . ."

"Help me check the garden for any snow flowers?" Caz asked Kiela.

"Can you research substitutes for lightning sand?" she asked Radane. She didn't know if Radane knew how to properly research anything, but she had been a student so she should understand the basics. "At least make a start. I'll be right back."

Leaving Larran to the fake walls and Radane to the spellbooks, Kiela followed Caz out into the garden. Meep was there, tossing bits of bread to the chicken, and then dodging out of the way when the chicken tried to peck them instead.

"What is it?" Kiela asked Caz. He didn't need her help to search for snow flowers. He knew far better than she did which plants were which.

"We need to talk Radane into another plan," Caz said. "Even if we had all the ingredients, I don't like the idea of trying a spell we've never done, especially with imperials in town. There's too much that could go wrong. Instead of saving Radane, we could be turning their attention directly on all of us. It would be a lot better if we could use a spell we've tested."

She agreed with that, but it wasn't as if they had an enormous repertoire. Curing storm sickness wasn't applicable, and the pine cone remedy wasn't going to hide anyone. "Making trees healthy isn't going to help, unless you want to pelt the imperials with fruit."

"No, but this has an extremely low probability of working."

He was right.

We need a Plan B. Or C. But what . . . ?

Kiela saw one of the small cloud bears flit from beneath the raspberry bushes and disappear in between the roots of the tree. *Huh.* She crossed to the garden and knelt next to the tree. She touched the mossy roots. "Tree guardian? Hello? Can I ask you a question?"

She didn't expect it to reappear, and she leapt back when a cloud taller than she was formed into the loose shape of a massive bear.

"Oh. Hello. Thanks." She licked her lips and told herself to sound calm. "Um, how do you stay hidden?"

"They're basically made of clouds," Caz said behind her. "I don't think their technique is applicable to flesh-and-blood humans."

Maybe. Maybe not. But all the folktales about so-called evil forest spirits . . . they centered around people who disappeared: men or women who wandered into the woods and didn't return, kids who vanished when they strayed from home, an old woman who was lured from the safety of her garden. Their loved ones searched, but it was as if they'd disappeared. A few tales emphasized how hard the searchers tried to find them. The few who returned couldn't explain where they'd been. How was that accomplished? Could it be done by a friendly forest spirit for a benevolent reason? Assuming they were friendly . . . *They are,* she thought. She believed that. "A friend of mine needs to hide. Can you help?"

Caz scooted closer to Kiela. "Are you sure this is wise?"

"It's no more dangerous than using an untested spell with inaccurate ingredients," Kiela whispered back. "Besides, we helped them. Perhaps they still feel some gratitude?"

"They already paid us," Caz said. "Remember the piles of supplies?"

"I can make more remedies," Kiela told the cloud bear. "I'll do it anyway if I'm not hauled off by the imperials for harboring a fugitive. Please, is there a way to hide my friend?"

Right in front of Kiela and Caz, the massive cloud bear melted into the bark. Just . . . melted. It slid directly into the wood as if the tree were absorbing it. A second later, it slid out and waited, looking down at her with its fire eyes.

"You could hide her in a tree?" Kiela asked.

Could it be done? She'd never heard of it, but just because she hadn't read about it yet didn't mean it wasn't possible. She wanted to ask if this was how it had been in the tales, to take notes on the process, and then search the texts, but for now . . .

Behind them, the cactus chirped, "Meep!"

"Meep will bring Radane," Caz translated.

Neither Kiela nor Caz moved from their spot. They kept their eyes on the forest spirit. Could they trust a wild grizzly bear made of clouds? *I followed them into the woods, and they didn't harm me.* Yes, the old folktales said they were amoral, dangerous, and un-friendly, but to her, they'd been friendly, and if *this* was how they made people disappear, then this could be the exact solution they needed.

She heard Radane and Larran come outside.

"What is it? Are the soldiers here already?" Radane asked.

"This might sound like an unusual idea . . ." Kiela began. *Possibly a terrible idea. Or a brilliant one.* "Unusual" was a fair enough word.

Radane halted. "Is that . . . Oh, wow, I've heard of them. I didn't think they let humans see them." Her voice was hushed, as if she were afraid a loud sound would frighten it away.

"I think this cloud bear can help hide you," Kiela said.

"What? How?"

The cloud bear demonstrated once again, slipping within a tree. Out of the corner of her eye, Kiela saw that other cloud bears had filtered into the garden—they lurked on the roof, between the vines, and on top of the chicken coop.

Radane shook her head. "I'm solid. Flesh and blood. I can't dis-appear into a tree— Oh, whoa." The other bears flowed toward her, surrounding her in their cloudlike bodies.

Caz hopped on his soil ball anxiously. "This won't hurt her, will it? I feel like there should be a lot more explanation. Or experimen-tation. Can we test this first?"

Radane looked at Kiela. "Do you trust them?"

Do I? She knew they'd want her to continue to make and use the remedies. But more than that . . . they'd allowed her to see a unicorn. "I have no idea if this is safe. I don't know how it works. I don't know what they intend or how to reverse it. But I do know they're willing to help. And I know we need help."

"So, you are saying it's a risk," Radane said.

"Trusting anyone is a risk," Kiela said. "But it's better than doing it alone." She looked over her shoulder at Larran, who had come into the garden too. The chicken was pecking at his boot. He shook his foot gently to dislodge her.

Radane eyed the cloud bears. "What about the spellbooks? I should help you finish hiding them . . ."

"I have a plan for that," Kiela said. What Caz had said about using a spell they already knew had given her an idea. "And bonus: if it works, I'll be able to make a lot more jam."

"Oh, in that case, fantastic." Radane rolled her eyes.

She thought about telling Radane it would be okay, that it was a better idea than an untested spell, that the forest spirits seemed friendly, but she didn't know if any of that was true. This had to be Radane's choice. Kiela wasn't sure what she'd do, if their positions were reversed. It depended whether Radane was more afraid of the forest spirits or of the imperials—

"Let us do it," Radane told the spirits.

The cloud bears swarmed her. Kiela could barely see Radane between the blur of their fog-like bodies. Larran jogged up toward the tree, stopping beside Kiela. He was tense, as if ready to dive in after Radane if she called out or screamed, and Kiela didn't doubt he'd do it.

But the cloud bears melted softly like snow under spring weather. In seconds, the bears—and Radane—had vanished.

"Wow, that's disconcerting," Caz said. He shivered and all his leaves rattled.

The cactus agreed. "Meep."

"Do we hide you the same way?" Larran asked.

Kiela shook her head. "It'll be less suspicious if only one new arrival has disappeared. What we need is for them to go away quickly. Besides, so long as they don't find the spellbooks, they won't want me." Briefly she considered asking the cloud bears to hide the books as well, but given that books were made from dead trees, that didn't seem wise—she had no idea how they'd react. "We just have to hide the books."

"What's your plan?" Caz asked.

She pointed toward the brambles. "Raspberries. A lot of rasp-berries."

CHAPTER THIRTY-TWO

While Caz and Meep went to retrieve duckweed from the pond, Kiela mashed rosebuds and elder-bush leaves together with a few drops of water.

"I'm sorry the false wall won't work," Larran said.

"It would have if we had more time," she told him. "You tried."

"We could put the books back in their crates and move them in the library boat . . ."

"To where?" Kiela asked. The cave hadn't worked; Radane had found it nearly instantly. His house was no safer than hers. Besides, this was her home. *I have to protect it.* She pricked her thumb and added blood to the paste.

He winced at the sight of her blood. "How can I help?"

"Can you board up the windows and doors?" Kiela asked Larran. She wasn't sure how enthusiastic the growth was going to be, and she didn't want it shattering the glass.

"But why . . ." He shook his head. "Questions later. Of course I can. Whatever you need." He disappeared out to the front yard, and soon she heard the sounds of sawing and hammering.

As she memorized the syllables of the spell, her heart felt like it was hammering. There were so many unknowns in her plan. She didn't know why the imperials had come or what they were looking for or how hard they'd look. She was working with limited information and that was uncomfortable. But she was going to try to keep the books safe. And her friends.

They finished at about the same time: Kiela finished committing the spell to memory as the plants returned with the duckweed and Larran finished boarding up the windows and doors. As soon as Kiela mashed the paste, the four of them gathered in the garden. Larran opened his mouth, but Caz shushed him, which was fine by Kiela. She was nervous enough as it was.

She'd start with the vines already on the house, she decided. Kneeling by the base of an ivy vine, Kiela placed the paste for fast growth. "Wish me luck."

Caz backed away. Reaching out a tendril, he pulled Meep back too. "Larran, you might want to give it some space."

Larran retreated. "What's going to happen?"

"Watch," Caz said.

Kiela recited the spell once, twice, and then three times. Quickly, she retreated from the vine. An instant later, it shot upward into the air. Vines sprouted out of it, and they spread over the roof. Without waiting, she moved on to the next vine. She repeated the process until the entire cottage had been engulfed in vines.

She then moved on to the brambles.

She selected a raspberry bush that was closest to the house. As she buried the paste, she hoped the brambles didn't subsume the entire garden. They'd worked so hard to tame it and had been making such progress. "Meep, can you release the chicken? I don't want her caught in this."

The cactus scurried over and unlatched the coop.

The chicken didn't budge. She clucked at the cactus, who meeped back at her.

Kiela began the spell.

As the brambles erupted, the chicken squawked and fled the garden, following Meep. The raspberry bushes grew larger and larger in bursts that shook the ground, until the whole of the cottage was obscured.

A few seconds later, they stilled.

She could barely see a hint of the roof or the walls. She swallowed hard. It had seemed like a sensible choice, but seeing her parents' home this way . . . *My home.*

"That should keep the books safe," Caz said with satisfaction.

Kiela reminded herself that was the point. *We can fix it later.* This wasn't permanent. After the warship left . . . After she was sure they were all okay . . . If that ever happened . . . What if the imperials saw through the lies?

Larran laid his hand on her shoulder. "Now, how do we keep you safe?"

She'd told him Bryn's original plan for Radane—lying about why she was on Caltrey and how long she'd been here. "There isn't enough time to convince everyone in town to say I've been here my whole life. But maybe there *is* a story that will throw them off the track?" She was going to have to think about it. Perhaps she could pretend to work at the bakery? That sounded harmless enough and not spellbook-adjacent. "In the meantime, we can't stay here. The imperials have to believe this place is abandoned. Caz—"

"We'll hide in the brambles," Caz said. "It's perfect."

Demonstrating, Meep darted beneath the raspberry bush, out of view.

"Stay safe," Kiela told them.

"You too," Caz said.

"Meep."

So anxious that she had to remind herself to breathe, Kiela strolled into town with Larran. It took every bit of courage she had to keep putting one foot in front of the other and not look as if she were screaming inside.

Maybe I should have asked the cloud bears to hide me too.

But that would've been shortsighted. She had to appear in town, act innocent, and not draw any suspicion to the cottage. She planned to slip into Radane's role at the bakery, as Bryn's assistant, and pretend she'd always worked there. With luck, the imperials would overlook her entirely.

She knew from her life in Alyssium that those in power, whether nobles or military, overlooked ordinary people. Librarians and shopkeepers were virtually invisible to them, just tools to complete a task. She could guarantee that, unlike Radane, no one on that ship was going to recognize her. *I left so little mark on anyone in Alyssium after years. Yet here, after only a few days . . .* Kiela looked at Larran and, despite everything, she felt like smiling. He was by her side, despite the risk and uncertainty.

Together they strolled past the mermaid fountain. It flowed with a cheerful burble, as if nothing was wrong. On the rooftops, the winged cats lounged in patches of sun. She kept reminding herself to look relaxed, casual, innocent, and she couldn't help but critique every step: Was it casual enough? Was her expression bland enough? Were her shoulders relaxed? What in the world was she supposed to do with her arms? Swing them or keep them still? She couldn't seem to remember how she normally walked. And what about her expression? Was her smile normal? Should she pretend to laugh at whatever Larran had just said that she completely hadn't heard because she was too focused on her own feet, hands, and face?

Larran squeezed her fingers as they approached. They'd taken too long at the cottage—the imperials were clustered around the bakery. The boy Tobin was scurrying between them, serving up muffins as quickly as Bryn could put platters on the counter.

If I can't claim I work at the bakery . . .

Plan B? Or were they up to Plan C? D?

Bryn waved cheerfully. "Hello, Kiela! Larran, we were just talking about you!" She bustled between the tables, distributing mugs to several imperials. They were dressed in military uniform, stiff tunics as red as the sails on their boat, with leather-armor-like pants and swords strapped to their waists. She counted three men and five women, but she didn't doubt there were others in the town. A ship that size typically carried a crew of at least two dozen.

One man with hair twisted in a spiral had gold stripes on his tunic—he had to be the captain, Radane's would-be fiancé. He was seated next to Eadie. "Ah, yes, there's Larran!" Eadie said. "He's the one who pulled that red-haired girl from the ocean."

"You said she was calling herself Radane?" the captain asked. "Can you describe her for me, as well as the boat she arrived in?" He stood, and Kiela noted that he was quite a bit taller than Larran, though skeleton-thin. He had thin, long fingers that he moved as he spoke.

"Of course. You are?"

He bowed slightly. "Captain Varrik of the *Alyssium Rover*."

"I'm Larran of Caltrey. And this is my wife, Kiela." He lifted Kiela's hand to his lips and kissed the back of it.

Kiela managed, barely, not to react. She knew it was just what Larran said to keep her safe, but she couldn't help a little birdlike trill that echoed in her head. Summoning a smile, she said to the captain, "Pleasure to meet you." She did *not* look at Bryn or Eadie to catch their reactions. She did hear Tobin let out a little gasp, then a yelp, as if someone had kicked him in the shin.

"We spotted the boat mid-storm," Larran said. "It was getting tossed around on the waves. Midsize, designed for one to four passengers. But with all the chaos of the storm, I couldn't get a good look at it. Did you, dear?" he asked Kiela.

"It had a mast," Kiela said helpfully.

"What color sail?" the captain asked.

Kiela frowned as if trying to remember. She felt as if the moment was seared into her memory—the scream of the wind, the fury of the waves, and how fragile the boat had looked. Of course she remembered every detail. "I didn't see a sail. I think the wind had ripped it away?"

"It was already half-capsized," Larran explained. "I rode one of my merhorses out to the wreck. Barely got there when the woman went under, but I made it in time. Got her inside and warm fast, and she recovered quickly. She wasn't in the water long enough for hypothermia to set in."

Fenerer lurched to his feet. "Go get her, Larran. She's staying at your house. Or is it in your bed? Tell us, Larran's *wife,* do you share your bed with Larran and the investigator, or do you clear out when the two of them are together?"

"She's not at Larran's," Bryn said. "She was staying in the empty room above my bakery, until she decided to leave Caltrey."

Eadie jumped in. "And just because you weren't invited to their wedding doesn't mean you can disrespect Kiela. You better watch your tone or Bryn won't give you any more of those biscuits you like."

Fenerer snorted.

Before he could speak again, Larran cut him off. "At first, she didn't identify herself, but after she recovered, she claimed to be an imperial investigator."

"Made a mess of my bakery, until things were sorted out," Bryn complained.

Captain Varrik said, "Sorted out?"

He's good. He hadn't said much. Just let people talk. Luckily, with the exception of Fenerer, Kiela's friends had stayed on script, which was remarkable given how little time they'd had to prepare. It helped that they were mostly telling the truth. She tried not to fidget.

"She found nothing suspicious," Bryn said. "In fact, she wanted to make amends, so she helped me clean up the bakery, and in return I offered her a place to stay."

Fenerer jabbed his thumb toward the bakery. "Nothing suspicious? Ha! I'd like to hear that from her own mouth. Bring her out! Why isn't she here briefing these fine soldiers? She should be reporting her finds."

"I would indeed like to speak to the investigator," Captain Varrik said, much more politely than Fenerer. Kiela wished there was a way to eject everyone's grumpiest neighbor from the conversation. With Fenerer here, everything was much more likely to go awry. She hoped no one got too extravagant with their lies.

Bryn shrugged. "She moved on, once she finished here."

"To where?" Captain Varrik asked.

Scooping up several empty plates, Bryn carried them back to the bakery counter. "She didn't say, but personally I don't see why anyone would ever want to leave Caltrey." There were ragged cheers from the other customers, all the Caltreyans. The other imperials watched the streets and the houses, as if on guard against attack. *From who?* she wondered. *The cats?*

"Have there been other recent arrivals?" Captain Varrik asked.

Kiela felt Larran tense beside her.

Before Fenerer could jump in with any kind of accusation, Eadie said, "We could help you better if we knew why you're asking. Who are you looking for?"

"Of course." He bowed his head politely. "We are looking for Ravandil Etra L'sari. Due to . . . recent events, she is currently the only living heir to Emperor Mevorin. It is imperative we find her."

They really were sent to find Radane.

"So you can crown her or kill her?" Eadie asked.

Bryn bustled out again. "Eadie."

"What?" Eadie asked. "I can't ask questions?" To the captain, she said, "Forgive an old lady's bluntness. We get so little news out here. How did you misplace the sole living heir? Seems like that's the sort of person one wants to keep track of. It's not like she's a pretty bauble that got stuck in a box."

"She's certainly not a bauble," Captain Varrik said. He touched his hair spiral as if soothing himself and then sighed. "Frankly, if she doesn't wish to be found, she shouldn't be. But I have my orders. And I come offering a substantial reward: a deed to a recently vacated palace in Alyssium. It comes with all the furnishings and treasures of its former owner, as well as the title Baron or Baroness."

Fenerer jumped to his feet and pointed at Kiela. "*She's* new to Caltrey."

Her heart clenched. *So much for that lie working.*

Larran stepped in front of Kiela, and she tried to look shocked. She did feel shocked. That was a very substantial reward. It could tempt anyone in Caltrey. Even Bryn or Eadie. She wondered if either of them had guessed that Radane was this heir. It was no more or less plausible than that she was an investigator who wanted to leave her job. Still . . . *They don't know where she's hidden.*

And besides, she didn't think either Bryn or Eadie wanted to leave Caltrey.

Captain Varrik crossed the courtyard to Larran. The two men eyed each other, and the captain said mildly, "I would like to speak with your wife."

Kiela laid her hand on Larran's arm. "It's all right. I'm obviously not heir to anything, except a cookbook." She stepped out from around Larran. "I'm Kiela Orobidan, daughter of Atlan and Binna. I was born on Caltrey." All true.

Varrik studied her for only a heartbeat—took in her blue skin, her hair, the shape of her face, her eyes, her new freckles—and dismissed her. "She's not the imperial heir."

She began to breathe normally again.

Fenerer shook his finger. "She's suspicious, though. Came to this island and things started happening. You should search that cottage of hers. She keeps unnatural things. Bet she knows what really happened to the imperial investigator. Probably did something unnatural to her, to make her stop asking questions."

Eadie smacked his finger with a napkin. "That's enough, Fenerer. Captain Varrik . . ."

At the same time, Larran said, "Captain Varrik . . ."

Bryn said, "Ignore Fenerer. He's suspicious of everyone."

Captain Varrik inclined his head. "My mandate does not include the investigation of local island matters. I have one priority."

"Mark my words," Fenerer said, "that woman is hiding secrets."

With the air of someone who was used to interviewing the islands' most irritating residents, Captain Varrik said, "Describe this investigator to me, please."

Fenerer happily jumped in with a description: height, shape, skin, eyes, hair. It was so detailed that he might as well have painted a picture of her. Kiela watched the captain and saw the moment that his suspicion was confirmed.

Until that instant, she'd had the sense that the captain was simply going through the motions, humoring the islanders while they discussed the latest event—the shipwreck and the absent imperial investigator. He hadn't truly thought it had anything to do with his mission. Now, though, he looked like a hunting dog who'd scented a rabbit.

Oh, this is not good.

"Who was the last to see her?" he demanded.

His sailors sensed the change in his tone as well, and they became more alert. Kiela noticed their postures straightening, their eyes darting to observe everything and everyone. She didn't doubt that they'd report back the slightest suspicion.

"That would be me," Bryn said cheerily. "She helped me out at the bakery before she went on her way, and I gave her a bag of cinnamon rolls for her journey. You need sugar for the sail to the next island in the chain—it's not a short journey, and my cinnamon rolls are the best. Would you like to try one?"

"What ship did she take, if hers crashed?"

Bryn glanced at Kiela, just a quick flash of the eyes, but the captain noticed it. He turned to Kiela. "How are you involved in all of this?"

She didn't think. She just answered. "I sold her my parents' boat."

"Did you now?"

"I didn't need it," Kiela said. "I'm not planning on ever leaving Caltrey." She smiled at Larran, and this time the smile was real. He smiled back at her.

"Eh, she's lying," Fenerer said. "That citygirl has no boat but the one she sailed in on—a kind of scow with a sail. Not Caltreyan. She's from Alyssium. I'd bet she knows everything about this heir of yours. I'd bet they're in cahoots. Or else sworn enemies. She did her in. Buried the body. Or transformed her into something nasty. A bit of moss. Or a slug. I'm telling you: she's brewing up illegal spellcraft in that cottage of hers. You need to arrest her."

Primly, the captain said, "I'm not in the habit of arresting civilians on no evidence. But that said, I must insist on seeing this cottage."

"I don't live there," Kiela said. "No one does. It's abandoned."

"You have a jam shop, run out of your cottage!" Fenerer cried. "Obviously a front for something shady. How can you survive just selling jam? Especially just one flavor."

Captain Varrik turned to him. "Is your accusation that she's a rogue sorcerer, a murderer, or a bad businesswoman? I am losing track of your complaints."

Fenerer drew himself up. "I am only saying that she doesn't belong here."

Bryn slammed a mug of tea down on one of the tables. "It's you who doesn't belong. Perhaps when Captain Varrik's ship leaves, you should be on it."

"Oh, I will, and you'll be calling me Baron. Because I'm telling you: there's something wrong about that blue-haired citygirl." He wagged his finger at Eadie then Kiela.

Larran stalked toward him. "Enough, Fenerer."

"She's spelled you too, she has," Fenerer said. "Otherwise you'd see it. She's the source of everything strange that's happened on this island. She's a rogue sorcerer. And I'll say it again: she knows exactly what happened to your investigator."

Captain Varrik turned to Kiela. "Forgive the imposition, but I must ask you to show us this cottage now." It was clearly not a request, but it was just as clear that he wasn't happy with the source of his inspiration. She hoped that meant they weren't doomed.

"Ha!" Fenerer said in victory.

In a low voice, Larran said, "You must see that Fenerer is . . . not our most reliable citizen. He's prone to paranoia, and he took a dislike to my wife from the start. An irrational dislike. He's chosen her as his scapegoat for everything from the tide to whether his fish stew was oversalted."

"Then it should be no problem to show us this cottage he speaks of," Captain Varrik said. "You must understand my position—my superiors have set a clear task, and no matter my personal feelings on the matter, I cannot be anything less than thorough."

"And what are your personal feelings?" Kiela asked.

"Irrelevant," he said. "Please, lead the way."

CHAPTER THIRTY-THREE

Kiela led the captain and his soldiers to the cliff stairs. "Watch your step." As soon as she said it, she felt silly—these were soldiers and sailors who were undoubtedly used to much more perilous conditions than wooden stairs in the breeze.

But the captain said courteously, "Thank you," and held the handrail as he began the climb. Overall, he didn't seem a bad sort. Of course, that wouldn't stop him for an instant if he guessed she'd hidden the heir or that she possessed stolen spellbooks and, worse, had used them. She was fully aware of this, no matter how polite he was. He didn't know her at all and would have no reason to hesitate.

Rather than joining them on the stairs, Larran said, "I'll catch up with you folks later. I've got to get the herd out to sea to help with the day's fishing."

"Now?" Kiela said. She tried not to let all her worries and fear seep into the one syllable, but she heard her voice squeak and knew she hadn't hidden it all well.

He shrugged casually. "Work doesn't stop because life interferes."

The captain looked back at Kiela. "Is there a problem?"

Only if you discover everything illegal I've done. "Of course not. I can take you to the old cottage while Larran tends his herd." She didn't need Larran with her. It wasn't as if he could do anything about a half-dozen trained soldiers if they decided to arrest her. Still . . . she'd expected him to come with her, at least for support and encouragement.

Frankly, it hurt that he was leaving.

She told herself it shouldn't, but her heart wasn't in the mood to listen. It was too busy thudding faster and faster. *Stay calm. You can handle this.*

Kiela continued her climb up the cliff stairs, while Larran trotted across the pebbly beach. Looking back, she saw him strip off his shirt, toss it onto a rock, and then wade into the water. He whistled for his merhorses.

At the top, the captain waited for Kiela and his squad to reach him. Hands clasped behind his back, he gazed out across the water and at the purple-streaked clouds on the horizon. In front of him, the roses bobbed in the breeze, and it all looked delightfully picturesque. "Quite the view," he said.

She caught her breath and nodded. "It's one of my favorite things about Caltrey."

"I can see why." Then he frowned at the sky. "We should move along. There might be a bit of unpleasant weather coming our way soon."

Kiela leaped on that. "Are you certain you shouldn't head back to your ship? Get clear of the island and to your next destination before the storm arrives?"

One of his sailors studied the clouds. "It's far enough away and not certain it'll develop into a storm," she said. "It could dissipate. We have plenty of time before we need to be concerned."

Well, it was worth a try, Kiela thought. "Just a warning: storms blow in quickly on the outer islands. These aren't like storms near the capital. You shouldn't underestimate them."

The sailor disagreed. "Not that quickly. We have time."

"Lead on," the captain said.

Kiela led them into the greenery, along the trail that Larran had blazed and that was now matted down from all the back-and-forth since she'd arrived. She hoped it wasn't suspicious that the trail existed in the first place. Maybe she should have cast a spell to swallow it up too. The imperials could have used their shiny swords to hack through the greenery—that would have really made the area feel uninhabited—but she hadn't thought of it. "I haven't lived in the cottage since I was little. I'm not sure why Fenerer thinks I do. He's clearly confused."

She stepped out of the green in front of the cottage.

It had been embraced by vines and brambles. Lush and verdant, they knotted around the entire house, blocking the doorway and the windows. The boards that Larran had hammered over the windows and doors weren't even visible. A few flowers bloomed on some of the vines that draped down over the walls.

"I should have maintained it," Kiela said apologetically. "But since no one lives here . . ."

"I see that," the captain said.

"I'm sorry to waste your time," Kiela said. "I did try to tell you."

The captain bowed his head politely, even sheepishly. "I do apologize for the intrusion, but since a lead was presented, it has to be followed."

"Of course," Kiela said. She could be gracious, now that he'd seen there was nothing here. "If we head back now, I'm sure Bryn will have some baked goods that you can take with you on your way to your next destination."

"As soon as we conduct our search, we'll return to town," Captain Varrik said. He barked to his soldiers, "Search the area." To Kiela, he said, "A formality, you understand. I need to report that we followed every lead."

Kiela tried not to let the panic show on her face as the soldiers split up, circling the house and tromping through the forest. If they looked hard enough, would they find Caz and Meep? She hoped the plants had enough sense to stay hidden. What if the soldiers decided to chop down the vines and break into the house? Why would they? It looked as if no one had gone inside the cottage in years. There was no reason to think they'd search inside, if they could even get inside . . .

She noticed that Captain Varrik was watching her carefully. *He knows. He sees it in my face.* She was certain he could tell she wasn't calm, but would he guess what she was hiding? He couldn't know Radane was here, and he had no reason to suspect the spellbooks. *Please, Caz and Meep, stay hidden.*

Her heart felt as if it were racing as fast as a hummingbird's wingbeat.

"What's your plan when you find this missing heir?" Kiela asked, trying to make her voice as casual as possible, as if she were just making conversation.

The captain shifted uncomfortably. "She'll be put on trial."

"For what?"

"To determine if she is a threat to the new government of the Crescent Islands." He turned to face the bramble-covered cottage. His soldiers were stomping through, branches snapping beneath their boots. A bird scolded them from the top of a pine tree, and Kiela glanced up at it—red feathers and an apple-blossom tail. She looked quickly away, hoping none of the soldiers noticed how unusual the bird was. This could all go so badly so very quickly.

Kiela thought about what to say. She had to choose her words carefully. And watch her tone. Lightly, she said, "Well, the woman who was here—don't know if she was the heir or not—but she didn't seem like a threat. She just wanted an ordinary life, she said."

"She did, did she?"

"It sounded to me like she never wanted to return to Alyssium."

"Ahh."

One of the soldiers headed for the stairs down to the cove. *Oh no, the library boat!* It was Alyssium-made. Any sailor would recognize it. He'd know it wasn't old and abandoned. Worse, the captain would know she'd lied. She'd said she'd never left Caltrey, plus that she'd sold Radane her parents' boat. There would be more questions, and she didn't know how to answer them. She clasped her hands behind her back so the captain wouldn't notice how badly she was shaking.

In a soft voice, Captain Varrik said, "She did always want her own life."

Before she could decide how to respond, she heard one of the soldiers swear and then call out, "Careful of the thorns!"

"You might want to call them back," Kiela said, "if you don't want them scratched up. The thorns are vicious, especially the deeper in you go."

She saw the captain's forehead crease as if he were thinking.

"Also, there's poison ivy. You're going to end up with a ship full of itching sailors."

He raised his voice and called to his soldiers, "Steer clear of any poison ivy. Don't touch shiny leaves if you don't want to itch."

I should have grown a lot of poison ivy. And poison oak. And maybe installed a beehive or two. Or a family of raccoons. "It's not always shiny. Best to avoid any leaves of three."

He relayed this to his soldiers.

"Give me a giant squid over this anytime," one of them complained.

Kiela knotted her hands behind her back and tried to concentrate on looking amused instead of terrified. "How can this 'heir' be a threat to the government if all she wanted to do was leave? That doesn't sound like someone they really need to be concerned about."

The captain nodded. "Politics."

"If she just wants to live out a quiet, ordinary life, isn't that best for everyone?"

He studied her for a moment and then raised his voice again, "If you see any red berries, you should retreat immediately." *Red berries?* she wondered. Of course there were red berries in a raspberry bramble—

"There are loads of red berries, sir," a soldier called, "but they appear to be raspberries."

"Not on Caltrey," the captain called. "Get out of there. That's an order—Caltrey is home to a red berry that resembles raspberries but is highly poisonous." He leveled a look at Kiela. "Our local can confirm that."

She met his eyes and hoped that she was understanding him correctly. "Absolutely," Kiela said loudly. "Even inhaling its odor can cause lasting damage to the lungs and kidneys and . . . spleen. It's terrible for your spleen."

He nodded. "You heard the local. I don't want you lot coming down sick when we're out in the ocean. You see those red berries, you come out."

At this command, the soldiers exited the brambles, as quickly as they could. They assembled in front of them. A few looked somewhat panicked and kept glancing at the raspberries that covered the cottage.

"It's why I had to abandon the cottage," Kiela explained. "The poison berries took root."

For a moment, she thought she was in the clear. The search was halted. The captain had, for whatever reason, helped her end it. *Now they'll leave, we'll be safe, and—*

She saw movement from the cove stairs, and she tried not to react as the sailor returned. Yes, the soldiers had stopped searching around the cottage, but if he'd seen the boat, Captain Varrik wouldn't be able to ignore the evidence. It was one thing to obstruct a search subtly; it was another to ignore direct evidence publicly. He'd said himself that he had to report back. There had to be a limit to how far he was willing to push against his orders—cutting short a search through thorny brambles was one thing, but publicly ignoring a lie was another.

Captain Varrik was watching her again. He'd seen her flinch.

He knows I lied.

"No boats in the cove," the sailor reported. He was holding a bit of rope. "Line is new, so there was a ship docked there not long ago, if I had to guess, but it's gone now."

Kiela wanted to cry with relief. They should have found it. They should've had questions. They should've poked holes in her story and reconsidered the accusations from Fenerer . . . but the library boat was gone.

Larran.

She suppressed a smile.

He must have realized as soon as she told the lie about selling Radane the boat that her boat was the weak spot in their plan. He'd taken a merhorse to the cove and moved the boat while Kiela and the soldiers climbed the cliff stairs and trekked through the forest. She made a mental note to kiss him extra for that. "I told you: I sold my parents' boat to Radane."

"And which way did she sail?" Captain Varrik asked.

"I didn't ask her destination," Kiela said, "but the closest island is Faysa. It's east of here." She added, as if remembering, "She did sail east, I think." And then: "If she switched directions later, I don't know. If she is this heir and didn't want to be found, she most likely did."

He didn't react to that, but he barked at his soldiers, "Report!"

Down the line, they reported: because of the poison berries, they could not conduct a thorough search, but from what they had seen, the cottage appeared to be overgrown from every direction, there was no clear entrance that had been used, the brambles were uncut and undisturbed, and the windows and doors were boarded up. One of the soldiers complained about a feral chicken in the midst of the overrun garden. None mentioned a talking spider plant or a mobile cactus or an apple-blossom bird or cloud bears or a lost heir. All of them were adamant that there was no sign that anyone had entered the house in months, and all were anxious to leave the poison-berry-covered cottage.

Kiela managed not to audibly sigh in relief.

The captain bowed toward her. "Again, apologies for the intrusion on your day."

She wondered again what it meant that he'd invented the nature "fact" about the poison berries. Was he actively trying not to find Radane? It certainly seemed that way. If so, how far would he go?

He asked, "Will you accept a cup of tea at the bakery, in compensation?"

"That would be lovely." Yet another lie, delivered with a smile. *Maybe I'm getting better at this.* She led them back through the greenery to the cliff stairs and wondered why he'd suggested tea. Did he want to interrogate her privately? Was she not yet in the clear?

The purple clouds on the horizon were massing, like a bruise in the midst of the blue—it looked as if the sky had been punched. She'd only weathered the one storm on Caltrey so she was no expert, but it didn't look like it was dissipating to her.

"Perhaps you shouldn't delay for tea?" Kiela suggested.

"Perhaps you're right," the captain said, eyeing the sky as well.

The sailor who'd dismissed the coming storm earlier agreed. "It has grown quickly, but we can still outrun it, if we leave now."

The captain nodded briskly.

Kiela fell behind as the sailors strode through town, calling for the others. She trailed them to the dock, along with Bryn, Ulina, and other townspeople. Fenerer emerged from his house lugging a trunk and carrying a pack on his back. He pulled it down the dock.

"Requesting passage to Alyssium!" Fenerer called.

"This is not a passenger ship," the captain informed him. Dismissing him, he shouted commands to his people as they swarmed over the deck, preparing to set sail.

"I request sanctuary!" Fenerer demanded.

Captain Varrik sighed. "On what grounds?"

"Danger of retribution."

Kiela had read enough legal tomes to know that fear of retribution from the accused was considered a valid reason for granting sanctuary on imperial property, but it was only used in cases where the accused had been found guilty. It didn't extend to instances of false accusations. In fact, there were laws that allowed those who were falsely accused to demand payment from those who had wronged them.

"Rejected," Captain Varrik said.

He clearly knew the law as well.

Hmm . . . If he knows the law . . . "Request for payment as the wronged party," Kiela said.

Fenerer squawked like a cat whose tail had been stepped on. "You can't!"

Ignoring him, Kiela said, "This man has leveled false accusations at me and wasted imperial resources and time. As payment, I request that he be removed from Caltrey and relocated to Alyssium."

Ulina chuckled.

"You dare—" Fenerer began, and then he shut his mouth. His eyes widened, and she could see what she'd said sink in. He turned to Captain Varrik. "Yes, that. That's fair."

Captain Varrik glanced at the growing storm. Kiela wondered if he was calculating whether it would be faster to let Fenerer on his ship or to continue the argument. "You may board," he said. "Understand that this is no luxury vessel. This is a working ship, and we have orders. We will reach Alyssium when our search is complete, not before, and you will pull your weight about the ship and will not complain about accommodations. Is that understood?"

Fenerer was already up the ramp and onto the deck.

"Thank you," Kiela said to the captain. "That's better compensation than tea. Good luck on your search. I hope you find whoever you're looking for."

Under his breath, he said, "I hope I don't." He waved to the townspeople who had gathered to see him off. "Thank you for your cooperation, people of Caltrey!"

He looked as if he wanted to say more, give a nice rousing

speech, but from the deck, Fenerer called, "Hey, where should I put my stuff?"

Captain Varrik sighed and boarded his ship.

Kiela stood on the dock, watching them row out of the harbor and raise the sails, while the angry purple clouds spread across the sky. A streak of silver lightning flashed in the distance.

CHAPTER THIRTY-FOUR

"Definitely going to storm," one of the fisherfolk on the dock said.

Kiela didn't wait for others to express their opinions. As soon as the imperial ship cleared the rocks that marked the mouth of the harbor, she ran down the dock, through the streets, and to the pebbly beach.

Seeing her, Larran waved from the jetty. He then signaled to the merhorses to swim out into deeper water before he strode across the stones and jogged along the beach. Reaching her, he caught her in his arms and swung her in a circle, pulling her close. "They didn't take you," he whispered in her ear. "You're safe. You're still here."

She wanted to kiss him. She wanted to thank him for moving the boat, for leaping to do what he could to keep her safe, for helping even when she didn't think to ask for help. She wanted to melt into his arms and stay there. But the purple clouds were blotting out the sun. "Storm's coming," she said. "With the cottage wrapped in vines, Caz and Meep can't get inside to safety. And Radane . . . What if the tree she's in is damaged in the storm? We can't leave her stuck in there."

He took her hand and, without a further word, ran with her up the cliff stairs. She clung to the railing with one hand and to his hand with the other, and she ignored the way the wind slapped into her—it was no longer a gentle breeze. The roses at the top swayed hard, and the pine trees bowed as they ran between them.

"Caz? Meep?" Kiela called.

Caz poked a tendril out from beneath the brambles. "Kiela! Are we safe?"

Without pause, Larran attacked the brambles that blocked the front door. He sawed away the thicker ones and yanked the vines back. He then switched to the hammer, using the back to pry off the boards that he'd used to block the door.

"The imperial ship is gone, but a storm's coming in," Kiela told Caz. "Where's Meep?"

Meep popped out from beneath the brambles. "Meep?" Behind them, she spotted the chicken. Somehow they'd prevented her from running away, even with the chaos of the excess growth and the intrusion of the soldiers.

"We need to let Radane out," Kiela said. "Larran, do you have—"

He produced clippers from one of his pockets.

"Perfect."

She ventured into the garden, using the clippers to cut her way through the brambles. She wished he'd had his scythe, but at least the clippers worked. It was incredible how thick the brambles had grown. She could see the spots where the soldiers had hacked through, but thanks to their captain, they hadn't ventured deep enough.

All the work she and Caz had done to clear space for new growth . . . They'd have to begin again, which was far better than being hauled away from this place altogether. *It's only time and sweat.* She told herself to be grateful it wasn't worse. "Tree guardians?" she called as she continued clipping. "Can you bring our friend back, please?"

What if the cloud bears didn't hear her? What if they couldn't or wouldn't release Radane? They'd been so desperate . . . *It worked.* But it was pointless if Radane was stuck inside a tree forever. She wished she could have asked more questions or done more research.

When this was over, Kiela was going to research nonstop: everything she wanted to know about forest spirits, everything about garden spells, everything about storms, everything about everything. She'd record all of it, of course—her own book about Caltrey.

Frankly, it sounded like the perfect life.

But first, Radane was still in a tree.

At last Kiela succeeded in climbing, squeezing, and cutting her way through enough of the growth to reach the tree that held Radane. Her arms and legs were crisscrossed with tiny scrapes, and her skin stung.

In the distance, she heard the rumble of thunder.

She knocked on the bark. "Radane? Can you hear me? They're gone. You can come out. Actually, you really should come out, because we have to get to shelter—there's a magic storm coming, and I don't know if it's a good idea to be inside a tree during it." She remembered her parents shooing her inside whenever thunder and lightning swept over Caltrey. They'd cautioned her never to stand under a tree when there was lightning. She wasn't sure if that applied to being *in* a tree, but she didn't think it was a risk anyone should take, especially since this wasn't an ordinary storm.

"Radane?"

No answer, and the garden was growing darker. She looked up in time to see a streak of silver zigzag above her, breaking the purple. Rain began to fall, hitting her face like tears.

"Radane!"

White fog drifted around the tree, and Kiela stepped back. The fog writhed, and she saw the flash of ember eyes. She couldn't tell where one cloud bear began and where they ended—they were a mesh of cloud.

A moment later, they parted, and Radane fell onto the ground at Kiela's feet, hands and knees slapping into the vine-covered ground. Kiela helped her stand. "Are you all right?"

"That was . . ." Radane sucked in a gulp of air. "Very, very strange. Varrik?"

"Gone." Kiela glanced toward the sea beyond the cove. She wondered if the ship was as fast and as sturdy as they claimed. She wasn't certain Alyssians knew how bad the storms could be in the outer islands. Maybe they should have stayed.

Except that was dangerous.

No, surely they knew what they could handle. "He was sent to find you."

"To kill me or crown me?"

"Kind of think the former." Kiela added quickly, "But I don't think he wanted to. I think he wanted you to escape." She helped Radane through the garden. It was slow going—Radane's legs wobbled as if she hadn't used them in months, and the vines and brambles were thick.

By the time they reached the front of the cottage, Larran had the door partway open. They all piled inside. Caz and Meep were already in the kitchen, along with the chicken, and Caz was lighting several of the lanterns with the fire-starter. Between the dark clouds and the vine-covered windows, it was nearly as dark as night within the cottage.

"It's going to be a bad one," Larran said grimly.

"Your merhorses?"

"They'll be fine. They'll dive."

"What about the village?" Kiela asked. A lot of the homes were close to the water. They'd mostly escaped damage during the last storm, but it was clear that a stronger one could rip the roofs off the buildings, bash the boats, destroy the dock—there was a lot of harm that strong wind and rain could do.

Using his hammer, he knocked a board off the front window.

"If it is as bad as all that," Radane said, sinking into one of the chairs, "are you sure you shouldn't leave the boards? I know that I feel safer with them."

"Just one. I want to see the sky." He peered out. "Whoa. Yeah, it's going to be a bad one. They'll have sounded the harbor bell. The villagers know to stay in." He didn't sound certain, though.

She wondered how bad a "bad one" could be. What if it flooded the village? What if it leveled it? What if . . . "What about the warship?" Kiela asked. "Do you think it got clear in time? Imperials don't know how bad the storms are out here. They don't have this kind of weather in Alyssium."

Radane waved her hand in the air. "Please tell me you are not really worrying about the people who came here expressly to bring me to my death?"

"Captain Varrik didn't want to," Kiela reminded her.

"Yes, but he was still going to follow orders if he found me."

She wasn't so certain about that. Maybe, but maybe not. He hadn't had to invent the lie about the poison berries, after all. And she had no idea what he would have chosen to do if he'd discovered her library boat. "You don't know that for certain. Sometimes we have to choose between terrible options. You don't know what pressures he was under." Kiela had absconded with crates of priceless books. Radane had impersonated an imperial investigator. Perhaps Captain Varrik had volunteered to search for Radane because he knew he was the only one who wouldn't try hard to find her. "He seemed like a good person."

Radane sighed. "He is a good person. But now his fate is up to, well, fate. I told you a single wind-speaker can't stop a storm. There's nothing I can do to help. We just have to ride it out and hope for the best—"

Kiela glanced at Caz.

Caz scampered into the back room and emerged with a slim volume: *On Storms.* Swinging himself up onto the table, he plopped it in front of Radane and opened it. "Do you know this spell? It says it's only taught to wind-speakers."

Radane peered at it. "Yes, but—"

"You need a coven to cast it," Kiela said.

"Exactly," Radane said.

Caz tapped his tendrils against the table. Agitated, Meep scooted around the table legs. It would be a risk, but was it a necessary risk? Kiela looked over at Larran. "Do you think the ship is in danger?" she asked him again.

He checked out the window once more. "Yes. A storm this size? Absolutely, they're in danger. If it capsizes, though, I can't save them all. There are too many of them."

"It will not capsize," Radane said. "It is a massive ship."

"It's a massive storm," Caz said. "I can feel it in my leaves."

Larran headed for the door. "I'll mobilize as many merhorses as I can—"

Kiela blocked him. "Their ship will be farther out than Radane's was. She was coming toward Caltrey; they had a healthy start away from it. You won't be able to reach them in that chaos." The waves, the wind, the lightning—he'd never make it.

"I can't just let them drown. If I can only save a few, then that's—"

She interrupted him. "I think the best chance of saving everyone on that ship and protecting everyone on the island is if we stop the storm."

Radane shook her head. "Absolutely not. Please, be practical. It takes an experienced, trained coven. You and I alone . . . Can the plants cast spells? Larran, do you have any experience with spellwork? Have you ever spoken a word in the First Language?" Without waiting for an answer, she turned back to Kiela. "This is not magic for amateurs. Do you have any idea of what can go wrong with a spell of this magnitude?"

Kiela crossed to the window and looked out the slit that Larran had opened. Between the vines, she saw a strip of angry purple sky. "Can we make it to the town? Bryn, Eadie, and Ulina—we need them."

Larran shook his head. "The stairs won't be safe."

She thought of Ivor. "Can we fly?"

"That's a terrible idea," Caz said.

The cactus agreed. "Meep."

"But it could work," Kiela said.

They didn't fly.

Instead they glided. Ivor produced a polished walking stick that he held horizontally. Larran grabbed one side, and Kiela and Radane held on to the other. Meep tucked themself into one of Kiela's pockets, while Caz wrapped himself around her neck.

"Hold on," Ivor said as he ran off the edge of the cliff.

The winds were smacking into the island, but Ivor knew how to ride them. He picked a current that was sweeping along the side of the cliff and used it to glide straight into town. Kiela felt the wind in her face, and she didn't know whether to scream or laugh as they sailed above the rooftops where the winged cats often sunned themselves. She'd never felt the world disappear beneath her before or been surrounded by forces that felt so immense. For the minutes they were part of the sky, she felt both unstoppable and incredibly fragile.

As lightning skittered across the sky, they landed near the fountain. Rain pelted the streets diagonally. All of them were soaked through. She felt Meep's prickles through her shirt but didn't complain—of all of them, they were the one least suited to a downpour. Ivor kept his wings spread to block the worst of the rain and led the way until they reached Bryn's bakery. He knocked on the door with his antlers.

Kiela heard a plaintive yowl from beside the steps and squinted through the rain to see one of the cats, a tabby with bright parrotlike green wings, huddled under the bakery window. "You shouldn't be—"

Throwing the door open, Bryn gawked at them. "What on all the islands—" She yanked Ivor inside by his antlers and then shooed the rest of them in. "Kiela, you too."

Kneeling down, Kiela called to the cat, "Get inside. Come on."

"Meep!" the cactus ordered, from within Kiela's shirt.

At Meep's command, the cat darted into the bakery, his wings plastered to his sopping-wet fur.

As soon as they were all inside, Bryn shut the door against the wind and demanded, "Why are you out in this? We're way past the harbor bell!"

Huddling together, they dripped on her floor. The winged cat hid beneath the counter, shivering, and Kiela wished she could join him. Now that they were here . . . *This is too wild a plan. It's too great a storm. We're too inexperienced.* But she'd dragged everyone this far. Kiela pulled a piece of paper out of a pouch and laid it on a counter, being careful not to drip on it. "Radane wrote out the spell, but it'll take all of us to cast it."

"It works if and only if it's done correctly," Radane said. "It'll stop a magic storm, but it needs to be cast by at least five sorcerers simultaneously."

Bryn peered at the spell. "It doesn't list any ingredients."

"We're the ingredients," Kiela said.

"It's explained in the papers of Ivini," Caz said. "Fascinating theory, actually, that the breath of the sorcerers acts as the ingredients, if every exhale is coordinated." Ivini had won a medal for his pioneering research. It was displayed in the North Reading Room—or it used to be.

"It's imperative that the spellcasting be absolutely simultaneous, including inhales and exhales," Radane said. "Usually the windspeakers practice for hours until they match one another in cadence. I think this idea is foolish at best. Reckless at worst."

"Like diving into the ocean during a storm to rescue a woman on a capsized boat," Kiela said, with a smile at Larran.

Smiling back, he didn't argue. "I'll bring Eadie and Ulina here."

Without another word, he headed out into the rain-drenched street. Wind slammed into the bakery door, flinging it open, and Bryn forced it closed. "The storm will pass," Bryn said. "We've weathered them before; we'll do it again."

"The imperial ship is out there," Kiela said. "It didn't leave early enough to escape. It's exposed, with no protection against the wind and the waves and worse."

"Are you certain we want to rescue them?" Bryn asked. "I mean, we just escaped them." Her gaze fixed on Radane, and Kiela could see the worry in her expression.

"They will guess we used forbidden magic," Radane pointed out.

It's what Larran would do. She couldn't put into words why it was important to do this, but if she didn't . . . if she hoarded the knowledge she'd taken and didn't use it to help, then she'd be no better than the emperor and his sorcerers. "We have the power to help. How can we not use it?"

"I'm just saying it's a risk," Radane said.

"We can't control what Captain Varrik chooses to do," Kiela said. "We can only control what we do and hope other people make the right choices." She did have hope, given his actions at the cottage, but it was a sheer guess that he wouldn't simply follow orders when faced with a more difficult choice.

"It's the right thing to do," Caz said. "I'm with you, Kiela."

"Obviously I am with you too," Radane said. "I provided the spell. I came to the bakery on his wings." She flapped her hand at Ivor, who'd helped himself to a cup of tea. His hands were shaking as he sipped it. "I simply want it clear that there could be consequences. For instance, if we save them and they return to 'thank' us, or arrest us, what will they do if they see me? What will they do to *you* if they know you hid me?"

"We won't let them see you," Bryn said.

"You will stuff me back in a tree?"

Bryn looked confused.

Before they could explain, Larran shoved his way back into the bakery. He had his arm around Ulina. Eadie trotted in behind him. She shook the water out of her mane and tail. "What's the emergency?"

"Did you tell them?" Kiela asked Larran.

"He said the words 'pine cone coven,'" Eadie said. "We didn't need to hear anything else." She flashed a smile at everyone who was crowded into the bakery, from Ivor to Radane to Meep and Caz. "I see our coven has expanded."

Kiela waved them all close. "Everyone, this is what we're going to do . . ."

CHAPTER THIRTY-FIVE

To ensure no mistakes, Caz copied the spell phonetically, because he had the neatest handwriting. Ulina agreed to conduct them—she'd signal for each syllable and each breath. Kiela formed a circle around the table with the spell. On her left was Larran. Bryn was on her right. Eadie, Radane, and Ivor were squeezed on the other side of the table.

"The storm needs to hear us," Radane said.

Bryn crossed to the window and door. "Ready?"

Meep and Caz sat on the corners of the spell to secure it. "Meep."

She threw open the window and door, and the storm roared into the bakery. A bag of flour plummeted from a shelf and broke open on the floor, and the tabby cat yowled. Flour whipped in a cloud around him and then was carried out into the streets.

"It's worse!" Larran shouted to be heard over the wild wind.

"There's flooding in the streets!" Bryn called.

"Then let's stop it now!" Kiela said. She joined hands with Bryn and Larran as they came back to the circle. "Ulina, lead us!"

Holding her neighbor's hands with one pair, Ulina used her other pair of hands to conduct. She raised them up, took a breath . . . and they began.

Verisinasa tri biasa
Sey hiavor cry tricoma
Suna wyri suna wira . . .

Outside, the howl of the wind sounded like a child's scream. The winged cat cowered behind the counter, shielding himself with his bright green feathers. She heard a crash—a tree falling? The dock breaking? A roof cracking open? Concentrating, Kiela pronounced each syllable as precisely as she could. Around her, the others did the same.

Virrinaya tri virona
Muria rysana verisinasa . . .

She felt Bryn's hand tighten in hers as they heard the rush of water on the streets outside. As Larran had said, this storm was worse than the last—they should get to higher ground. But not until the spell was complete.

Sey govana
Suna wyra veri myana!

They reached the end, raised their faces, and looked at one another.

"Again," Kiela said.

Verisinasa tri biasa . . .

Kiela felt wetness on her toes. She looked down to see seawater seeping into the bakery through the open door. The level of water in the street had risen to the top of the steps. The town was flooding. Soon it would be inside every house. And she didn't know when it would end. Perhaps not until all of Caltrey was swept away.

She spoke the words louder.

Beside her, she heard Eadie's voice hitch as she stumbled over a syllable. The winged cat darted toward her and curled around Eadie's front hooves. Strengthened by the encouragement, Eadie continued, her voice clear and strong.

They kept going.

A third time.

And then: silence. The wind's screams died to a whisper. The water on the floor of the bakery receded, and Kiela glanced to the door to see that the flooding was flowing out of the town like it was being pumped back into the sea.

"Did . . . did we do it?" Ulina asked. Her voice was rough. All of them had been shouting. Kiela hadn't even realized she was too. She swallowed. Her throat felt raw.

Slowly, they released one another's hands.

Eadie sat down hard on her hindquarters. "I faltered. I failed."

Kiela shook her head. "I think it worked." She didn't hear the storm screaming anymore. The wind was dying, and the walls were no longer shaking as if the world wanted to tear them apart. At her feet, the tabby with green wings purred. Picking up the cat, Kiela cuddled him as she took a deep breath and then exhaled. The air tasted like the salty sea.

Bryn rushed to the door and peered outside. "The sky's clearing! It's . . . well, there's no rain and thunder." Her voice shook a little.

Raising her head, Eadie asked, "What is it?"

"Come see," Bryn said, stepping outside.

Carrying the cat, Kiela followed her, with Larran. Caz and Meep scooted outside at her feet. They all emerged into sunshine. Everything was dripping wet—from the roofs, down the walls. The stones glistened with water. And flowers were falling from the sky.

Blossoms of white, pink, blue, purple, and yellow drifted down in lieu of the rain and lightning. It looked like a celebration. With a delighted *rrr-eow,* the tabby cat leaped out of her arms, spread his green wings, and flew into the petal-filled sky, catching blossoms in midair. Laughing, Kiela stretched out her arms and spun as the flowers danced all around them.

"Everyone will know it's magic the second they see this," Radane said quietly. She hadn't left the bakery. She hovered by the doorway, just out of sight.

"They'll know it's magic the second they realize they didn't die." Kiela caught blossoms on her open hands. She lifted them to her face and inhaled the soft perfume. It smelled like the heart of summer. "Come and see this!"

Shaking her head, Radane retreated into the bakery.

With a worried glance toward the dock, Bryn followed her inside.

Out on the wet cobblestones, Larran caught Kiela's hands and swung her in a circle. A half-dozen cats swooped and danced above them. Consequences might come soon, but for now . . . flowers were falling like the miracle they were, and Caltrey was safe.

Pulling on his hand, she tugged him toward the dock. All around, villagers were coming out of their houses and marveling at the blossoms. Even more winged cats had returned to their rooftop perches and were batting the flowers out of the air as they fell. Larran had them in his hair, and she knew she did too. It made Kiela think of festivals and of weddings. She felt her cheeks blush.

"Let's see what we saved," Larran said. Still holding her hand, he led her toward the dock. The flowers kept falling, but her heart sank as they drew closer.

Ships in the harbor had been tossed around. A few were beached. One had been smashed against the rocks. Blossoms floated on the lapping waves and on the damaged ships.

"We weren't quick enough," Kiela said.

"It's not all the ships," Larran said, "and they can be repaired. We saved the homes. And the people. Even them." He pointed to beyond the harbor, where the warship with its white hull and red sails was listing to the side as it headed back toward Caltrey. "You were right. They hadn't escaped the storm. If not for the spell—"

"They're coming back," Kiela said. A piece of her had hoped they'd accept the miracle for just that and continue on to their next destination.

"There's time to hide you and Radane," Larran said.

She shook her head. "Radane, yes. Me, they met. They know I'm here. Hiding would only look like guilt. Besides, you cast the spell too—and Ivor, Bryn, Eadie, Ulina, Caz, Meep. We're all in this. If we all disappear . . . I'm not leaving all of you to face this."

Larran looked worried. "Maybe we don't need to make it easy for them, though?"

"Oh, yes, we should absolutely lie our faces off."

Holding hands, they watched the imperial ship sail into the harbor. One of its masts had snapped, and a sail was torn. Clearly it hadn't gone through the storm unscathed. *Maybe it's only here for repairs. Maybe they won't ask questions.*

And maybe the chicken will start talking.

Of course they'd ask questions.

Kiela was aware that others were scurrying over the dock. This time, though, the villagers weren't gathering to greet the ship. Everyone was focused exclusively on cleaning up from the storm. People were working together to patch their boats, to pull them off the rocks, and to sweep up from the damage—and from the flowers.

Only Kiela and Larran were standing still, watching the wounded ship come in.

Kiela knew she should help too, but she felt rooted to the dock. *Maybe I should hide us all.* Maybe she should grow more plants and stuff everyone behind them. She didn't think that would work this time. What they'd done was too large to ignore.

The ship limped into the harbor.

Halfway between the breakwater and the dock, it dropped anchor. Shortly after, a rowboat was lowered, and she saw the captain and several sailors rowing toward them.

When they reached the dock, Larran reached a hand down and helped them tie off to the piece of the dock that was still sturdy.

The captain, Kiela noted, had flower blossoms in his hair, as did the rest of them.

"Everything okay with your ship?" Larran asked. "Need any help with repairs?"

Captain Varrik climbed out of the rowboat and ordered his sailors to remain by their oars. Kiela wondered if it was a good sign that he didn't have them disembark and immediately begin an investigation. "My crew is already working on it," he said. "We returned to ensure that your island survived." Walking to the very end of the dock, he surveyed the harbor. "I see there's been some damage."

Larran shrugged. "We'll manage. We always do."

"You've had storms of this magnitude before?"

Joining him at the end of the dock, Larran said, "The storms have been worsening ever since the capital stopped sending its sorcerers around. The outer islands have suffered the most. We depend on the sorcerers maintaining a balance in the magic, to offset the miracles they make in the capital. I'd planned to visit Alyssium and appeal to the emperor, but given the mess in the capital . . ."

"I have reason to believe the situation will improve," Captain Varrik said.

"Oh?" Kiela asked. "Will sorcerers be sent on circuit again?"

"I don't believe that will be the solution." He looked at her, and she wished she could read what he was thinking. It was the kind of look with unspoken words behind it. Her heart thumped faster and harder, and she hoped he couldn't hear it. "The laws *are* changing, but unfortunately, they are changing slowly."

She wanted to ask which laws precisely, but she wasn't sure she dared. Asking could be tantamount to admitting that they'd broken several laws, and she wasn't sure that was wise. It had to be a good sign that he hadn't immediately arrested anyone.

Fortunately or unfortunately, she didn't have to ask.

"So, did they repeal the law saying only approved sorcerers can perform spellwork yet? Specifics, please." It was Caz. Kiela hadn't seen him come down the dock, but here he was, his tendrils wrapped tight around his soil ball. It was remarkable he was here, willingly, with water sloshing underneath the boards, but as proud as she was that he'd overcome his fear, why hadn't he stayed hidden? He knew he was difficult to explain. Granted, he had every right to be here, but convincing the captain of that, in the wake of the abrupt and flowery end to the magic storm, could be a challenging task. It would have been better if—

"Meep," the cactus added, poking themself out from beneath Caz's leaves.

Now it's over.

Captain Varrik gaped at them.

Running down the dock, Tobin skidded to a stop in front of them. "Caz! You're in town!" He boasted to the captain, "This is my friend, Caz. He's a *Chlorophytum comosum*—see, I learned how to say it."

Bryn called from the foot of the dock, "Tobin, come help with the nets!"

Tobin groaned and then trotted back. Over his shoulder, he said, "Caz, come to Aunt Bryn's bakery sometime. I'll sneak you pastries."

All of them watched the boy scamper away down the dock to rejoin Bryn and the rest of the Pine Cone Coven. Side by side, her friends stood at the end of the dock, watching, waiting, ready—and Kiela realized they'd sent Tobin intentionally, to show Captain Varrik that she, Larran, and the plants weren't alone. *Or to remind me.*

She had no idea what they intended to do if she needed to be rescued, but she wasn't going to let it come to that. *I won't let Captain Varrik take any of them.*

In the moments it had taken Tobin to cross the dock, Captain Varrik had composed himself again. She couldn't read his face to gauge his reaction to the presence of a sentient plant who was clearly not native to Caltrey when Radane was supposedly the only recent arrival. *He must know we lied, even if he doesn't know about what or why.* Now if she could just think of what to say to explain everything in a way that would make the imperials leave . . .

Before either Kiela or Captain Varrik could speak, Caz informed him, "I was created illegally by a librarian in the Great Library of Alyssium. I was granted citizenship, but she was arrested and executed."

"Transformed into wood," Kiela clarified.

"Executed," Caz said firmly. "She couldn't speak or move, and when the library burned, she couldn't call for help or run to safety. If she hadn't burned in the fire, she would have rotted where she was placed, as her body of lifeless wood decomposed—and through it all, she was aware of her fate, helpless and trapped and forgotten."

Kiela stared at him. He *never* spoke about his creator. She'd never asked, not wanting to upset him with talk of what neither of them could change or fix. She hadn't realized he'd understood her fate when the North Reading Room burned.

"Her name was Terlu Perna, and she was kind and soft and had a fuzzy voice. She wouldn't squash bugs because she didn't want their families to be sad and lonely. But she was tortured and killed for giving me life, and she told me before they took her that she didn't regret what she'd done for a second. She regretted that she wasn't sneakier about it, obviously, but she told me that I was the best thing she ever did, and that if the emperor and his sorcerers didn't see that, they were small, selfish people who didn't care about anyone but themselves."

Kneeling next to Caz, Kiela said softly, "I didn't know she made you on purpose."

"She did," Caz said. He wrapped a tendril around Meep, as if for comfort. Meep pressed closer to him. "She was lonely, and she wanted someone to love. She made me out of love, and the empire destroyed her for it."

"I'm so sorry, Caz."

"The law against unofficial sorcery doesn't exist to help people," Caz said to Varrik. "The revolutionaries were right—yes, I read their pamphlets, and I agree with them. The laws were created to consolidate power among the already powerful, and the people in charge didn't care who else they hurt. They didn't care about a lonely librarian who was doing no harm to anyone, just as they didn't care about thousands of islanders left in the lurch, who are bombarded by storms that their misuse of magic caused."

Captain Varrik said, "As of now, that law still stands. Please know that I didn't write the laws, and I have no power to change them."

Kiela looked from the spider plant to the captain and didn't know what to say. This felt much bigger than a single spell to stop a storm, or even a bedroom full of illicit books.

Larran jumped in. "But you do have power to choose what you do next, whether to follow orders or your heart," he said. "You could choose to sail away. You have no direct proof that any illegal spellcasting happened here."

Standing up, she gawked at him for a moment. He was so nice to everyone that she hadn't expected him to argue with an imperial captain, even on her behalf. The fact that he did heartened her. *We can convince Captain Varrik to do the right thing, if we only can find the right words.* As the fake poison berries proved, he *wanted* to do the right thing—that had to matter, didn't it?

Mildly, apologetically, Captain Varrik said, "There are flowers in my hair and on my ship. It would require a complete lack of attention to not realize magic was at work, and there are no approved sorcerers on either my ship or on Caltrey."

Caz pointed out, "You have no proof of who worked this magic."

"We could, with an investigation," Captain Varrik said.

"Is that part of your mandate?" Kiela asked. "Your mission is to find the emperor's heir. Surely your superior officers would deem that more important and wouldn't like that you delayed your mission to act as an imperial investigator on a minor island."

"Such a spell could only have been conducted by someone with the knowledge of wind-speaking, which the heir possessed." Again, he sounded apologetic. "One could argue that investigating this lead is directly related to my mission."

"Or one could choose *not* to argue that," Kiela pressed. "Yes, you have your mission, but it's up to you how you fulfill it." She pitched her voice even softer. "It's your choice whether there are poison berries or not."

He shook his head. "It's not that simple—"

"Meep," the cactus said.

Caz translated. "They say to tell you that one could argue that whoever cast this spell to disperse the storm could have let you and your crew drown. They chose not to, which would imply that it wasn't cast by your target."

"They said all that?" Captain Varrik asked.

"Meep."

Caz translated again. "Yes."

"Whoever cast this spell clearly cared more for what was right than what was the law," Kiela said. She'd thought before that he seemed like a good person. She hoped with every bit of her heart that she'd been correct and hadn't misjudged him. He had a choice here, whether he saw it or not. He could think for himself and decide what was right. "You can care too."

Captain Varrik looked back at his ship. In a low voice that didn't carry beyond them, he asked, "Tell me: Is she safe? Is this the life she wants?"

"It's certainly better than the alternative you're offering," Caz said.

He nodded, looking unhappy. "But if it wasn't . . . If I came offering the crown . . ."

"She doesn't want it," Kiela said.

"You're certain. She won't—"

"She neither wants to overthrow the government nor die from it," Kiela said. "She told me she wants an ordinary life." He could make the right choice. She knew he could. If he wanted to badly enough. "But you know her a lot better than I do. What do *you* think she wants?"

"She never wanted power," Captain Varrik admitted. "Or anything that I could offer her." He sighed heavily, and Kiela began to hope. She glanced at Caz, who was vibrating slightly with either worry or fear—she couldn't tell which. Kiela held out her hand, and Caz reached up a tendril and took it. Larran took her other hand.

They waited, hand in hand and hand in leaf.

Raising his voice so that others on the dock could hear, Captain Varrik said, "I've received word that a traveling sorcerer was able to dispel this storm. We're all quite grateful for that bit of luck. His timing was excellent."

"It was excellent luck," Kiela agreed loudly.

He strode back to the rowboat and began barking orders—two of them would row him back to the ship, while the rest would assist the fisherfolk. "I'll send some of my crew to help with storm repairs, at least until we are ready to proceed on to the next island."

As the sailors climbed out of their boat to assist, the Caltreyans on the dock cheered. Shortly, they were all working side by side. Once his men and women were all assigned to useful tasks, Captain Varrik climbed into the rowboat and returned to the ship, leaving Kiela, Larran, and the two sentient plants on the dock. He did not look back.

"Meep?" Meep asked.

"He chose kindness," Kiela said. She wanted to sink into a puddle of relief. She smiled down at the spider plant. "Caz, you did it."

"We did it," he corrected.

"Meep," the cactus agreed, as Larran wrapped his arm around Kiela's shoulders and kissed her cheek. She hugged him back.

Kiela offered to Caz, "Want me to carry you back to solid land?"

"I've got this," he said confidently.

As one of the fisherfolk hauled a boat closer, the water sloshed beneath them. Caz clung to the boards of the dock with his leaves. "If you don't want—" she began.

"Yeah, just carry me."

Bending down, she scooped up her friend, while Meep climbed up into the pocket of her still-wet skirt. Her arms full of leaves and Larran by her side, Kiela walked off the dock and through the flower-strewn town.

CHAPTER THIRTY-SIX

Kiela stirred what was supposed to be apple jam and wondered if she'd mashed it too much. *Can't mash it less now.* Caz peered into the pot. "It looks like applesauce," he said.

"I guess we could sell applesauce."

"It's a jam shop," he pointed out. "Says so on the sign."

"Maybe it will transform into jam soon." She kept stirring. Outside, Larran was working in the cottage garden again. It had taken a lot of effort to tame the yard into anything reasonable after what Caz dubbed the Great Brambling. Occasionally the members of the Pine Cone Coven had pitched in, along with Larran. Sometimes with Ivor but always with Bryn, Eadie, Ulina, and Radane, they met twice a week to assemble more remedies and learn new spells for healthier plants and trees, kinder weather, and better fishing— Caz would take copious notes for the spellbook that he, Kiela, and Meep were writing, a compilation of the spells of Caltrey. Afterward, the coven would help out a bit in the garden. Kiela always gifted them with extra jam as thanks. It seemed most people in Caltrey were quite fond of jam, especially when combined with Bryn's pastries. Once word got out about the extra jam, Tobin frequently joined them too. Ulina and Caz took turns playing the harp while the others worked.

Caz swung down from the counter and then up onto the table where he'd left his harp. Using his leaves, he began plucking out a melody. A few more leaves, he added another harmony. Kiela swayed to the music as she stirred. Their newest addition to the family, the tabby cat with green feathers, purred on the hearth along with the music. He'd moved in shortly after the day of the flower storm, and since then he'd become nicely plump and his coat glossy, thanks in part to a steady supply of fish from Larran.

Hearing voices rising above the harp, she glanced out the front window to see the core members of the Pine Cone Coven coming out of the greenery: Bryn, followed by Eadie, Ulina, and Radane. They were carrying baskets of ingredients that they'd gathered, and talking and laughing as they walked.

Larran came inside through the back door. As he removed his gardening gloves, he kissed Kiela's cheek. He peered into the pot. "Delicious-looking applesauce."

She sighed. "Thanks." Moving the pot off the stove, she wondered whether to bother pouring it into jars or just start over. Spooning a bit out, she tested the viscosity. Edible, but it was much closer to applesauce than jam. *Tomorrow I'll try another batch.* "The coven's here. Caz and I were thinking of experimenting with a new water-desalinating remedy. If it works, we can give the fisherfolk and boaters the ability to create as much drinkable water as they need."

"Sounds useful."

"Do you want to stick around or—"

"Not today," Larran said, with an apology in his voice. "I'm going to go down to the cove and check on Sian and the others." Six of his merhorses were pregnant with foals, and Larran had been hovering as if he were the father. He'd brought them to Kiela's cove so they could be sheltered from the wind and waves as they neared birthing.

"Who's with them this morning?" Kiela asked.

Before he could answer, a high-pitched shriek cut through the air. Abandoning the applesauce, Kiela rushed to the door. Larran made it out first.

"Meeeeeeeeeeeep!"

Without pausing, Larran barreled past the cactus and down the steps.

"Is it the mares?" Kiela asked. "Is one of them giving birth?"

The cactus bobbed their top half so hard in a clear nod that they fell over. Caz helped them steady themself on their roots, while Kiela dashed back inside to the bookshelves. She pulled out the notebook where she'd compiled notes on how to help with merhorse births. She'd studied it backward and forward already, but now wasn't the time for error.

"Caz, ingredients!" she called.

"On it!"

She and the plants had set the ingredients aside in a basket, ready to go at any moment, enough for all the mares. Caz retrieved the basket from the cabinet beside the sink, while she got out the pestle and mortar. He dumped in the carefully selected leaves, berries, and seeds.

At the window, Eadie stuck her head in over the counter. "How can we help?"

"Which one of them is giving birth?" Kiela asked Meep.

"Meep, meep, meep," they said. And then: "Meep."

Kiela froze in the middle of mashing the ingredients. "Four? Four of them at once? Okay, yes, definitely need help. Thank you, Eadie. Caz, please show the coven the spell."

Bryn claimed the spellbook from Caz. "We'll practice."

"I have never seen a merhorse give birth," Radane said.

"It's wet," Eadie said. "Very wet."

Outside, the women sat in a circle and began to memorize the syllables. Kiela called out corrections on pronunciation while she prepared the paste. It had to be fresh or she would have had it premixed. She hoped they were quick enough.

As soon as the paste was ready, she rushed outside. Everyone in the coven got to their feet (and hooves), and they all hurried down to the cove.

Larran was hip-deep in the water already, switching from merhorse to merhorse, trying his best to soothe them as they flailed and whinnied in pain. "Kiela!"

"We're here!" Without bothering to kick off her shoes or undress, she waded directly into the water. It was, thankfully, warm today. Seaweed brushed against her ankles, and the bottom of the cove clung to her shoes. "Help me rub this on them. Anywhere on their scales. They just need to absorb it through their skin into their bloodstream." She reached for the nearest merhorse, but the mare bit at the air and slapped her tail against the water.

"I'll steady them. You smear the stuff." Larran caught the mare's torso against his chest and began to rub her neck, making soothing crooning noises.

The merhorse's kicking slowed, and Kiela was able to move in closer. She applied the paste as quickly as she could. "Start the spell," Kiela ordered Eadie, Bryn, Ulina, Radane, and Caz. Meep held the paper with the spell aloft with his needles.

Together on the dock, the Pine Cone Coven began to chant as Kiela and Larran moved on to the next merhorse. When they got to the end of the spell, Kiela said, "Again."

Restarting the chant, they continued to cycle through the spell as Kiela applied the paste to all four of the merhorses. The other two mares who were not yet in labor treaded water in the deeper part of the cove, watching with wild eyes. At the mouth to the cove, several mermaids and mermen had gathered. The merbaby that Kiela had once saved hoisted himself onto a rock for a better view. He'd grown over the past four months, and his tail sparkled with new flecks of gold and silver.

The horse-fish with teal scales—her name was Amarin, Kiela knew; she'd learned all of their names—twisted and cried out. Larran positioned himself beside her. "Shh, shh, that's it, mama, you're doing great. You can do this. Breathe." He stroked her throat slowly and steadily until her breathing matched his strokes. She flailed less. "That's it."

As he calmed her, he positioned himself behind her.

In the same soft, soothing voice, he said, "Kiela, stroke her neck and keep her calm. Watch for her teeth. She may try to bite. She won't mean it, but it'll still hurt."

The coven kept chanting as Kiela crooned to the mare.

"Contraction coming," Larran warned.

She dodged in time to avoid the mare swiping at her with her teeth.

Three more contractions, and a foal with an emerald fish tail slipped out into Larran's arms. "Good job, mama!" He rinsed the foal off in the water and guided him toward his mother. The foal immediately latched on and began to drink, and Larran turned to the next mare.

"Oh, that is amazing!" Radane said, after the last syllable of the spell.

She and the others started immediately into the next recitation as the second merhorse, Marri, gave birth to a little filly. Sian was third with a colt.

In the space of a single chaotic hour, all four babies were born. Larran cut the umbilical cords, helped the mothers pass the afterbirth, and checked over each mare and child to ensure they were all healthy—all were. By the time Kiela and Larran climbed out of the water, all four newborn foals had nursed for the first time and were now resting close to their mothers. Cooing and crooning, the mermaids and mermen swam around the mares, delivering seaweed for them to eat once they'd recovered enough and marveling at the foals without disturbing them.

Kiela flopped onto the dock. Her friends were all drenched from the amount of splashing. Caz and Meep had kept clear of the splash zone, she was happy to see.

"Rest," Eadie ordered. "We'll make dinner."

"That's okay," Kiela said. "You don't have to—"

Eadie snorted. "Of course we don't have to. We choose to. Don't argue. Unless you mind us using your kitchen and ingredients? May we?"

She waved her hand. "It's fine. But thanks for asking." It felt like a lifetime ago that she'd snapped at Larran for cooking with her stuff without permission, but she still liked to be asked. It was her kitchen, even though it was filled with memories of her parents—or perhaps *because* it was filled with them.

"I'll bake dessert," Bryn offered as they climbed the stairs out of the cove. "Radane, I'll mix the batter if you make the cream. Strawberry flavored?"

"Strawberry and honey, I think," Radane said. She'd been working at the bakery with Bryn, and Bryn insisted she was a genius with flavors. Apparently, their customers agreed—they'd even had a few orders from nearby islands. One batch featured Kiela's jam.

"I'll do a salad," Ulina volunteered.

Caz offered to help her, insisting it was self-preservation, not altruism.

After a few minutes they were gone, leaving just Kiela and Larran with the sleepy merhorses and the delighted merfolk. Kiela lay where she'd flopped after coming out of the water, on her back looking up at the clear blue sky.

"Four babies," Larran marveled. "Four healthy babies with healthy mamas, thanks to you." He turned his head and smiled at her as if she'd gifted him with the sun, the moon, and all the stars.

"It was everyone," Kiela said. She, Caz, and Radane had perfected the birthing spell; she, Caz, and Meep had located the ingredients; and the full coven had made it possible for her to apply the ingredients while the spell was cast. And of course Larran had been midwife to the mares. It wouldn't have been possible without him coaxing the mares through it, catching the foals, and cutting the cords.

Larran lifted her hand and kissed her knuckles. "It was you.

You, caring enough to make things better, brave enough to try. You brought hope with you in that library scow. You, Kiela. I love you."

"I love you too," Kiela said. She searched for the words to say exactly how he'd changed her life. She'd come to Caltrey with a plan to hide in her parents' cottage, seeing no one and befriending no one, and then Larran had showed up with his ridiculous scythe and a cinnamon roll . . . and suddenly it wasn't about escaping or hiding anymore. *Find someone who will be there for you,* her father had once told her. *Someone who will laugh with you through the years. Someone who makes you happy day-to-day.* "You built me bookshelves."

"And jam shelves."

"Can't forget the jam shelves," Kiela agreed.

"Will you marry me?"

Kiela propped herself up on her elbow and stared at him. He was looking at her with the most vulnerable expression in his beautiful eyes. "I'm not leaving my cottage. It has my jam shop and my library and my garden." Plus it was Caz and Meep's home. And the chicken. "And you can't leave your house by the shore. Your merhorses need you."

"So?" he asked. "I'm not asking our houses to marry. I'm asking you to be my wife. If you'd like to. If you don't want to, I love you just as much. You can forget that I asked, and I'll pretend I didn't, and we can continue on exactly as we were. Either way, we can sleep and eat and live wherever, whenever we want, together when we want or not. I didn't mean to make you uncomfortable or push before you—"

"Yes," Kiela said.

"Yes?"

"Yes, I'll marry you."

"Oh. Yes." He smiled like the sunrise, bright and unstoppable. "Good."

Kiela scooted closer to him. Both of them were still sopping wet and exhausted, but he wrapped his arm around her, and she curled against him. One of the merhorse foals drifted toward their feet, which were dangling off the end of the dock. He nuzzled against their toes.

"You're a miracle," Larran said.

She wasn't certain whether he was talking about her or the foal, but it didn't matter. It was all equally wonderful. They lay in each other's arms as the merhorse mares and foals floated in the cove, and the sunset spread across the sky above.

"What are you thinking?" Larran asked her.

She kissed him and then said, "I'm happy I'm home."

ACKNOWLEDGMENTS

This book began with hot chocolate.

It was November, a little bit chilly, not quite cold enough to justify hot chocolate, especially the really good hazelnut hot chocolate that uses three overflowing tablespoon-size scoops, but I made myself a mug anyway, sat down at my computer, and thought, "I want to write a book that reads like drinking hot chocolate." Or eating really good raspberry jam. Or a fresh-baked pastry, with hot chocolate and maybe some raspberry jam on the side.

I wanted to write a book that felt like a warm hug.

The Spellshop is special to me because it's filled with things that bring me joy. As I wrote each chapter, I'd ask myself, *Does this make me smile?* I've always believed that the classic writing advice "Write what you know," should really be "Write what you love," so I've filled this book with every bit of joy and delight that I could pour into it.

We've all been through a lot over the past few years. This book is my gift to anyone who wants to escape and sink into a world filled with kindness and enchantment.

Thank you to my amazing agent, Andrea Somberg, and my incredible editor, Ali Fisher, as well as the wonderful Dianna Vega, for believing in Kiela, Caz, and me! Thank you to artist Lulu Chen and designer Esther Kim for the gorgeous cover! And a huge thank you to Julia Bergen, Rafal Gibek, Will Hinton, Jim Kapp, Megan Kiddoo, Greg Collins, Christina MacDonald, Monique Patterson, Caro Perny, Devi Pillai, Chris Scheina, and all the other phenomenal people at Bramble, Tor, and Macmillan for bringing this book to life!

And thank you with all my heart to my husband, my children, my family, and my friends. You are my happiness, my life, and my raspberry jam!

ABOUT THE AUTHOR

SARAH BETH DURST is the author of more than twenty-five fantasy books for adults, teens, and kids, including the Queens of Renthia series, *Drink Slay Love,* and *Spark*. She has won an American Library Association Alex Award and a Mythopoeic Fantasy Award and has been a finalist for the Andre Norton Nebula Award three times. She lives in Stony Brook, New York, with her husband, her children, and her ill-mannered cat.